EYES OPEN AT DAWN

By P. Katherine Barkley

ISBN: 978-0-9848721-1-4

HANSON AND KRIPTER: END-LIFE INVESTIGATORS

Hanson and Kripter had been the best End-Life investigators in the whole star system. They had been an unstoppable pair. And now they weren't. But even though all good things end before their time, sometimes they go on in unexpected ways. Hanson and Kripter were no longer an unstoppable pair, but they were still unstoppable.

How it had all happened was easy to explain to the Sangi authorities. It was the why that was posing a problem. That's why they were sitting in the office of Kripter's oldest relative now. The short, greenish, scaly, disgruntled man looked very displeased, but to whom else could they turn? They couldn't afford a more impartial barrister, and he couldn't turn down family, no matter the circumstances. He shook his bulbous head as if disbelieving his own eyes and settled into the comfy chair behind the ornate iron desk. They sat in silence in the dark office for more than a minute while he deliberated. The bare walls and musty stacks of books and papers framed his calculating features perfectly, and for a single moment, there was doubt about whether he would risk censure by refusing familial ties. After all, very few would blame him personally, despite the official sanctions.

However, the old Sangi was not entirely without compassion. He finally sighed and nodded in agreement, a slight whistle escaping from his nasal orifice. This indicated complete acceptance, and Hanson sighed in relief. He spoke, his human voice sounding very odd to his human ears in this dark place that smelled of Sangi. The pungent odor was comforting and headache-inducing at the same time. This dichotomy was now a part of daily life, but it was still too early to think of getting used to it.

"We thank you," said Hanson, suppressing a cough. "We will repay you, Uncle...I mean, Gripnor Singlah."

The old Sangi ignored his human gaff politely and spoke with a gruff yet musical voice, "Family need not worry about such...details. Now tell me the whole story. You may speak in English if you like. Your tongue is not yet accustomed to Sangween."

Hanson relxed a bit and thought back to the beginning of the story. When had it really begun? It felt like a lifetime ago. Was it the end of the Banjee case? Or before that? It was before; it must have been. The business card had been the first clue, although neither of them knew it yet.

Kripter picked up the card, plain and white, with one word printed in embossed lettering: Feeshar. It meant "service" in the human English. It meant nothing, but Kripter slipped it into his coat pocket anyway. He had a feeling there was more to it. He pulled his collar up and shivered in the cold rain. Sangi Prime was never warm, and he had spent too much time on the warmer Sangi Reesha in the last few years. But you go where the clients send you and where the cases take you. The Banjee case had brought him home to Sangi Prime. It was a bittersweet homecoming. But Hanson seemed to be enjoying himself.

Kripter glanced at his human companion, stamping around in the puddles and checking the windows of the surrounding buildings for clues or witnesses. His pale skin and dark hair seemed at home in the dank of the city. He always turned red in the bright sun of Sangi Reesha.

A car floated past them on the street, and Hanson instinctively stepped back into the shadows. The homeless squishy humans were not well-liked on Sangi Prime, even those like Hanson who had earned their freedom from the slave collars. He had learned to stay out of the way of Sangi who lived their lives on the homeworld. He paid his fees once a year at the End-Life Center, took his serum, and did his job. That had been the extent of his interaction with Sangi until ten years ago. Meeting Kripter had changed everything. Kripter was the first Sangi to show any respect for humans. He seemed to sympathize with them, so Hanson built up the courage to speak with him about sponsorship for freedom.

Kripter had seen the young human working so hard around the End-Life Center and knew there was something special about him. He had proven his mental capacity on numerous cases, and he was eager to escape the confines of his job. He spoke to him on occasion about working independently and applying for a free life license. Over time, they became the closest of friends, and Kripter sponsored Hanson for freedom. They became inseparable and unstoppable, solving End-Life cases together and becoming the most decorated team at the Center. Some Sangi still refused to acknowledge Hanson's contribution to their partnership, but he worked more for his own satisfaction than that of anyone else. He thirsted for knowledge and for success. He asked so many questions. Some were simple enough to answer, like where did humans come from? "A planet far away that died many years ago."

But some questions were more complicated, like why do Sangi hate and enslave humans? Or why are humans allowed only one year of life at a time, while Sangi can live multiple lives? There was a lot of history in questions like those, but Kripter did his best to condense it.

"Lives are full of memories, and these memories are sacred. They are a gift. To let those memories end, die....This is felt to be obscene. Humans live one short life, and then your memories are gone. You cannot help this, but still the Sangi resent you for it. Therefore, shortly after the humans arrived in our system, it was decided by the authorities that you should repay the universe for your profane existence and the Sangi people for your economic burden. I have argued personally before the End-Life Council that there would be no human burden if you were allowed to work and contribute on your own, but they will not hear me. The enslavement of your people continues as it has for decades. The only good that comes of it is that the money you pay each year to continue your life and escape the grip of the bakra poison is used for environmental projects and to support your own people. Small comfort, perhaps, but better than none. I hope that someday we will be able to save all humans permanently from the poison that is given to them at birth and the antidote they must take each year to continue their lives and the indignity with which they are treated by my people. There must be some compassion amongst the Council, for they once ruled that humans have the right to mate and form comforting family units. It's not much, but it's something to begin with."

Frank discussions like this served to deepen their friendship, making both their lives and their jobs not only easier but also more fulfilling. They became like brothers, each willing to do anything for the other. Thoughts of Hanson's eventual demise were tempered by the knowledge that Kripter's memories of him would be passed on to future generations.

"How many lives have you lived?" Hanson had once asked. It took a moment for Kripter to count them. His first had been many centuries ago. Each life was distinct, with its own flavor, so to speak. Each layer of memories added through the End-Life ritual changed the flavor a bit. Ensuring that these memories were passed on properly was just one of the duties of an End-Life investigator. After counting the lives in each of his progenitors' lines, Kripter answered, "One hundred and seventy-four. Including this one."

Hanson was awed by this ritual of passing life memories to another at the end of one's life. He often seemed sad when investigating a murder case, knowing that the victim had no time to pass on his memories. His sympathy for his people's slavers was quite moving.

Murders were committed only by young Sangi, those with no wisdom passed to them by previous generations. This actually made them more difficult to track down. Multi-life Sangi registered themselves voluntarily with the End-Life Center, but the newly born were unregistered and virtually untraceable. Hanson and Kripter were the best in the business of tracing the untraceable. Between Kripter's lifetimes of knowledge and wisdom and Hanson's uncanny natural intuition and intelligence, they had the best track record in the system: zero cases lost.

And the Banjee case was turning out to be no different. They had all the evidence on this murder case collected. The last piece of the puzzle was tracking down the perpetrator of the brutal crime. The meager trail had led them to this dark side street. So there they were in the rain, waiting for some sign of their young quarry. Kripter was having doubts, but his instincts told him to trust his partner. And Hanson was sure the guy would show up there sooner or later.

Two hours of cold, wet waiting finally paid off when the young Sangi appeared at the end of the street. He trudged through the darkness as if toward his own funeral, which was not entirely inaccurate since the punishment for murder was death without the End-Life ritual.

Hanson hid in the shadows of a building, and Kripter stepped forward, assuming the posture of a man just passing through. He casually pulled a packet of smokesticks out of his pocket and asked the approaching stranger for a firelight. The man obliged, and Hanson slipped noiselessly out of the shadows to flank him. He never knew what hit him. It was the end of an easy, clean case.

But something about it bothered both of them. Hanson felt that they'd missed something, and Kripter kept going over the evidence in his mind, sensing a mistake but not seeing one. They received the usual congratulations from the Council and returned to their office to await another assignment. Kripter sat in his swivel chair, playing with the white slip of paper he'd picked up on the sidewalk before they apprehended the Banjee murderer. Feeshar, service. It meant nothing. So why was it on his mind? It was an odd message, to be sure, but not important. At least, not yet. He slipped the card back into his pocket, and the two of them ordered in a late dinner.

Hanson preferred to eat in the office and avoid the stares that he always met in public places. Some Sangi were still openly hostile to him. If he didn't have his best friend with him, solving cases would be nearly impossible. They enjoyed dinner in silence, each mulling over the day's events and the case's conclusion. At the end of their meal, they both glanced up at the same time and knew what the other was thinking.

"It's out there," Hanson nodded.

"The answer," Kripter agreed.

With one purpose, they strode from their office and back out into the cold rain of Sangi Prime. Their first stop was at the home of the man who had hired them to track down Banjee's killer, the chief barrister of Sangi Prime, Fazeray. The old man answered the door himself.

"I already received the announcement from your superiors," he said, eyeing Hanson suspiciously. "You are to be commemorated for your work, but I haven't the time for house calls. We are still in mourning."

"Pardon the intrusion, Morgla Fazeray," Kripter replied with deference, "but we fear that the case may not be entirely closed. Something does not fit."

The chief barrister glanced past them to the dark, wet street, then motioned for them to step inside the well-furnished mansion. He was no longer concerned by the presence of a human; instead, he seemed agitated by the darkness outside his door. He slammed the door and asked gruffly, "What do you know?"

Hanson and Kripter exchanged a glance and remained silent. The chief barrister of Sangi Prime seemed remarkably eager to discuss something that they knew literally nothing about. He was frightened. But of what? Or whom?

"What we know isn't important," Hanson replied with ease, adopting a relaxed pose. "What's important is that there may be trouble heading this way."

The barrister seemed to weigh his options. There weren't many apparently, for it took him only a moment to start spilling out everything he knew. Interrogation tactics were quite unnecessary. Unfortunately for the detectives, he didn't know much.

"I received the note two days before the murder," he said quickly. "I thought it was a joke, I swear, or I would have contacted the Council immediately. I couldn't tell anyone afterwards; my career would have been decimated. I was foolish, I admit. But I have nothing left but my work now that my nephew is dead. You have to believe me, I had no idea there would be another murder so soon or that they would be somehow connected."

Hanson tried not to show any surprise. They hadn't been told about any other murders recently. Kripter and he glanced at each other and knew they were thinking the same thing. There was much more to this story, and it wouldn't be easy tracking it down.

"We'll need the note for evidence," Kripter said to Fazeray. "Don't worry, your name won't come up unless it's absolutely necessary. You have our word. And I would advise you not to speak to anyone else about the second murder, not even the victim's family."

Fazeray nodded and left the room quickly to retrieve the note.

"Nice try," Hanosn remarked under breath. Kripter's attempt to draw out information about the second murder victim had failed, but at least the barrister hadn't deduced that they knew nothing about the case.

Fazeray returned with a carefully preserved piece of paper and handed it to Kripter.

"Thank you, Morgla," the investigator nodded and slid the note quickly into his pocket. "We won't bother you any further."

He led Hanson back out the front door, making sure not to glance back. Once they were some distance down the street, they began speaking in hushed tones, planning their next move.

"The Council won't tell us anything they haven't already."

"We need to find a sympathetic party."

"Someone on the inside, but not too far in."

"We could search the records ourselves."

"It may not be in the records, and if it is, it may be beyond our clearance."

"We have no other options."

"We could leave it alone. If we haven't been informed, there may be a reason."

"We could....But we won't."

Illegal record searches were best done by night, so the investigators returned to the Center and stalked silently through the building until they reached the records room. A vast computer filled most of the room, and no one else was there. Hanson checked the other door, while Kripter sat at the control console. He pulled out the note and read it aloud softly, "Banjee is dead. His memories die with him."

"Not much to go on," Hanson sighed. "What do we even look for?"

"We'll start simple," Kripter stated with resignation to a difficult search. "Recent murders."

They searched the computer's records for the next few hours, finding little of use. No recent murders or even suspicious deaths on file. No mysterious announcements or messages from higher-ups. No odd assignments given out or retracted. Everything appeared to be clean. They had only two options available to them: search the High Council's private files in person or find someone who had the information they needed and wasn't afraid to share it. Neither task would be easy.

"When was the last time you spoke with Kleena?" Kripter grinned, his clean yellow teeth taunting Hanson.

The human shivered a little and shrugged before saying, "It's been a while. She's so...clingy."

They stared at each other for a minute, each daring the other to force the issue. Finally, Hanson blurted out, "She creeps me out, okay? She got this...fetish for humans, and I'm as interested in her as I am in...you! I don't have a problem with the inter-species maters; I'm just not one of them. She'd never tell me anything, anyway."

"She would if you...you know," Kripter grinned again, and Hanson growled back at him, "I'd rather search the Council's private files."

"If we were caught, it would be death," Kripter reminded him.

"Still preferable to a night with her," Hanson insisted.

"Fine," Kripter sighed. "Death, it is, then."

The Council's private files were kept in a secure room on the top floor with two guards outside. Hanson and Kripter's usual ploy to slip past people in that situation wouldn't work since the guards would recognize Hanson and know that he wasn't some vagrant human. So they would have to try something different.

"Is that room secure?" Kripter barked at the Sangi men.

"Of course, sir," one of them sneered.

"Don't use that tone with me," Kripter straightened to his full five-foot stature and glared at the guard on eye level. "We've received word that there may be an attempted break-in tonight. Double-check it. Now!"

The guards reluctantly keyed in their personal pass-codes on the door, and it clicked. Kripter brushed past them, pushing the door open, and stepped around the filing drawers in the room.

"You're not allowed..." one of the guards started to say.

"Help me check the room!" Kripter feigned exasperation.

The guards stepped inside and started searching around the room. It was narrow but long, and the cabinets created a lot of places to hide. Hanson slipped in behind them and pretended to join the hunt. He checked the dates printed on each drawer until he found the most recent one.

Kripter was leading the guards further away, so Hanson knelt down and quietly pulled the drawer out. It was full of organized computer chips, filed by date and cross-referenced by case type. Hanson grabbed the last half-dozen and closed the drawer. Slipping the chips into a pocket, he hastened to catch up with Kripter. One of the guards was saying, "There's no one here."

"Good," Kripter nodded, catching Hanson's eye. "Keep it that way. Hanson, let's check the air ducts."

They left quickly and headed toward the next hallway on their right. The only terminal authorized to read the Council's classified files was in the Council chambers. They would be empty at this time but guarded and monitored by an electronic security system. Breaking in there would not be so easy.

"We can't do this on our own," Kripter mumbled pointedly.

"We'll find a way," Hanson whispered insistently.

"We don't have that kind of time," Kripter hissed. "It's already after 26 hours. The sun will be rising in less than four hours."

Hanson stopped walking and sighed. He mulled the situation over for a minute and finally relented, "I'll call her."

Kripter handed him his PCD, and he made the call. Kleena's voice practically purred on the other side, "Hanson, I've missed you! You should stop by. I have a new piece of artwork to show you. My husband's out of town next week, you know."

"The whole Council is," Hanson sighed. "That's not why I'm calling."

"You need a favor, I know," Kleena giggled. "It's the only reason you ever call."

"We're outside the Council chambers..."

"Say no more! I'll be right there!"

There was a beep, and Hanson sighed heavily, "She could've turned off security from her rooms."

"Then she wouldn't get to see you," Kripter chuckled. "Relax, she won't attack you while I'm here."

Hanson wasn't so sure about that, but he had no choice. The six-foot, grey-scaled, red-eyed Sangi beauty was already slinking around the corner to join them. She pressed herself up against Hanson and ran one hand through his hair, purring, "You are as handsome as ever. Handsome Hanson."

"We, uh, need to, um…" Hanson stuttered, aware that her other hand was sneaking down his side and heading for his hip.

"I'm afraid we need the Chairman's personal codes," Kripter interrupted.

"My husband has many personal codes," Kleena grinned and playfully nipped at Hanson's ear.

"Please, Kleena," Hanson begged, edging away from her.

"Fine, but you owe me dinner," she whispered. "My place. Next week."

She marched over to the Council chamber door and punched in a code. The door swung inward, and she marched inside and punched another code into a large computer terminal.

"Now you can look at whatever you want," she announced, stalking back out the door. One shoulder of her leather dress slipped down, revealing the darker scales on her upper chest and lower back. "Anything at all," she purred and winked at Hanson. "Don't forget our date."

Then she was gone, and Hanson let out the breath he'd been holding and leaned against the doorframe. "That woman's going to be the death of me," he said aloud. "I'll either die of fright, or the Chairman will catch her crawling on me one day and have me executed."

"Nonsense. The Chairman knows about his trophy wife's…uh, appetites," Kripter said dismissively. "You'd get off with an empty warning at most. Now let's see what we've got, before some patrolling guard decides to follow a different route tonight."

They huddled around the terminal, inserting chip after chip. Every documented murder case was well-known, except for one. A young Sangi woman named Sempa had been strangled the day before. The case had been quickly classified. A reference name was at the bottom of the file: Krupik. There was a relocation address, as well.

Kripter was in shock. This man had to be a witness, but why was the whole case being covered up? Neither the victim nor the witness was a member of the upper levels of society. Hanson observed his partner's agitation and suggested they get some rest. It was too late to pay this Krupik a visit now, and they would be very busy the next day.

Krupik turned out to be a nervous little Sangi with no mail slot. So much for the mail delivery scam. Luckily, when he answered the door, he said, "Did the Chairman send you?"

Kripter and Hanson smiled and nodded. He let them inside, and the three of them settled into a comfy living room with cushions and pillows everywhere.

"We need to discuss a few things," Hanson started to say, but Krupik interrupted, "I was told I wouldn't have to deal with humans anymore. It's why I requested this neighborhood."

Hanson grunted, but he knew the drill. He let himself out and waited outside. Kripter was annoyed as well and said the first thing that popped into his head, "I need you to tell me what you saw that day."

Krupik snapped to attention and eyed him suspiciously. "I was told never to discuss that with anyone. Not even the Chairman himself."

Kripter felt panic welling up. He had let his emotions distract him, and now his chance at interrogation was slipping away.

"I…I meant," he stuttered in Sangween, grasping for words, "that we should talk about your feelings. About what happened. To make sure you're adjusting. I'm a psychologist."

Krupik relaxed a bit, although he continued to tap his fingers on his arm, as if he were impatiently waiting for something. He whistled through his nosehole, and Kripter breathed a sigh of relief.

"It was terrifying," Krupik began. "I was just doing my job, supervising the humans at the janitorial adjunct, and it happened. People like me don't see such things. So why?"

Kripter shook his head sympathetically, and the nervous little man continued, "I tell you, my confidence in the system was nearly broken that day. If the Council hadn't acted so quickly, I don't know what I would have done. I still fear for my life. He's out there. Sitting in his mansion. Working for them! And I'm the one who gets sent away. I'm such a nervous wreck because of all this!"

Kripter listened to another hour of complaining, but no more helpful information was revealed. He joined Hanson on the front door steps and whispered, "The murderer is one of the elite."

Back in their office, Hanson exploded, "How's that possible?! All that stuff about memories and wisdom!"

"I know," Kripter sighed. He was out of answers. And out of leads. With Krupik refusing to say more, they were at a dead end.

Hanson knew it, so he decided to make a huge sacrifice. He breathed in deeply, hardly believing his own conviction, and said, "I'll visit Kleena."

The Chairman and his wife lived on the top floor. The Council were in their chambers, reportedly discussing how a handful of their private files had been accidentally left in their chambers the previous day. Loud voices could be heard all the way down the hall.

Kleena answered the door and purred, "You're a week early, Hanson, but I love surprises. Come in!"

Like a man resigned to death, Hanson stepped through the doorway and spoke in a low monotone, "It's urgent, Kleena. There's something monumental going on, and your husband's a part of it. We need information fast. What did Krupik see two days ago? Who killed Sempa?"

"I haven't a clue," she whispered in his ear, wrapping her arms around him. "But I did hear my husband mumbling in his sleep about this Krupik the other night."

"What else did he say?" Hanson asked through a clenched jaw as her hands slipped into his coat and her breath started to make him nauseated.

"Ohh, something about a theft and a service and a man named Rikken," she answered softly.

She began to slip her dress off her shoulders, and he stepped toward the door. But she moved quickly to intercept him and said, "I think that information must be worth a little something." Horrified, Hanson fumbled for the PCD in his pocket.

"Just a kiss, perhaps?" Kleena pouted and leaned into him.

"Just a kiss?" he repeated, glancing desperately at the door.

She nodded, closed her eyes, and leaned closer, her grey, scaly lips puckered.

Hanson took a breath and dove in, pressing his lips against hers. She was surprisingly warm, and her scales were soft. It wasn't so bad, at least until she tried to nip at his lower lip playfully. She drew blood, and he shouted involuntarily.

"Sorry, I forget myself," she smirked. But she stepped aside and let him leave.

Back at the office, Kripter had ordered lunch. He chuckled at Hanson's lip, and his human friend glared at him. "Alright," he acquiesced. "Was it worth it?"

"Yeah, I guess," Hanson admitted, sitting down and wiping away the blood. "I got a name: Rikken. Also, there's something about a theft, but I don't remember the murder having anything to do with a burglary."

"Hmm, no," Kripter agreed, chewing slowly. "But it must mean something."

"Oh, and a service," Hanson added, digging into his lunch. "Some kind of service. Whatever that means."

Kripter stopped chewing. He swallowed hard and slowly pulled the white notecard from his coat and laid it on the desk between them.

"Feeshar," he said. "Service."

There was a connection.

The holding cells were in the basement of the Council building. Banjee's killer sat in a corner cell on the second level, awaiting death calmly. It wasn't unusual for an investigator to request a visit with a criminal he helped imprison, so they had no trouble getting in to see him privately. His name was Saffon.

"Feeshar," Kripter hissed, sitting on a stool on the other side of the metal bars. "Service. What does it mean?"

"You came here for a school lesson?" the young Sangi smirked.

"No games," Hanson growled, stepping out of the shadows.

"What is this thing doing here?" Saffon addressed Kripter.

Hanson stepped between them, towering over both of them and spoke softly but darkly, "There are no guards down here. Would you like to find out why your people so often call humans 'animals'?" He finished by cracking his knuckles, and Saffon actually jumped.

Kripter stifled a laugh and added, "I'll unlock the door if you don't cooperate."

Saffon retreated to the back wall of his cell and said, "Fine, alright, but you can't tell anyone. The Council will do worse to me than you ever could."

Hanson backed away, and the young man continued, "It's the Council who should be in here. They hired me. That's what the card means. It's a sign that I'm doing their bidding. It was supposed to protect me. Fehklah!" He crossed his arms and sulked.

"Who on the Council hired you?" Kripter asked tensely. He didn't like this turn of events.

"I spoke only to an intermediary," Saffon shook his head. "And I never saw his face. But he had the Seal of the Council."

"Do you know the name 'Rikken'?" Hanson asked.

"No, I don't," he shook his head again.

"Why?" Kripter whispered. "Why did you do it?" His face was twisted with turmoil, and Hanson put one hand on his shoulder comfortingly.

"I told you, the Council hired me," Saffon answered.

"I don't care if you were working for the old gods themselves!" Kripter shouted. "Why did you kill that young man?!"

There was a moment of stunned silence before Saffon answered, "Because he was unworthy, and the Council agreed with me."

"Unworthy for what?" Kripter seethed.

"The End-Life ritual."

Later, Hanson and Kripter sat in their office, unable to say anything. He was unworthy? It was confusing. They had to keep digging. But where now?

"I'll check public records," Hanson said aloud. "You should go back to Barrister Fazeray and find out if he knows who the Council might send on a secret errand."

Kripter nodded and gripped the white notecard tightly. He was determined now to get to the truth more than ever.

"We'll avenge the loss of these people's memories," Hanson stated sympathetically. "Who better than us?"

Kripter gave a half-smile and said, "Thank you, old friend. You always know what to say. Sometimes I think you care more than any Sangi. You understand somehow, don't you?"

"I try," Hanson shrugged humbly. "I couldn't do it without your patience. Now, let's go, before things get sentimental."

Kripter chuckled and stood up. He turned his PCD to automatic and handed Hanson a new one. "Just in case," he winked. "Council rules be damned."

They split up, and Hanson walked the half-block in the drizzling rain to the Public Records Office. If any person named Rikken ever existed in the Sangi system and participated in the End-Life ritual, he would be in the records.

The clerks glared at him as he walked in, but they knew he worked in the Council building and left him alone. On the second floor was a terminal registered for the investigators to use. It gave them access to every file at once. He sat there and typed "Rikken."

There was only one entry, and it was over 200 years old. Rikken had been a barrister for the Council. He worked his way up to Chief Barrister, despite never having participated in the End-Life ritual. He was apparently quite brilliant. But he had a strange political view that led the Council to fire him, something they hadn't done before or since to the Chief Barrister. He believed that only the worthiest, most carefully chosen candidates -- chosen by him, of course -- should have the honor of going through the End-Life ritual. He tried to create a class for new investigators that would teach them how to judge the people. The Council, and the people, refused to let this happen. Rikken vowed that he would return one day in a new, unrecognizable body and become Chief Barrister again and find a better way to implement his ideas. No one believed him because he had no family, no friends, and no supporters. Who would share their memories, their lives, with him?

Then, an incident two years later changed everything. Rikken was spotted *forcing* someone's memories out of their body, something that wasn't considered possible. The ordeal appeared to be quite painful for both of them. The victim died, and Rikken vanished again. He popped up again at random points in history, killing young Sangi and taking memories. His behavior became more crazed with each forced ritual.

About 20 years after the first incident, he disappeared for good. His body was found in a back alley, abandoned. The eyes were black, like the eyes of one who had passed on his memories through the ritual. But they were singed around the edges, as if by fire. As if it had taken a great deal of force to make it happen. Council investigators tried to track him down, but they failed time and again. Scientists studied what little data they had and determined that the force Rikken used to perform the ritual against his victims' wills was twisting their memories and actually pushing him further beyond the boundaries of insanity.

A trail of murders stopped cold about 20 years ago. Nothing more was known.

Hanson felt a chill go down his spine as he finished reading. He knew that Rikken must be behind all this. As a suspicion began to form in his mind, his PCD beeped, and he heard Kripter's voice say, "...Rikken?"

"How did you guess?" said another voice. "I must say, this game was fun. This body's mind really had no idea, so it was amusing to see you stumble over his honesty. But it's old. Time to get a new one."

"Why? Why did you kill them? Why did you hire Saffon? Why did you play this stupid game with us?"

Hanson raced down to street level as he listened to the conversation. His suspicion was confirmed. Fazeray was Rikken. Or at least Rikken's twisted memories and motivations.

"They were not worthy!" Fazeray shouted. "Saffon was going to be my next body after he killed Krupik, when I let him out tomorrow. But since you've arrived ahead of schedule, you'll have to do. I planned for you to take a fall for murder. Instead, you'll take a step up in society."

Hanson put on a burst of speed and ran into the middle of the street. A car halted abruptly in front of him, and he ran to the driver's side and pulled the shocked Sangi out and took his seat. He struggled with the controls for a moment since he'd only driven a couple of times, but he managed to get the car to rise eight feet and speed off.

"You can't force it," Kripter protested.

Hanson knew he was worried about all of the people who came before him, all the memories that would be lost when he was lost.

"I can," Fazeray gloated.

"Ask him how," Hanson muttered. "Stall him."

"That's impossible," Kripter said. "How?"

"I have made my own ritual," Fazeray chuckled. "Now, no more stalling."

"But what hold do you have over the Council? I must know!"

"Only the hold of bribery. Once I am in power, I will make the Chairman my second in command. Give up now, and you will rule this system."

"I'll never give up!" Kripter yelled.

Hanson heard a series of thuds and shouts and knew there was a fight going on. He could see the house just a block away.

There was a crash, and Kripter moaned loudly. Hanson barely slowed the car down. He lowered it enough to jump out and left it on its own. It crashed into an office building with a spectacular explosion, but he barely noticed.

"You fool!" Fazeray was shouting. "Now you can die without passing on your memories to anyone!"

Hanson was in the entranceway, having found the front door wide open. He snatched an expensive-looking antique sword from the wall and raced around a corner. Fazeray was coming down the hallway, mumbling to himself. He didn't notice the intruder until it was too late.

Hanson ran as fast as he could at the old barrister, the sword between them. It slid surprisingly easily into the old Sangi's gut. It went in up to the hilt, and purple blood spilled copiously onto the hardwood floor. He fell to the floor with a shocked expression on his face, and Hanson jumped over him and continued to the living room. There, he found Kripter bleeding from the chest, among the wreckage of broken furniture and glass.

"Hold on, friend," Hanson said, kneeling beside him. "I'll get you to a physician."

"No time," Kripter choked, grasping at Hanson's collar. "I'm hurt too badly."

"But your memories!" Hanson tightened his eyes, fighting tears.

"I know there's no one better to trust them with. Please, old friend, take me with you."

"But I'm human! How can…?"

"I think it can work. You understand more than most young Sangi. If Rikken can force it, you can allow it."

"Then I'm honored," Hanson bowed his head slightly and sighed with acceptance. He held Kripter's weak hands and looked into his eyes. They widened, and a greenish mist seemed to issue from them and enter Hanson's eyes. He felt a sting but resisted the urge to blink.

Suddenly, it was over, and Kripter's empty body slumped forward.

But it was really just beginning. A flood of alien memories began to flow through Hanson's mind. He was a young Sangi girl and then an old chauffeur and then a young investigator watching a young human who seemed to be determined to make something of himself. The weight of it all felt like it was going to split his head in half. He lay on the floor groaning for what seemed an eternity.

Finally, everything seemed to settle. But he forgot who he was for a moment and was shocked to see his own body dead beside him. He reminded himself, "I am Hanson."

Fazeray was dead as well, and Rikken with him. The Council would want answers, especially once they learned of the Chairman's betrayal. In the meantime, everything was new and different. The rain was a little bit colder than he remembered, the smell on the air a bit more appetizing, and the language of Sangween made more sense, felt more familiar. Memories of places and people were still shuffling through his mind, and Hanson wondered what he should do. But he already knew, because Kripter knew. They went to see his uncle.

Singlah sat and stared. He didn't even breathe for nearly a minute. Then, he sighed, shook his head, and said, "The Council will want to cover this up. But they can't cover you up."

Slowly, Hanson realized the implications of this. He could almost hear Kripter's voice in his head, saying, "The word will get out that humans can be a part of the End-Life cycle. It's a new era for your people. For our people."

Hanson smiled and said, "We're counting on it."

Just then, there was a loud knock at the door, and a figure burst in. It was the wife of the Chairman herself.

"I heard what happened," she gasped. "Where's Kripter? Are you alright?"

"We're fine," Hanson said, admiring Kleena's curves for the first time. "I'm fine."

"Kripter gave his memories to Hanson here," Singlah explained. "Things will be changing. And from what I just heard, your husband will not be going along for the ride."

"Gave his…? Oh my!" Kleena gasped, then with a dismissive wave of her hand, "Oh, I wouldn't worry about the Chairman. He can talk his way into or out of anything. But what can I do to help you, Hanson dear?"

Hanson realized he'd been staring. Kleena seemed extremely attractive all of a sudden. Images flashed through his mind, and he knew why. Kripter found her attractive.

"Well, actually," he grinned, "if your husband's going to pull himself out of this, perhaps he could give us a hand. We're going to start a revolution in human relations."

"Mmm," she grinned back. "I like the sound of that. He'll help. Or else."

She ruffled his hair, and for the first time, he didn't pull away. His headache was starting to ease, as well. Things were looking up as much as they could without Kripter.

"But I'm still here," Hanson thought to himself in Kripter's voice. "And I always will be. And so will all the rest of us. And when it's time, we'll pass on to someone new. All of us."

Hanson and Kripter were no longer a pair. They were hundreds. And they were, and would always be, unstoppable.

KITTEN'S PATH

She had known that this day would come. She had prepared for the tournament nearly her entire life. And yet here she was, standing before the crowd, holding her breath as if she could hold back the moment. But Time will not be held back or controlled. And so the tournament bell rang, and the competition began. And she was the first competitor. The eyes, and the fate, of a nation were upon her.

"It is time for the battle we have been waiting for for over thirty years!" the announcer shouted. "Meet our first competitor: Kitten Izzill!"

The crowd sniggered at the sound of her name, but she ignored them. She had endured the tauntings of the public for too long to let it bother her now. She knew her father had given her the name of a weakling in order to make her strong. She stepped confidently into the center of the ring, and a hush fell over the people. They recognized her immediately. How could they not? She had the trademark blood-red hair of the Warrior Clan, the last of her race and the last hope of the people of the Cantari Nation. No one was laughing now.

"And her competitor: Bushah Killrod!" the announcer continued. "Both fighters have trained for more than fifteen years for this day! Let the battle begin!"

Kitten stepped forward to meet her opponent, a giant of a man with a smirk on his face. He was apparently one of the few there today who did not realize who she was. No matter, she would soon show him. Stepping back with her right foot, she assumed the traditional fighting stance and beckoned Bushah forward with a single wave of her hand. He obliged by racing at her headlong, as would a bull in a mating pen. This was going to be easier than she thought.

"And Bushah makes the first move! But Kitten appears to have kept the advantage to herself! She's holding her ground! It seems she knows exactly what she's doing!" The announcer droned on, narrating the fight for the people in the stands.

Waiting until precisely the right moment, Kitten executed her first move perfectly, just as she had practiced it a thousand times. She vaulted over her opponent, springing over his head and delivering a hard kick to the small of his back that sent him reeling into the force field barrier that surrounded their battlefield. He was several feet taller than she, but she managed to do this easily. She focused on each subsequent move as if she were still back at the training grounds, ignoring the roar of the crowd. She ducked under his massive fist and swung her leg into his feet, bringing him down hard onto the ground. He wasn't very quick. She obviously had little to fear from this one. As he turned to get to his feet, she ran and jumped onto his chest, slamming him back onto the ground. Standing on top of him, she leaned down and gripped his throat with one hand. When he tried again to get up, she squeezed at just the right spot, immobilizing his left arm. Her eyes squinted at him, but he was apparently unaware that he had been beaten. He reached for her with his right arm. She squeezed again, and it went limp. Eager to end this pointless struggle, she reached back with her free hand and smashed her fist into his face, breaking his nose and knocking him unconscious. The crowd screamed with excitement.

"And in the first battle of the day, Kitten beats her first opponent into the ground! The crowds are going wild! Whether you were rooting for the young Miss Izzill from the Cantari Nation or the champion of the Brunt people, this has been quite a match, folks! And we've only just begun! Stay in your seats! The second match is up next!"

Kitten stepped off of the stage and breathed a sigh of relief. Perhaps this would not be as difficult as she had supposed. Perhaps she stood a chance at saving the people of Cantari. They were all counting on her. Few of them knew her name, but all of them knew that the last member of the Warrior Clan would be competing in the tournament in order to win their freedom. The pressure was frightening, but she maintained a brave face. Until she saw him walking towards her. He stepped out of the crowd like some otherworldly creature come to call on her. He nearly floated over the ground. When he smiled, his teeth glinted, and his eyes flashed. He stood in front of her and spoke with an aristocratic accent and the confidence of a man who feared nothing and no one.

"You did well in your first match. Of course, I would have expected no less of you, Miss Izzill. Especially considering the rather paltry display of brute strength your opponent presented you with. But mark my words, my little warrior girl, there will be far greater men than that to oppose you over the next few days. Do not become overconfident. I would hate to see you knocked out of the runnings before I had a chance at you myself."

"Just remember not to be overconfident yourself, Vincoral," she countered. "I plan to make it to the end of this tournament; even so, you may not get the chance to fight me."

Kitten spoke with more confidence than she felt. This was a creature to be reckoned with, she knew. He was an opponent to be feared, no matter how much training you had gone through, no matter how strong and skilled you were. She knew he could see right through her bravado, but what else could she do? His eyes bored right through her skull and seemed to read her mind and her very soul. She could feel the power emanating from his skin. He was one of the most powerful wizard warriors in the land. How could she expect to defeat him? And yet she had to try. It was what she had been preparing for since the day her parents had died in the Great Schizm. She forced herself to look away from those dangerous eyes, and she saw her little squire approaching.

"Come on now, no time to chat," he spoke softly and took her hand. "You've got to get ready for the next fight. You're up again in one hour. That's not much time. Come on now."

Kitten let Zharran lead her away. He was her best and only friend and the world's best actor. She knew that he was really quaking in his boots at the sight of Vincoral the Demonic, but he could hide it better than anyone. She glanced over her shoulder once to see the wizard standing amidst the unknowing crowd, and then he was gone, having disappeared into thin air. She relaxed somewhat and focused on the upcoming battle. There was already another fight going on inside the force field. Whoever won would be her next opponent. One man was a blue magic-thrower from the snowy regions of Mithar; the other was a human fighter from the realm of Edging. Either one would be easy for her to defeat. But they were certainly smarter than the Brunt. It was true that the battles would get more difficult as the tournament went on. She must prepare.

"And that's the end of the second match! Gleeca of the Mithar magic-throwers has defeated Tahj of the Edging fighters! That makes him the next opponent of our youngest and only female warrior here today, Miss Kitten Izzill! The third match will begin in half an hour while the two fighters rest up a bit!"

"Sit down, Kitten!" Zharran spoke over the blare of the latest announcement and pulled her into her tent. "You need to prepare for the next match! Pacing and stalking like a caged dornak will do you no good."

"I can't help it, knowing that he's out there, waiting, watching. It drives me crazy," she gritted her teeth and paced in front of him. "Besides, I can't relax now. I've got to stay tense; I've got to stay ready. What would you have me do? Take a bath? Just quit worrying over me; you'll make me nervous."

Zharran shook his little brown head and ran to fetch some drinking water. Kitten went over the next battle in her mind. Magic-throwers were smarter than Brunt warriors, much smarter. Simple speed would not be sufficient to win her the next match. However, she was no dunce when it came to using magic, either. It might be time to put those skills to use. He would be well-defended against physical attacks, but he probably wouldn't be expecting her to use magic, too. She smirked a little but quickly lost her grin when she caught a glimpse through the tent curtain of Vincoral the Demonic's robe passing by. Perhaps it wasn't his, only a look-alike. Either way, he was back in her thoughts, sending shivers down her spine and doubts through her mind. Her magic could surely defeat a lesser wizard, but the Demonic One himself? All the training in the world couldn't prepare her for going up against the likes of him. Her father had been one of the best in the land, and he hadn't stood a chance against Demon Vincoral. What could she do?

"I won't let him demoralize me, that's what!" she answered herself out loud. "Even if I die the death of my parents, I will not let him take my spirit as he has taken the spirit of the people of Cantari! I can't! I've got to show them that we can fight!"

"Take your seats, folks! The next match is about to start!" the announcer shouted.

Zharran rushed into the tent with a mug of water, and Kitten took a swig of it before stepping towards the battlefield. She refused to let herself look around for the watchful eyes of the Demonic One. It made no real difference whether he was nearby or not; he could see her anywhere. Only the people of Cantari were aware of his full abilities, having witnessed them firsthand over the last thirty years. It had started before she was born, but Kitten had listened to the stories by the light of the fire at night, surrounded by the elders of her village and her family. Shortly thereafter, she was unfortunate enough to see these stories come to life and take the lives of her parents and everyone else in the village. His siege of the Cantari Nation had been completed by the utter destruction of the Warrior Clan. She alone had been left alive by virtue of Vincoral's impatience. She had hidden in the woods, protected by a magic shield left behind by the village shaman, and Vincoral could not see her. Rather than waste any more time, he abandoned the search, assuming that a little girl no higher than his boot could pose no threat to him. Of course, she intended to prove him wrong.

"And the third match begins! Kitten in one corner, Gleeca in the other! Warrior against wizard! Fighter versus magician! This match is guaranteed to be as exciting as the first!" The announcer's words flowed over her like water as she took her place in the ring. She ignored the screams of the crowd and focused her energies on her opponent.

Kitten stared down the blue man from Mithar. His eyes were red. He looked back at her calmly, assessing her as she did him. With the slightest movement, almost undetectable, he flicked one finger. Kitten suppressed another grin. She knew what he had just done. He had activated his independent, invisible personal force shield. It would protect him well against all but the strongest physical attacks. He took one step forward, and she did the same. He seemed to gain confidence and reached slowly for his belt and unclipped a magic dagger. He was in no hurry. Now was her chance. Quick as lightning, Kitten dashed straight into him. He made no move to stop her, knowing his force shield would most likely hold against such an ill-timed move. But she had more than that planned. She pounded her left shoulder into the shield and reached under her arm with her right hand. A simple thought was all it took. She had practiced such disarming techniques often enough. A nearly invisible spark flew from one finger, and the shield gave way. Too surprised to react in time, the magic-thrower stood with his dagger held above his head, ready to throw a spell at her. But she rammed into him with her left shoulder, and he fell without any resistance. She had caught him so off-guard that she was able to snatch the dagger away and pin him to the ground before he could even move.

"Looks like it's all over, folks!" the announcer said with a hint of annoyance in his tone. "Miss Izzill sure knows how to finish a fight! That one was as quick as her first match! But wait a minute! Something's happening!"

Something was happening, indeed. Gleeca seemed to be melting away in Kitten's fingers. Of course! The magic-throwers of Mithar were snow people. They could melt their bodies and reform them elsewhere. It was too late to stop him now. She leapt to her feet and stood ready to repel his attack. He reformed right in front of her. As the announcer described in disbelief what was going on to the crowds, Kitten herself felt somewhat shocked. She had known the Mithar people could do this. Why had she not been prepared for it? She had been distracted and overconfident. Silently, she berated herself for letting her guard down. Stupid mistakes like that would take her out of the tournament. She nearly chuckled at the irony that Vincoral had been the one to warn her against her own tendency toward overconfidence. But she would not let this temporary setback defeat her. The wizard now knew that she could use magic, too. She no longer had the element of surprise. But that did not mean she was finished yet. He would be expecting her to take advantage of the magic dagger she still held in her hand. But she had never liked such props. She felt that they interfered with a more direct and accurate use of magic. She preferred the personal touch.

She raised the dagger into the air, as if preparing to throw a spell at Gleeca. He reacted by throwing up his hands, ready to cast a counter-spell. He did not reset his shield. It was a mistake he would regret. Kitten pulled a dagger from her own belt. It was not magic, but that didn't matter. She threw it with a perfect aim that sliced off one of the wizard's fingers and sent the blade deep into his chest. She dropped the magic dagger and blinked her eyes once, slowly. A faint glow appeared around Gleeca, holding him down so that he couldn't cast any spells with his hands. He seemed to rely on his hands and his dagger to do all the work. Another mistake. Kitten had long ago learned to cast spells with a simple thought. It had saved her life many times. She stepped over to the wizard, reached effortlessly through the glow, and pulled out her dagger. The wound in his chest healed almost immediately, as the skin melted and reformed together. The hole apparently remained only as long as the offending object was in place. It was a good thing she had thought to place the binding spell over him.

"What an exciting match!" the announcer seemed to have recovered his interest in the battle "We couldn't have seen that coming if we'd had a crystal ball! Up next, it's the fourth and final match of the day! Don't go anywhere, folks!"

Kitten stepped into her tent in a daze. Only her second fight in the tournament, and she had made a mistake. She couldn't afford to let down her guard like that. She couldn't afford to make assumptions. She couldn't afford to forget things. She promised herself that it wouldn't happen again. As Zharran bustled around, getting things ready for tomorrow and preparing dinner, she reached into the bag she carried with her everywhere and pulled out a letter that had been written long ago. She read it silently, although she didn't really need to see the words. They had quite some time ago been permanently burned into her memory.

"My dearest daughter, I am writing this letter in case the tyrant Vincoral the Demonic succeeds in destroying our people and crushing the Nation of Cantari. I want to make sure that you know that I never gave up and that I will always believe in our people's right to freedom and their ability to win it back. I knew from the day you were born that you would have a special part to play in the protection of our people, and I have the utmost confidence in you. I know you will be strong for all of us; I know you will never forget why we have fought so long and so hard. Even if we lose the upcoming battle with the Demon, we will return to fight again until he is banished from our land. You may have to continue the fight after your mother and I are gone. I know you will make us proud. I love you always, your father."

Reading the letter from her father always gave Kitten the confidence and determination to face another day. Now she took a deep breath and vowed once more to avenge the deaths of her parents and everyone in their village. She would not rest until Vincoral had been defeated. After all, that was why she was here. Thirty years ago, he had offered the world a chance to defeat him, and thirty years ago, no one had stepped forward. As time passed, Vincoral had relaxed his relentless campaign to rule the world and settled into a role as ruler of Cantari. It hadn't taken long for the people who had not seen his power firsthand to forget how dangerous and destructive he was. The stories of the tournament had become tales of amusement among the children, and Vincoral found that it amused him to set up another tournament, exactly thirty years after the first. Kitten had always suspected that he had chosen that date because it would give her enough time to mature and prepare. He seemed eager to prove once and for all to the people of Cantari that they had no savior and no hope.

But the stories of the last survivor of the Warrior Clan had spread once she had taken up residence in the village of Moonsea, where the greatest martial arts teacher of the entire land lived. From that time on, the people had begun to think that perhaps the war was not yet over. Only the Cantari Nation seemed to be aware of the true purpose of the tournament. Vincoral himself would be fighting, disguised as one of the contestants. There was no doubt as to his ability to make it to the final match, when he would reveal himself to the crowds. And if he won, the people of Cantari would suffer even more. He had promised to slay one Cantari citizen for every second that the final match lasted, unless he was defeated. Why, no one knew but Vincoral himself. If Kitten managed to slay him first, she would be the hero of her people, a true champion. If she did not succeed, more blood would be spilled than she had seen on the day that her village had been slaughtered.

"Wake up, Kitten! It's nearly time for your first match! Hurry!"

Kitten leaped to her feet. She had dozed off in her tent after a light breakfast, waiting for the tournament to begin again. She could now hear the announcer outside, urging people into their seats. Zharran stood by her side anxiously, waiting to follow her to the battlefield. She stepped outside and looked up to see her next opponent already in his position. He was dressed in a martial artist uniform, but she didn't recognize the design. He could be human, for all she could tell. She knew she would have to stay on her toes, not knowing anything about the man ahead of time. She hurried into her place, and the announcer introduced her to the crowd.

"And Miss Kitten Izzill finally makes it to the stage, folks! I guess she slept in this morning! No matter, she and her opponent are both ready to go now! So let's get this fight started!"

Kitten took a moment to study the fighter at the other side of the field. He was only a few inches taller than she and appeared to be human. The martial artist uniform indicated that he was well-trained in physical fighting, but that didn't rule out magic skills. Kitten disliked going into a fight without knowing what to expect, but if she couldn't handle this situation, she was unlikely to be able to handle Vincoral the Demonic. So she gritted her teeth and stepped forward. She waited for him to make the first move, but he seemed to be waiting for her to do the same. The crowd began to get impatient. She had to force herself to wait longer; she didn't want to rush in and make another mistake.

The man seemed to decide something. He dashed around to her left, and she spun to face him. He came at her, and with a flick of his wrist, he sent a jolt of electricity into her left hip. Her leg locked up, and she stumbled to the ground. Quickly, she cast a counter-spell, but he was already standing over her, his fist held ready to strike. She reached to block the blow with her left arm and punched at his knee with her right. He staggered backwards but immediately regained his balance. She stayed crouched low and waited for him to move again. This time, she didn't have to wait long. He leaped over her, spinning in

26

the air, going higher than she could have possibly jumped, and landed behind her. Hoping to catch him before his feet touched the ground, she turned and ran towards him, jumping and kicking into the air. But she seemed to pass right through him and landed awkwardly on the ground, barely escaping a twisted ankle. She looked back and saw the man vanish like mist. Behind him, where he had been before he jumped, he still stood. In the blink of an eye, he was running straight toward her. She rolled forward on the ground, forcing him to jump over her; then she spun on her back and kicked him. He fell into the force field, and she jumped to her feet and grinned. Now she knew what he was. A technique like the one he had used was unmistakable. The stories had said that the Ninja Clan had died out hundreds of years ago. Apparently, the stories were wrong. He was Cantari, a Cantari ninja.

"Have you ever seen anything like that in your life, folks?!" the announcer asked rhetorically. "I know I haven't! Whatever Raisa just did, it was unbelievable! I don't blame Kitten for falling for it! I sure did! That was incredible!"

Kitten made a mental note to try not to injure this opponent too badly; she had questions for him. She thought back to her training and readied herself mentally to fight a ninja. He seemed to be unaware that she had figured out his secret. He crouched low, ready to strike again, and jumped forward spinning around and around, faster and faster, until he was a blur, like a little tornado. She recognized this technique too. It was meant to frighten opponents into attempting to dodge or escape. At the last second, he would reach out and catch the victim unawares. Instead, Kitten held her ground and waited for him to get close, then she reached into his vortex and grabbed him by the collar of his shirt. He was surprised but not unprepared. He grabbed her wrist and spun back the other way, throwing her off her feet and onto the ground. She quickly grabbed his wrist and pulled, using him as leverage to jump back on her feet. Then she pulled him close to her and held her palm up to his face. She cast a spell and pushed him away from her again, ready for him to counteract it. But he seemed stunned. She had cast a misting spell to temporarily blind and deafen him, and it had apparently worked better than she had expected. He stumbled, with his hands ready to repel an attack, but he seemed uncertain what else to do. He obviously had no magic skills of his own. Kitten walked straight up to Raisa and punched him in the jaw with her best right hook. He fell to the ground unconscious, and the crowd around her roared with excitement.

"Amazing! Simply amazing! Kitten Izzill is rocketing to the top of the tournament charts! She's beaten her third opponent! Raisa is out cold! Unbelievable!"

Kitten watched the doctors take the ninja away to the recovery tent and followed them slowly. Her next match would be coming up soon, but she hoped to speak with Raisa before then, before he got a chance to leave. The tent was dark, and several doctors were watching over their patients, healing them with the red glow of their magic. In one cot was the Brunt warrior she had fought in the first match. Next to him was the human who had lost the second match. On the other side was Gleeca, and next to him, a black Shifter lay moaning. The doctors were just placing Raisa onto an empty cot, and Kitten stood nearby, waiting for them to finish. One of them laid a hand over the ninja's face, and the red glow engulfed his features. In moments, he was regaining consciousness. He immediately shooed the doctors away and sat up. He looked right at Kitten and spoke in a respectful but vaguely annoyed tone.

"You fought very well. I had thought I was prepared for your magic, but I have had little practice in repelling it. My people do not use magic. Your physical prowess was not lacking, either. How did you know how to stop the Tornadex?"

"I practiced with the last martial arts teacher known to my people in the village of Moonsea," Kitten answered quickly. "He prepared me well for every possible situation. Including encountering a ninja. Although at the time, I had doubted the use of such practice, I now see that it has saved me a great deal of trouble. You are a great fighter, as well. We had thought that all ninjas had died long ago. Can I convince you to tell me your story? It may be helpful to both of us."

"I will tell you my story if you will tell me yours. Sit. The reason the people of Cantari have thought for so long that the ninja clan had died off is that we went into hiding. Three hundred years ago, the elders of my village received a vision that told of a powerful tyrant who would crush all who stood in his path and destroy the people of Cantari Nation. He would destroy the Ninja Clan as well if he were not stopped. The elders chose to hide our people rather than face the evil that was approaching. Three hundred years was enough time to convince the world that we were gone forever. The Demonic One came and took the freedom of the Cantari people, and we were protected by the stories of our disappearance. We hid in the Forest Beyond the Mountain and did nothing when Vincoral and his soldiers passed by. It is for that cowardly behavior that I have come to the tournament myself and left my village behind. We have worked hard to perfect our skills, hoping to one day defeat this madman, but I can see now that we have been too long away from the people of the outside world. You easily defeated me, and I am one of the elite ninjas in the bodyguard troop of the elders. Perhaps we have been wrong to deny ourselves the use of magic, as well. I came here to stop Vincoral and bring peace back to Cantari so that my people may return to the outside world. But I see now that I never stood a chance in this competition. Perhaps you will fare better."

"I hope you're right, Raisa. Vincoral is the most poweral wizard warrior this world has seen," Kitten looked away and sighed. "I may not stand much of a chance, either. But perhaps, you can help. Your people may have developed some techniques in the last few centuries that I wouldn't know. If you could teach me, I would at least have the advantage of a little knowledge. And knowledge is power."

"I would be honored to teach you anything you wish to know," Raisa bowed his head. "If I can be of any assistance in the defeat of the Demonic One, I would give my life to do so. It is a shame the other contestants in this tournament are unaware of what is at stake. But I suppose we should not yet enlighten them. Anything that goes against Vincoral's plans may cause him to abandon the entire event."

"I must prepare for the next battle. I see the doctors bringing in the contestant who lost to my new opponent. Meet me in my tent this evening. We will talk more over dinner, and I will tell you about myself. Then we can discuss my training under your tutelage."

Kitten left the recovery tent and hurried past the doctor's new patient, a ranger from the hills of Sheela. Outside, she looked to see who her next opponent would be. The man was cloaked in a black robe with a hood that covered his head. Only his chin peeked from underneath the cloth, and it was deep purple. She knew he must be a wizard from Howerth Lake. They were an elite group of magic-casters who considered themselves the best wizards in the world. She would test that theory today. The ranger certainly hadn't stood a chance. His magic arrows and knives couldn't have defeated a magician of this caliber.

Kitten watched the wizard carefully, hoping to see a sign of which hand he favored or where a weak spot might be. But he was careful to avoid her gaze, as if he knew she was watching him. For a moment, the thought crossed her mind that perhaps he did know. Perhaps he could see her in the crowd of people milling about. Perhaps he knew who she was. Could this be Vincoral's disguise? But, no, that would be ridiculous. Why would he disguise himself as another wizard? It would be much too obvious. Of course, he might anticipate that sort of reaction and choose to disguise himself so in order to fool her. Kitten shook the doubts from her head. Now was not the time to think in circles. She had no way of knowing whether this was him or not, until she was face-to-face with him. In the meantime, it did her no good to speculate and confuse herself. She walked quickly back to her own tent for a gulp of drinking water and then took her place just outside the battlefield. She watched her new opponent carefully, waiting for the match to begin. The announcer in the unseen paddock was already droning away, trying to pump up the crowd. But the crowd was already excited.

"Are you ready for the third match of the day?! Our two contestants are! Kitten is back on the battlefield once more to match skills with the great and powerful Howerth wizard, Draegor!"

Kitten watched the wizard step forward to meet her. He showed no hesitation and no fear. He slowly pushed back the hood of his robe and looked her over once. He seemed to dislike what he saw. Kitten wasn't any happier. She began to worry that perhaps she wasn't strong enough to stand up to an elite wizard like this. But now was no time for hesitation. She moved one finger and set up her own invisible shield, like the one that Gleeca had used. But this one was fine-tuned to work against magic, although it probably wouldn't hold against the powerful magics of Draegor. He surely knew it was there and could disarm it easily. Kitten decided to take the offensive and threw her right arm in front of her, pushing a spell from the palm of her hand. The streaks of lightning flew toward her opponent, and he deflected them without even blinking. Kitten began to seriously worry.

"It doesn't look like this match will go well for Miss Izzill! She may have finally met her match!" the announcer sounded relieved at the thought.

Kitten told herself to focus. She just had to win this one; she just had to! She decided not to give Draegor time to breathe. She ran through her most powerful spells in her mind, casting each one in turn. He blocked most of them without moving. Some of them he had to actually counteract with a spell of his own. Only one hit him directly. It was an icy wind spell, and it blew him back against the force field. He seemed angered that she had found something that could touch him. He waved one hand, and she was thrown backwards. She hit the force field, and the wind was knocked out of her. She lay on the ground recovering, but Draegor was already preparing his next attack. His next spell yanked her up into the air and threw her back down again. It did this over and over until she lost count and nearly lost consciousness. Finally, he seemed satisfied that she'd had enough. He dropped her roughly back onto the ground and strode slowly towards her.

"Well, folks, this match is all wrapped up! The mighty Kitten has roared her last in this tournament! It looks like she'll be lucky if she can move enough to go home now!"

No! It can't end like this! I won't be beaten! Especially like this! Kitten's thoughts were angry and red. She felt tears welling up her eyes. She hovered on the edge of consciousness. Her focus wavered between the slow, methodical steps that the wizard took across the ground toward her and the crowd of people beyond the force field. Her vision blurred and cleared. She saw the sloping hill behind the seated audience and the strip of beach where the hill met the ocean about a mile away. She saw a few ships on the water, and her attention lingered on them as they passed each other. A muffled voice interrupted her thoughts just before she faded out, and she found herself being pulled back to reality. The wizard had grabbed her with his bare hands and pulled her to her feet. He seemed angry. She snapped back into focus.

"Is this the best you can do, little girl?! I expected better, considering how far you've come in the tournament. Why did you waste my time? Fine then, we'll consider this match over."

Draegor dropped her unceremoniously and started to walk away. Kitten could feel her temper rising. How dare he act like that? Like she was some novice fighter with no skills, not worth his time? She dragged herself to her feet, and the crowd gasped. She summoned her strength and cast another icy wind spell just to get his attention. Then she flew across the ground and tackled him. He seemed to slither out of her hands, and he appeared quite annoyed that he still had to deal with her. She cast a powerful blizzard spell. Ice and snow blew horizontally around them, but she barely felt it. He staggered into the force field, which held the storm in so that it didn't touch their audience. His skin was beginning to look scaly, like a snake. Kitten hesitated a moment, wondering if this might be a significant development. She just didn't know enough about Howerth wizards to be sure. They kept to themselves too much for her to learn any of their secrets. She cast a second blizzard spell, intensifying the storm, and approached him cautiously. He didn't even see her; his eyes were closed. She reached back to hit him as hard as she could with her right fist, but suddenly he was gone. His robe had dropped to the ground, and he was simply not there. She heard a heavy breathing sound and turned quickly to face it. There, behind her, standing several feet higher, with claws bigger than her head and teeth as long as her arm, was a great purple dragon. She suddenly realized what one of the secrets of the Howerth wizards must be.

Outside the protective force field, the announcer spoke in awe, "I can't believe it, folks, I just can't believe it! This tournament keeps getting better and better! Looks like Draegor had a little something up his sleeve, but don't count Kitten out yet! She's shown us time and again that she's not leaving this tournament without a fight!"

Kitten knew she was in trouble now. A dragon was not a creature to be taken lightly, whether it was a real dragon or one transformed from a wizard. It was likely that he breathed fire and that his skin was poisonous to the touch and that he had perfect vision and hearing to keep track of her movements. It was certain that his claws and fangs were razor sharp and that smoke was now pouring out of his mouth. He threw his head back, and flames shot upwards, fanning out over the inner surface of the force field. Suddenly, her blizzard spells were gone, and the air around them was as hot as a bonfire. His head swung back down, and he squinted at her, as if daring her to try something else. So she did.

Kitten threw a quick iceball spell at his eyes to distract him and ran around to the side. She passed his long neck and ran right up to his left front claw. He started to reach for her, and she jumped onto the back of his paw and ran up his arm. He twisted his neck around to see her, and she could see the smoke starting to pour out of his mouth again. She timed it in her head just right and leaped over the flames when they shot from his throat. She rolled over his back and dashed back up towards his neck. He made another attempt to scorch her, but she was too far behind his head this time. He reached back with both front claws, trying to grab her, but she dodged every swipe. She raced up his neck, defying gravity, until she reached his head. He shook back and forth, trying to throw her off. She kept her balance long enough to cast a quick stick spell, and her boots stuck to his scaly skin. But the poison started to eat through the material; she could feel it beginning to boil. She knew she had to hurry. He reached for her with both claws again, and she ducked under one of them and stabbed the other with her dagger. Then, she quickly cast an ice spell directly into his eyes. The orbs were immediately frozen solid, and he yowled in pain. He swiped at her blindly. When she couldn't duck quickly enough, she stabbed his paw with her dagger again.

The soles in her boots were nearly gone before she got an opportunity to finish her plan. She ran a hand over the blade of her dagger, covering it in a special magic coating that could sedate dragons. She raised the dagger high above her head and brought it down on his forehead. The blade went in up to the hilt, magically passing straight through the thick bone of his skull. Kitten unglued what was left of her boots and jumped off. She rolled away to avoid being crushed as the dragon fell to the ground. He struggled for just a moment longer and went limp. A hush fell over the crowd. They sat in shock for nearly a minute. Even the announcer was silent. Kitten breathed deeply, her head swimming with relief and excitement.

Then, the people screamed. It was the loudest response she'd heard yet. They all stood up, some of them jumping up and down. The announcer's voice was drowned out. The doctors stood by in shock. The moderators of the tournament, normally neutral, shouted congratulations to Kitten and cheered along with the crowd. She looked around at everyone and smiled, spotting a family of Cantari origin nearest the battlefield. They looked at her with tears in their eyes, as if they finally knew that their freedom was within sight.

It was almost thirty minutes before the crowd settled down enough to even hear the announcer's voice. He was starting to sound hoarse. "There's one more fight coming up, folks, but we'll give you some time to settle down! I need some time myself! That was the most incredible thing I've ever seen! This tournament is full of surprises, but nothing could possibly top that!"

Kitten spent some time in the recovery tent before returning to her own for an evening meal. Zharran was waiting excitedly for her, and Raisa soon followed her inside. He congratulated her on her victory and helped get dinner ready. Zharran talked almost nonstop about how amazing the last match had been. It was the most Kitten had ever heard him talk at once. He finally silenced himself when Raisa began to speak.

"You may be even more talented than I had thought, Miss Izzill. Very few have ever faced a wizard of Howerth or a dragon and survived with all of their limbs intact. You managed to fight both in the same being and not only survive but triumph. Of course, he wasn't a winged dragon, or it might have been far more difficult to deal with him. But it was still quite a feat. You are as agile as a ninja, if I may say so. I would be happy to teach you whatever I can to help you defeat Vincoral the Demonic. I'm certain you have a very good chance at success. We shall begin tomorrow when the sun rises. Now, if you feel well enough, I would like to hear more of your story, as you promised."

Kitten told the ninja her life's story as they finished their meal. She told of the village she lived in as a child, the death of her parents at the hands of the Demonic One, the atrocities she had seen him commit, the training that she began at such an early age in the hopes of freeing her nation, her time at Moonsea and the time she spent elsewhere training with other fighting masters, and how she met Zharran in one of the villages she lived in for a while and how he had been helping her ever since. When she had told him everything that she could think of, she closed her eyes and waited for him to respond.

"That is a very painful story," Raisa's voice was quiet and respectful. "Ninjas are trained to live on their own and be independent, but we always have the support of the village. You pushed yourself to do the work and to move forward when others would have given up in despair. Your determination will likely be one of your greatest assets. Thank you for sharing your story with me. I am honored."

Kitten smiled. Just having someone acknowledge her hard work was enough to warm her heart. She knew she now had two friends she could count on. She was so happy, she laughed out loud. Zharran grinned at her, the tanned skin on his face wrinkling in a way that she seldom saw; he knew what she was thinking, and he agreed. Even Raisa found her laughter infectious and joined in.

"You must get some rest now," he said at last. "We will train in the morning, and you will still have one fight tomorrow. If you win that one, you will advance to the final match. There are not many fighters left. One of them must be Vincoral. But we'll worry about that in the morning. Get plenty of sleep tonight. I will come for you at dawn."

As Raisa was preparing to leave, the three of them heard a commotion outside. There were some screams and what sounded like a cannon firing. Raisa threw open the tent flap, and they saw people running. He disappeared into the crowd, heading towards whatever they were running from. Kitten motioned for Zharran to stay behind and followed the ninja. The people were running away from the beach. She almost expected to see Vincoral there, but she knew that would be unlikely. He had no reason to start any trouble until he had at least fought Kitten. She reached the edge of the sand and paused. In the water, close to shore, was one of the ships she had noticed earlier in the day during her fight with Draegor. She now saw that it had fired on one of the other ships in the inlet. The second ship was taking on water and being boarded by men from the first. Raisa appeared next to her, and they looked at each other, wondering what to do.

"All right! Everyone listen up! We're here to take what was taken from others by Vincoral the Demonic! This is his ship, and these are his lackeys working it! If no one else interferes, no one will get hurt!"

Kitten and Raisa heard the voice coming over the loudspeaker from the ship, and they both chuckled a bit. It was amusing to see someone attacking Vincoral in such a blatant manner. They seemed to have no fear of reprisals. Did they think that the Demon would be too preoccupied with the tournament to notice his own ship being attacked? Were they daring or stupid? Or both? Kitten's first thought was to stand by and watch events unfold. Vincoral hadn't shown himself yet; maybe he wasn't going to. In that case, she could watch these pirates leave with whatever treasures Vincoral had brought with him on his ship. On the other hand, whether they got away with it today or not, he wasn't likely to forget such a sleight. He would hunt them down at a later time and slaughter each man mercilessly. He might show up any second now, and the bloodbath would take place in these waters. Either way, Kitten didn't want more people to be killed while she stood on the shore and watched. She'd made up her mind; she had to take action.

"I can't let them get killed! I'm going to get on board that ship!" she shouted above the din.

Raisa nodded as if he had planned on doing the same, and she ran down to the edge of the water. The rowboats were a little farther down the beach, in a row next to a dock, but taking one of them somehow didn't seem like the best strategy. On the other side of the beach was an outcropping of rock, like a little cliff. Just a few feet from it was another rock just as high in the water. And next to that was Vincoral's ship, connected to the pirate ship now by a plank, across which men ran back and forth with chests, sacks, and hostages.

Kitten ran to the cliff, climbed up to the top, and leaped across the gap to the rock tower in the water. She looked down at the first ship. It was about a ten-foot drop and about five feet away. But the mast with its furled mainsail and rigging was closer. She backed up a little and ran and jumped off the edge. She caught hold of a rope in mid-air and slid down to the deck. Two looters were on board, and they both dropped what they were carrying and faced her. She didn't think it was likely that they would listen to what she had to say. Each one of them drew a sword. She had to get to their leader, their captain. He was probably on the other ship. She would have to dispose of these underlings and cross the planking. One of the pirates, slightly to her left, pointed his sword at her, and a flash of light flew from the tip of it. Kitten dodged to the right, barely missing the spark. It hit the rock behind her and seemed to have no effect. The second man threw a spell at her with his hand. She ducked under the glow, a binding spell, and ran around him. She cast a spell of her own, a wind spell to blow them off their feet. They both tried to throw more magic at her, but it was blown back at them by the force of her magic. The first man stiffened as if he had been frozen, and the second was bound tightly and fell to the floor.

Kitten turned and raced across the planking to the pirate ship. The other men had seen what she had done, however, and were gathered around her, ready to fend off her attack. She paused momentarily. She didn't want to hurt them, but she couldn't freeze all of them at once. And if she were captured herself, it was unlikely they would let her talk to the captain. They probably thought that she was a member of Vincoral's crew. As she debated, the men prepared to strike at her. But before anyone could make another move, one man stepped out in front and motioned for the others to back down. He was a human and had an air of authority about him that told Kitten he was the man to talk to here. He rested one hand on the hilt of his sword. On the other side of his belt was a whip. He wore no captain's hat but rather a simple headband. When he spoke, she knew that his was the voice that had been on the loudspeaker earlier.

"You're not one of Vincoral's cowering servants. You don't work for him. So why are you interfering here? Who are you?"

"I am Kitten Izzill, one of the contestants in the tournament, the one who is going to defeat Vincoral and win back Cantari Nation's freedom," she spoke confidently. "I came here to warn you. Although I don't disapprove of you looting one of his ships, you won't get away with it with your lives. Even if you leave now before he shows up, he'll chase after you another day. And he will find you."

The man laughed at her and asked, "What would you have us do then? Return his gold to him and beg for his forgiveness? I appreciate your concern, but we are here today for the same reason you are: to bring down the Demonic One. We intend to destroy him by taking away the gold that finances his domination of your nation and others. We have a magic shield set up in a secret place, where we will hide until his attention is gone from us. Now, I will offer you the chance to leave my ship peacefully, if that's all you came to say."

"That is all I came to say. But before I leave, I'd like to add one thing: You can't defeat Vincoral the Demonic by picking away at his wealth. He is one tyrant who doesn't depend on riches to keep his rule over people strong. He doesn't need money. He conquered my nation without it, and he can rule without it. He only keeps it in order to remind people that he's in charge. You may get lucky when you hide behind your magic shield; he may, indeed, lose interest in searching for you. But that will only be because he doesn't consider his wealth that important. The suffering of other people is far more entertaining to him. You could take every gold coin he owns away from him and strip his castles bare, and it wouldn't change a thing."

The pirate captain seemed to think about this for a moment. He looked her over as if deciding whether or not she knew what she was talking about. Meanwhile, she caught a glimpse of Raisa climbing up over the side of the ship behind the captain and his men. She motioned quickly for him to wait before attacking. If this could end without any further violence, she would prefer it that way.

"You may be telling the truth," the captain said slowly. "You certainly seem to know the Demonic One well. You've seen his destruction firsthand, I assume, since you are from Cantari, where he spends most of his time. But, I repeat, what would you have us do? We don't have the power to stop him ourselves."

"You seem to have plenty of manpower, and you have some magic. There must be something more useful you could do. There are rebel groups who fight Vincoral's troops; perhaps, you could join them. They sometimes send in spies to try to find a weakness in his armies or his personal defenses."

"An easy way to end your life, which is not something any of us are interested in," he shook his head. "But your determination is admirable. I truly wish there were something we could do to help you in your quest to stop Vincoral here in the tournament. But I fear determination will not be enough to end his reign of terror. You are obviously talented, but I'm not sure you will be able to defeat him. However, as you said, we do have some magic. I myself know a particular trick that is rather rare and unknown by most magic-casters. I learned it from my father, who learned it from his father. I would be happy to teach it to you in order to assist you. It's the best I have to offer."

"Why, thank you. I would appreciate your assistance. But you'd have to stay here to teach me. I can't leave; I have a fight tomorrow," she reminded him.

"Then I will stay. My men can take the ship and its new cargo to our hiding place and await my return. I had nothing else planned after this little adventure anyway."

He smiled at her, and the pirates began making preparations to leave. Kitten sighed with relief. Things had worked out better than she had expected.

"I should probably take a moment to introduce you to my friend then," she waved at the ninja. "This is Raisa. He is going to train me in some special ninja techniques."

The pirate started and spun around to face the ninja, who stood calmly at the side of the ship. The captain laughed and shook Raisa's hand warmly.

"I am very happy to meet you. That was quite a trick. Perhaps, you can teach me something while I'm teaching your friend something."

Raisa nodded politely, and the pirate looked at them both and grinned. He waved at one of his men, who then approached them.

"Get my things from my cabin and inform Binthor that he'll be in charge until I return."

The man nodded and disappeared through a door into an inner chamber of the ship. His captain nodded at Kitten and Raisa and led them to the starboard side of the ship, where a small rowboat was fastened. He quickly lowered it to the water and threw a rope ladder over the side so they could climb down. Raisa went first, and Kitten followed him. The captain came after with a bag slung over one shoulder. He waved a kind of salute back at the men on the ship and then took the oars. He rowed them to shore and stored the boat behind a nearby rock so that it was out of sight of most of the tournament grounds. They could see the pirate ship heading out to sea now.

Kitten led the way back to her tent, taking a more circuitous route than the one she had taken to the beach. She wanted to make sure they weren't spotted by any of Vincoral's lookouts. It was possible, even probable, that he had seen everything with his all-seeing eye, anyway. But it was worth a try. They made it back to her tent without any trouble, and Kitten introduced her new friend to Zharran. They all sat down to rest, and the captain took the opportunity to officially introduce himself.

"My name is Markuss. I am a pirate by trade and a rebel at heart. There's not much more to tell really. I've sailed the seas with my men for the last ten years, ever since Vincoral destroyed my hometown on the coast of Argull. He was passing through on his way to Cantari, as I understand it."

"He has destroyed many lives and many villages. Most of the world is now linked in some way through him," Kitten said sullenly.

"Indeed," Raisa agreed. "But to save that world, we will need our strength. I suggest now that we all get some sleep. You are welcome to share my tent, Markuss, unless you have one of your own to pitch."

"Thank you, I'll be happy to take you up on that offer, my kind ninja," the pirate grinned. "Good night, Miss Izzill, Zharran. I'll see you bright and early in the morning."

"It is nice to have some help from others and to see other people with an interest in what we're doing, isn't it?" Zharran smiled at Kitten.

Zharran continued smiling as he set up their cots for a night's rest. Kitten sighed contentedly. He was right, of course. But she worried that their help still wouldn't give her enough of an advantage against Vincoral.

"Time to get up, Kitten! The sun's nearly up. Raisa should be here to fetch you any minute."

Kitten opened her eyes slowly. She hadn't gotten up at dawn for training in years. She shook herself awake and grabbed a light breakfast and some water. She was just finishing when Raisa poked his head into the tent. She nodded at him and followed him outside. He led her over a small hill to a little valley that formed between the hills of the region and a nearby forest. Markuss was waiting for them, resting under a tree with his eyes closed. For a minute, Kitten thought he might be sleeping, but he opened one eye and grinned at her when they came closer.

"I thought I'd tag along, but Raisa will handle your first lesson. Right, Rais?" he winked mischievously at the ninja.

"Ahem, yes," Raisa cleared his throat and turned away from the rogue. "There are two specific techniques that have been developed recently enough in my village that you couldn't possibly know them. The first is the Raptor Strike."

Raisa demonstrated the first technique by running at Kitten and jumping as high as her head. She steeled herself and tried to block any hits, but he landed on her shoulders and immediately jumped off again. He flipped over in mid-air over her head and came down again on his hands. His feet fell forward in front of her and met the ground, and his hands pulled her down with him. He flipped her quickly up into the air over him, and she landed on her back. He followed without letting go of her shoulders and landed with his feet on her legs. He seemed to be pressing her into the ground with greater force than she expected. He quickly released her, stood up, and helped her off the ground.

"Of course, at the end of that move, in a real fight, I would have stabbed daggers hidden in each of my shirtsleeves through your shoulders, pinning you to the ground. It's quite an effective technique," he added calmly.

"Yes, I see," Kitten gasped. "It felt as if you were pushing me into the ground harder than I would have expected you to be able to do in that position."

"It's the virtue of that particular technique. It allows one greater use of force in unexpected ways. It takes a great deal of practice to get it right. One must learn to align one's flow of energy properly."

"Sounds a bit like magic. Are you sure ninjas don't use magic?" she grinned at him.

"Well, perhaps we use something similar that you would classify as magical but we would not. Let me show you the second technique, and you can make up your own mind," he nodded.

Raisa seemed to concentrate on something for just a second, then he walked slowly around Kitten until he was standing behind her. He suddenly grabbed her head and clamped one hand over her mouth. She tried to remember not to struggle, since this was only a demonstration, but it was difficult. Her head was beginning to spin, as if she were swimming with her eyes closed. She began to get the distinct sensation of gulping down water into her lungs every time she took a breath. She couldn't understand what was going on, but she felt as if she were drowning. She began gasping for air. Raisa's hand didn't cover her nose, but she couldn't seem to breathe properly. She tried to move her arms, but they moved slowly as if through water. Raisa let go of her, and she fell to her knees, choking and gasping. Her head began to clear, and in a moment, he helped her to her feet again.

"It's called the Watergod," he explained. "I would have used it on you in our match together if I had been able to get close enough. But it requires immense concentration, and you were a little too quick for me."

"Well, that definitely felt like magic," she gasped. "I think you ninjas are learning how to use magic on your own in some way that's unrelated to the way the normal casters learn to use it. In that case, I think I might be able to improve upon it and make it easier to use. I'm a bit of a natural at making spells easier to cast without all the frills of props and dramatic preparations. Tell me how you do it."

"Again, it's a matter of focusing one's energy, this time focusing on the water energy that's inherent in the body and directing it through the opponent's mind. You must make them believe that they are actually in a pool of water. You can see why it takes so much concentration. I direct the flow through my hands, but perhaps you can find a more efficient way."

"I think I can. But I don't know if I could use it on Vincoral. He would probably have a defense against that sort of thing. Maybe if I just took the principal of the technique and adapted it to him specifically, I could come up with something that would get through his defenses. But first, I'll have to learn the basics."

Kitten practiced the Raptor Strike and the Watergod all morning under Raisa's instruction. It didn't take her long to perfect the alignment of her energy. She could focus and direct it much faster than

Raisa could. The Raptor Strike was easier, but Watergod didn't take her much longer to learn. By lunchtime, Raisa had decided that she could learn no more from him. They went back to her tent for something to eat, which Zharran had prepared while he was waiting for their return. The first match of the day had already been held, and the second, Kitten's only match that day, had been announced.

"You're fighting in an hour, so you'd better hold off on any more training until afterward. Your opponent is a new fighter. His name is Akkanar," Zharran told her.

"The final match is tomorrow," she mused. "Either my opponent today or the man who won the first match today is Vincoral the Demonic. Who won the first match?"

"I believe his name was Seelis," he answered. "He won the fight very quickly. I was in the tent, but I no sooner heard the bell than the announcer said that the fight was over. I didn't get a look at him."

"Sounds like Vincoral, all right," she grimaced. "But no sense taking any chances. I'd better be ready for Akkanar just as if he were the Demonic One. He might find it amusing to knock me out of the tournament without letting me get to the final round."

Kitten was the first to the battlefield that afternoon. As she waited patiently for her opponent to show up, the announcer introduced them both to the crowds, although by now, an introduction for Kitten Izzill was entirely unnecessary. Nearly the entire audience roared with applause when they heard her name.

"You all know the young Miss Kitten Izzill from Cantari Nation! You're about to meet her final competitor before the last match of the tournament: Mr. Akkanar! Little is known about the man, but you'll see him for yourself in just a moment!"

Kitten watched as the next competitor entered the battlefield. He wore a heavy black cloak that masked his face. He brought a walking stick with him, and he leaned on it heavily, as if he were old and decrepit. Kitten knew better than to fall for a trick like that, but she wondered why he would bother. Surely, he didn't think she had made it this far in the tournament only to be defeated by such a crude ploy! But he just stood there, and she could make no determination from this distance.

"I have been greatly impressed by your skills in your previous fights. I look forward to this battle."

He spoke slowly and softly, his voicing cracking as if it hadn't been used in years. Kitten felt somewhat confused about her opponent but determined not to let him distract or trick her. She nodded back to him and took her fighting stance.

"And here we go, folks! You better get ready!" the announcer shouted.

Akkanar made the first move, without hesitation. He leaped toward her, showing no sign of decrepitude or excessive old age, and swung his walking stick downward. Kitten jumped out of the way just in time, and the ground broke open where she had been standing and where the stick had struck. He ran at her again, without pausing or even slowing down, and Kitten realized that if she were going to get anywhere in this match, she was going to have to get back on the offensive.

"And Akkanar makes the first move! Kitten seems to be on the defense, but I'm sure she's just looking for an opportunity! So far, there's been no show of magic, but that will likely change soon!"

Kitten threw a blinding spell, but Akkanar ran right through it and seemed unaffected. She threw a sticking spell, but he dodged it and continued chasing her across the battlefield. She cast a fire spell, but he passed right through the flames. Nothing seemed to affect him, and he was too fast for her to avoid forever. She resolved not to panic and cast another spell, an illusion spell. A fire-breathing beast appeared between them, but Akkanar leaped through the illusion, and it dispelled.

Kitten decided to quit running and try a different approach. She turned and ran back toward him, but he didn't even pause. She whipped out her dagger and slashed at him. He blocked it with his stick, and for a moment, they both stood still, staring at one another. Kitten knew that this was not the Demonic One, but there was still something sinister about him. She swung at him with one fist, and he dodged effortlessly. He swung his stick at her, and she ducked and jabbed at him with her dagger again. He backed up one step, and she tackled him. He threw her off and cast a spell. Several vines grew out of the ground and wrapped around her ankles, holding her to the spot. He raised his stick, ready to strike.

"Kitten has taken the offensive, but Akkanar has maintained the upper hand! It looks like the incomparable Miss Izzill has finally run out of surprises!"

"Don't count on it!" Kitten whispered under her breath with a grin.

Kitten reached out one hand, pointing her fingers toward Akkanar's mouth. She focused her energy and sent it to him. He paused in surprise. His stick lowered in his hands. His eyes grew wide, and he began choking and gasping for air. He clutched at his throat. He threw himself into her, and the vines gave way. They both tumbled to the ground. Kitten pushed him away and stood up. He breathed deeply, recovering. She kicked his stick away and stood ready to repell any additional attacks. She was not disappointed. He leaped to his feet and reached out with his hands, preparing a spell. She did not intend to give him a chance to finish it, however. She ran toward him and jumped up into the air, landing on his shoulders. She finished executing the Raptor Strike with perfect timing and, with the final move, pinned him to the ground. She opted to use the original dagger technique this time but pinned him by the hands, instead of the shoulders, since his spells were channeled through his hands. He didn't even scream from the pain. He leaned back, and the hood finally fell from his face. Kitten gasped. The audience gasped. Even the announcer was speechless. They all stared at Akkanar. His skin was browned and shriveled. His eyes were sunken in. His nose was cracked at the base, as if it were ready to simply drop off. He was a zombie. He cackled hoarsely and spoke again.

"I'm not really dead, or undead. I've kept myself alive with spells and treatments for decades. I have long sought an opponent more skilled than myself, and I am happy to have found you and proud to have fought you. I can rest in peace now, knowing that the world is in good hands. I will trust its well-being to your capable skills. I only hope that my meager energies can lend you some assistance. Please accept them. And good luck, Kitten Izzill."

Akkanar pulled one of his hands free of the dagger without so much as a grimace of pain and pointed a finger at Kitten. For a moment, she worried that he still meant her harm, but she felt certain now that the only thing sinister about him was his appearance. A bright light grew at his fingertip, and it floated gently away from him and toward her. It touched her chest, and she felt a warmth fill her body. His remaining energy was definitely good. She closed her eyes for a moment, savoring the feeling of pure energy infusing her veins. She felt invincible. When she opened her eyes again, Akkanar had dropped his hand to his side, and he was no longer moving. A healer approached the battlefield reverently and scanned his body quickly with one hand. He announced softly that Akkanar had died. It had not been the injuries he sustained in the battle that had killed him. He had simply ended his life with a thought. Kitten thought about how tired he had seemed before and after the battle. As the crowd sat in silence in deference to this obviously great wizard, she wondered if she would ever know his story. After a few minutes, the healers took his body away, and Kitten walked away from the field and back to her tent. Akkanar had seemed to put a great deal of trust and faith in her abilities. It seemed that he knew about Vincoral and his plans. Once more, Kitten felt the weight of the world pressing down upon her.

"Well, that's it then," Markuss said, stepping into her tent. "Seelis must be Vincoral. He's the last one. At least, there's no wondering now."

"Yes, I suppose you're right," Kitten took a deep breath. "I'll have to be ready. Show me that trick you were talking about. Tonight."

Markuss looked at her in surprise, but Kitten nodded grimly. She didn't care how tired she was. She had to be as well-prepared as it was possible for her to be for this fight. She would need all the help she could get. He sighed and led the way outside to a spot behind her tent where they were mostly out of anyone's line of sight.

"This is a trick I only resort to if there is no other choice in a given situation. It can take a lot of energy and do a lot of damage," he spoke solemnly.

Markuss raised his hands to the sky. Slowly, Kitten began to see a glow around him. The hairs on the back of her neck stood up, and she felt the electricity in the air coursing through her skin. The wind began to whip around them, as if a storm were building. It was concentrated on their little circle of ground, however; the trees a mere twenty feet away were undisturbed. There were no clouds in the sky, but she had the distinct impression of a shadowy darkness rolling over them. The glow around Markuss brightened, and he seemed engulfed in the light. There was a bright flash, temporarily blinding Kitten, followed quickly by a crack of thunder louder than a giant's drum. She cast a vision spell to clear her sight and saw a spot on the ground nearby smoldering. A small boulder was split in two, and the ground smoked.

Markuss lowered his arms and collapsed onto the ground. He lay there for a moment, breathing deeply. Kitten inspected the target spot and found that the rock was still hot to the touch. She was impressed. It was a very good "trick."

"That was incredible!" she grinned. "You brought the power of real lightning straight down from a clear sky! If we could channel those sorts of pure, unfiltered elements without the use of substitute spells -- they only give you an imitation that can replicate only a fraction of the power -- we...we could wipe Vincoral and his evil from the face of this world! Do you have any idea what you've been holding onto all these years? The secret that your family has kept could change the world!"

Kitten paused to take a breath, and Markuss sat up and looked at her bemusedly. She helped him stand up, and he laughed out loud.

"Didn't you see how much effort and energy that took from me? I don't think it's practical to call upon the powers of pure elements on a daily basis. As I said, I only use that trick in extreme emergency circumstances. If I really put my back into it, I can call up a storm big enough to capsize any vessel. Once, I caused a tidal wave that took out a rival pirate's stronghold. But I was laid up for a week after that!"

"I found a better way to do Raisa's techniques, and I can find a better way to do yours. It's just a matter of better energy control, I'm sure of it! I don't think you realize what we have here! You must be sent from the gods to have arrived here at exactly the time that I would need you! I just need time to practice! I'll work on it for a while tonight. Tell me what you did."

"Well, the key is to attract the energy of the lightning with your own energy. It's all connected anyway. Everything in this world is connected. But you have to align your energy just so to bring it to you without actually hitting yourself with it. Mentally, I picture sending a spark up to the atmosphere, a message to get the attention of the electricity floating around up there. Then I picture where I want it to go. It takes a lot of concentration to make sure you don't call down too much power or send it off in some wild direction."

"I understand," Kitten nodded reassuringly. "I have a knack for focusing my energy quickly, efficiently, and accurately. Don't worry. I'll have this down in no time, and I think I'll be able to improve on it while I'm at it."

Markuss bid her good night and left her to her practice. It was pitch black by the time she decided to take a break. Most of the landscape behind her tent was quite charred. She went inside and collapsed into her cot. Zharran was already fast asleep. Her mind raced over tomorrow's events, but luckily, she was exhausted enough to fall asleep quickly.

"Well, folks, it's time for the final match of the tournament, the one that will decide the champion of the century! Our two contenders are Kitten Izzill and Seelis! The match starts in one hour, so you'd better get ready!"

Kitten waited as calmly as possible on the battlefield. She heard the announcer, but she knew that Seelis' real name was Vincoral. This was it. The culmination of what she had been training for. This was the battle that would decide the fate of her nation. And it would likely decide the fate of her life as well. She closed her eyes and focused her concentration. Fear was not an option. Hesitation was not an option. Failure was not an option. She opened her eyes when she sensed him approaching. He stepped onto the battlefield and met her glare. He didn't look like himself. He had transformed his image with a spell so that no one knew who he really was. But Kitten would recognize him anywhere. That icy stare, that cold aura, his very spirit surrounded her and pressed her spirit down. She shook off the feeling and held her head high, determined to show him that she would not be beaten.

"A pleasure to see you again, Kitten dear," his voice was ice-cold. "This should be a most interesting match, wouldn't you agree? Are you prepared to face me? I'm ready for you. Let's not keep our audience waiting."

"Wouldn't dream of it!" Kitten responded more confidently than she felt. "Let's get this contest started."

Kitten drew her sword and raced toward Vincoral. She was determined not to let him get the upper hand. She knew she could maintain pace with him if she never paused, never hesitated. For a moment, catching a glimpse of his ice-cold eyes, his merciless grin, she felt that there was no way possible she could defeat him alone. But she steeled herself, reminding herself that even if she couldn't survive this fight, she could still take him down with her. Vincoral stepped aside gracefully, allowing her to pass him without harming him. But she had expected him to do just that. She stopped mid-lunge, sliding briefly on the dirt, and flipped up into the air, jumping over him. She swung her arm back, nearly hitting him with her sword. But still he was too fast for her. He dodged and jumped away from her, laughing.

"You can't defeat me with those pitiful tactics, Kitten! I am a master of warfare! I was fighting while you were still in diapers!"

Kitten didn't bother to answer. She knew better than to let him draw her into an energy-sapping shouting-match. She needed to save her breath for more important tactical maneuvers. She kept her feet on the move, wary of any sudden moves Vincoral might make. She had circled him fully when she threw out some magic sparks to catch his attention. He remained focused on her, just as she had expected. She knew he would never fall for such cheap distractions. That was why she had done it. At the last second, she focused additional energy into the small sparks, which were floating swiftly in Vincoral's direction. They turned into large balls of energy and smashed into the ground at his feet. He must have seen them coming in his peripheral vision; he jumped out of harm's way in time to avoid singed feet. But Kitten hadn't expected to hit anything vital; her plan was still to distract. She hoped to throw so many distractions at him that he would lose track of where she might attack next. It was an exhausting method, but she hoped that it would be exhausting for him, too.

"Kitten seems determined to finish this final match off quickly! She's not giving Seelis a moment to rest!" the announcer's voice was a mere buzzing in Kitten's ears. "But he hasn't even attempted a single attack yet! The fight has so far been entirely one-sided! When will Kitten's opponent make a move?!"

Kitten reached for her dagger and threw it at Vincoral. He dodged it, of course, and as it struck the ground, she threw a magic force from her hand directly at him. He held out his hands to halt it, but it still pushed him back a few inches. She allowed her invisible energy to flow past his own defensive shield and then pulled it back toward her so that it slammed into his back. Without missing a beat, he flew forward, just as she leaped out of his way. He still didn't attempt an attack. She wondered if he were simply gauging her power, waiting to see how much she would throw at him. Kitten didn't want to give him a chance to wonder for long. She grabbed her dagger and ran towards Vincoral again. She swiped at him with her sword and jabbed at him with her dagger. He dodged each attack effortlessly. While she was still attacking him physically, she sent a binding spell to surround his feet. He walked backwards right through it without so much as a stumble. At the same time, she sent an electric shock through the air and into his body. He didn't even shiver. He continued staring at her almost placidly, grinning. She wanted nothing more at that moment than to wipe that grin off of his face. She focused on his eyes and forced her thoughts toward him, concentrating on water. She seemed to hear him laugh again, as if he were in her mind. Then, she felt as if a great wave of water had been pushed back over her. It crashed over her head, sucked the breath from her lungs, and caused her steps to falter. She leaped backwards and ran off to the side. He simply continued watching her. The Watergod had failed.

"Please do not insult me by playing such idiotic mind games," his voice remained as calm as ever. "If you can't do any better than this, I should end this pointless exercise now."

Kitten could feel him gathering his power. He was ready to strike. Vincoral looked straight into her mind, and his eyes flashed. They seemed to hold her, slowing down her movements. She struggled to break free of his mesmerizing stare. Something seemed to pierce her heart; she gasped for air, her feet frozen in place, unable to run. He laughed and let go of her. She fell to her knees, clutching her chest. He hadn't even broken a sweat, and already, she was struggling to maintain consciousness.

"You see, my dear, your life is in my hands. It always has been. The mere fact of your current existence is due to my own allowance of it. I allowed you to remain alive all this time for my own amusement. You could alleviate your own suffering by simply joining me. I could use someone as tenacious as you."

"Never!" she coughed weakly. "What...could you possibly want...with me anyway? I thought the great...Vincoral...needed no one!"

"You're right....So, of course, I don't need you, whelp!"

Vincoral fairly glowed with anger. Kitten hadn't expected such an emotional response from him and took advantage of it. While he was dashing toward her, she jumped up and leaped over his head, delivering a quick kick to the back of his head on her way. He didn't even flinch. She threw her dagger at him again, and he dodged it. But his responses did seem to be slowing down somewhat. He focused on her, coming at her with lightning speed. She avoided his gaze, knowing that meeting his eyes again could be fatal. He threw a blinding flash of energy, like red lightning, at her, and she barely managed to dodge it. The ground where it struck exploded in a spray of dirt and rocks and was scorched as if by fire. She stayed on her feet, expecting another attack, but once more, he laughed.

"It looks like Seelis is finally settling down to business, folks!" the announcer shouted excitedly. "But something tells me he hasn't even begun to show us the extent of his power! Kitten may be in for it this time!"

"You silly little girl! If I wanted to destroy you, I could do it with a thought! I don't need to even try!" Vincoral raged at her.

Kitten blushed, knowing it was true. Of course, she couldn't possibly catch him off-guard with petty emotions. Even if she managed to anger him, he was too powerful for her to trick him that way. She took a deep breath and focused her thoughts once more. It was time to try out another technique. She knew that nothing that she had used previously in the tournament would work now; it had to be something Vincoral hadn't seen, something more powerful than he would expect from her. Without raising a finger, she called on the power of the lightning from the sky. She called it down to her with a thought, directing it at Vincoral and his energy aura. He sensed something coming and darted to the side, but she made sure that it followed him. It appeared in the form of a great dragon, a lightning dragon, shooting through the sky, coming down to the earth to smite the evil Demon. It spun through the air, curling around in great arcs over their heads. It passed right through the force shield that surrounded the battlefield and chased Vincoral, matching his every move, countering his every dodge. Kitten put all her energy into that strike, knowing it was her last chance. Vincoral seemed genuinely surprised when the dragon hit him squarely in the chest, knocking him into the ground and sending waves of electricity through his body. It seemed to short out his illusion spell, for suddenly his true form was visible to everyone. The crowd around them gasped audibly and seemed to shrink back from the stage, even those who had known what to expect. The announcer remained silent. Kitten stayed perfectly motionless, afraid that even her most powerful attack would not be enough. But Vincoral lay still.

Finally, the announcer found his voice and broke the silence, "Um, I think it's over....Yeah, it seems that Seelis, er, Vincoral the Demonic has been...defeated!"

Kitten breathed a sigh of relief and looked around for her friends. Zharran, Raisa, and Markuss were standing near the battlefield, waving at her. She waved back but paused when she sensed a movement behind her. Then, that laugh reverberated through her skull. She spun to face him and saw Vincoral rising to his feet. He didn't seem affected in the least by her great lightning dragon. He laughed cruelly and looked into her eyes. She felt the world closing in around her. Her lungs stopped moving, and so did her heart. Everything disappeared. She could see and hear only Vincoral.

"How very stupid of you. I am master of all elements. None can harm me. You know, I could force you to serve me, control your body and your soul, your every movement and whim. I could make you mine. But as fitting an existence as that would be for you, I think you would serve me better at this time as an example. An example to anyone who thinks that I am vulnerable to anything. To show the world what will happen to all who oppose me!"

Kitten felt her life draining away, but her consciousness began to return. Her heart began to beat slowly. Her lungs filled with precious air. She struggled to clear her vision and saw everyone around them staring at her. In an instant, she realized what her fate would be that day. Her fate was to be the same as all the other warriors from her village who fought so valiantly against Vincoral all those years ago. She would die today, and her blood would stain the ground on this spot from the volume of it that would be shed. She turned her eyes to face him. His own eyes were blazing. He didn't move, didn't take a single step toward her. His thoughts surrounded her with the red lightning. It flashed around her entire body, and she felt a pain like no other fill her every nerve. She screamed at the top of her lungs, unable to move, unable to stop it. She knew her heart would give out first. She struggled to remain calm, to soothe the pounding beat inside her chest, but the intense pain filled her thoughts and beat back all other concerns. She couldn't stop screaming.

Razor-sharp spikes formed out of the red lightning and slashed at her skin, cutting her ten, twenty, thirty times and more. Her blood poured out, down her face, her arms, her legs, flowing out over the dirt at her feet, pooling in a nearly perfect circle. Her life ebbing from her, she could still think of nothing but the intense pain. She couldn't even hear her own voice, crying, screaming. She didn't feel the liquid pouring from her eyes; blood or tears, it didn't matter. She began to forget everything she had ever known. Vincoral waved one hand, and a sudden waterfall drenched Kitten and vanished. It washed some of the blood from her skin, which was quickly replaced by more. He sent a blast of lightning into her body. She shook uncontrollably, held in place by his red energy that cut her more deeply each time she moved. He laughed again, relishing the sight of her blood on the ground, the sound of her screams of agony.

"Heed this lesson well, my subjects! None can defeat me, and it is beyond foolhardy to try! I slaughtered this girl's village in this same manner, and I will do so to anyone who dares to stand against me!" Vincoral's voice didn't even echo in her ears now. Instead, she heard something else.

I have the utmost confidence in you. I know you will be strong for all of us; I know you will never forget why we have fought so long and so hard. I know you will make us proud. I love you always...

Kitten heard her father's voice. It echoed through her mind, drowning out the pain, the screams, even the voice of Vincoral. She could remember nothing but the voice of her father and his face, his smile whenever he looked at her. She knew she had the strength to try one more time. She called to the lightning. She called for its help to defeat the Demonic One. Light could still end the reign of dark. Her mind reached to the sky, to the heavens above, to the very stars. She was not disappointed. Her dragon returned, bigger and stronger and brighter than before. But it was different this time. It radiated an energy more powerful than the lightning that it had come from. This was no electrical energy; this was something more, something incredible. It appeared between Kitten and Vincoral in the blink of an eye and surrounded him in less time.

Kitten dropped to the ground, released from the hold of the red lightning. She shielded her eyes as the dragon grew so bright that it seemed to outshine the sun. Vincoral fought against it, casting spells and shouting incantations. Black energy seemed to emanate from him, but the dragon absorbed it all and grew in both size and brightness. It radiated heat, light, and a crackling sound that filled her ears. It hid Vincoral from sight, and Kitten had to close her eyes. The light was too bright to look at even indirectly. Suddenly, there was silence. Kitten looked up. The dragon was gone. And so was Vincoral. Afraid to believe it might be true, Kitten waited, shivering, in the silence. Her wounds were already healing, though she would be severely weakened for a long time. She felt drowsy and exhausted, but she was determined to wait for a sign that he was really gone. The force field was lowered, and her friends rushed to her side.

"That was like nothing I've ever done!" Markuss' voice came slowly to her ears, as if they were reacquainting themselves with external sounds. "That was not my lightning technique! You changed it completely! That was incredible!"

"That, I believe, was a Light Dragon," whispered Raisa in awe. "A very rare, very difficult to execute technique that has not been seen in these lands for millennia. Its secrets were lost to the ages. You seem to have rediscovered them. Congratulations."

"I...I had no idea....I didn't meant to…" Kitten choked on the words.

"Sssh! Don't try to speak!" Zharran interrupted. "And don't move! We'll carry you back to your tent. You've lost too much blood. Raisa, please take her."

"No! Wait! I need to know....I need to see..." she tried to object but was too weak to say any more.

Raisa nodded and lifted her carefully. He carried Kitten to the spot where Vincoral had been standing when the dragon surrounded him. He knelt down and gently turned Kitten's body in his arms so that she could see for herself the scorched ground. She winced slightly and closed her eyes. It wasn't the ground she wanted to see. She wanted to see his spirit leaving this world. She could only catch a glimpse of that with her mind's eye. She felt around for his presence, but she couldn't sense anything. Perhaps, he was indeed gone. Gone from this world forever.

Just as she was ready to accept this possibility, however, she felt something else that told her that the war with the Demonic One was not over. A shiver went down her spine. Even Raisa felt it. It was like a voice on the wind. It seemed to tell them that he would return. Kitten opened her eyes and saw the head of Vincoral's cane lying on the ground where there had been nothing a moment before. She heard his cruel laugh in her head again and knew that her struggle wasn't over yet. He would return, stronger than ever, no doubt. He was taunting her, knowing that she had used the last of her strength to simply wound him and chase him away. No one had ever done that before, but he would come back with more powerful spells and techniques. He would shore up his power and resources for the day when they would meet again. On that day, he would crush her once and for all. And there was little she could do to prepare.

But Kitten gritted her teeth, took a deep breath, and resolved then and there to improve her powers and her techniques even more than Vincoral could improve his. She promised herself, her father, and their people that she would still defeat him, that she would fulfill her promise to rid the world of Vincoral the Demonic, no matter how long it took, no matter how much strength it took from her, no matter if it took her life. She would train until she was stronger than Vincoral. She knew now that he could be beaten back. And she knew that she would do it again. And again, if necessary. And again, until he could no longer return to fight and the world was safe.

"We'll find him. I will help you. We will find him," Raisa vowed softly.

"He's not gone yet, huh?" Markuss sighed. "Well, you can count on me, Kitten. I'll stick with you, too."

"You're not alone," Zharran said reassuringly.

It took days for Kitten to recover from the tournament. She tried to be patient with the healers, but she hated being in bed for so long. All she could think about was the fact that Vincoral was still out there, and while she was healing up, so was he. Her friends tried to keep her occupied, but she just couldn't concentrate on anything else. She wanted to get started on tracking him down right away. She didn't know where to go for additional training, however. She needed to improve her skills, but she had already worked with one of the best martial arts teachers in the world. Raisa volunteered to look for some leads while she was abed. Markuss volunteered to get a head start on tracking Vincoral. They left Zharran to look after Kitten. While the healers were doing their work on her, he packed her things up and got everything ready to leave. He knew that she'd want to get out of there as soon as she could walk.

"We'll meet Raisa and Markuss at the entrance to the campgrounds. They should be back anytime today," she said to him once she had pulled herself to her feet.

Zharran nodded and collected their bags. He followed her through the deserted grounds of the tournament. Most of the tents were gone, but the few stragglers who remained stared at Kitten as if she were a ghost. One man had the courage to smile at her, and she smiled back and nodded. They stopped at the entrance to the grounds, set between two hills. Gazing inland, Kitten rested against a tree and watched for her friends to return.

"I am here. I have found a lead."

Raisa appeared around the edge of the closest hill. He had approached without Kitten seeing him, but she wasn't surprised by that. She was a little surprised that he had found a possible lead on learning new techniques. He sat under the tree, and she followed suit.

"There is a land very far from here known only as The West. It lies farther west than anyone has ever been. But the stories say that a magical people live there who know more about martial arts and spells than anyone else in the world. Some say they are even immortal. No one knows much more about them, but the sages and seers of many places agree that they and their land exist. It is not much to go on, I know. But my instinct tells me that this is the direction to take in your journey."

"I agree," she smiled enigmatically at the horizon. "I don't know why, but I think you're right. I've got a good feeling about this West land. But how will we find it?"

"They say that the traveler will know when he has reached it. But I would propose a more direct approach. I have found a magic-caster who specializes in traveling spells and is willing to transport us all there for no fee. It seems that he is eager to further the cause of the warrior who plans to defeat the Demonic One. He says that his spells can take you anywhere, even to places that have no specific location."

"Excellent work, Raisa! I almost can't believe our good fortune! I hope Markuss has had such luck."

The three of them waited there for Markuss to return. A few hours later, they spotted him crossing the valley. He met them with a grin on his face and nodded triumphantly to Kitten.

"I tracked Vincoral back to Cantari, but I couldn't cross the border. He's got that place extremely well-guarded. I think he's bulked up the security since his defeat here. Most of the soldiers I saw didn't even look mortal. I think he's pulled them from some other dimension to help him. But he's definitely in his fortress. He took a peek at me when I got close enough; I could feel it. I'm sure he recognized me, but he didn't do anything. He must still be too weak. We could attack him now, but I doubt we'd get past those guards easily."

"No, we wouldn't," Kitten said darkly. "And I'm not certain I could defeat him anyway. He's on his own turf now; his magic will be exponentially more powerful. He'll at least have enough to protect himself until he's strong enough to take me. I've got to improve my own powers before attempting a siege like that. And it wouldn't hurt to have reinforcements. But few people in the known lands would dare to join us in such a foolhardy effort. Perhaps we will have more luck in The West."

She explained to Markuss about the West land, and he agreed that it seemed to be the best place to start looking for help. Since they were all ready to get going, the others followed Raisa across the valley to a little town on the edge of a forest. It was night by the time they arrived, but a man with a long white beard and dark blue robes was waiting for them at the entrance to the town. He was blind, but he seemed to see them coming, speaking to Kitten before she had even gotten within ten feet of him.

"I am glad you have come so quickly, Kitten Izzill. I am prepared to transport you and your friends immediately. Time is of the essence, as I am sure you are well aware. I have been watching your progress. I saw your temporary defeat of the Demonic One. You cannot attack him again so soon, but you must use this time to ready yourself for the next opportunity. Are you ready to go?"

Kitten was rather surprised that the old magician had recognized her without his sight and knew so much about her efforts. But she agreed with him that time was an important factor in her journey, so she took only a moment to glance at her companions and make sure they were ready. Then she nodded at the man, and he took a glowing orb out of a deep pocket in his robes. He tossed it towards them lightly, and there was a bright flash. Kitten blinked, and when she opened her eyes, they were in a new area. The trees around them grew closely together and were taller than she could see. She couldn't recognize any of the plants or insects, and the sun was still in the sky. They were clearly in a new land. Everything about the place felt infinitely more magical than anything Kitten had ever sensed before. She knew they had come to the right place.

"The sun is setting....Again," Markuss commented quizzically. "We should find shelter. We don't know what to expect from this land."

"I don't think we have anything to fear," Kitten smiled. "I think we should look for the people of this land right away. Time is of the essence, you know. We're here to ask for their help; there's no reason to put that off. They might not think our problem is urgent if we spend too much time just hanging around."

The group of travelers picked their way through the trees and underbrush of the new forest, looking for signs of civilization. Kitten had the odd feeling they were being watched, but she couldn't figure out where the spies were. When the sun had nearly disappeared behind the horizon, she paused and motioned for the others to wait a moment. She shimmied up a tree trunk and climbed as high as she could. She was thirty feet off the ground before she stopped, and she still couldn't see the top of the trees around her. She had hoped to get a better view of the land, but the trees were too thick. She started climbing back down to the ground, but ten feet from the bottom, she heard a tiny voice in her ear, as if someone were speaking to her from far, far away. Kitten paused on a branch and glanced around. She saw nothing but foliage and insects. A big red dragonfly sat on her knee, and she stared at it in surprise. Suddenly, the voice came again, this time from a definite direction: the dragonfly.

"I've been watching you, traveler. Tell me why you have come to these lands, and perhaps I will introduce you to my lady, the queen."

Kitten stammered, "Uh, well, I am a warrior from the Cantari Nation. My name is Kitten Izzill. I have come here to search for help in defeating Vincoral the Demonic One. Have you heard of him here?"

"Indeed, we have," the dragonfly shivered a little. "His evil deeds are famous the world over. But he had best never try to invade these lands, or he will find himself the object of our wrath. If you are attempting to defeat him, I am sure my lady would be happy to lend her assistance. Follow me."

The little bug flapped her shimmery wings and took off quicker than Kitten could see. She climbed down the tree and ran off in the direction she thought the dragonfly had gone. Raisa, Markuss, and Zharran followed her, shouting questions and trying to get her to stop. She spotted the red dragonfly, though, and ran faster to catch up with her. After running for more than twenty minutes, the dragonfly paused on a tree trunk, and Kitten and the others collapsed at the base of it, gasping for breath.

"Remain here, while I announce your arrival." The dragonfly flew off and disappeared into the trees, and Kitten sat up against the tree trunk. Markuss was staring in the direction the insect had gone. He seemed to have lost his voice.

"I see you finally heard the voice of the red dragonfly," Kitten laughed. "She said she would introduce us to the queen of this land and that the queen would help us fight Vincoral."

The red dragonfly returned in only a moment and fluttered about Kitten's head, then flew back in the direction she had gone earlier. Kitten took that as a sign to follow and pulled herself to her feet. She waved her hand at the others, drawing them toward her, and walked softly into the trees. At first, this part of the forest seemed like all the others, but soon, Kitten noticed that something was different. The trees were lighter; the very air seemed less dense. Everything around them felt as if it were alive and sentient. The dragonfly led them into a small clearing. Two people, more beautiful than any people Kitten had ever seen before, although she couldn't think of why or how, were standing in the clearing, watching them. The woman had long gray hair, but she appeared to be younger even than Kitten. Her violet eyes seemed to look deep within Kitten's soul. For a moment, Kitten worried that they had come to the wrong place, but the woman smiled, and everything felt calm and peaceful again. The man next to the woman held her hand and stood back a step, eyeing the newcomers with uncertainty. His green hair blended in with the foliage around them, but his clothes were blood red. They both had pointed ears and delicate features, but there was a strength about them, as if they could snap any mortal being in two with only their gentle fingers. The woman began to speak, and the forest became quiet.

"My dear Red has told me why you are here, and I have consented to help you. We too desire the defeat of the Demonic One. He has destroyed that which nature has created for far too long. I am the ruler of these forests. I would tell you my name, but it is unpronounceable in your tongue, and it would take more than an hour to speak in mine. You may call me Queen Mellah. This is my co-ruler; you may call him King Lendril. You have already met one of our other co-rulers, Red Dragonfly. You will meet the fourth member of our group shortly. Come to the throne hutch, and we will talk further."

Kitten and her party followed the queen and king in awe. The two of them seemed to float just above the ground, and the tree branches seemed to part for them. The forest was quiet except for the buzz of Red Dragonfly's wings, and Kitten kept silent for fear of disturbing some unspoken law of this strange land. They passed into another, smaller clearing and into the base of a large hollow tree. The tree was large enough for two people to enter side-by-side, but the interior was even bigger. Kitten stood near the entrance in disbelief. It was not elaborately decorated, as one might expect for royalty, but its plain, simple elegance was impressive in its own right. And the sheer size of the interior area left no doubt as to who lived here. At the far end, two thrones sat; they seemed to be made of wood, but the wood seemed to be still alive, still part of the tree they were standing in. Queen Mellah and King Lendril crossed the room and sat in the thrones. Red Dragonfly flew next to them and seated herself on a tiny throne atop a table next to King Lendril's chair. Another table sat on the other side of Queen Mellah, but it didn't appear to have anything on top of it.

"The fourth of our number will be here shortly. In the meantime, please, sit and tell us more about yourselves."

"Yes, please do," King Lendril spoke for the first time. "We will need to know all we can if we are to help you."

Four chairs rose up out of the floor facing the thrones, forming themselves out of the wood of the tree. Kitten sat and motioned for the others to do the same. She spoke in a slow manner, as if she were in a dream. She couldn't shake the feeling of awe that she had. She told the King and Queen everything that she could think of about her efforts to defeat Vincoral, especially about the recent tournament. When she had finished, Raisa and Markuss added a bit about their own stories. Then, they waited in silence.

"You see, my queen, it is as I told you. They are worthy," Red's soft voice reached them from her throne.

"Yes, you may be right, Red," King Lendril nodded. "Perhaps I underestimated these mortals. They speak the truth, at least."

"Of course, they do. I would not have allowed them to come so far in my forest if they were unworthy and deceitful." The voice seemed to come from nowhere. Then a shape moved like water right through the wall of the tree. It formed vines and wrapped itself around the table next to Queen Mellah. The voice had come from this plant-like creature, Kitten was sure of that. It formed a vague sort of head, like a large blossom without petals, and spoke again, projecting the words into their minds.

"I was watching you the whole time, weighing your souls. If I had found you unworthy, my trees would have halted your progress before little Red had even seen you. I am the fourth ruler of this land; you may call me Thorn, as I will sting you sharply if you betray us."

"Two of my companions are not quite so easily won over as the third," Queen Mellah smiled behind one hand. "But you have convinced us all, and we will help you. First, we will rest for the night. When the sun rises again, we will teach what you will need to know."

Queen Mellah indicated that they should follow Red Dragonfly into another room, and Kitten led the way. There was a smaller room connected to the main one, and four beds had been prepared ahead of them, formed right out of the walls and floor. There was no door, but a curtain of vines pulled itself across the doorway, shielding the rooms from one another. Silently, Kitten made herself comfortable on one of the beds. The others had barely spoken since their arrival here, and now was no different. The night passed quickly and quietly for them.

"Awaken, please. It is morn."

Kitten opened her eyes and saw the red dragonfly hovering over her head. For a moment, she wondered where she was and what was going on. But as Red woke everyone else, she recalled the previous evening's events. Kitten scrambled out of bed and ran to the doorway. She peered out into the main room and saw that the other three rulers of this land were seated on their thrones already. She wondered if they had ever left. These otherworldly creatures seemed capable of anything. Red lighted upon her shoulder and spoke softly.

"The others are waiting for you. First, a morning meal, and then we will speak more of helping you on your quest."

"This is the weirdest adventure I've ever been on," Markuss whispered. "But it's all for the greater good, I suppose. So, let's go eat breakfast with a bug, a plant, and two immortal elves."

Kitten led the way into the main room, with Red on her shoulder. She bowed stiffly to the three beings on the thrones and noticed that a table had been set out with fruits and vegetables. Queen Mellah smiled and waved her hand, indicating that everyone should sit down. She and Lendril rose from their thrones and seated themselves at the table, and Kitten and her friends followed suit. Thorn remained on her table/throne, while Red stayed on Kitten's shoulder for some reason.

"After your meal, you may use the bathing pool outside to clean up if you'd like," Queen Mellah spoke. "Red will show you the way. Then, we will begin your training. There is much to teach you and very little time. Things move slowly in this land, but the people of your world continue their own journey at their own pace. We must work quickly."

"Thank you very much," Kitten said reverently. "But if you don't mind my asking, what exactly do you plan to teach me?"

"Our particular style has no name here in our land," King Lendril said vaguely. "It is simply a way of moving, a way of existing. And few people from your land have seen it, let alone named it. There are physical techniques, and there are what you would call spells. And there are things which have no counterpart in your land. You will see."

The table fell silent, and Kitten decided to hold off on any more questions for now. She would see soon enough what they had planned for her. After eating, she followed Red to the bathing pool and cleaned up. Then, while her friends were doing the same, she waited in the throne room with the rulers. There, Queen Mellah began to speak of what they were going to teach Kitten that day.

"To fight like one of us, you must very nearly become one of us. Others use magic, bend it to their will, utilize cause and effect. We are magic; we are both the cause and the effect. To make something happen, we simply will it so. I sense great capacity for magic within you. I believe it is possible for you to do what others of your race would fail to accomplish. We begin now."

King Lendril took up the dialogue: "It will help you to get into a frame of mind similar to our own. You will understand that the reason we are so protective over our humble abode is that it is not simply the place we live in. It is us; we are the land, the trees, the sky. It is all as much a part of us as your fingers are of you. Because of that, we can use any part of our surroundings to defend ourselves and our home, just as you would use your hands to cast a spell or hit an opponent. We could have stopped you from entering our forest if we had so desired. We saw you approaching through the old man's spell before you set foot on our land, as you would see a butterfly before it landed on your shoulder."

The co-ruler Thorn then spoke with her peculiar telepathy: "I embody this way of life, as I myself am one of the plants of this forest, literally. But make no mistake, my companions are just as much a part of this land as I am. I simply appear more so to your eyes because of my current physical form. I could take another form, but I prefer this one. You must learn to be a part of this world, as well."

"The same is true of me," Red's tiny voice came close to Kitten's ear. "I am one of the insects of the forest, which to your people might seem insignificant, but I have more control over my environment than they have ever had. Are you ready to learn to be what we are?"

Kitten nodded slowly. She was a bit overwhelmed by everything they had just told her. She was worried about changing herself to become one of them. What that meant, she had no idea. But she was determined to go through with it. She took a deep breath and steeled herself as Lendril rose from his throne and approached her.

"The best way to fight something is to understand it, and therefore, the best way to understand something is to experience it, or fight it, as the case may be. You will fight me. It will teach you more about what we have told you; it will help you understand it."

Shocked, Kitten took a step backwards. She had no idea what to expect in a fight with Lendril, and that worried her more than she would have cared to admit. The walls of the room seemed to expand around them until the floor space was twice what it had been. No one moved a muscle, waiting for her signal. His argument made sense; she just wasn't sure she was ready. But surely he wouldn't actually try to harm her. Although she wasn't really ready, Kitten nodded again and took a defensive posture. Lendril nodded. In the blink of eye, she was ten feet off the ground. Or rather, the ground was ten feet from its former position. A hump in the floor had risen beneath her feet. She teetered for a moment and forced herself to remain calm. She reached for a nearby vine and began sliding down it. The floor returned to a flat surface as soon as she stepped off of it, and the vine moved in her hands, snaking around her body and lifting her higher into the air. She considered using a fire spell but worried about whether or not that would hurt her teachers.

"You're holding back," Lendril said disapprovingly. "Don't. You won't learn that way."

Kitten let loose a volley of fireballs in two directions. The first consumed the vine, and the second flew at Lendril to distract him. The vine dropped her, and she used a quick wind spell to cushion her fall, landing gracefully on her feet. However, Lendril had not been daunted by the simple fire spell. He seemed to have absorbed the flames into his body; the last of them disappeared as she stared at him. He walked toward her and reached for her with his right arm. Kitten grabbed it by the wrist and swung him around. Rather than fight it, however, he leaped into the motion as if they were dancing, spun around, and delivered the hardest kick she'd ever felt straight to her head. She nearly fainted at that moment, but Lendril waited for her to recover and get back on her feet. She shook herself and nodded. She decided her best strategy at this point would be to stay on the move. She ran to her left and nearly collided with a wall that hadn't been there before. She turned and faced Lendril. She was tired of trying all the amateur moves and getting shut down. She concentrated and called down a bolt of lightning from the sky. It passed through the walls of the tree and hit the spot where Lendril stood. But he was unaffected. He reached up and grasped the lightning with one hand. It retracted into a ball of energy that he threw at her. Kitten dodged, just barely missing what would have been a deadly blow. She was beginning to lose her temper. Obviously, elemental attacks were of no use against this man.

She summoned all her strength and called upon her Light Dragon. It appeared before her and lunged at Lendril. He didn't try to harness it this time, but the dragon was unable to touch him. A bright red force field had appeared around him. The dragon tried to engulf him in its light, as it had done with Vincoral; there was a screeching sound when it attacked the force field, and smoke filled the room. When the noise and the smoke had gone, Lendril stood calmly. His force field dissipated, and he smiled and nodded at Kitten. She collapsed into a chair that appeared behind her, exhausted and in shock.

"I...I can't believe it. Even Vincoral couldn't stand up to my dragon like that. How?"

"Light is a part of our world," he answered. "I could have absorbed it like your fire and lightning spells. But I wanted to show you that we have other defenses, as well. I wasn't using my full power, of course. You would have been killed several times over. I am still impressed, however. No one from the outside world has known how to summon a Light Dragon in millennia. You are more powerful, indeed, than I at first supposed. Have you learned anything from our sparring?"

"I have learned that I couldn't fight you for two seconds at your full strength," she grimaced. "And I have learned that I came to the right place to learn how to defeat Vincoral once and for all. But I don't know how I can become more like you. How can I master the elements as you have?"

"By becoming those elements. As I said, we are a part of this world, this land. You will become part of it, too."

"The ritual will go a long way toward helping you achieve that," Mellah spoke again. "You already have some of the abilities. You are in tune with your magic. You just need to take the next step. Come closer."

Kitten hesitated, then steeled herself for whatever was about to happen. She stepped up to the queen's throne and gazed into those beautiful, cool eyes. Queen Mellah smiled softly and whispered words in an ancient-sounding language that Kitten had never heard before. The words seemed to surround her and pass through her. She felt as if she were floating. She sensed the king stepping up behind her, and Red the dragonfly hovering on her right, and Thorn the living plant snaking to her left side with a mass of vines. They all began repeating the words that Mellah had spoken, and Kitten felt herself falling into the Queen's all-seeing eyes.

It began slowly at first; then, everything seemed to rush at her. The words, the people, the air, the stars, the world. She could feel everything around her. She felt the distinctions between separate objects fall away, as if they were nothing more than a veil, a lie. She knew that they were; she knew that everything was one. She knew where each molecule of air was hovering, what the tree that they stood in was feeling, what the ground on the other side of the world was doing, where the stars above them were heading, and how it all connected. She could see and feel each person, animal, plant, and particle in the entire universe. It all fit together like a puzzle, each piece necessary to complete the picture. And she saw how some pieces did not fit together. How some magic-users tried to use their talents to force the world into a shape they desired. How some people, even normal humans, tried to control the world, or at least the pieces around them. It created friction and slowed the turning of the universe. And she saw the void that hovered over the Cantari Nation. That was the worst violation of all. Vincoral had done more than torture and kill mortals. He had tortured the world. He had violated the laws of all that existed. He had sapped the energy from all that he had touched. The universe, unseen by mortal eyes, was collapsing around him. Before long, there would be nothing left to save.

Kitten found herself crying. She didn't know whether they were real tears, but she was crying with the universe. Waterfalls cascaded through her, and she felt the pain of every thing that Vincoral the Demonic had touched. She felt the sorrow that the universe felt each time a piece of itself was lost forever, and she felt the agony of each of those lost pieces as they died or vanished from existence. Vincoral had done more than conquer the mortals of Cantari; he had attempted to conquer all that existed. And he was winning.

The pain was becoming more than she could bear. She no longer simply observed and felt the rest of the world. Now she was the world. She was the air being sucked into Vincoral's rotting lungs. She was the fly on the back of the horse in the farmer's field. She was the woman giving birth in her ancestral home and the baby being born there. She was the boy hunting his first dornak, the dornak evading the boy, and the tree that the dornak was hiding in. She was the ground on which her friends stood near the bathing pool, and she was the water with which they were bathing. She was Kitten Izzill. She was Zharran. She was Raisa. She was Markuss. She was Queen Mellah, King Lendril, and their co-rulers, and she was their beloved homeland. And she was Vincoral. She felt the coldness within him more keenly than ever before, because it was suddenly the coldness within herself. She thought his thoughts, and they were her thoughts. She felt his pain, and it was her pain. Her blood boiled with anger and fear. She felt both a desire to own everything and the emptiness of the world around the Demonic One. She felt her father's spirit and her mother's energy, both part of the universe still, part of her now. She was her father's spirit and her mother's energy. She was their confidence in her and their love for her. She held their memories and thoughts in her mind, and they were her memories and thoughts. She was the living and the dead and the undead. She was magic and energy. She was good and evil. She was light and dark. She was the Ancestral Dragon. She was the energy of the earth. She was the worm in the ground, and the sun in the sky. She was all of these things at the same time. It was nearly too much. Then, it was perfect. Everything was perfect. It all made sense. It all felt real. It felt...like home. She was home.

"Is she gonna be all right?" Markuss' voice floated from her lips. Slowly she began to realize that he was speaking above her, with his own lips. She felt the ground beneath her, soft and warm. It still felt like a part of her, but it was more distant now. She opened her eyes and looked up at her friends.

"She will be fine," Red's tiny voice echoed through her mind and through the walls of the throne room. "Give her a moment to collect herself. She has been on a journey."

"She didn't go anywhere," Markuss objected.

"A journey of the mind, my friend," Raisa whispered. Kitten could hear his thoughts. Or were they her own? She wasn't sure. She tried to speak.

"I...we...," the words came with difficulty. She wasn't sure which ones to use. Was she a single person? Was she the tree? Was she the sky?

"Give it time," Queen Mellah seemed to imprint the words upon her mind. Or were they thinking them together? "You have felt the connection between all things in this world. You have felt the falseness of the separations mortals impose upon these things. You have felt the oneness that we have lived for centuries. You have been that oneness. No mortal being has ever done this. You must give your body time to catch up with your mind."

Kitten closed her eyes and saw herself through her friends' eyes. She felt their concern for her, and she tried to impress upon them her own calmness and certainty. She knew that she would be all right. She floated above the clouds and through the trees and into the ground and out into space, where the blackness surrounded and filled her. But this blackness was nothing compared to the empty void that surrounded Vincoral. Above the atmosphere of the planet, there were still thoughts and feelings and specks of dust. Near the Demonic One, there was nothing. Even he was not yet aware of the damage he had inflicted. Kitten let the peace and warmth of the rest of the world fill her and give her the strength to face Vincoral, not only in person but also within his soul. Even Vincoral had a soul, she knew now. A rotten one, falling apart and barely hanging on to the body that he inhabited, but it was there. And she would have to deal with it when she dealt with him.

It was the chirping of the birds above her that finally woke Kitten this time. She looked around and saw her friends sleeping peacefully in the beds around her. She reached out with her newfound powers of thought and feeling and looked into their dreams. Zharran dreamed of the desert land from which he had come as a young boy, forced to travel by the uncaring stepfather who planned to sell him as a slave to Vincoral. Zharran saw the beauty of the sands and the brilliance of the sun. He became a desert lizard and sat on a rock, bathing in the light.

Raisa dreamed of a dark forest, not ominous or frightening, but beautiful and full of life. Raisa became a tree-dweller, living off of the land and communing with nature. He saw the world move around him and time pass him by, and he enjoyed living his life without either one of them.

Markuss dreamed of a house on a cliff and a little path that led down to the water, where a boat was moored, waiting for the master of the house. Markuss saw himself walk through the house and down the path, stopping at the water's edge to admire the sunset. He heard someone laugh, and he turned to see them, but their face was blurred. The warmth and love was unmistakable, though.

Leaving her friends to their dreaming, Kitten stood and re-entered the throne room. She knew that the rulers of The West would still be sitting there, waiting for her. She also knew that they were the ones who gave her friends the pleasant dreams. She wanted to thank them, but before she had uttered a word, she knew that they had already felt and acknowledged her gratitude. She knew so much now that her head nearly ached. But she knew that she would adjust, and the discomfort would go away.

She also knew that her hosts did not need to hear words from her lips to understand her, but she spoke anyway, partly out of habit and partly because it made her more comfortable.

"I understand everything you were telling me," she said, sitting on a chair that rose up out of the ground to accommodate her. "But I still need practice."

"You will practice on your way to Vincoral's stronghold," Queen Mellah spoke aloud, as well. "There is no time left. The world has continued to turn while you have been here."

"I know," Kitten sighed. "But can't you transport me straight to Vincoral's throne room? I know you have the power."

"Under other circumstances, we could and would," King Lendril shook his head. "But you know now the state of the world around him. Sending you there with such powerful magic could damage both you and the world itself, causing the very thing we are trying to prevent: the destruction of the fabric of the universe."

"I understand," Kitten said thoughtfully. "But then how can I fight him in his stronghold if using magic there will cause further damage?"

"By doing the only thing that will both weaken Vincoral's hold on this world and put right what he has done wrong," Mellah explained. "You must reverse the damage he has caused and replace the pieces of this world that he has erased. We would do it ourselves, but it would be easier for Vincoral to sense our arrival than yours. He knows of our power, and he has long watched for us to interfere in his plans. He fears us more than any other creature in the world. But he will not expect you to come bearing the gift of our power, the power of the universe. He will expect you to be small and weak, especially so soon after your last battle with him. You will be able to reach his throne room undetected, if you are careful."

"But he always knows where I am!" Kitten protested. "Since my childhood, he has known. I've felt him watching me all these years. Why should he stop now?"

"Because he does not know where you are right now," Lendril smiled slyly. "The magic of our land shelters you from him, and he will not know which direction to watch for you. That is why we sent our messenger to transport you to The West, so he would no longer be able to track you. You can sense him now, as well. You will be able to watch his spying and detect where he is looking for you. You will be able to keep yourself and your friends safe."

"How can I replace the pieces of the world that he destroyed?"

"The world will do that for you if you give it a little push," Thorn's thoughts flowed directly into Kitten's mind. "Give it power and energy, and it will grow. It will grow into the void. All you have to do is stop Vincoral from destroying it again. Once the growth has begun, you will be able to perform any necessary magic and call on any of the mystical powers. We will come to your aid if you need us at that time."

There was still one thing that Kitten did not know. She looked at the Queen and King, and they knew what she needed to ask. But they couldn't answer her question.

"We don't know," Red's voice said softly, as she lit on Kitten's shoulder. "We don't know whether you will win this fight. It all depends on how quickly you can help the world re-grow what it has lost."

"Now you must be on your way," Mellah said. "There is no more time. We will transport you as far as we can without touching on the borders of the void and without alerting the Demonic One to your presence. Your friends will go with you; they may yet be of some further use."

On cue, Zharran, Raisa, and Markuss came wandering sleepily out of their room, yawning and glancing questioningly at their hosts. Kitten thanked the immortals profusely with her thoughts and feelings and stood next to her friends. Aloud, she said, "We will win this time. We must."

Mellah smiled sweetly, and Red fluttered up to the ceiling, spinning in circles and dropping glittery dust over the travelers. "Farewell!" she shouted, as the room began to blur before Kitten's eyes. There was another bright flash, and the world moved around them until they were in a forest glen just outside of the village of Gollbrook, which lay nearly a day's journey to the east of Cantari. The sun was setting, although they had just woken up mere minutes ago.

"What was all that?" Markuss asked, sitting down on a fallen tree. He was annoyed. Kitten could both see it and feel it. "I thought we'd have more time. Did they teach you anything?"

"I have to practice," Kitten told him. "But there's no more time, so I have to do it on the way to Vincoral's stronghold."

She reached out with her mind to sense Vincoral's gaze, but it was not on her at that moment. He seemed to be watching the west, beyond the sunset.

"Practice what?" Zharran asked. He was concerned and uncertain, but hopeful that Kitten's trust had been well-placed in the immortals.

"You needn't worry," she smiled and looked at each of her friends in turn. "I have what I need. I just need to control it. In the meantime, let's start walking. We have a long way to go yet."

"We should gather supplies," Raisa suggested, his mind a turmoil of curiosity and urgency that belied his calm demeanor. "I am familiar with this town. We can get what we need from the night market."

"Agreed," Kitten nodded and sauntered forth with authority. She led them down side streets that she had never seen, feeling her way past the untrustworthy denizens of the town's criminal populous and finding a clear path to the night market. It stood in an open square, about twenty dealers and merchants displaying their wares and a handful of shoppers strolling quietly under the moonlight.

Raisa approached a man near the entrance to the square and spoke to him in whispers for a few moments. He returned to the group, and Kitten knew that he had negotiated the price of some new weapons for them all.

"We will be well-armed," he said. "My friend there will sell us the best weapons we could find for the promise of a favor."

"I don't like favors," Markuss hissed suspiciously.

"His daughter was captured by Vincoral's men years ago, and he needs to know if she is still alive and whether we can rescue her," Kitten told him reproachfully. "We will do what we can. If you don't want to join us on our quest to the stronghold, you may leave at any time, pirate."

Markuss was ashamed of himself suddenly, but he didn't show it to the others. He asked loudly, "How did you know all that?"

"She has the benefit of the immortals' wisdom and power," Raisa answered him, his mind finally grasping the truth that he had been considering since their arrival outside of Gollbrook. "She knows things that no mortal has ever known."

Zharran suddenly looked up at Kitten with a question in his eyes. He would not speak it in front of the other men, but Kitten knew what it was and how important it was to him. She laid a hand on his shoulder to reassure him and spoke to Raisa, "You've told him that we will do what we can. Now tell him that we need the weapons tonight."

Raisa bowed respectfully and returned to the merchant, who looked back at Kitten with a mixture of hope and awe. Markuss mumbled something about getting some food and blankets at the next stall and left Kitten and Zharran to themselves. They ambled away from the market and sat on a bench outside of a darkened tavern. Zharran waited as patiently as he could, fidgeting with his belt and watching Kitten anxiously. She sighed and gave him the bravest smile she could muster before speaking.

"Your mother is no longer in this mortal world. I'm so sorry, Zharran. I wish we could have found her before the tournament began, but she died many years ago."

Zharran dropped his gaze to his knees, but his voice was steady. "I knew it was likely that we would never find her. I knew that she could not have survived in the desert without a family or a village to take care of her. My stepfather knew that, as well. There are nights when I am glad that the traders killed him."

Kitten felt the anger and pain in his heart, the betrayal of a trusted elder, and the sorrow at the loss of his mother. She knew that he had still hoped. She felt the heavy burden of being the bearer of such sad news. But Zharran deserved the truth. He had been loyal to her from the day they met, when she and her mentor had stopped the band of traders that had killed his stepfather from taking him to the border of Cantari. She had promised him then that if it were possible to track down his mother, left to die in the deserts of Shar-rah by her greedy husband, they would do so. But now she knew that they had never had a chance of finding her before her death. She passed away in the heat of the desert sands mere days after losing her son, his name on her lips as her last breath left her body.

They waited there together for a few minutes, Zharran soaking in the impact of the news of his mother's death, and Kitten traveling through the night air. Mentally, she checked on Vincoral again, but he was still gazing at the west. Perhaps, he suspected that her sudden disappearance was connected to the immortal beings that he feared so much. She checked on Raisa, who was enjoying a reminiscent chat with his friend, the merchant. She checked on Markuss, who was gathering supplies, hoping to redeem himself after his petty outburst. He did not regret joining them on their journey; perhaps, he was not quite a true pirate at heart. Then, Kitten checked on her former home, the village of Moonsea. Her mentor there had died shortly after completing her training, but she still felt his presence there. In fact, she felt it within herself, as well. He was lending her his own strength. She thanked him and smiled.

"Can you see everyone?" Zharran asked suddenly.

Kitten pulled herself back to Gollbrook and looked at him. He was calmer now and genuinely curious about what she knew of the world.

"I can feel your mother's spirit around you," she said softly. "She has been with you since the day she died, watching over you and encouraging you."

"I think…I always knew that," he said, looking up at the stars. "Who else can you see?"

"I can see my parents and my teacher," she began. "I can see our friends in the market and Vincoral in his castle. I can see the immortals in The West and the Cantari people in their hovels, praying for salvation. I can see you and me, and I can see people who haven't been born yet."

"Is it hard? Do you have to concentrate very hard to see all that?"

"Not at all. It's more like suddenly realizing I had an extra hand all along, but I'm only just now able to see it. We're all a part of each other. Seeing everyone else is like feeling a part of myself."

"I like that," Zharran laughed, something he didn't do often. "It makes me feel safer. I feel closer to my mother thinking of it."

"You are close to her," Kitten nodded. "She is a part of you. And a part of me. And a part of that tree and this town. Just like you are. Just like I am. That's how I know we can defeat Vincoral. Because this world is bigger and stronger than he'll ever be. And we're a part of it."

She felt Markuss approach them, bags of food and blankets slung over his back. He walked slowly and looked at her expectantly.

"Good job," she said to him encouragingly. "We're almost ready to leave."

He relaxed a bit and set the bags down next to the bench. A question formed in his mind, and it was strong enough that Kitten could feel it without looking into his thoughts. She answered before he spoke.

"Your crew is safe. They made it to the cave without encountering any trouble from Vincoral's men."

Markuss stared at her with shock and relief. She wondered for a moment how long she would have to put up with these confused reactions. Raisa exited the market square, carrying a small crate full of weapons. The rest of them gathered around him as he opened the crate and handed out the forged blades that would be their traveling companions through the next part of their journey.

Kitten received a Volcanic Blade, a special sword forged from a metal so hard that the heat of volcanic lava was needed to melt and reform it. Only a few had ever been successfully completed, although hundreds of attempts had been made. The blacksmiths who worked the volcanic fires deep in the bowels of the earth usually died there before they could complete their task. Kitten held the blade reverently and vowed that she would use it to avenge all the people that Vincoral had sent to their deaths beneath the fiery mountains in an attempt to obtain one of these weapons himself. She sensed the power within her new sword. The magic inherent within the metal felt ancient and connected directly to the power of the earth.

Markuss was given a sword forged by the Howerth wizards in the days when they still deigned to mingle among common mortals. It held the power of protection, serving as both shield and weapon. Very few blades of its kind remained in human hands.

Zharran received a short sword suited to both his stature and his ancestry. It came from the desert lands he had once called home and had been imbued with the power to sap energy from all who opposed its master. Few desert-dwellers practiced the ways of magic, but those who did preferred such parasitic spells, drawing water from sand and energy from enemy nomads.

For himself, Raisa kept the legendary Ninja Star, a weapon so steeped in myth that Kitten was the only member of their group who had known it really existed. It was said to fly with deadly accuracy, regardless of the thrower's aim, and to return to the thrower's hand once it had hit its mark. It was also said to multiply itself into five or even ten when necessary, but even Kitten wasn't sure whether it could actually do this. Created by the first ninja, the Star had been passed down through the Ninja Clan of Cantari until a great battle with a mysterious, unnamed enemy had resulted in its loss. For centuries, many ninja families had sought its power, but it remained hidden from them, and eventually its absence was thought to be proof of its nonexistence.

"How did this merchant get all these weapons?" Markuss asked suspiciously. "Some of them have been lost to the world for ages, and some are impossible to obtain unless you have family connections."

"My friend the merchant has many secrets," Raisa answered. "Some he does not even tell me."

"They showed up on his doorstep mysteriously one afternoon many years ago," Kitten smiled knowingly. "A gift from an old friend."

"Who?" Zharran asked. Her three companions looked at her questioningly.

"Akkanar," she spoke softly, sensing the old wizard's spirit, feeling the energy he gave her pulsing within her veins. "He didn't know at the time what use they would be, but he sensed that they would best be kept in the hands of a merchant who happened to know the only ninja to leave his hidden village in centuries. He didn't know how close he was to sensing the oneness of the universe at that time. But at least he was able to contribute to our quest. His life's goal was to destroy the evil of Vincoral."

"This is a little…creepy," Markuss commented. "How could he know that we would need these or come here to get them?"

"As I said, he was very close to sensing the connections between all things and all time," Kitten smiled. "He had worked very hard his whole life to gain magical power. It is bound to leave a mark on one's soul. Now, we should leave. Time is running low."

She could feel the void around Vincoral growing again. He was regaining his power and stretching out with it to search for her and to feed on the energy of those around him. She could feel his guards and soldiers shivering within their souls, fearing their master and his whims. She could feel the people within his dungeons, cold and without hope, crying out for an end to their torment. She could feel the people of Cantari, abandoning their homes in the hopes of crossing the border to safer lands, or staying and fighting the daily intrusions of Vincoral's army. She could feel the daughter of the merchant in Gollbrook, waiting for them. She, out of all the others, was not afraid. Her pain was not brought by torture or loss. Kitten could see her story and knew why she was waiting for them. As she led her friends through the forest toward Cantari, she knew this girl would be one of many trials ahead of them before they reached Vincoral on his throne of power.

They had walked in silence through the dark forests outside of Cantari Nation for a couple of hours before Kitten spoke. She wanted to warn her friends of the dangers ahead. They were all expecting a tough battle and many dangers, but she knew specifically what they would be up against. She could see the placement of soldiers and the wanderings of unknowing travelers in her mind. She couldn't know what would come tomorrow, but she could see what lay on the path before them tonight and guess what they would be facing once they reached the border.

"You all know this will not be easy," she began, startling Zharran and Markuss. "But there is more ahead of us than you could guess. I want to warn you."

"We may die on this quest," Raisa interrupted. "We are each aware of this. It matters not how, only that we fight with all our strength."

"I want to give you the chance to fight with your minds, as well," Kitten said. "If you know what is coming, you will be better prepared for the battles ahead. You must have guessed that Vincoral would protect his domain with spells and with soldiers, but we will be facing more than the average warrior within the borders of Cantari. The Howerth wizards have aligned themselves with the Demonic One in the hopes of seeing the humans wiped from this planet."

There was an audible gasp as her companions realized what this meant. With the Howerth wizards on Vincoral's side, they would be hard-pressed to sneak through the hills of Cantari unchecked. Not even the great magic master of Moonsea was said to have had the power to equal a Howerth wizard.

"Can't you shield us from them or something?" Markuss asked.

"I dare not use any magic once inside the borders," Kitten sighed. "It will attract Vincoral's attention and may further damage the world there. We must find another way. There are also creatures from other worlds. Dimensions that we could not possibly comprehend. These things will be the most difficult opponents we face outside the castle walls because even I can't tell you anything about them. Their worlds are completely cut off from ours, so I can't sense anything from them. I can only see the voids in the air where they stand. I see them moving and feel the coldness emanating from them, but I can tell you nothing more."

She waited a moment for this information to sink in and then continued, "Raisa, I'm afraid I must give you bad news. Twice over, as well. The girl, the merchant's daughter…"

"She has aligned herself with Vincoral, as well, yes?" the ninja said softly. When Kitten was silent, he added, "I suspected as much when you did not say whether she was alive or dead. Had she been dead, you would have told us right away. Had she been alive and in the dungeons, you would have devised a plan to rescue her. But you were more cryptic in your reply."

"Yes, she has chosen to fight on the Demon's side," Kitten confirmed. "When she was kidnapped, he offered her the chance to save herself from the ravenous claws of his minions, and she took it. Who can blame her? She was barely fourteen years old at the time and no fighter. He taught her some of his magic and molded her into a willing slave. She desires his conquest of the world nearly as much as he does now, if only to punish it for allowing her to be torn from her home and her father."

"And what is your second piece of bad news?" Raisa asked.

"The ninjas have left your village," Kitten said simply.

Their group was silent. They all knew that she would not have mentioned this fact if something big hadn't happened to the ninjas, and there were only two possible conclusions to take from this. Either Raisa's people had died fighting Vincoral, or they had joined him as the Howerth wizards had. After a few minutes, Raisa asked with a voice that was calmer than he felt, "Do they live?"

Kitten trembled a moment before answering. Either way, it would be difficult for her friend to deal with this news. Either all of his friends and family were dead, or they were working for the most evil warlock in history. But he needed to know the truth; they would all be facing it soon enough.

"Yes," she stated quietly.

They spent the next hour in silence. But they were not idly wandering through the trees. Kitten spent the time focusing her newfound power with her mind, touching the plants that they passed in the darkness and helping them grow, forging connections between pieces of the world that had gotten separated by Vincoral's passing through this forest on his way back from the tournament. It became easier as she practiced, and she needed all the practice she could get before they reached the border. She checked on Vincoral every now and then, but his gaze never left the western horizon. She pulled energy toward herself from all over the universe, asking the stars for help, taking strength from the earth. Once or twice, she even found her consciousness drifting so far from her body that she nearly forgot who she was supposed to be. But she never forgot her purpose, her goal.

Raisa was thinking beyond his physical being, as well. His thoughts were on strategies to defeat his own people. Saddened as he was by their betrayal of the principles he held dear, he knew that they would have to be fought, for once the ninja people put their minds to a task, they could not be stopped. He steeled himself for the battle ahead and prepared his mind for the appeals his people would most likely attempt on him.

Markuss considered ways to get them all across the land of Cantari and into Vincoral's stronghold without magic. He hadn't used magic much himself during his time as a pirate, but he knew how easy it was to rely on it for emergencies. Now, they needed to rely on their wits, something all pirates learned to use, especially when they were trying to avoid being burned alive by an all-powerful dictator.

Zharran thought mostly of his mother, feeling her love and her strength more strongly than he had in years. He asked her for guidance and help in the challenges ahead, and he felt her confidence bolstering his own. He knew he was not as strong a warrior as his companions, nor as experienced, but he felt he was ready to face his fears. Kitten had trained him somewhat during their time at Moonsea, teaching him some of the things she learned and encouraging him to improve his abilities. Soon he would know if any of it had truly become a part of him.

They were approaching the border of Cantari Nation by midday the following morning. Everyone instinctively paused on the top of a small hill overlooking the valley that led into the land. They could see no guards or patrols of any kind. But that did not mean there was nothing there. Kitten could smell magic in the air. She was prepared to deal with spells that Vincoral had laid as traps for trespassers, however. She looked into the past connected with this spot of ground, hoping to see what magic spell he had cast on the valley below. But there was nothing to see. Whatever he had done, he had done it from the comfort of his own throne room.

"I can't tell what has happened here, but there is magic all around the border," she told her companions.

"We will have to test it," Raisa spoke, moving forward a step.

"We can't risk losing one of our own," Markuss protested.

"How else would you have us get past the border?" Zharran spoke up.

"Enough," Kitten said softly, but her voice carried such spiritual force that her friends were startled. "I will ask for help. A volunteer."

She reached out to the world around them, the plants and animals and rocks. A cohen remembered passing through the area the previous day and encountering some sort of barrier, but a birchee recalled no such thing when he flew by that same day. He volunteered to try it again and did so with no trouble. The cohen refused to repeat his excursion, however, and the other animals followed his example. The plants felt the magic but could tell nothing about it. Finally, however, Kitten noticed something unusual in the air. Over the hill, the wind blew free, and the air flowed normally. Near the border, though, just on top of the ground, it was stagnant and very nearly frozen. Each molecule that touched the ground seemed to be moving only a tiny distance over the course of minutes. The air above it moved freely and rustled the grass, but the grass moved slower than it should have. It was as though the ground and everything touching it around the border were in a completely different time frame than the rest of the world.

"It's some sort of slowing magic," Kitten spoke at last, having been silent for several minutes. "I believe it affects only those things that touch the ground around the border."

"If the forest extended farther, we could swing through the trees," Raisa said thoughtfully. "Is there another spot at which we might cross?"

"Yes, but it is two days' walk from here," Kitten told him. "We must find another way."

"How much does it slow?" Markuss asked. "Perhaps we could simply walk through it."

"It takes a single air molecule minutes to cross a space less than the span of my hand," Kitten shook her head. "It would take us weeks, perhaps more, to cross the border that way."

"Can you stop the magic?" Raisa asked the obvious question.

"That would alert Vincoral to our presence," Kitten gave him the obvious answer.

They were running out of options. No magic of any kind could be used this close to the border without giving away their position. It seemed impossible that they could cross the border in time to stop Vincoral.

"On my ship, my crew swung from place to place with the greatest of ease," Markuss commented.

"But we have no trees," Zharran reminded him.

"Yes, little one," Markuss grinned. "But we have each other. I assume, Kitten, that the spell does not affect things that touch objects already on the ground? Such as the birds sitting in that lone tree near the border?"

When she nodded, he continued, "I propose a test of acrobatic skills. Pirates use such skills every day in the running of their ship and in taking over other ships. Ninjas are well-known for their athletic prowess. And our fearless leader is a genius in many areas. What about you, little one?"

"Zharran was more acrobatic than I when we met," Kitten smiled at the young man. "I believe he can do what you are thinking."

"Then let's go, before I change my mind," Markuss nodded

Kitten grinned and took off at a run toward the border. As she felt herself approaching the magical barrier, she leaped high into the air, careful not to jump too far and put herself out of reach of her friends. She flew through the air at lightning speed, flipping over once, until she landed on the ground, about ten feet from her starting point. As soon as her foot touched the ground, she slowed to nearly a complete halt. Her flaming hair hovered in the air behind her, her right foot held still just above the ground, and her breathing slowed to a whisper. Everything seemed to slow down in her mind, as well. The world appeared to be moving very quickly around her. To regain some sense of control, she concentrated on her connection with the universe.

Meanwhile, Markuss quickly explained their goal to Raisa and Zharran, although Raisa had already guessed it, and took a leap of his own into the air above the border. After an artful flip in the air, he landed on Kitten's shoulders, steadied himself, and leaped farther into the barrier. He landed about the same distance from Kitten as she had landed from the beginning of the barrier. He reached the approximate location of the actual Cantari border. He, too, slowed to a near halt, one foot held just above the ground, his mind slowing to match the speed of his molecules. So far, no one seemed to have noticed their haphazard passage of the barrier.

Raisa nodded at Zharran, who ran and leaped without hesitation. He flew a bit far, however, and nearly overshot his first landing point. He halted himself in mid-flight by twisting around, grabbing onto Kitten's shoulders, and putting his entire weight onto her frame. Keeping his feet from touching the ground, he pulled himself up, literally climbing the body of his friend and mentor. When he had gained his footing on her shoulders, he perched there a moment to steady his nerves. This time, he leaped more carefully and with more control, landing atop Markuss' broad shoulders without a single mistake. He then jumped toward his own station, landing midway between the border and the point at which the magic barrier should end. Once he touched ground, he felt himself slowing to a stop, as if he were in a dream. He wondered briefly how long it would take for Raisa to reach him, from his perspective.

Raisa copied the path his friends had taken, jumping quickly and lightly from ground to Kitten, from Kitten to Markuss, and from Markuss to Zharran. To err on the side of caution, his final leap was his farthest. He pushed himself to the limit, aiming for the farthest piece of ground he could possibly reach, even if it meant an awkward landing, just to be sure that he passed the edge of the magic. He flew through the air nearly twenty feet before coming to a landing. It wasn't awkward; however, it was very slow. A single toe touched the ground, and his last thought before he slipped farther into the quagmire of time that they all were now stuck in was that the magic barrier had unfortunately been much wider on this side of the border than anticipated.

With her connection with the universe, Kitten sensed what had gone wrong. She knew that even if Raisa were mere inches from the edge of the barrier, it would take him precious hours to finish crossing under his own power. Being just outside the border herself, she decided that she would have to chance a little magic of her own and hope that Vincoral didn't notice it. In fact, she hoped that if she chose a solution that appeared to be a natural accident, he wouldn't notice anything at all. She focused her energy on the most innocuous of allies, the air. She called up a gale wind from high in the mountains, and it rushed at them with the speed and force of one of the long-dead Sky Dragons. It blew all four of them straight up into the air and tossed them high over the land.

Raisa, Zharran, and Markuss landed safely beyond the magic, but Kitten landed just inside it. She lay on her back, immobilized. Her friends shook themselves out of their stupor. They didn't know or understand what had happened, and their minds were still re-adjusting to the passage of normal time. After a few moments, however, they realized that Kitten was still inside the barrier. Raisa produced the lasso he would have used to pull all of them to safety if their plan had worked and used it to capture Kitten's raised right arm. He pulled her quickly and carefully through the grass until she began moving and breathing again.

"That was a close one," Markuss sighed. "What happened?"

Before answering, Kitten checked on Vincoral. He hadn't yet seen them, but he was searching the land of Cantari methodically. He had sensed the magic but not the direction from which it had come.

"I had to do a bit of magic to get us out of that," Kitten said quickly. "Now we must find a way to hide ourselves before Vincoral spots us."

"We cannot stay hidden and continue our journey to the castle at the same time," Raisa reminded her.

"We'll have to find a way!" Kitten said, growing nervous as she watched Vincoral's gaze approach them. Then she noticed something and pointed. "There's magic beyond those trees in the distance. Perhaps, we can hide there. Run!"

Her friends followed at their fastest gait, covering a hundred yards in seconds. On the other side of the small stand of trees she had indicated, they found a group of ordinary-looking peasants. Four men sat on the ground, consulting with one another in hushed tones. When they heard the newcomers approaching, they looked up. One grinned and stood. He folded his arms and waited for the interlopers to approach. When Kitten stood a few feet in front of him, he spoke with a voice as harsh as sandpaper.

"No one's allowed in or out, pet. Those are the rules. Looks like you just volunteered to feed me and my men tonight."

He licked his lips with a very non-ordinary tongue, forked as it was and green. The other three chuckled and stood behind him, pulling swords out of their belts.

"Are they...?" Markuss started.

"Not human," Kitten answered simply, drawing her own blade.

Her friends followed suit, and they ran at their opponents. A simple swordfight ensued. If they had magic, these four creatures were not using it, and Kitten and her followers were reluctant to do so after so recently attracting the Demonic One's attention. Kitten watched Vincoral's eye with her mind and saw his gaze grow steadily nearer. This fight had to end quickly.

The creatures were good with swords, parrying and slashing with perfect timing. One of them backed Kitten into the trees. He lunged, and she spun around one tree and ducked behind another. He chased her, but she was quicker than he and caught him by surprise.

She approached him from behind and slashed quickly with her sword, severing his head from his neck. Instead of blood, a fountain of green ooze flowed from the body, even as it fell to the ground. It all seemed to gather into a single puddle, and Kitten plunged her blade into it. There was a sizzling sound as the blade grew hot, and then silence.

Meanwhile, her friends experienced similar incidents with their opponents. Raisa threw his ninja star and watched it multiply into three exact duplicates, flying at his enemy with impossible speed and accuracy. They hit their marks, cutting through the creature's neck at once and removing the head from the body. Their job done, the stars vanished before they hit the ground, reappearing in Raisa's hand. The green ooze flowed from the fallen body, puddling on the ground at Raisa's feet.

Markuss fought his opponent with amusement. His weapon was proving to be more than the creature could handle. Its inherent shielding kept the enemy sword from laying a single blow to either Markuss or itself. He stood for a moment and laughed at his opponent's frustration, until the creature stopped, widened its eyes, and screamed. The sound was like a hundred dornaks screeching in pain inches from one's ear. Markuss clutched his head in agony, although no one else seemed to have heard the noise. Satisfied with its victory, the creature raised its sword to strike at Markuss, but the pirate's eyes were not damaged by the terrible screeching. He raised his own sword to fend off the creature and took a single swipe at it, slashing open its gut. Green ooze began pouring out of the wound and pooling on the ground. The creature opened its mouth to scream again, and Markuss swung his blade and took off its head.

When the others had all finished their battles, Zharran was still struggling with his own. He had kept the fourth creature at bay, but he was finding it difficult to finish the fight. It felt as if his sword were fighting against him as well. Kitten rushed out of the trees and plunged her blade first into the green puddle at Raisa's feet and then into the one at Markuss' feet. Finally, she turned to Zharran and saw what was happening. His sword was becoming darker and heavier, and he was becoming tired and slow. He summoned all of his strength and took a final swing at his opponent, lopping off its sword-arm. The creature stumbled backwards and sat on the ground, green ooze pouring out of its shoulder. Kitten ran to Zharran's side and touched his blade with her own. The Volcanic Blade grew hot, and Zharran's sword became lighter in both color and weight. Then, she turned to the creature.

But it was no longer a creature. It was the body of a man. He lay on the ground, next to the puddle of green liquid, gasping and twitching. As the four travelers gathered around him, he found his voice and whispered, "Kill...me....Kill..."

Zharran's eyes widened in horror, and even Raisa looked astonished. Kitten raised her sword and sliced off the man's head, quickly and cleanly. Only blood dripped from the neck this time. She plunged her blade into the green ooze once more, waiting until the sizzling noise had stopped, and then turned to her friends.

"I will explain everything, but first we must act quickly to avoid being discovered. Take the clothes from the bodies and put them over your own. The magic aura from the creatures will last long enough to protect us for the rest of the day. Hurry!"

Each of them undressed a body and threw the robes and pants on over their own. Then they waited by the trees, waiting for word that they had been noticed or not. Kitten stared off into space, watching Vincoral carefully. His gaze approached them, looked at them, and passed over them, moving on to the next hill. She took a breath and sighed. The others relaxed when they saw her do this.

"I was afraid all that magical weapon activity would result in Vincoral bringing us a new welcome, personally," Markuss shook his head.

"The magic in the weapons is an inherent, natural ability that would not catch anyone's attention, unless they were looking for it," Raisa explained.

"I'm afraid that magic nearly got one of us killed, nonetheless," Kitten looked at Zharran with affection. "Those creatures were from another world. They had the ability to take over a human's body and control it, living inside of it and slowly killing it with their poisonous blood. That green ooze was their natural form. My Volcanic Blade was the only thing we had that could kill them for good. Zharran's sword has the ability to sap energy from its opponent. Unfortunately, the energy it was sapping came from a creature that took energy from others, as well. This created the effect that we saw, the changes in the sword and how it affected Zharran. If we run into more of those things, you would be wise, my squire, to hang back and let us do the fighting."

He nodded with understanding and said, "No wonder that man wanted to die. His body had been host to such a demon and, no doubt, had been damaged beyond repair."

"He was in considerable pain," Kitten agreed. "Also, once these things take your body, they can track you and kill or recapture you if you escape."

"How do you know all this?" Raisa asked, as they all stepped away from the trees and headed towards the castle once more.

"I touched the men's minds," Kitten answered. "Their minds were still intact, although damaged and frightened beyond sanity. I saw what they had been through. It was horrible." She sniffed and wiped away a tear. "The physical pain of the poisonous blood coursing through their bodies, the mental suffering caused by seeing everything that the creatures used their bodies to do, killing and raping and destroying. The creatures made them believe that it would be like that forever, that they would be forever trapped inside their own bodies, listening to such depraved thoughts and feeling themselves slip into insanity day by day. That is the sort of thing that Vincoral causes that I hope to put an end to. That is the sort of torture and despair that he uses to keep people under his control." Her voice cracked a little as she concluded, "Welcome to Cantari Nation."

Her three friends realized then that it was not only physical danger they were putting themselves in by going on this quest. They all risked such torture. But they knew that there was no turning back, even if they could pass through the barrier at the border again. They would stop this madness, no matter what the cost.

They could see the top of the castle in the distance, dark and strange. It had several towers at odd points, not at the apparent corners of the outer wall but rather inside the building itself. The walls were built of strong, heavy stone, and they were darker than they should have been with the setting sun casting its rays over the countryside. But the stronghold was even darker than could be seen with the naked eye. Kitten could see the underbelly of this part of the world, the unseen insides. She saw the cracks in reality and the void that grew darker and stronger the closer they got to the castle. The world was in pieces here, and the pieces were growing smaller and weaker with each step they took.

They still wore the filthy robes of the creatures they had killed at the border. The land had been strangely devoid of activity since they had left the bodies behind. Kitten had kept one eye constantly on Vincoral, but he had shown no sign of having noticed their presence. Still, something was odd about the lack of resistance they were encountering. Her friends sensed the strangeness of this, as well, silent though they were on the subject. They followed her footsteps without saying a word, eyes on the castle ahead, ears pricked to any noise that might alert them to an ambush.

As they approached a dark swath of forest that stretched between them and the stronghold, Kitten held up one hand to halt the party's progress. A small, dingy hut stood at the edge of the trees. There didn't appear to be anyone at home, but Kitten saw a lifeforce inside, huddling behind the door. It was a small girl, frightened that the footsteps she had heard might be the Demonic One's soldiers come back for what they had left behind on their last visit. The bodies of her parents still lay just outside the back door to the hut. The girl considered running out that door but hesitated because of the carnage she had witnessed there. She was only eight years old.

Kitten decided to chance making a sound and called out to the girl, "We are friends. We mean you no harm, and we may be able to help you. I will come inside, alone. The soldiers are not here, but they may return. Do not run, and we will take you away from here."

She stepped up to the front door, motioning for her friends to remain outside. She pushed the door open slowly and heard the girl scamper underneath a bed on the other side of the one-room cabin. Every other piece of furniture there was overturned, broken, or both. Blood stained the back wall and drenched the back door, which stood ajar, a pool of blood congealing on the floor around it. Kitten sensed the spirits of the girl's parents trying to protect her, but there was nothing they could do should the soldiers that killed them return. They had left the girl there on purpose, perhaps as an example to the citizens of Cantari, as a storyteller to spread the word of what they were capable of.

"My name is Kitten," Kitten said softly to the dark space under the bed. "I want to help you. Please come out."

She tried to project a sense of calmness and safety to the little girl to encourage her trust. It seemed to work, as the girl peeked out from her hiding spot and then slowly emerged. Her clothes were dirty and ragged, and she was thin and frail. Obviously, her family had not had enough to sustain them for some time. It mattered not how close a member of the Cantari Nation lived to the border; none were allowed to escape, although many tried.

The girl cradled one arm at an odd angle, and Kitten realized that it was broken. She offered a smile and knelt down on the floor, holding out one hand. The girl approached cautiously, sniffing the air like an animal. She was sniffing for the telltale scent of Vincoral's army: old blood and gore, filth, rusted armor, and ancient magic, which smelled oddly like burning sulfur. Her parents had taught her well. Perhaps, they had been among those who opposed Vincoral vocally, and that was why they had died.

Once she was satisfied that Kitten was no foe, the girl came close and whispered in a tiny voice, "Will you take me away?"

Kitten's heart nearly broke. She realized that taking the girl with them to the castle would be a death sentence for her, but they couldn't break off their journey now to take her back to the border. She was torn and uncertain what to say. So instead, she gently took the girl's broken limb in both hands, closed her eyes, and concentrated on healing it. It was a risk, but whatever happened, she had to have the girl in good health for traveling. She kept one eye on Vincoral, and when he appeared to be swinging his gaze toward her, she stopped, mid-healing. The break was nearly healed, so she wrapped a bandage around it and tied it over the girl's shoulder and left it at that.

While the girl marveled at her nearly healed arm, Kitten looked around the nearby countryside, hoping to find a relatively safe spot where they could leave her. There was a cave full of refugees a few hours from the cabin, but it was south and would mean a deviation from their course. Feeling there was little choice, she led the girl outside and told the others what they would be doing. Markuss and

Zharran seemed hesitant. If Raisa felt the same, he did not show it. But they all nodded silently and followed her away from their previous direction, turning their gazes from their true destination.

After the first hour of walking, the girl began to falter, and Markuss picked her up and carried her. She did not protest and seemed to trust all of them since they were with Kitten. However, near a small stream at the bottom of a hill, she began squirming and pointing away from it. Kitten stopped and sniffed the air. She sensed that this spot was well-used resting ground for more otherworldly creatures. She could tell nothing about them, however, so she turned to the girl.

"What comes here?" she asked.

The girl's face showed her fear, but she finally answered in a whisper, "The Barking Shadows. They kill animals and steal babies." She began to cry but added, "They'll come when they hear us."

"Can we sneak through if we're really quiet?" Kitten asked hopefully.

The girl seemed to consider, but she was uncertain. No one had ever tried. The soldiers were enough for the people to fear. No one would risk death at the claws of strange, alien creatures that seemed invincible.

Kitten considered their options. They were losing time on this diversion already; they couldn't afford to lose much more. She motioned for everyone else to stay back and approached the stream on her own. Closer to the water, the land reeked of something foul and evil. Darkness seemed to close in around her, although the sun had not yet fully set. But there were no creatures there yet. They had left behind a scent and a feeling, but they were not there. Kitten motioned for the others to follow carefully and slowly. They tiptoed through the dead grass and reached the edge of water just when the sun dipped below the horizon.

Suddenly, the world seemed to turn upside-down. Kitten felt disoriented, and her eyes went dark. The girl screamed, and something flashed by them, a scout of some sort, followed by the pack. A strange sound assaulted their ears, a sort of barking noise, but with a hissing in the background. Kitten focused her eyes and recovered her vision. The others stood with their weapons drawn, the girl between them, crying. But none of them could see. Kitten saw them, the shadows. For shadows, they were, flitting along the ground in strange, ever-changing shapes. They seemed to be avoiding Kitten, but they were growing closer to the others, teasing them and reaching out to touch the girl. She appeared to be growing cold, shivering and sinking slowly to the ground. Her eyes went blank, and her skin became paler and paler.

Kitten dashed to the girl, picked her up, and thrust her into Raisa's arms. "Go!" she shouted, spinning him to point him in the direction they had been headed. She knew that if anyone could outrun such beasts, besides herself, it would be Raisa. Indeed, he took off like an arrow, splashing through the shallow stream and leaping as best he could without seeing the ground. Once out of range of the "barking shadows," his vision would return. In the meantime, Kitten, Zharran, and Markuss would have to deal with the dark creatures that surrounded them, angry now that two of their prey had left them. A few of them tried to chase after Raisa, but Kitten could see they weren't nearly fast enough and would lose his scent once he took to the trees in the forest before the cave.

"I can't see anything," Markuss whispered.

"Do as I say," Kitten instructed, swiping her sword at a passing phantom. "Zharran, put your back to Markuss and swing your blade low to the ground. Let it draw in the energy of anything it touches. Markuss, use the protection of your sword to surround us. You'll feel a glow, but don't be alarmed."

To herself, Kitten prayed to the gods that her plan would work. No physical attack would work against such beings, and if she used any more magic, she was certain that Vincoral would spot her. Once Markuss and Zharran were in place, she held her Volcanic Blade against Markuss' sword and willed it to use its own magical abilities. First, it grew warm, as it had when killing the green ooze creatures earlier. Then, it began to glow. The hotter it became, the brighter it glowed, until the glow extended through the outer edge of the invisible protective shield that Markuss' sword extended around them. It became a bubble of light, protecting them from the shadow creatures, which nipped at the edge of their circle, whining and barking.

The shapeless things spun around them, faster and faster, becoming more and more desperate and angry. Kitten focused the energy of her sword and, through it, Markuss' sword. The bubble of light grew brighter and hotter, until even her blinded friends could see. They squinted into the light, as it grew outward. Suddenly, it shot away from them on all sides, growing large in an instant and absorbing the darkness of every creature around them. There was a final screeching howl, and the shadows vanished.

Zharran and Markuss stood blinking in the moonlight, and Kitten searched the surrounding landscape with her mind for signs of the creatures. There were only the few that had followed Raisa, and they were wandering aimlessly through the distant hills. The light had dissipated once the immediate danger had been destroyed, and Kitten felt certain they would not need it again soon. She could still smell the death and darkness that had become a part of this area because of the creatures' presence, but the shadows themselves were definitely gone.

"What happened?" Zharran asked in wonder.

"I combined the power of my blade with that of Markuss' sword," Kitten said briefly. "Come, we should rejoin Raisa at the cave as quickly as possible."

The three of them raced across the stream and followed the ninja's invisible trail over the hills, through the trees, and into the opening in the rock at the base of a small mountain. It took them less than an hour, now that they were running. Here, the trail led down into the earth. Kitten sensed that there was magic in the rocks, magic that would shield them from Vincoral's sight, and she relaxed somewhat. At least, here, they would be safe for a moment.

The sound of whispers reached her ears, and Kitten listened to the voices and thoughts of the people of Cantari who had come to this cave to hide from the Demonic One and his rage. They left the cave for only minutes each day to forage for what sustenance could be found in the trees. They were fearful after Raisa's bold and sudden entrance, but some of them recognized the girl and were tending to her. It took a few minutes to reach the main cavern, then Kitten stepped slowly into the firelight and looked into the faces of her people. There were audible gasps from many of them when they saw her face and her bright red hair. They knew who she was and what she was doing there.

A woman in bright robes, who seemed to be the leader of the group, approached Kitten and spoke for the others, "We thought perhaps your friend was the vanguard of Vincoral's invading army. But we see now that he spoke the truth. You are, indeed, the warrior for whom we have waited."

A few in the room sighed with palpable relief, and one woman burst into tears of joy. Kitten felt uncomfortable under the gaze of such hope and admiration. She had known what was expected of her, but she had not realized that the people would look on her with such joy and gratitude. She looked into each face that gazed up at her and nearly cried herself. They were tired and hungry, each of them. The stories of want, abuse, and fear were etched into them. Most of the people had a wound of some sort, a broken limb or a deep cut or worse. But they all hoped. Each one of them had hope shining in their eyes behind the fear and exhaustion.

"The savior of Cantari," someone whispered, and the chant was taken up by every man, woman, and child, until the cavern was filled with voices repeating those words over and over.

"Please," Kitten held up one hand. "Please. I wish only to leave the girl here with you and continue on my mission. Time is running out."

"We understand," the leader said. "We may be of some help to you. I see you are wearing the clothes of the Swamp Men, I presume in order to slip under the Demonic One's search for alien magic. But the effects will wear off very soon. We have collected armor from the few soldiers that we have managed to slay. Take it, and you may be able to approach the castle without further obstacles."

She waved at two men, and they pulled a collection of rusted armor from a niche in the rock wall. It was bloodstained and worn, but

Kitten could smell the stench of Vincoral's army on it. It would help them get closer to the castle walls. She smiled and nodded, and she and Raisa took the armor and distributed it among their group.

Once they were outfitted in their new clothing, Kitten thanked the woman and her followers, speaking in the Cantari formal language, which was known only to the Warrior Clan and the Ruling Clan. The woman nearly choked on her own tears. The rest of the refugees remained silent, but the look in their eyes was enough to give Kitten further resolve to complete her mission. She turned and led her friends back out into the night. She whispered only one word: "Run." She knew that Vincoral's evil would become unstoppable by tomorrow midday. She sensed the progression of his power, and her stomach churned at the sight of the pieces of the world that had already been lost, never to be recovered. She ran back to the hut in the trees where they had found the girl, her friends at her heels, and led the way on toward the castle.

Their new armor took them nearly to the castle gate. Numerous monsters and demons and nameless creatures prowled the grounds around the stronghold, but they paid no attention to the four unknown guards running over the dreary terrain. They smelled like members of the evil army, and it was too dark to see their faces underneath the low brims of their leather helms. The otherworldly things ignored them and went about their business, eating their bloody meals, fighting amongst themselves, and patrolling the overgrown paths through the trees. Kitten and her crew remained on guard for any sudden attacks, but nothing happened until they were a mere twenty yards or so from the castle gate.

The four of them came to a sudden halt when they saw the group of soldiers at the gate, checking each demon and searching each guard. It looked as though Vincoral had become somewhat more cautious during the time he had spent healing and watching for Kitten's approach. Kitten briefly considered fighting the guards and storming the castle, but that would give Vincoral time to mount a defense. She wanted to hang onto the element of surprise as long as possible. She motioned for the others to follow her silently and sneaked around the side of the gate, following the wall and looking for another way in. She mentally examined the stronghold from other vantage points and found nothing but mouse holes. They had gone halfway around the outer wall when it occurred to her that there was something strange about the mice that made the mouse holes in the rock at the base. She paused at the next one they passed and reached out to the mouse that lived there.

So they still existed! Stories of the changelings that lived in the land of Cantari ages ago had been circulated by the peasantry for decades. But no one had believed that they could still exist. No one had seen a changeling in centuries. Yet, here they were, masquerading as simple mice in the castle of Cantari's greatest enemy. Kitten saw immediately why she hadn't noticed them before, during her initiation ritual in The West. When a changeling became something, it became that thing totally and completely. This changeling was a mouse. The only reason she could see the truth now was that it wanted her to see it. It sensed her connection to the world when she was still in the Land of the West, and it and its brethren had made their way stealthily to Vincoral's castle and slipped inside. As mice, they could explore and learn secrets without being noticed. Even Vincoral had no idea what they really were.

"Genius," Kitten whispered. Her companions waited for an explanation while she communed with the changeling that was now peeking out of its tiny tunnel through the wall. After a moment, she stood and spoke, "We have an ally. He will use his inherent magical abilities to transport us one by one through the castle wall. Once inside the courtyard, we'll be on our own, but Vincoral won't notice our entrance."

"Why is that?" Zharran asked with a cryptic smile. He had already guessed what she was going to say. His people had known of the existence of changelings for many years, and for a moment, Kitten and he shared in the wonder of it all in their thoughts.

"We will be mice, my little friend," Kitten winked at him. "But it will only work while we are in direct contact with our ally here. You can see why that would be too awkward to continue past the courtyard. But once inside, our armor should be enough to finish the job. Let's get going."

The mouse dashed out of its hole and touched her foot, and she vanished, replaced by another mouse. The two rodents quickly ran into the tunnel through the rock and out the other side. The changeling hurried back outside to get the rest of the group, and Kitten hid herself in the shadows of an outhouse nearby. One by one, her friends appeared inside the castle wall, slightly disoriented, but no worse for the experience. They hid with her until all four of them were safely inside. Kitten mentally thanked their new friend and sent him on his way. Then, she led the way across the courtyard toward the main building of the castle.

Demons and otherworldly creatures slunk around the shadows of the yard, but they didn't appear to be as alert as their counterparts outside. They didn't look twice at the group of four soldiers who marched slowly and silently across the dirt yard. Training dummies were set up everywhere like so many bedraggled scarecrows, torn to shreds by the newest recruits. It looked like a graveyard of some sort with makeshift markers for headstones. Kitten shivered a little at the thought. She checked Vincoral again, but although he was searching the land for any sign of her, he was not looking within the walls of his own castle. She then checked on her companions. They were not doing so well. They had all been awake and traveling for more than a full day, and they were very tired. She had kept herself going by drawing on the energy of the world around her, but now that they were so close to the center of the void that surrounded the Demonic One, she felt the drain on her energy, as well.

Once they reached the relative safety of the main building, they huddled in the shadow of the corner farthest from the creatures that stalked the courtyard. Some of the beings walked on two legs, some on four, some slithered on bellies, some floated through the air, and some seemed to simply appear and disappear at will. There were at least two score of them, though there may have been more beyond the light of the moon. Kitten checked the area around them for spies and then pointed at Raisa's pack. He had carried a bag full of supplies from Gollbrook. They had used little of it other than the food during their walk to Cantari. Now was the time for the special drink that Raisa's merchant friend had included for them.

"I had hoped we wouldn't need this," Raisa whispered. "It has an unfortunate side effect."

"We have no choice," Kitten sighed. "We are all tired, and now that we are within the void's area of effect, we will have even less energy to draw upon. Drink. Everyone, drink."

Raisa took a single sip of the small blue vial and handed it to Markuss, who looked askance at the strange liquid but took his sip, as well. Zharran took his, and Kitten drank the last. Markuss was about to ask what the unfortunate side effect was when the magic began to take hold. A surge of energy coursed through each of their bodies, renewing their depleted reserves and filling them with hope and excitement. A glow seemed to surround them, shining brightly at first and then settling into their eyes.

They stared at each other and wondered for a moment at the light that shined from all of their eye sockets. They would have to make their way through the rest of the stronghold without any guards noticing the strange sight. Kitten pulled the brim of her helm down as low as it would sit, and this was enough to hide the light as long as she didn't look up. The others followed her example, and they all tiptoed silently along the wall of the main building.

There were no windows, but there were three doors. Kitten checked each of them with her mind and found the entrance to the soldiers' barracks, the dungeon, and main door used most often by Vincoral and his personal attendants. The main door was well-guarded by soldiers conducting the same search they had seen at the front gate. The other two were more easily accessible, but the soldiers' barracks were cut off from the rest of the building by solid walls. There were no doors to lead from the barracks to the other rooms. Inside the dungeon were people that Vincoral had tortured for one reason or another. Some were dead, some were dying, some were held in a sort of suspended animation so that they could not die. Kitten's heart went out to them, and she knew that they had to help them. Ninjas were guarding the dungeon, but the armor might be enough to get her and her friends past them. Since the dungeon was their best way into the main building, anyway, it seemed a simple thing to help the prisoners escape before continuing on to Vincoral's throne room.

Kitten led the way through the dungeon door. Inside, the air smelled dank and rotten. The stench of blood and offal hung throughout the dark halls, and only a single torch shed any light on the slick masonry in each tunnel. The ninjas were nowhere to be seen, but Kitten knew they were there, hiding in the crossbeams overhead and around shadowy corners and in dark closets where tools of torture were kept. She sensed some trepidation in the minds of many of them, uncertainty that this was what they should be doing with their time. Many of them doubted the orders of their leader to follow Vincoral's commands, but they were loyal to the end. She noticed that some of the ninjas seemed to be shielding their minds, hiding themselves from her own probing thoughts. That was strange and disturbing. But they had already been spotted and had to continue their trek through the dungeon.

Kitten walked slowly down the first hall, her friends in step behind her, and passed the first few doors. One or more prisoners were behind each lock, but they were being watched by unseen eyes. She began to doubt that they would be able to free anyone before the destruction of the Demonic One.

Before they could round the corner at the first intersection, a ninja dropped from the ceiling to confront them. But he didn't speak to Kitten. He stood before Raisa and used the ninja code language to say something that Markuss and Zharran couldn't understand. He seemed to be asking a question. Raisa answered in the common tongue.

"No, brother, you are the one who has betrayed the Ninja Clan."

At those words, a dozen more black-clad warriors appeared from everywhere at once and surrounded them.

"I must apologize, Kitten," Raisa said sorrowfully. "A challenge must be met. But perhaps this incident does not need to result in our discovery."

"Perhaps not," Kitten agreed and then spoke directly to the first ninja who appeared before them. "I sense your doubt. Your brother has pointed out that he may not be the disloyal warrior. Have you considered where your loyalty should lie? With a leader who has led you to ally yourselves with the destroyer of our people? Or with the brother who has laid his life on the line in order to fight for our people's freedom and survival?"

"Our tradition dictates that we must follow our leader," the ninja said behind his mask, but his voice, and his thoughts, wavered.

"The act of following a tradition means nothing if that tradition means nothing," Raisa said softly. "Our people have been dedicated to protection and survival for centuries. But we have lost our way because we became too concerned with our own protection and survival. We have forgotten what it means to be the Ninja Clan of Cantari."

His voice was filled with pride, and it seemed to speak volumes to the silent ninjas in the dungeon. They listened to both his words and his intent. Many of them seemed to make a silent agreement among themselves that today would be a new day for the Ninja Clan. The one who seemed appointed to do all the talking for them said, "We have lost our way, that much has been clear to many of our number for some time. But we still need a leader. Will you lead us, Brother Raisa?"

Raisa hesitated, worried about what such a decision would mean for Kitten and her mission. But Kitten smiled and nodded at him, and he bowed low before her and his clan. The other ninjas took this as a sign that he had accepted their request, and they took up positions around him, ready to receive orders and protect him and his friends. Others appeared from the shadows and joined them, making their little group larger by dozens.

But some of them did not seem interested in joining the quest. A few ninjas remained apart from the rest, and a few more joined them, until there were about ten of them standing separately in the middle of the intersection of hallways. Half of them were hardened warriors, ninjas who had come to believe that their true path lay along Vincoral's swath of destruction. They were certain that the ninjas would rise to power if they sided with the most powerful wizard they could find, and they were tired of hiding in shadows and protecting weaker clans. The other half was a mystery, the ones who had somehow shielded their minds from Kitten. They almost seemed to not be there at all, like the alien creatures from other worlds. She felt uneasy looking at them and knew that their troubles were not over.

"Will the great Ninja Clan split itself in two?" the nameless ninja asked, looking at his brethren who remained apart from the group.

"The Ninja Clan will live on with us," one of the separatists said. "You will perish on your erroneous quest, and we will make the Clan great once more."

Raisa sighed sadly and motioned for everyone to leave, but the ninjas who still followed Vincoral positioned themselves in front of him.

"You will perish," the one who had spoken before said venomously. "Here. Now."

He whipped out a sword, and his followers did the same. In the blink of an eye, everyone in the hall was armed and ready to fight. But before they could get started, half of the traitor ninjas, the half that

Kitten had been unable to read with her mind, pulled off their masks and revealed themselves to be Howerth wizards in disguise. The deep purple of their skin could not be mistaken, and they looked upon everyone else with contempt. One of them spoke, something Kitten had not heard often before. The Howerth wizards did not often bother speaking to anyone outside their clan.

"You have two choices, little ones," he hissed. "You can surrender and live long enough to see the Demonic One become your new ruler, or you can die now."

Kitten knew which choice her friends would take if they had the time to consult one another. They would never surrender to Vincoral or his lackeys. The wizard seemed to hear her thoughts and nodded.

"Very well. Your lives are forfeit."

He cast a spell, and a flash of light blinded everyone. But it was only a distraction. Kitten sensed the real magic coming from behind them and turned in time to see another group of wizards throwing lightning at them. She ducked and pulled Zharran down with her. Markuss had his shield, and the ninjas were all quick enough to avoid getting hit. The hall was wide enough to dodge but too narrow to avoid getting hit for much longer. They needed a plan that didn't require the use of magic.

The ninja closest to Raisa threw a key to Kitten, said a few words in the ninja tongue, and led the others in a charge to fight the traitor ninjas and the Howerth wizards. Kitten rolled across the hall, unlocked a door, and ducked inside. Fire spells were now flying through the air, and Markuss and Zharran barely missed getting turned into cinders. Raisa remained in the hall with his fellow ninjas, fighting as best they could against the overwhelming forces of the wizards and their allies.

"We need to help them without using magic," Kitten said breathlessly, slamming the door shut.

She walked over to the lone piece of furniture in the filthy room, a table on which a peasant lay, chained and bleeding and dying. He was too weak and in too much pain to even speak, and his eyes looked right through her. There was nothing that could be done for this one, so Kitten took the lamp that sat beside his head and blew out the candle. The man exhaled for the last time, and Kitten closed his eyes with one hand. The lamp had been a magic one that kept the man alive long after he would have otherwise perished. There were more like it elsewhere in the dungeon, and Kitten was determined to put them all out.

"How can we fight wizards without magic?" Markuss asked.

"Remember how we combined my weapon with yours to defeat the shadow creatures?" Kitten said, turning to face him. "I think we can do something like that again. But this time, we'll use Zharran's sword with yours."

"I think I understand," Markuss said, grinning.

Zharran nodded silently, and the three of them steeled themselves for battle. Kitten opened the door, and Markuss led the way with his sword held before him to protect them all with its shield. It was chaos in the hallway. Ninjas fighting ninjas and wizards, spells flying through the air, dead bodies piling up. And from the look of things, most of them were ninjas.

One of the ninjas still loyal to Vincoral fell into Kitten, and she turned to defend herself. He spun and looked into her eyes with contempt. One hand twitched, and Kitten barely managed to dodge the knife that flew from his fingers. He threw himself at her, and she fell back against the wall, grabbed his shirt, and flung him to the side, using his own momentum to propel his body. Markuss and Zharran remained behind the invisible sword-shield, fending off attackers with their backs to the wall.

"Wait for my signal!" Kitten shouted above the fray. She wanted to make sure their allies were out of the way.

A paralyzing spell flew just over her head, causing some of her hair to stand on end. Kitten mentally pinpointed each friendly ninja, including Raisa. Most of them were at the other end of the hall. She motioned for Markuss and Zharran to follow her and crept around the flying fists and spells. Halfway to the position she had chosen, another ninja attacked her. With lightning speed, his foot hit the back of her head before she noticed he was there. She had been too focused on making it to the rendezvous point. She slipped to the floor, one hand on the wall, and the ninja tried to pin her. She spun and delivered an elbow to his nose. But he was ready and managed to grab her arm before it made contact with his face. She ducked a bit and punched him in the gut, but he barely flinched. A couple of plain metal ninja stars appeared out of nowhere and struck her in the shoulder. The ninja took advantage of her surprise and hit her forehead with the palm of his hand. A brief flash went through her brain, and she found herself dazed and unable to decide what to do next. Then, a fist connected with her chest, and everything came back to her. But she was too winded to raise herself to her feet again. She rolled out of the way, and another ninja jumped into her place. This one was a female ninja on Kitten's side, and she seemed better prepared to handle this enemy.

Markuss' hand reached down and raised Kitten to her feet. She gasped for air, refocused herself, and led him to the spot in the hallway that stood between most of their allies and most of their enemies. Some would remain on either side, but the risk had to be taken. She nodded at her friends, but before they could make a move, a trio of combatants attacked them from three different sides. Two ninjas pulled Markuss and Zharran apart in an attempt to divide and conquer the group. The wizard cast a holding spell on Kitten to keep her from doing another.

"Coward!" Kitten shouted. "Fight me like a true wizard of Howerth Lake!"

Her challenge did the job, and he extinguished his spell and came at her with his staff. Kitten grabbed hold of it and swung both of them away from the others, who were holding their own for the time. She slammed the wizard into the wall, and he lifted his staff, pulling her closer to him. He raised one leg in an attempt to kick her, but she let go of his staff, grabbed his foot and flipped him onto the floor. He jumped back up before she could attack again and jabbed at her with the staff, its tip glowing with the green aura of a poison spell. Kitten dodged, jumped, and flipped through the air, her feet landing on the wizard's chest and pushing him away. She spun in midair, landing on her feet again, and charged quickly, head-butting the wizard in the stomach. He hadn't been expecting such an unsophisticated attack and went down easily. She wrested the staff from his grasp and broke it over her knee, making it unusable.

The wizard growled in anger. A Howerth staff was not easily replaceable, although the wizards could do magic without it. His hands glowed red, and he advanced towards Kitten, speaking arcane words that hadn't been heard outside of Howerth Lake in centuries. The words seemed to appear in the air, glowing and encircling her. Kitten knew she had to act fast. She jumped as high as she could, landing on one of the ceiling beams, and propelled herself out and down, towards the wizard's head. She kicked at him, sending him reeling backwards. He recovered quickly, but the mysterious words and glow had disappeared. Kitten swung a fist and then a foot, trying to keep the wizard off balance, but he parried each attempted blow with barely any effort at all. Tired of the battle, he held up one hand and cast a spell. Kitten felt herself flying upwards. Her head hit a ceiling beam, hard, and she found herself losing consciousness.

No! I have to finish this! Kitten drew on the energy around her, careful not to take too much and hoping that the overwhelming chaos was enough to keep her hidden. The wizard threw her into a wall, and she landed on top of a dead ninja. Scrambling to get out of the way, she just missed getting hit by the wizard's next spell, an explosive one that took out a wall and buried several ninjas in rubble. As the dust settled, Kitten stood angrily in front of the wizard, determined to end this battle.

The wizard threw a spell, but Kitten dodged it, running towards him. At the last moment, she spun, avoiding his block attempts and hitting him with her arms. She spun around and around him, faster and faster, in a version of the ninja Tornadex, lashing out when he least expected it. She finally had him off his guard. He cast a shield spell, and Kitten paused long enough to draw her sword. It began to glow as she spun around the wizard again. The magic of the Volcanic Blade allowed it to heat up enough to pass straight through the shield spell. As this realization dawned on the wizard, his face froze in a contortion of horror and surprise. His skin began to scale, as he prepared to transform into the dragon form, but it was already too late. Kitten spun close enough to hit him with the sword and sliced his head clean off.

Her battle done, she turned to check on her friends. Markuss and Zharran had been unable to defeat their opponents. She dashed over to them, dodging more spells and weapons. Without missing a beat, she jumped and slid sideways through the air, knocking both ninjas off their feet. Without standing up, she jabbed her sword through one ninja's head and kicked the other in the back of his head. She got to her feet, grabbed the ninja by the shirt, and hissed in the ninja code language, "If you want to live, stay down."

She dropped him and backed off, but the ninja was stubborn and pulled himself up by the wall. He was angry that she had used their sacred language and that she had taken him by surprise. He called two of his fellows to his side, and the three of them advanced on Kitten and her friends.

"We don't have time for this!" she shouted in frustration. "Raisa! Get over here!"

Her ninja friend appeared out of nowhere, his armor colored with fresh blood. He was breathing heavily and favoring an injured right arm, but he prepared himself to fight Kitten's attackers. Instead, however, she pulled him behind Markuss and shouted, "Now!"

This time, Markuss and Zharran were ready. They held their swords together and concentrated the magic. A few of the nearest ninjas backed away, realizing that something incredible was about to happen. The wizards looked up in wonder, throwing up shield spells to protect themselves. The glow from the two swords spread throughout the hallway in front of them. It looked as though someone had simply opened a window to let in the light of the sun. But something strange was happening to the ninjas and wizards who stood before them. Everyone was becoming pale and weak. Ninjas dropped to their knees, reaching for each other. Wizards struggled to remain on their feet, leaning on their staffs and adding power to their shields. But nothing worked. The power of Zharran's sword, magnified by the power of Markuss' blade, was sapping the strength and energy, both physical and magical, from every person in front of the shield. A handful of friendly ninjas were among them, but Kitten hoped to stop the process before they were killed. Those behind the shield were unaffected, but the friendly ninjas had already taken out most of the enemies at that end of the hallway.

One wizard farthest from them raised a hand and said weakly, "The prophecy!" He dropped to the floor, and everyone else did the same. Kitten held out her hand, and Zharran and Markuss separated their weapons. A couple of ninjas close to where they were standing had died, drained of every drop of life energy, but everyone else remained alive. Kitten picked her way through the bodies to the wizard who had spoken. He looked at her with tired eyes, unable to even raise his head.

"What did you mean?" she asked, reaching out to him with her mind. She saw him standing at the edge of Howerth Lake, an older wizard at his side. The older wizard was telling of an ancient prophecy written in the oldest Howerth magic books. It told of a reunion between the Howerth magic-casters and the rest of the world. This reunion would be triggered by the appearance of a powerful Howerth weapon in the hands of an outsider during a time of great chaos and conflict. But it could be easily undone if the holder of the weapon abandoned the first wizards to see the fulfillment of the prophecy. Kitten watched the memory for a moment longer and then turned to Markuss.

"You must stay here," she said.

"What?" he responded. "Why? Shouldn't I be at your side?" He seemed hurt.

"It is more important that you stay with the wizards," she assured him. "This is the most helpful thing you can do right now. They will follow you. Because of the sword. If you do this, they will help us fight Vincoral's armies. They can use potions to recover their strength, and they will fight the demons that would otherwise storm the castle once I confront the Demonic One. In their dragon forms, they will easily be a match for the creatures. But you must lead them."

Markuss nodded with determination and said, "I'll see you after we save the world."

He knelt next to the nearest wizard and helped him extract a healing potion from a pocket. Zharran and Raisa stood ready to follow Kitten farther into the castle. But she had a job for one of them, as well.

"I need one of you to remain in the dungeon and release the prisoners," she said. "Some of them you'll have to kill by blowing out the magic candles that keep them alive. Others will survive with proper care."

"There are many here," Raisa said. "My fellow ninjas and I will clear the dungeon. It will take all of us to get everyone out before the final battle. I will see you afterwards, as well."

Kitten nodded and smiled, then led Zharran around a corner to a stairway. She knew her squire would follow her through the rest of her journey, but she worried that it would be too dangerous for him. He would not be deterred, however, and the two of them crept upstairs and through the next floor to another stairwell. On the third floor, they spotted a few burly guards patrolling outside a door. Kitten knew it was Vincoral's throne room.

They walked nonchalantly down the hall towards the guards, who paid them no attention until they noticed that the strangers were covered in fresh blood. One of them grabbed Zharran's arm and snatched off his helmet. Kitten kicked the guard in the face, and Zharran stumbled backwards, drawing his sword again.

These soldiers looked to be mercenaries from the Brunt region, so Kitten didn't expect brilliant martial arts from them. But having been surprised a few times already on this quest, she prepared herself for anything. The soldier she had kicked was already on his feet and growling at her. He made a dash forward and tried to grab her around the waist. She ducked to the side, but he recovered quickly and swung one fist at her head. She ducked again and swept her left leg along the floor, tripping him. He fell with a loud thud, and she glanced at the other two guards. One had Zharran pinned against the wall, fighting with sword and dagger, while the other was advancing on Kitten. She pushed off with her right foot, sliding forward on her left and ducking down. She slid into the second guard's feet, and he fell right on top of the other guard's legs.

There was a scream, and Kitten turned to see Zharran's blade sticking out of his opponent's back. The man tried feebly to swipe at Zharran with his own sword, but Zharran pushed him away, and he fell to the floor, bleeding and gasping. He would be dead in moments.

Kitten returned her attention to her own opponents, who had stood and drawn their swords. She feinted to the right and rolled to the left, slashing at one guard. He dodged, and the other one jabbed at her with his sword. The first guard brought his sword down from overhead at the same moment, and Kitten blocked it while jumping out of the path of the other blade. She pushed the first guard back, jumped into the air, and landed on the second guard's shoulders. She finished executing the Raptor Strike, pinning the guard to the ground with a quick thrust of her favorite dagger into his throat. Leaving him there, she leapt through the air again, kicking the first guard in the head. She landed on the floor beside him and punched him quickly in the side and the back of the knee. He fell to the floor but struggled to regain his balance. Kitten jumped up, spun, and gave him a quick spinning kick, sending him into the wall. He didn't get up again, but she knew that he would eventually, so she brought her blade down on his head, splitting it in two. The other guards were already dead, so she retrieved her dagger and turned to look at Zharran.

"I will watch the door," he volunteered, sensing her hesitation. "I know you think it is too dangerous for me to face Vincoral at your side, and you are probably right. I am not half the fighter you are. But I can help by staying here to make sure no other guards attempt to interfere with your battle."

Kitten smiled, grateful to have such an understanding friend. She told him, "You are brave and strong, and someday you will be as great a fighter as any of the Cantari Warrior Clan. Thank you."

"I will see you after you have restored the world," Zharran bowed.

Kitten took a deep breath, steeled herself, and opened the door. A young woman sat on the floor next to a throne, crying. It was the merchant's daughter, and they were false tears, Kitten knew. She closed the door behind her and walked slowly up to the throne.

"You don't have to make a scene for me," Kitten said. "I know who you are and why you are here."

The young woman raised her head and then raised one arm. It was chained to the throne. "Please, help me," she begged pitifully.

Kitten decided it would be best to play along for the moment. She approached the woman cautiously, pretending to look over the chains shackled to both of her wrists. But she was ready for an attack, and she did not have to wait long. The young woman flicked one wrist and cast a paralyzing spell, but Kitten dodged it and slammed the hilt of her Volcanic Blade into the back of the young woman's head. Reeling, the woman leaned on the throne. The chains on her wrists vanished, and she floated into the air. Her voice changed into something hard and angry, and she shouted, "You will not touch my master!"

The young woman's eyes blazed, there was a flash of lightning, and Kitten felt herself fading out, as if she were going to faint. She shook herself out of it and said, "Why don't you actually try to kill me? Wouldn't that please your master? Or maybe he doesn't think you can do it."

"You don't know anything!" the woman screamed, casting a firebolt spell.

Kitten dodged left and right and said calmly, "I know that you were kidnapped by Vincoral, and he convinced you to fight at his side. I know that you are angry with the people who let you be taken by the Demonic One's army, so you hope to help him destroy the world. But your father still loves you, and he will take you back. There was nothing he could do to protect you, but you have protected yourself. Now you have a chance to return to your home and family."

"Shut up!" the woman screamed, holding her head. She dropped slowly to the floor, and a genuine tear fell from one cheek. For a moment, Kitten hoped that the girl could be turned away from the Demon's path. But the anger returned, stronger than ever, and the merchant's daughter stood and said with an icy voice, "This world does not deserve me or my pity."

A gale wind rose up in the room, and Kitten struggled to keep her footing. The woman cast a red lightning spell that Kitten was all too familiar with. She dodged, but the lightning followed her every move, coming closer and closer. There was little she could do to defend against it. The young woman was concentrating very hard on the spell, though, and Kitten hoped that would give her a small window of opportunity. She dodged and ran straight at the woman, the red lightning right on her heels. She leaped at the final second and tackled the woman, pulling her down to the floor. The woman screamed as the red lightning surrounded them both and pinned them together, sucking energy from them and cutting their skin in little slits.

"I am not weak!" the woman screamed, but the spell was wavering. She couldn't keep it up much longer.

"I'm afraid you are, my dear," an icy voice said from behind the throne. "I had hoped you had come far enough in your training to handle this yourself, but it would seem my confidence was misplaced."

"I...I can...," the woman choked. The red lightning vanished, and the wind died away. The woman began to sob, and Kitten stood to face Vincoral. He stepped out from behind the throne, fully healed and ready for her.

"It ends here," Kitten said with conviction.

"I agree," Vincoral hissed.

The woman stood behind Kitten and readied another spell to attack with. Kitten saw into the girl's mind and knew that she would never leave the Demon's side. Now that the element of surprise was gone, though, she could use her magic. With a thought, she called on the Light Dragon once more. It appeared in a flash, bursting through one wall of the room, leaving a gaping hole to the outside. The girl screamed, as the dragon engulfed her, taking her to the next world or perhaps to nowhere at all. They both vanished, leaving Vincoral and Kitten alone. Neither of them had flinched or blinked during Kitten's display of magic power. She knew that the Demonic One would not fear her connection to the elements. But she had another trick, this time.

The sun was beginning to rise, and the sounds of battle floated up to the room, now open to the outside world. Purple dragons could be seen swooping down on otherworldly creatures, ninjas were stealthily conducting prisoners across the courtyard, and loyal guards battled them all, dying in the shadows. Silently, carefully, Kitten reached out to the pieces of the world that still existed at this spot in the center of the void. There was almost nothing left. She pulled strands of energy together, connecting this piece and that piece. Vincoral remained unaware of her efforts for the time being.

He cast his red lightning at her, but Kitten was ready for that, and a magic shield protected her. The red lightning strained to squeeze the energy out of her shield, but it was too strong this time. Vincoral seemed surprised at this. He squinted and growled at her, and the room became dark. He was drawing energy from the world again. But Kitten was ready for this, too. She was strengthening the pieces of the world underneath the visible, and she was doing it faster than he could undo it.

"Why don't you attack me!?" he shouted angrily. "What are you…?" Realization came into his eyes, as it occurred to him what she had been doing. "You did go to The West," he whispered. Then, he screamed, a powerful, overwhelming scream that brought the darkness closer to them both.

But a circle of light remained around Kitten's feet. She smiled to herself. He couldn't touch her now, she thought. He ran at her, drawing a sword from the air around him. He slashed at her, and she dodged, sensing that this blade might cut right through her shield. She drew her own sword but kept her focus on healing the world around them. The more energy she could deprive the Demon of, the easier it would be to stop him for good.

They fought hand-to-hand for a few minutes, Vincoral stabbing at her with a recklessness she hadn't expected from him, Kitten dodging and blocking. She didn't even try to attack; she kept her mind on her real work. But it was becoming difficult to maintain her concentration. Vincoral threw a few fire and lightning spells and made one final jab at her. This time, it hit, slicing through the outside of her right leg. She cried out and dropped to one knee. Vincoral laughed and raised his blade to strike again. Kitten rolled out of the way and kicked at his feet. He jumped and came at her again. She pulled herself to her feet and mentally drew energy from the universe to heal herself. Now her mind was pulled in three directions, and she knew she couldn't continue for much longer. It was time for backup.

Kitten paused everything else in her mind and called out to her friends in The West. It took only a moment, but that was enough time for Vincoral to catch up to her and stab at her with his blade. It would have gone straight through her chest, but an invisible barrier suddenly materialized. Four figures appeared behind the Demon, and a calm but angry voice reverberated through both of their heads, "You will not harm her."

Queen Mellah and her co-rulers stood in the room, light emanating from them, stretching out into the farthest corners of the shadowy architecture.

"You have no place here!" Vincoral shouted, but fear cracked his voice. He cast a dark spell that seemed to snake around the immortals, trying to contain them. But Lendril held up one hand, and the spell dissipated.

"Neither have you," he said with a sneer.

Thorn's tendrils moved quickly and surrounded the Demonic One, holding him in one spot. Kitten slipped to the side, returning her mind to her task. The world was nearly halfway healed. She couldn't believe how quickly it had all happened. But it wasn't over. Vincoral would not go down without a fight to the death. He called on every dark force he had access to and blasted through the vines that held him. Kitten felt Thorn's pain, and it broke her concentration.

"Don't stop!" Mellah shouted and added her own strength to Kitten's efforts.

"Destruction is more powerful than creation!" Vincoral laughed. "I will win in the end. You are wasting your time!"

Red flew to Kitten's side and lit on her shoulder, adding her own energy to the mix. The healing of the world sped up, and Kitten watched the cosmic tapestry fly through the void, filling it with life and light. She laughed giddily, and Vincoral spun to attack her again. A flash of energy shot out from King Lendril's hand, and Vincoral screamed in pain. It had hurt him; Kitten could hardly believe it. She stood, stronger now that the world was nearly healed around her.

Vincoral muttered a few arcane words and stepped out of his own body. He did it again and again, until there were five of him standing in the room. One of them attacked Queen Mellah with a sword of darkness, one of them attacked King Lendril with a similar blade, and one of them attacked Thorn with a sword of fire. The other two attacked Kitten. Each of the immortals held his or her own against the Demon's clones, but he was matching them spell-for-spell now. Desperate as he was now, he was drawing on the energy of the universe as quickly as Kitten could replace it, and his magic became as powerful as the Light Dragon.

Red Dragonfly flew off of Kitten's shoulder and hit one of the clones with a light spell. The two of them wandered off to another corner, battling with magic and leaving Kitten to deal with the final clone. Kitten maintained her concentration on the cosmos, but she blocked each of Vincoral's attacks with her sword or her magic. She could draw no more power from the world without detracting from its healing efforts, and her own seemed to be dwindling. Vincoral's fists seemed to appear out of nowhere around her, and she slapped each blow away as he advanced on her, backing her into a corner. A grin appeared on his face, and Kitten felt herself slipping out of consciousness. She was fading into the universe. Her efforts to heal the cosmos were pulling her own body into the void to bridge the last of the gaps. She couldn't prevent it. She pushed the palms of both hands forward, casting a force spell that pushed the Demon back. It gave her enough time to call on the most powerful element she could think of: a Star Dragon.

It flew into the room faster than lightning, and its roar was painful to her ears. But at the sight of its brilliant light, each Demon clone paused in his attacks, giving the immortals the chance to kill them. Each one vanished in a burst of fire, leaving one final Vincoral standing before Kitten. She spun and kicked him in the head, and he stumbled backward, straight into the waiting maw of the mighty Star Dragon. He made one last grab for her, snatching at her arm, but she twisted away from him and sent another force spell at his chest. He fell back and vanished into the light.

The scream was agonizing. Kitten felt Vincoral's pain as he was devoured by the most powerful light force in the universe. The Demon's power was too weak from the loss of his void and from splitting his efforts into five copies of himself. His energy dissipated, and he was lost in the void of space, searching for a way back into the physical realm. Any small chink in the armor of the universe would give him a chance to return. The only way to make sure he would drift harmlessly and unconsciously for the rest of eternity would be to fill each corner of the cosmos with more energy than it had ever held.

Kitten dropped to the floor and observed with some dispassion that her own body was fading away into space. Her Star Dragon disappeared, and the immortals came to her side. She watched the last threads of the universe wind themselves around her and use the last of her energy to fill the last of Vincoral's void.

"You have saved the universe, Kitten Izzill," Mellah's thoughts drifted into Kitten's consciousness, as her physical form disappeared. Some of the Queen's energy sifted into space, helping to fill it with the energy it needed to protect itself, melding with the last of Kitten's energy.

Kitten expressed her own gratitude for their help and her sorrow at not being able to stay. But she knew that the world couldn't have finished healing without her. Not completely. It needed her energy to fill its darkest corners with light and keep Vincoral from ever returning again. The immortals knew this and watched the last of her energy fade into the air, before they returned to their lands in The West.

Kitten took one last look at her friends. Zharran had fought several soldiers in the hall outside the throne room and was now entering the doorway to find her gone. She sent a message of regret and love into his mind so that he would know she was all right. Raisa and his brother ninjas had gotten all of the prisoners out of the dungeon safely, just before an explosion caused by one of the otherworldly creatures caved in half of the tunnels. She touched his mind as well to let him know that she was at peace. Markuss had led the Howerth wizards in a glorious rout of the demonic creatures and Vincoral's armies, and nearly every enemy had been killed or chased back to their own dimension. She knew that a new era of cooperation had been born that day between the Howerth magic-users and the rest of the world, and she touched Markuss' mind to let him know that and to encourage him to carry on as a leader of the people.

Kitten looked over her homeland and saw the people coming out of hiding and seeing that they were finally safe. She looked into the future and saw the prosperity and happiness that would soon result. She smiled to herself and knew that she had finally fulfilled her quest. She felt her parents' energies join her as she drifted around and through the world. They would be together forever now, and they could watch the universe and make sure that the Demonic One could never return to the physical world. She stretched her consciousness all around the universe, communing with the dragons that no longer lived, the elements that filled every living thing, the immortals in The West, and each life that grew on the planet. It was finally over, and she was at peace.

ORPHAN SIGHT

Marilee poured the tea carefully from the antique pot, one hand resting lightly on the top. Sunlight streamed into the room through the worn curtains, giving her dirty blonde head a bright halo as the dust motes swirled around her. Everything in the room was antique, except for Marilee and her silent guest. He glanced at his own reflection in an antique mirror above the fireplace and saw a young man in his mid-twenties with a straight back, an expressionless face, and black hair and eyes.

Lula poured the tea slowly from the makeshift teapot, built from an old paint can and some discarded scraps of metal. The sun beat down on her chestnut head and reflected off of the collection of objects on the rug that was spread upon the ground. Everything was salvaged and reformed into something new, even Lula herself, who still bore the scars from her Voluntary Repair surgeries. Her silent guest gazed at the paint can/teapot and noticed his reflection staring back at him – a young man with an expressionless face and dark hair and eyes, slightly contorted by the curvature of the metal can.

He had no name and no home in the traditional sense. The people around him had always called him "Orphan," and it had become his name. The people who had known him from birth had allowed him to stay in their homes. He had no other family. Marilee was like a sister to him. Lula was like a sister to him. But neither young woman had ever met the other, or ever would. And he couldn't tell them about each other because he had been mute since the day he was born. He was not dumb, however, simply silent. He knew both Shakespeare and Hawking but couldn't recite either one. He could laugh and cry and moan, but he couldn't use words. No one knew why, least of all him. He thought of himself as an Observer. He still interacted with the people around him, but less than he would have if he had been able to speak. He never wished that he could speak, though. The thought of wishing for something that the medical physicians of the day couldn't give him had simply never occurred to him.

Marilee smiled softly at him and spoke as though her voice would shatter the teacups if she raised it much higher. "I'm glad we have a chance to spend some time before everyone else gets here. We've been so busy lately with Events. I suppose the political climate these days is to blame. It keeps Boryn busy churning out new Lesson Events and Example Events." She paused to sip her tea, and he did the same, savoring its robust flavor.

Lula took a deep breath and began her pre-tea chant. She always said that chanting a little before doing anything would

mentally prepare one for the task. He waited patiently until she had finished, then they sipped the tea together. It was sweeter than he liked it, but it was the company he had come to enjoy.

For a brief moment, he marveled at the sensation of two flavors tickling his tongue at the same time. But he had grown used to such oddities years before, and the moment passed quickly. There were four oddities in his life that he had more or less surrendered to, one after the other.

The first, his lack of a proper name, was something he had never given much thought to. Considering his nomadic lifestyle, it seemed rather appropriate.

The second, his lack of a proper home, was something he had never felt a need for. Welcomed into any of his friends' homes, he did not desire to own a building or vehicle.

The third, his lack of words, had been confusing at first. He had spent about ten years trying to change his luck, visiting doctors and healers of every kind. No one could help him or even tell him why he could not speak. Eventually, he accepted his fate and even found some comfort in the silence. People tend to be more honest with those who do not speak, and consequently, he learned more about his friends than their mothers knew.

The fourth oddity was more difficult to understand and had taken over twenty years to come to terms with. Even now, he did not know what it meant or if it meant anything at all.

Marilee continued speaking, staring into his eyes as if she could see his thoughts there. Sometimes, he thought that she could. "I wonder if we're making an impact. If I just knew that we were at least entertaining someone..."

She sighed and continued, "Sometimes, I miss my days at the theatre. You always know where you stand with an aware audience. But Boryn does such good work, and Amay and Roosh and the others are so passionate! I don't regret anything. I just wish....Well, maybe we could tell the watchers after....But, no. I know Boryn is right; it wouldn't have the same impact."

Lula's eyes wandered for a moment, touching on the horizon, roving over the distant treeline, and finally settling on his head. She often stared at his hair, his jawline, his nose, studying his features as if she were trying to memorize them. When she spoke, her voice was bright and clear, even though she seemed to be speaking to his chin.

"I'm glad you're here. Soran's angry with me today. I guess he wasn't calm enough to hear another rejection. I don't know why he thinks we should spend time together in his home. We don't have the same interests, and we don't agree on anything. Even the lust we felt for each other is gone. There's nothing between us. He doesn't even drink tea."

She smiled briefly and took another sip. "He won't do the chants or talk to the air. He won't even pretend that he believes in society anymore. Why does he think that we should try to make a match? I don't love him, and he doesn't love me. If he wanted children, I might consider it. But he doesn't want anything. Even love. Maybe he wants something I can't understand."

In the brief pause that followed, he considered what Marilee had said and what Lula had said. The fourth oddity of his life made it difficult to respond differently to individual people. Luckily, his inability to speak made it easier, since no one expected a verbal response. He watched Marilee sip her tea and watched Lula swirl hers around the cup with a spoon made out of clay. Neither woman knew the other existed, and yet they sat in nearly the same spot, relative to his position. Things usually happened in unison in the two perceptions of Orphan. He had no trouble understanding them because he was in two places at once.

When he was young, he had tried to explain the phenomenon to two doctors that he had gone to see simultaneously. He had written words on paper, drawn pictures and diagrams, and gestured wildly. But each doctor told him that the other did not exist and that he should focus on the real world. But both were real as far as he could tell. A search in Lula's hometown in Marilee's world had uncovered no Lula, and a search through Marilee's city in Lula's world had found no Marilee. Was he insane? Was he somehow existing in two parallel dimensions at the same time? Or perhaps in two time frames in the same world? Or on two planets? The questions no longer seemed as pressing as they once had been. He cared about the people in each reality, and they about him. Perhaps, he was lucky to have two families.

Sometimes, he felt as if he had two bodies and two minds, as well. But they seemed to be identical. Each processed and interacted with its world, and he experienced the perceptions of both. His reflections were the same; his thoughts were the same. He was the same.

A doorbell rang in Marilee's world, and her face brightened.
A voice called in Lula's world, and her gaze darkened.

Timing in parallel worlds was always impeccable, uncanny even. He braced himself for the intrusion of other people into his two private little conferences with his two favorite people.

Four familiar faces bounced into Marilee's antique sitting room, laughing and chattering like squirrels.
One familiar face stepped up to Lula's rug of refurbished items.

Many things were the same in each world, but more things were different. Although events, situations, and actions were often identical or similar to one another, despite the vast ocean of time and/or space that seemed to separate them, and despite the fact that they often occurred concurrently in each world, so much was different about each place.

In Marilee's world, she worried about her life's goals and supported her friends. In Lula's world, she cared about the state of the world and did not worry about her friends. In Marilee's world, she had been married twice, each union ending in a painful separation and resulting in her hiding deeper in her life of antiques and theatre. In Lula's world, she had never married, for she had never loved anyone enough to prove it. In Marilee's world, capitalism ruled the globe, and political unrest encouraged her group of theatre junkies to perform skits on the street in order to make points and teach lessons. In Lula's world, a sort of democracy affected most of the globe, and the people were generally content with the way things were run since anyone was free to do almost anything. In Marilee's world, they would have called Lula a hippie and a bleeding heart. In Lula's world, they would have called Marilee a prude and a savage. In Marilee's world, men were considered superior to women in most ways, animals were slaves or food, and the "nuclear family" was sacred, though a bit more rare than it used to be. In Lula's world, men, women, and animals were equal, and love was more important than contracts, which meant that families were a bit more fluid but also, by his observation, happier. In Marilee's world, attending church was expected of most people. In Lula's world, there was no such thing. In Marilee's world, everyone had to live with the bodies they were born with, regardless of poor health or physical agility. In Lula's world, Voluntary Repair surgeries were typical and could involve anything from skin stitching to organ and appendage replacement. In Marilee's world, appearances were everything, and doing what everyone else did was a life goal. In Lula's world, appearances meant nothing, and people did anything they desired as long as it didn't harm anyone. In Marilee's world, technology was advanced but sometimes abhorred because of its negative effects that went unchecked. In Lula's world, technology was an integral part of everything and was used to fix anything that it may have affected negatively. The list went on and on.

Marilee's friends greeted him, while Lula's visitor ignored him.

"I've got something brilliant this time, Mari," Boryn called out, grinning. "Your friend Orphan will play an important part."

Marilee squealed excitedly and glanced at him. He nodded encouragingly.

At the same moment, he was nodding at Lula, who had asked him his opinion. Soran had told her that she was being unreasonable by rejecting his overtures. Lula had insisted that Soran was the unreasonable one for expecting her to continue a

loveless and lustless relationship. She asked Orphan for his opinion, and he agreed with her by nodding his head.

Most of the time, his responses were appropriate in both places. This was a great comfort to him since he could not communicate his reality to anyone else.

"You'll be the heroic victim this time, if you're interested, Orphan," Boryn said enthusiastically.

"What does he know? He doesn't even own a house!" Soran's voice burst in on his thoughts violently.

"This'll be great, Orphan!" Marilee gushed.

"He knows more about real love and friendship than you do!" Lula insisted quietly.

He listened silently to the simultaneous chatter that was comprised of Boryn's and Soran's voices and Marilee's and Lula's voices. It was like a symphony of opposites: Boryn's gentle, excited tones sounding through the same space as Soran's rising, angry punctuations; Marilee's soft, dulcet notes clashing with Lula's bright, sharp crescendos. It was the music of life. He was almost sorry that he was the only human who could hear it.

"You'll be the silent Everyman, taking it on the chin and finally rising to the occasion," Boryn said at the same moment that Soran thundered, **"The kind of love you want is nothing! I want passion!"**

"This'll be your biggest Event yet!" Marilee sighed at the very moment that Lula trilled, **"Your passion is dangerous and hurtful!"**

"Look it over," Boryn handed him a copy of the latest Event.

"We're not happy together," Lula shook her head sadly, not noticing the movement of his hand as he took the sheaf of papers. **"Leave me alone."**

"We should all start rehearsals," Marilee stood quickly and straightened her dress.

"Give me a moment to compose myself, Orphan," Lula slumped, as Soran stalked away from her.

Orphan stood and walked through Marilee's back door and past Lula's vehicle. He entered a personal garden and a public park. Both had a bench on which he could sit and contemplate. He was glad to help out Marilee's friends, and he enjoyed their Events. But he was uncertain whether he could react according to the Event's script without disturbing Lula's reality. His choice was simple: refuse to play his assigned part in the Event or take the risk of affecting Lula's world and his place in it. He knew what he would do even before he read the script. He couldn't refuse Marilee and her friends, but he would probably be able to avoid any confrontations in Lula's world by keeping his performance low-key. He lowered his gaze to his hands. In Marilee's world, he began reading the Event script. In Lula's world, he appeared to be studying his hands, but no one would much care.

In Marilee's world, voices from outside the garden were carried through the foliage by a light breeze. In Lula's world, a few afternoon joggers wandered among the meditators and the nude sunbathers in the grass. Time passed quickly, and he was just finishing his reading when both Marilee and Lula approached him.

"Are you finished?" Marilee asked.

"I'm finished," Lula stated.

He nodded his head at them both and folded his hands over the pages of the script that didn't exist in Lula's world.

"I'm so happy for you," Marilee sighed, her eyes twinkling in the sunlight.

"I'm so happy with you," said Lula with a sigh, her eyes shining with tears.

"We're having a pre-show dinner inside in an hour," Marilee added. *"Please join us."*

"Happier than I've ever been with anyone else," Lula continued more slowly. **"Will you join me?"**

Marilee turned and walked back into her house, while Lula sat next to him and waited for a reply. He considered his choices for a moment: join Lula in her home for the night to warm her body and her mind or avoid the possible embarrassment this could cause since Lula's bed was in the same spot as Boryn's bed in Marilee's world. But he could no more refuse Lula than he could have refused Marilee and her friends when they asked for his participation in their Event. He nodded and smiled, and Lula kissed him lightly on the cheek and whispered, **"Tonight."**

Marilee would never have considered inviting him to have sex with her. Their relationship was strictly platonic, according to the rules of her world. But in Lula's world, relationships were more fluid. They could be friends who sometimes had intimate relations, and that was healthy. As Lula sauntered back to her rug of items for sale or trade, he wondered at the differences between the two worlds once more.

In one hour, after he had read through the script a few more times, he walked back into Marilee's house and back to Lula's rug. He sat with Marilee's friends in the sitting room to join them for dinner and sat with Lula as she spoke to buyers and traders who wandered past them. Marilee's friends chattered about the Event, and strangers haggled over Lula's prices. He tuned out most of the cacophony and enjoyed his dinner: the roast that Marilee had prepared and the instant stew that Lula had brought for her day at the edge of the park.

"Where are you staying tonight, Orphan?" Marilee's voice cut through the noise.

He looked inquiringly at Boryn, who smiled, swallowed the bite he had been chewing, and laughed, *"Sure, man! Glad to have you. You can have my bed for the night, and in the morning, we'll go over your part in the Event. Good plan!"*

The usual chatter resumed in Marilee's world, and he noticed a familiar couple of women approaching Lula's rug. Lula squealed with excitement and jumped to her feet. She embraced one of the women, and he remembered that they were sometimes lovers.

"Seena, it's so good to see you!" Lula stepped back to admire her friend and saw her companion. **"And who is this? Cora? You've dyed your hair! It's beautiful!"**

"Thanks, I changed it to commemorate our union," Cora smiled and brushed her purple hair with one hand. **"We made our marriage promises last month."**

"I'm so happy for you!" Lula exclaimed, hugging them both.

"There's nothing like love," Seena said, gazing adoringly at her companion. **"You should visit us in our new home sometime. You can stay in my room."**

"Yes, you can meet my lover Max," Cora nodded enthusiastically.

"Tomorrow," Lula agreed. **"I have plans with Orphan tonight."**

"Oh, hello, Orphan," Seena smiled down at him. **"Enjoy yourselves. We'll see you tomorrow, hun."** She kissed Lula on the mouth and waved before walking away with her new spouse.

Orphan thought briefly about how marriages in Marilee's world were strictly regulated to be between a man and a woman, while in Lula's world, men married men, women married women, men married women, and people sometimes even had multiple spouses and lovers at the same time. He wondered if this might be related to how sex was restricted to married couples in Marilee's world, due to the influence of organized religion. In Lula's world, sex was something married people rarely, if ever, did with one another. Love and lust were seen as two very separate things. They often occurred together; after all, he and Lula cared deeply for one another and often shared a bed. But love and lust were usually independent of one another. This seemed more practical to him, and he thought it might explain why people in Lula's world were generally happier and could maintain multiple intimate relationships without dealing with jealousy and bitter divorces. The divorce rate in Marilee's world was a hundred times that of Lula's world. But not being married himself, he couldn't be certain of the true issues at stake. He sometimes wondered if he should marry, but no spouse would understand his odd behavior without explanation. Besides which, the two people he loved, Marilee and Lula, would not marry him, the first because she loved him only as a friend and the second because she was too attracted to him physically. Had their homeworlds been reversed, he might have been married to both women by now. But the union with Lula would likely have ended in tragic divorce, and for that reason, he was glad that things were as they were.

Life in both worlds passed around him until the sun began to set. When Lula began to gather her unsold items to store in her water-powered vehicle, he rose and waved to her and to Boryn. Lula smiled and waved back, and Boryn nodded and spoke a few words to Marilee. Lula knew that he would walk to her home. He never rode in vehicles. No one knew the reason except for him. He had ridden in a vehicle once as a child, and the resulting confusion had taken nearly six months to rectify. In one world, he was in a park, while in the other, he was in a building. Trying to find a way out of the park without walking into the walls of the building was a puzzle exceeded only by the difficulty of catching a ride to a spot that would match his two worlds up again. If only his relative state of motion in each world weren't so important. If he could sit in one world and walk in the other, there would be no problems. How strange it had been watching the world pass by through the vehicle window, even though he wasn't moving in the other world. It had been an adventure, but one that he was not interested in repeating. So he walked. He followed Boryn home and walked alone to Lula's apartment.

The night passed without incident. Boryn slept on the couch in his living room, and Lula didn't ask why he insisted on shutting the bedroom door. She also didn't question why he was paying rapt attention to a particular chair in the kitchen the next morning. Boryn went over the details of the next Event, and by the time he was done and everyone had eaten something, Lula was ready to leave for the park. Once again, he walked, with Boryn at his side in Marilee's world and alone in Lula's world. This time, though, he stopped at a particular intersection as Boryn walked on. He sat on a bus stop bench in both worlds and waited.

In Marilee's world, the stone bench was on an industrial intersection with skyscrapers and heavy brick buildings all around. A light smog settled on the streets, and oil trickled into the gutters. Everything was in shades of gray and brown, including the people who hurried past him on the sidewalk, dressed in business suits and overalls. Men and women with scowls on their faces ignored him or glared at him. Most of them looked tired, as if they had already worked a ten-hour day. Noisy vehicles sped down the streets, horns honking and radios blasting. One woman in ragged shirt and jeans led two small children to the bus stop and waited without sitting down. One of the children was crying, but the woman didn't seem to hear. When the bus stopped, she dragged the children aboard, and someone in the back yelled for the child to stop crying. The bus driver waited a moment and then drove on.

In Lula's world, log cabins and offices lined the roads at the intersection. Trees grew taller than the buildings, and a stream could be heard trickling on the other side of an open market square. People dressed in bright dresses and half-bottoms ambled past him, smiling and talking with one another or on their hand-coms. Silent vehicles drove slowly down the clean, paved roads. Birds chirped in the trees and fluttered down to land on a woman's hand when she held out some breadcrumbs. A dog dashed down the street and rounded the corner at the market. A woman with two small children walked behind the wooden bench and met a man in a skirt and tie. They embraced before picking up the smiling children and walking towards the market. The air-bus stopped in front of the bench, waited a moment, and drove on.

In Marilee's world, a gruff-looking young man dashed up to the bench, swore at the bus in the distance, and kicked a tin can into a puddle of oil. In Lula's world, a gruff-looking young man dashed up to the bench, swore at the bus halfway down the block, and kicked a rock into the grass. A few people stared but didn't stop to talk to him.

Orphan blinked. He seemed to be seeing double, or in his case, single. This young man not only looked the same in each world but also moved the same. His motions and words synced up perfectly, right down to the impatient tapping of his right foot in a perfect one-two rhythm. He thought to himself that perhaps he didn't know everything about living in two separate worlds yet. Perhaps, there were some things identical in each world, after all. He jumped slightly when the young man turned to see him staring. The man's face grew even darker, and he reached up to straighten the tie he was wearing in Marilee's world. Oddly, he conducted the same exact action in Lula's world, despite the fact that he was wearing only a loose toga top there. The irony did not escape Orphan's thoughts, and for a moment, he was distracted from what the young man was doing. Could it possibly be that someone else existed in both of these strange worlds at once? Someone besides himself?

The young man approached him and shouted something. Orphan had to wrench himself out of his reverie in order to consider and comprehend the words. The man had said, "What are you staring at?" It took Orphan a moment to realize the implications of the words and respond. The man seemed to get impatient and growled, "What're you, an idiot?"

Two voices, the same voice, speaking in unison. Even music had more variation in it between worlds, even the same song sung by the same singer. It was like having radios playing the same tune into both of his ears in both worlds. He blinked again, shook his head, and motioned with his hands to explain that he couldn't speak.

The young man looked disgusted and turned away to watch a woman walk by him. In Marilee's world, she was rail-thin and stern, with blonde hair and a gray suit. In Lula's world, she was average with brown hair, a green dress, and a smile. Both women walked by at the same pace, their legs occupying the same space and moving in exactly the same way. But at the last minute, as the gray-suited woman continued walking, the other woman paused just a moment and waved.

The young man waved back in both worlds. After she had gone, he turned back to Orphan, narrowed his eyes, and said just loudly enough for everyone on the corner to hear, "I suppose you're on welfare too, huh?"

The people in Marilee's world frowned knowingly, and the people in Lula's world looked at one another quizzically. There was no such thing as welfare in Lula's world; those who might have needed it could rely on personal gardens to feed themselves and the sale of excess produce to provide additional financial support. Everyone received their own tract of land at birth and agricultural supplies and education at the age of 12.

Orphan shook his head, and the young man grumbled, "Of course, you are. We work ten-hour days to support trash like you. You should be grateful enough to treat us with respect. But, no! You're all alike, acting like the world owes you everything!"

Orphan held up his palms in protest and shook his head vigorously, but the young man went on, pacing quickly in front of the bench. A few people in both worlds were watching him now. "You should pull your own weight! Haven't I got a family of my own to support? I shouldn't have to pay for the life of a stranger, too!"

In Marilee's world, people were nodding their heads gravely. In Lula's world, people looked confused and concerned, and one man spoke up, saying, **"Sir, what are you talking about? Are you ill?"**

The young man ignored everyone but Orphan and shouted, "We'd all be better off without leeches like you around! Your parents should have drowned you like a sack of kittens and saved us the trouble of dealing with you! You bastards are the ones keeping us from rising to a higher economic level."

"Yeah!" someone shouted in the growing crowd in Marilee's world.

"Now that's enough," said a woman in Lula's world. **"Have you lost your mind?"**

"We should put him out of our misery," shouted someone else in Marilee's world.

The young man stepped toward Orphan and pulled his right fist back. Just before he was able to swing it at him, a young woman stepped out of the crowd in Marilee's world, grabbed his arm, and shouted, *"Don't you dare, Corran!"*

Orphan recognized her as Amay, a friend of Marilee's and one of the four who had come to dinner last night. He looked around and saw Boryn, Roosh, and one other, Trav, in the crowd, as well. Marilee stood on the other side of the street, awaiting her cue.

"This doesn't concern you, Amay!" Corran whispered loudly. In Lula's world, he was speaking to thin air, and the people were gathering closer around him, ready to hold him down if he turned violent.

"Doesn't it?" Amay cried out, a tear falling from one eye. *"My eyes keep me from working, yet you support me! Should our mother have drowned me like a sack of kittens as soon as she learned that I was mostly blind?"*

"That's different!" Corran spluttered. "Th-that isn't your fault! And you can still work with your hands."

"So can this mute!" Amay said. *"And it's not his fault, either."*

"Calm down and come with us, please," said a man in Lula's world quietly. He indicated two others who waited to escort Corran away.

"You're more use to society than idiots like him will ever be!" Corran pushed Amay and the man away, and a murmur went through both crowds.

"Everyone has a place," said the man in Lula's world.

Amay started crying, and Roosh dashed up to her and said, *"You shouldn't treat your own sister like that."*

"It's none of your business!" Corran shook a fist at him.

"Actually, it is," said the man in Lula's world. **"I'm a peace officer, and you're disturbing the peace."**

"He started it!" Trav shouted, pointing at Orphan.

Corran turned and prepared once again to strike him. The peace officer grabbed his arm and pulled him back. In Marilee's world, he appeared to fall backwards for no reason at all. At the last moment, he kicked at Orphan's head. His foot missed by inches, but Orphan pretended to be struck, anyway. He flung himself over the side of the bench and lay motionless on the pavement.

"Nooo!" Marilee screamed and ran through traffic to reach him.

The crowd in Lula's world gasped in horror, and the peace officer's friends knelt beside him to check for trauma. Marilee and one of the men both checked his pulse.

"He's dead!" Marilee wailed. *"You've killed my husband!"*

"He's all right," said one of the men. **"Probably more startled than anything."**

"He got what he deserved!" Corran yelled, struggling against nothing in one world and the peace officer's grip in the other.

Marilee sobbed over Orphan's body, and the peace officer's friends tried to revive him. The crowds in both worlds looked horrified. A siren approached in Marilee's world; someone had called the police and an ambulance.

"We're, uh, we're better off," Trav chuckled nervously. *"Right?"* No one seemed willing to agree with him.

"You're an idiot," Boryn muttered, and several people next to him nodded assent.

The police car and ambulance screeched to a halt next to the bench, and the uniformed officers and attendants jumped out of their respective vehicles.

"All right, show's over," said one policeman authoritatively, as he pushed through the crowd to get to Corran.

The ambulance attendants checked Orphan before ushering Marilee to the side. He pretended to be unconscious, and the men lifted him off the ground at the moment that the peace officer's friends did the same. He was carried into two different vehicles and followed by a sobbing Marilee into one of them. The policeman and peace officer dragged Corran into two other vehicles and left with him.

As soon as the vehicles were a couple of blocks away from the scene, Orphan sat up and gestured to indicate that he was well enough to get out and walk. He was eager to escape the vehicles before they headed in different directions. The peace officer's friends were obliging once they were convinced that he had suffered no injuries, but Marilee had to intervene on his behalf with the ambulance attendants. Once he had exited both vehicles and gotten his bearings, he considered everything that had just happened. The Event had gone mostly according to plan, but Corran had been a surprise, to say the least.

"You were wonderful!" Marilee gushed, as the vehicles left them behind. She hugged him tightly, and he wondered if she had noticed Corran's strange behavior. The man was supposed to have hit Orphan with a fist. Instead, he seemed to throw himself backwards and fling a sloppy kick at Orphan's head. Orphan had never met the man before, so he must be new to the little theatre group. So perhaps, little slip-ups like that would not be noticed just yet.

"Come back to my house, and I'll introduce you to Corran," Marilee took his hand and led him down the sidewalk. He walked alone down the quiet lane in Lula's world toward the park. *"He's a cousin or something of Amay's,"* she continued jovially, her feet almost skipping down the pavement. *"He couldn't come to dinner last night, or you would have met him then. He was all right today, but you were the star of the show! I think we really made some people think this time, don't you?"*

She glanced at him expectantly, and he smiled and nodded. What else could he do? He wasn't as sure as she was about the Event, but she needed his agreement at the moment. She sighed contentedly and leaned her head on his shoulder for the rest of their walk.

Boryn was at her house with the others before they arrived. A noisy celebration commenced immediately.

In Lula's world, Orphan sat in the peace and quiet of the park, next to Lula and her collection of odds and ends. She smiled at him, then continued her meditations. Oddly, Corran sat near her, on a large rock that corresponded to his seat in Marilee's house.

"We had a time getting Corran out of police custody," Boryn laughed, slapping the young man on the back. *"But it was worth it, wouldn't you say, folks? This was our most successful Event yet!"*

There was a chorus of cheers, but Orphan sat still and quiet and stared at Corran. It was like watching a movie reel of a single individual imposed over two other different and separate reels that were running at the same time on separate screens. The young man seemed no worse for wear and was laughing and talking with the theatre group. And there he was in Lula's park, laughing and talking with no one at all. The people passing by stared at him but said nothing. Lula was busy meditating and didn't notice him. Eventually, Corran noticed he was being watched and began staring back. He winked once, and Orphan blinked in surprise.

"Did you lose your balance or something?" Roosh was asking.

"Are you all right, sir?" said a stranger in the park.

"Something like that," Corran smiled. "Everything's all right. If you'll excuse me a moment…"

He gave a curt bow, glanced meaningfully at Orphan, and sauntered out to Marilee's garden and over to the park bench. Obviously, Orphan was meant to follow, so he did, waving briefly to Marilee and Lula. He sat on the garden bench and the park bench and watched Corran intently. The young man paced in front of him, seemingly deep in thought.

"Stick out your tongue and wave your right arm," he demanded suddenly.

Orphan reluctantly obliged, wondering if this little demonstration was going anywhere. Corran nodded slowly, leaned down, and whispered, "You see both worlds, don't you?"

His eyes bored into Orphan's, and they remained motionless for a moment, searching each other's faces, attempting to search each other's minds. Orphan looked past the sandy-colored hair and pronounced cheekbones and saw his own face reflected in Corran's bright blue eyes, a pale, intelligent face with average features and slightly sunken eyes. He watched his head nod slowly before Corran drew back and showed a wide, toothy grin.

"I've theorized for years that I couldn't possibly be the only one," he said quietly. "I can't tell you how pleased I am to finally find you."

A breeze floated through Marilee's garden, rustling the tree branches. In Lula's park, a few joggers passed by them. They were alone enough that Orphan felt comfortable attempting to communicate. He bent over his own knees and drew words in the dirt of the garden with one finger. He couldn't draw in the grass of the park, but it would do.

" 'How did you know?' " Corran read the words aloud, then answered them with a smile, "The way you looked at me, as if you saw me better than anyone else did. And the way you moved. It was identical in both worlds, more so than anything ever has been. I just wish you could talk so we could discuss this! Cruel irony, eh?"

He sighed loudly and stared up at the sky, which was cloudy in one world and bright blue in the other. Orphan wrote another question on the ground; this time it was "How did you escape the peace officer?" Corran looked down and chuckled.

"I simply explained that I'd been experimenting with social psychology tests and took it a bit too far," he said. "Once I'd talked it out with them, they let me go. Luckily, Boryn got to the jail in time to help me leave. Funny how things usually converge like that in both worlds, isn't it?"

Orphan smiled and chuckled a little himself. He knew all about these convergences. They were convenient but mysterious. He scratched out a new question on the ground.

" 'Why?' " Corran repeated thoughtfully. He turned away and mumbled, "Why. That's the question, isn't it? Why are we so special? Why are these worlds so alike and yet so different? And let's not forget 'How.' How is any of this possible, and how does it work?"

He turned back to face Orphan and said with confidence, "I don't have the answers to any of these questions. But now that we have two minds to work on the problem, maybe we can compare notes and figure it out."

He seemed to be getting excited, but as he finished speaking, Orphan was distracted by two voices. One belonged to Boryn, and he was calling them into the house for lunch. The other was Soran's, and he was shouting at Lula. Orphan stood and started to walk towards the two men. Corran stopped him with one hand and asked, "Is she a friend?"

Orphan knew he meant Lula and nodded before proceeding to his place at the sides of his two best friends. Boryn was serving plates of homecooked casserole in the sitting room, while Soran was dishing out a strange tirade to Lula and anyone else within earshot.

"You speak of happiness, but I say that what you're really talking about is being content!" Soran shouted. **"I'm not satisfied with that, and you shouldn't be, either. Real happiness can only come from experiencing pain and strife. How can we know whether we'll make a good match if we don't go through some difficulties together?"**

Orphan found himself paying more attention to Soran's dialogue than the chatter that was going on in Marilee's sitting room. Something important was going on; he could feel it. It was like an electricity in the air, but it affected only the park.

"You don't love me, Soran!" Lula protested.

"You didn't give me time to learn whether I could!" Soran responded. "That's the problem with this whole planet! You all think you know everything!" He made a sweeping gesture with his arms to include the entire park in his argument and, by extension, the world. "Anyone can do anything, right? Except struggle! Except see what they're made of! Who are you? Do you know? I know who I am! I've been through a struggle; I know what I'm made of."

"Your wife," Lula said quietly. "But the accident was..."

"My fault," he said with a sigh. "Yes. But it showed me what I could do. I could push the limits of travel. I could make mistakes. And I could recover from them."

Orphan remembered that Soran had been a test pilot for experimental vehicles at some point. Lula had confided in him that this part of Soran's past had affected him deeply enough that their relationship was crippled in some way because of it. Now that cryptic piece of information made more sense. Perhaps, Soran was mentally unstable because of grief and stress.

"But I don't think you ever really did!" Lula stood on her feet and pleaded with him to understand. "You've been mourning her loss ever since the crash, and...and maybe you saw some of what you loved about her in me. But I'm not her."

"I'm not trying to replace her!" his voice burst into the air around them. "You could never take her place!" He took a deep breath and composed himself before continuing. "I want more, Lula. I want to be more. I want more than what everyone else has. I want to struggle and earn my reward."

"I don't understand," Lula shook her head. "What do you want to have? You can do anything you want!"

Orphan thought he understood. He didn't agree, but he thought he understood. Soran wanted pride. Not pride of accomplishment, which could be achieved here, but pride of ownership. It was hard to achieve that in a world where anyone could have anything. Most people didn't even think about it, but Soran seemed to view the world differently. He wanted to own things, and he wanted to own himself in a way that the peaceful, contented people of this world couldn't comprehend. And, it seemed, he wanted to own Lula. That would be not only undesirable but also dangerous. He hoped Soran didn't take his argument too far.

"Anything I want?" Soran smirked. "Can I take you with me to a secluded island and live there for the rest of our lives, alone? Can I build a collection of land tracts and establish my own city? Can I get everyone to understand why their lives are boring and stale?"

"You-you're crazy!" Lula started backing away, fear in her eyes.

112

"You see, there are things I can't do," he sighed. "And they're the very things I want to do. When everyone has the same possessions and the same positions and the same power and the same opportunities, there's no room for change or struggle. Why work hard when everything comes easy?"

"But equality is a good thing!" Lula protested.

"Up to a point," Soran pointed one finger at her, then glanced around. His audience was growing, and the peace officer from the morning's Event was approaching from the street side of the block. Soran turned to face the crowd and continued, **"What good is equality if you don't know who you are, if you don't know your limits?"**

A few people in the crowd seemed to consider this, so he went on, **"What good is contentment if you're never truly happy? We should have a choice as to how we want to live! We should be allowed to struggle and face real challenges. We should push the limits of whatever has become stagnant."**

"Is there a problem, sir?" the peace officer asked Soran. He glanced at Lula's frightened face and down at Orphan and Corran, recognition dawning in his eyes at the two men's faces.

"Let him speak!" said a man on the near edge of the crowd. **"He has the right, and we want to hear what he has to say."**

The peace officer left Soran and knelt in front of Orphan. Indicating Corran with a jerk of his thumb, he asked, **"Is this man bothering you again?"**

Orphan shook his head, and the officer sighed and walked over to a park bench. He sat down but kept an eye on both Soran and Corran.

"You don't agree, Orphan?" Boryn asked.

Orphan was startled. He had completely lost track of what was going on in Marilee's world and didn't know what Boryn was talking about. Corran spoke up for him with a chuckle, "He was responding to me, Boryn. I whispered a question in his ear."

Luckily, no one in Lula's world seemed to notice the odd bit of dialogue. Soran was arguing passionately for changes in government, culture, and society. All eyes were on him. Lula began gathering her things together quickly and stopped to say, **"I don't want any part of this. Do you hear me, Soran?"**

Soran paused in his oration and gazed at her. He looked almost hurt. **"But I need you,"** he pleaded. **"You're my inspiration."**

"If you want to struggle so badly," Lula shook her head, **"then you can struggle to do whatever it is you're trying to do, without your 'inspiration.' "**

Anger seemed to rise behind Soran's eyes, but he didn't make a move to stop her. She finished packing, and he turned back to his audience.

"Come with me to Seena and Cora's home, Orphan," Lula whispered. **"Bring your friend, there. We'll make it a party."**

She smiled, but her eyes looked sad. Orphan nodded without a moment's hesitation. He rose to follow her to her vehicle and heard Marilee's voice say, *"Leaving so soon, dear? Stay for drinks."*

"Yes, stay," agreed Boryn and the others.

Orphan considered his options. Lula needed his company right now, but he didn't want to be rude to Marilee and her friends. Corran seemed to realize his dilemma and spoke up, "I'm the one who has to leave. I have a previous engagement, and Orphan has kindly offered to keep me company on my way."

"In that case, enjoy yourselves and hurry back," Marilee smiled.

Corran stood, winked at Orphan, and led the way to Marilee's doorway and Lula's vehicle.

"Will you be walking?" Lula asked.

"Vehicles make me nauseated," Corran smiled and winked again at Orphan.

Lula drove off in the direction of Seena's house, and Orphan and Corran began their walk. The silence felt like a relief at first, but Orphan had questions that he hoped Corran could answer. He gestured with his hands to simulate writing, and Corran, with a bemused expression on his face, dutifully produced a pad of paper and a pen in Marilee's world. He had nothing like that on him in Lula's world, but it would do. Orphan wrote a question down, and Corran read it silently and answered, "I imagine there are many more worlds out there. I guess we're lucky that we only have to contend with two. Otherwise things would get confusing."

He laughed loudly, picked up a rock in both worlds, and tossed it off to their left. In Lula's world, it skipped across a stream and came to rest on the other side, but in Marilee's world, it skipped across a street and struck a woman on the shin. She shouted something at them in another language, shook her head, and walked on. Orphan quickly wrote "Shouldn't you be more careful when you affect both worlds?" on his paper and held it up.

Corran gave a half-smile and said, "We can't help but affect both worlds; we're in both worlds. We can't worry about it too much, or it'll drive us crazy. Aside from avoiding oncoming traffic and car rides, I don't see any reason to obsess over every potential consequence of every little action. Loosen up a bit; you'll enjoy life more. So tell me a bit more about these friends of yours I'm going to meet."

They spent the rest of their walk discussing Lula, Seena, and Cora, but Orphan had a nagging feeling in the back of his mind that Corran was taking their place in these two worlds too lightly. He planned to ask more questions later. He spent an enjoyable evening with Lula and her friends but left before the sun set. Lula and Cora's lover Max were going to stay the night, but he wanted to talk to Corran some more without worrying about anyone else paying attention.

As the two of them left, Corran paused to whistle at a young woman walking past the empty lot in Marilee's world that corresponded with Seena's house. She ignored him, but in Lula's world, a stray dog heard him and came running. It ran past him and bounded excitedly into Seena's living room.

"**I'm allergic!**" Cora shouted.

Lula chased the dog out, and it ran back the way it had come. Meanwhile, in Marilee's world, an identical dog ambled down the road toward them. Orphan watched it pass quietly by and watched the dog in Lula's world run in the opposite direction and chase a cat into a tree. He saw a boy appear from around a corner in both worlds. In Marilee's world, he was carrying a cat, and he passed them by without a single word. In Lula's world, he stopped at the tree and started calling for the cat. The two boys' paths diverged now, and something about that bothered Orphan. He paused on the sidewalk to see if Corran would do anything, but he walked away from the tree, completely unaware of the trouble that he seemed to have caused. Orphan followed him reluctantly.

The two of them ended up on the bus stop bench at the site of that morning's Event. As the evening shadows crept around them, Orphan tried to pinpoint the thing that was making him so apprehensive. He had a sense that something was wrong, and he knew it had something to with Corran and his lack of interest in the welfare of the worlds around him. Orphan scribbled on his pad of paper and held it up. Corran read it, and his brows knitted as he considered his answer.

"You're worrying too much about this," he said finally. But if you must know, there have been a few occasions when I've seen our two worlds diverge somewhat after something I've done. But it's no big deal, man. What's the worst that could happen?"

Orphan wasn't sure about the answer to that one, but he felt certain that it wouldn't be good. He decided to press the issue a bit further and wrote out another question. Corran sighed and rubbed his fingers over his eyes. Finally, he said, "I find it hard to believe that anything I could do would change the world that much. Orphan, we're just two people out of billions. We have a unique perspective, yes, but that's all. We don't have any special power over these worlds just because we can see them. I've never caused anything really bad to happen by messing with the convergences. And some really interesting and entertaining things can happen, instead."

Orphan considered this, but it still didn't seem worth the risk to him. He took a deep breath and decided to let the subject drop for now. He asked Corran about his family and childhood next.

"My parents had a hard time with me, I guess," Corran looked down at his shoes while he talked. "All four of them. They couldn't see each other, but I reacted to all of them. Made it hard to know which parent to obey when one told me to go to bed and the other said to take a bath. They looked exactly alike, but they were so different. In one world, they were married, living together, and miserable. In the other, they lived apart and were best friends. Unfortunately, in that world, my father lived in a house that belonged to a stranger in the other one." He looked up suddenly, and Orphan saw turmoil in his eyes. "I threw a fit every time we visited because the stranger wasn't happy to see me barge into his house, and my other parents couldn't understand why I was going there in the first place. Eventually, my mother stopped taking me, and my father stayed with us, instead. But they never got over it, none of them. And things between us…well…"

There was a pause, then he laughed and said, "But all that's long past. Let's talk about now."

"Do you have any friends?" Orphan asked on paper.

"The same ones you have, my friend," Corran grinned broadly. "But you will be my best friend."

He clapped Orphan on the back and laughed. But Orphan felt somewhat ill at ease. He was sympathetic towards Corran's rough childhood but wasn't sure that it justified his relaxed attitude towards the laws of cause and effect.

"Tell me about your life now," Corran insisted.

Orphan wrote on his pad until well past midnight, telling about his life up to that day. The thought occurred to him that Corran might learn something from his more cautious approach to life in these two worlds, but he wasn't sure the lesson would stick, anyway.

Once they had both tired of sitting under street light and moonlight, Corran offered Orphan a place to sleep for the rest of the night and walked him to his own house, which also happened to be an abandoned building in Marilee's world. This led to a rude awakening the next morning when they and a few homeless people taking shelter for the night were routed from the building by the police. Corran laughed as if it were a game, but Orphan wasn't amused.

On the way to the park and Marilee's home, they stopped at a street vendor and an outdoor diner for breakfast. There, Corran cut in front of a man in one world and a woman in the other. The man shrugged to his friends and stepped aside obligingly. The woman argued with Corran for a minute and then walked away. Orphan began to write a few words of protest on his pad when he noticed a familiar face on the video screen atop the street vendor's cart in Lula's world. It was Soran, and he was on a news report.

"…the biggest outbreak of violence in centuries," the reporter was saying. **"This man, known as Soran, somehow managed to incite a crowd of over fifty people to violence. The**

group stormed the local Peace Building and threw out the twenty-two employees who were inside at the time."

"What's going on?" Corran asked, chewing on a breakfast sandwich in both worlds. He followed Orphan's gaze upward to the screen, as the woman reporting from the scene continued, **"Seven people were injured in the struggle, including one of the mob's own. They are being treated at Sansea Hospital. Meanwhile, Soran and his followers are refusing to leave the building until they are allowed to broadcast a speech to the entire planet to express their desires. The arrangements for this are being made immediately. The last time Soran spoke to us through the front window of the building, he had this to say: 'We want real freedom, not just peace. And we're not alone. Our needs will be met, or there will be war.' "**

A murmur went through the crowd around the vendor at the word "war." It was an unholy word in Lula's world, feared and despised. There had been no war of any kind in nearly 1,000 years. Orphan's throat went dry, and his vision blurred for a moment. He ignored the people around him in Marilee's world and stared unblinking at the screen. Images flashed by of people's reactions, peace officer's speeches, and more commentary from reporters. In the midst of what felt like pure chaos, Corran's voice hit his ears like a jackhammer: "I never thought he'd have the guts."

There was an odd chuckle, and the voice went on, "He said something to me about all this a day or two ago, when Boryn was telling me about the Event. I told him he wouldn't have the courage to do it, but that I'd like to see it done. This oughtta be real entertaining. I think I might've mentioned something about how this kind of stuff, you know, the unrest and revolution kind of stuff, used to start wars."

Orphan couldn't believe his ears. He knew what he had heard, but his brain didn't seem able to understand it. How? Why? Questions raced through his mind. He felt dizzy. Finally, he was able to tear his eyes away from the screen and look at Corran. The man appeared perfectly calm and unconcerned. He even seemed amused by the story. Orphan felt a sudden rush of anger. He grabbed Corran by the arm and stared into his eyes, willing him to understand the damage he had done.

"What?" Corran asked innocently, then, "Oh, you're worried about that? Pssh! Come on! Don't you ever want to see something different around here? It's good for things to get shaken up a little every now and then."

Orphan had finally had enough. He pushed Corran away and ran to the park. Angry and frightened, he needed a friend to help him make sense of the chaos. But Lula wasn't in her place, and Marilee wasn't in her house. He was alone. He sat on the benches, hoping to calm his mind and find some peace and quiet.

But the breeze carried strange noises today. In Marilee's world, a police car stopped outside the garden wall, and two officers sat there discussing an arrest they had made that morning: three men and two women who were thought to be terrorists because of their association with a known trouble-maker who had only been identified last night by an informant. Orphan heard the story but not the voices. His feelings kept him from registering details. Fear was mixed with confusion in his mind, and it was all overwhelmed by the shock. Marilee and her friends were in jail? Because of Corran? This was madness.

In Lula's world, two joggers paused by Lula's usual spot to ask each other why she wasn't there. One of them said that he'd heard she was too frightened to come out today since her former lover had become violent. The other said that he'd heard she had gone to join Soran in his insurrection. Orphan knew neither of these rumors could be true.

Everything was happening too quickly. He didn't know what to do. Then he heard one of the policemen talk about searching the house, as he approached the garden gate. Panicking, Orphan stood, ran through Marilee's house, exited through a door on the other side, and kept running. He didn't know where he was going, but his feet took him to the site of all the trouble. Having passed blindly through streets in both worlds, he found himself in front of the police station in Marilee's world and the Peace Building in Lula's, both imposing edifices. He froze in place and gawked at the buildings.

The police station was quiet. Only the usual day workers passed by him on the streets and sidewalks. The Peace Building was comparatively chaotic. Crowds were gathered to watch how the peace officers and the Committee of Peace would handle the situation and what else Soran would say.

Orphan walked up to the front doors of the buildings and considered his options. He could enter and try to convince both the police and Soran that they were doing the wrong thing, or he could wait and do nothing. Neither option seemed likely to yield positive results. Suddenly, he noticed that he was still holding the pad of paper in one hand. Badly crumpled, it might still prove useful. He searched his pockets for the pen but came up empty-handed.

"Looking for this?" sounded a voice in his ears. He turned to see Corran holding the pen out. "Take it," he said. "You might need it if you're going in there. I heard about Marilee and the others. For what it's worth, I'm sorry. I know they meant a lot to you. I didn't know I was being watched so closely."

Orphan snatched up the pen and scribbled out, "Turn yourself in!" When Corran read the note, he sighed, lowered his gaze, and shook his head. "I can't do that," he whispered almost apologetically. "I wouldn't survive prison. I need excitement and life. And I haven't really done anything wrong; I'm just a disturber of the peace, you might say."

Orphan felt his anger rising again and turned away to write on the pad. He wrote, "The man you want is outside. Please, let Marilee…" He paused a moment to remember her last name; there were no last names in Lula's world. "…Winston and her associates go free. They've done nothing wrong." He pushed open the doors and stepped through.

Inside the police station, a handful of officers stood at the front desk, filling out paperwork and talking to the officer behind the desk. Everything seemed very normal. Inside the Peace Building, Soran and his mob of followers stood in the main hall, staring at him. It made the hairs on the back of his neck stand up. He walked up to both the front desk and Soran and held out his note. The officer took it, and Soran stared at his empty hand.

"Gene, go check this out," the officer handed the note to one of his colleagues.

"I know who you are," Soran grumbled. **"No need for introductions. Are you here to stop us?"**

Orphan nodded, as Gene exited the building. He tried to ask for pen and paper, but Soran didn't seem to understand. He only looked frustrated and turned to one of his followers for help.

"You can't speak?" the desk officer asked, before being interrupted by Gene from outside, yelling, *"I need some help!"* Two more officers followed him outside, and the desk officer ignored Orphan's nod.

"Use this," Soran said and tossed a pad of paper and a pen at Orphan. Orphan quickly wrote, "People will get hurt if you persist. Please, consider a more peaceful method of negotiation." Soran read the note and laughed, **"Ha, you must be joking. This complacent society will never listen to our demands unless we show them how serious we are. Go back and tell…"**

He paused in mid-sentence when the front door opened again. In Marilee's world, the police officers were dragging Corran inside. He was handcuffed but still struggling against them. In Lula's world, he appeared to be struggling against ghosts or having a seizure of some sort.

"You bastard!" he shouted at Orphan. "I can't believe you'd do this! We were friends!"

Orphan shook his head sadly. The officer at the front desk whistled and said with wide eyes, *"Well, I'll be damned. Son, you've just turned in a man we've been tracking for months. Do you know how dangerous he is? He caused the deaths of three people four months ago. If your friends in our cell didn't know about that, they'll be free to go. They're in interrogation now."*

Meanwhile, Soran was saying, **"He hasn't done anything. He can't stop us. You're free to join us if you're all right."**

In Marilee's world, Corran was dragged into another room and locked inside. He shouted through the glass at Orphan, but he was audible only in Lula's world, where he was standing in the open doorway of a closet.

"Do you have any idea what you've done?" he seethed with anger.

The officer at the front desk left to speak with someone at the back of the large room, and Soran pointed a finger at Corran and said, **"You'd best calm down and step away from that closet. We've got some sensitive equipment in there, and I won't let you mess with it."**

Corran started giggling strangely, and Orphan looked helplessly at Soran. There was nothing that could be done at this point. In Marilee's world, Corran was behind a heavily bolted door. Any attempt to walk him out would meet with failure. But perhaps, he could be moved out some other way. Orphan thought about the time that he took a car ride and gestured to Soran that he could lift Corran up and move him bodily away from the closet. Perhaps then, Corran would take a minute to calm down.

Soran considered the idea and instructed two of his followers to try it. They lifted Corran by the elbows and set him down in front of Soran. Now, Corran seemed to be standing in two different spots. It was a bit disorienting to Orphan, but at least, Corran seemed to be a bit calmer now.

"Now perhaps, you can tell me," Soran growled, **"why you burst in here like that and stood in front of that particular door."**

"You wouldn't believe me," Corran grinned. "But I'll tell you that this man is not to be trusted. He'll betray even his friends."

Corran glared at Orphan, and the tension in the room rose even higher. Soran watched them both for a minute and then said to his followers, **"Put them both somewhere we can keep an eye on them until I can figure out what they're up to."**

"Wait, Soran!" shouted a voice from the front door. Lula stepped inside, and Orphan waved his hands to warn her away. What was she doing? The situation was getting worse and worse. He felt his heart lodge itself in his throat, and he wondered if both of his worlds were about to crumble around him.

"All of this started because I refused you," Lula said as she approached, attempting to maintain a calm demeanor. **"So let's start over. I'll marry you, and we'll live on that island somewhere. The peace officers outside have assured me that if you all leave peacefully, nothing will happen to you. Just let Orphan go, please!"**

"Is this a trick?" Soran asked with a sly glance at Corran.

"Hell if I know," Corran mumbled, sulking.

"No tricks, I just want the violence to stop," Lula pleaded. **"Let him go, and his friend, too; and I'll stay."**

"So you don't know about the explosives," Soran said, watching her carefully.

"Explosives!?" she repeated, her voice cracking.

Orphan's mind raced. What explosives? He glanced toward the closet and the "equipment" that Soran had mentioned. All he could see were boxes and wiring, but he couldn't take the chance. He grabbed Lula's arm and tried to pull her to the front door. She yanked herself out of his grasp and said, **"Please, Soran, don't do this!"**

"Hey, buddy, where you going?" a policeman called. *"We're letting your friends out of custody and booking your terrorist."*

Orphan saw Marilee, Boryn, Amay, Roosh, and Trav being led to the front desk, while Corran was being removed from the locked room. He waved at Marilee, hoping that Lula would follow him, too.

"I'll let your friend Orphan leave if you stay here," Soran said.

"All right," Lula nodded. **"We'll talk some more. We can work this out."**

Orphan shook his head frantically, but two of Soran's people approached to take him outside. He backed away from them, tripped, and fell. After that, things seemed to happen in slow motion. He saw every head in both worlds turn and look at him. Marilee stood in front of him with the others, and Corran was just behind her with two policemen. Lula and Soran stood where Marilee was, with his followers and Corran behind them. Orphan's head began to ache, and he knew that something big was about to happen.

Suddenly, Corran pulled away from his escorts. One of them pulled out a gun and pointed it at him. He yelled something, but Orphan didn't hear the words. Soran reacted to the sudden movement by reaching for a pocket in his toga top. There was a clicking sound, and everyone froze.

In Marilee's world, the policeman with the gun fired it at Corran, who ducked in the nick of time. The bullet must have hit Marilee, because she fell forward and lay prone on the floor of the station.

In Lula's world, Corran ducked just as a bright flash of light came from the closet. Panicking, the two men on either side of Orphan picked him up, set him on his feet, and propelled him backwards through the front door. His eyes were frozen on Marilee's body and on Lula's feet, which, for some reason, weren't moving.

Everything felt like it took hours to happen, even though Orphan knew the real time elapsed amounted to only a few seconds. He had barely made it to the street, pulled by Soran's two followers, when the Peace Building erupted in fire, smoke, debris, and noise.

Thrown to the ground, Orphan remained motionless until all he could hear was the sound of a woman sobbing. He stood slowly and stared at the wreckage and rubble that rested in the same spot as the intact police station. Two worlds diverged.

After a few moments, Orphan's legs began to move. They took him back inside the police station and into the charred rubble that used to be the Peace Building. Marilee and Corran both lay on the floor in the station. Blood pooled from Marilee's body, and she wasn't breathing. Corran looked as though he had suffered third-degree burns over every inch of his body, with nothing left to identify it as his. Lula and Soran and the others were nowhere to be seen in the area where the Peace Building had been, and Corran's body was missing from that scene as well.

"What happened to him?!" a policeman was shouting, as Boryn knelt over Marilee. Other voices hovered in the air, but he didn't hear the words they spoke.

Orphan turned around and started walking. He didn't know where he would go, but his feet took him to Marilee's garden and Lula's park. His vision blurred as he nearly fell onto the benches. Tears flowed from his eyes, and he reached up to wipe them away. It was only then that he noticed a wound on the side of his head. Staring at the blood on his hands, he made the first wish that he had ever made in his life. He wished that it had been him, that he had been standing in Marilee's and Lula's spot. He slid off the benches, collapsed on the ground, and sobbed uncontrollably.

A breeze brought the sound of voices, and he looked up to see that many hours had elapsed since he arrived at the benches. The sun had passed the peak of its path, and footsteps were approaching. Boryn entered through the garden gate, followed by Amay and Roosh. Two joggers came towards the bench from the other side of the park.

Boryn froze when he saw Orphan, and after a moment, he said quietly, *"We came to get some of our things. We, uh...we'd like you to come with us back to my place. We'll be planning the, uh, funeral. And we'll continue the Events in a week or two. I think Mari would've wanted that. Will you join us?"*

The two joggers were close enough for Orphan to hear their words. One of them was saying, **"The news says a couple of them escaped and got away from peace officers."**

"Yeah, I heard," said the other woman. **"And they've already sent a threat to the Home Peace Building that if they don't get what they want there'll be more explosions. It's unbelievable! It's scary. It feels like the whole world is changing. What's happening?"**

"I don't know," the first jogger shook her head, then halted, pointed at Orphan, and exclaimed, **"Hey, isn't that...?"**

"Aren't you the guy they pulled from the Peace Building this morning before it exploded?" the other jogger asked him.

Orphan stood, nodded to both Boryn and the joggers, and walked slowly into Marilee's house and out of the park. He waited while the others recovered their possessions and followed them back the way they had come. At the gate, he paused to take a final look at Marilee's home and Lula's favorite spot in the park. These people would never be seen there again, and the places would change. But no matter how different they would be now, he would always think of his two worlds as Marilee's world and Lula's world.

EYES OPEN

"This is all I know. This is what I have to do."

"Why? You'll get yourself killed, and then who'll be around to keep me company?"

"I won't get myself killed. I can't. I have work to do."

She disappeared into the shadows of the night, her feet mere inches off the ground, leaving her companion in the alley to ponder her words. But Chyrit wasn't one to ponder the mysteries of life for long. Dystra was right; they had work to do, whether it made a difference or not. She didn't really care if it was all pointless; Chyrit just wanted to roll some heads. She lightly jumped into the air, rising until she was several feet above the treetops and peered across the cityscape beyond the park's edges, searching for a sign of her fellow fighter. She caught a glimpse of light, flashing bright enough to wake the sun. She vanished.

The park was empty of all but the wind. A streetlamp flickered and doused its light. A voice whispered so softly that no one but the listener could hear it. The listener responded softer still.

"They continue the hunt."

"They always will."

"Not for long. He will stop them. Come, we have work of our own to do."

The city was noisy, its residents unaware of the eyes that watched them from the clouds. The neon lights, billboards, and streetlamps left no shadowy oasis for the darkness of night. A young man's quick footsteps were barely noticeable in the din of the sidewalk's pedestrians, but he himself couldn't hear anything else. The thud of his shoes on the concrete filled his ears. He didn't hear the laughter of lovers walking slowly, arm-in-arm, in the opposite direction. He didn't hear the beep of the car horn that came to a screeching halt at the intersection. He didn't hear the snap of the streetlamp that went out just as he passed beneath its glare. He didn't hear the distant thunder or feel the light touch of a drizzling rain that began to fall after the echoes had faded. Suddenly, he didn't hear his footsteps, either. He waited a moment, pondering, and then looked up.

He stood beneath an awning. The window was dark, but he could read the name of the shop: "Pira's Electronics." For a fleeting moment, he considered the name, then his eyes were pulled beyond the glass to the television flickering in the darkness of the building. A reclining chair obscured part of the screen, but the bright colors seemed to shine through it. Happy faces flashed past his eyes, and he could almost hear the music. His foot started tapping, and it startled him. He looked down at his shoe and back up at the chair. There was someone there, but his foot was not tapping. The young man shook his head and turned to rejoin the throng of travelers on the sidewalk.

"Angel! Wait up, Angel!"

The young man paused on his doorstep, the key in his hand. He waited pensively for the young woman to catch up.

"I've told you before not to call me that. My name is Andrel."

"But you're such an angel."

The young woman beamed at him, her smile lighting up his doorway. He sighed, resigned to another evening of happy talk about happy things. She came over nearly every night; he should be used to it by now. Somehow, he wasn't.

"Smile, Angel. It's a beautiful night, and we're together."

She took his arm as he opened the door and led the way into his darkened apartment. She flicked on the lights and ran to the window, shrugging off her raincoat and dropping it on the floor. She parted the dingy curtains and opened the window to let the moonlight and night air into the stuffy little room. He shuffled toward the refrigerator, but she waved a finger at him and grinned.

"I'll make dinner tonight. I've been studying hard just to impress you. Sit down and relax, and I'll have it ready in a jiff."

He sighed and followed her orders. There was no point in arguing about it. She would have her way. He wondered what that would involve tonight. Burnt meatloaf? Soggy taco salad? And after dinner? Sometimes she would turn on the stereo and insist that he dance with her. Sometimes she would leave the dishes on the table and lead him straight back to the bedroom. Sometimes she would say that the couch was just as good as the bed. Sometimes she stayed all night, and sometimes she left before the sun was up. He watched her set dishes on the stove and counter, humming a tune he'd never heard, and he was struck with that feeling that he often encountered on rainy nights like this when she was in his kitchen and he had nothing else to think about. It was a sense that something was out of order, that he didn't belong or that she didn't belong, that something was missing or that something was there that shouldn't be. He could never quite pin down what the problem was, but it always left him feeling that this world he lived in was alien to him.

He watched her mix ingredients in a bowl and tried to focus on the day's activities. He knew he had gone to work in the morning, walking his usual route with all the other pedestrian commuters. He knew he had eaten lunch outside the office on the park bench next to the hot dog vendor. He knew he had come home by the same familiar route that he took every evening. But he couldn't recall anything that made today different from the day before, or the day before that, or the day before that. The routine was as familiar to him as the young woman in his kitchen, and also just as alien. It all felt like a role he was playing without an audience. She was his co-star in the play that they were secretly putting on in his apartment every day.

Why?

That question echoed in his mind every day, even when he didn't realize he was thinking about anything at all. Now it thundered through his head, drowning out the rain and the noises in his kitchen and the sound of his shoes tapping on the hardwood floor.

Why? Why was he in this place? Why was she with him? Why did he go to work every day? Why did she visit him every evening? Why did he do the same things every day? Why was this his routine? Why did this life belong to him?

"You're more spaced out than usual tonight. It's the rain, isn't it?"

She was setting plates on the card table in front of him, and he realized that he'd been lost in thought for more than thirty minutes. He offered a slight smile and stared into her eyes. Sometimes he thought that if he stared long enough, he could almost remember....

"Let's eat. Then you can have dessert."

She smiled mischievously and hurried back to the kitchen to get the pan from the stovetop. He watched her spoon some sort of casserole onto his plate. Her dark blonde hair fell over her shoulders as she leaned over, and she tossed her head and smiled at him, her green eyes bright and her freckled nose wrinkling up with the effort.

"It's Italian. I know how you love international foods. Would you like me to turn on the TV?"

She pushed the button before he could respond, and the screen flickered to life. The same program that he had glimpsed through the window on his way home was playing. Happy faces and bright colors. He noticed a look of concern on the young woman's face. She looked uncomfortable.

"I guess there's nothing on," she whispered and turned the television off again.

He wondered for a moment if she had sensed the same wrongness about it that he had sensed earlier that day. He tried to look into her eyes again, but she bowed her head and sat quickly in the chair to his left.

"You haven't said anything tonight. Say something." She turned toward him, leaned close, and whispered, "Tell me you love me."

He looked at her and smiled. She always said that when she was feeling uncomfortable. It was her security blanket, letting her know that the world was in order. He wasn't sure it was, but he placated her anyway. It was habit, routine, even if he didn't know why.

"I love you, Frina."

She sighed happily and leaned on his shoulder, poking at her dinner with a fork. She ran one hand through his dark brown hair and then rubbed his shoulder a little.

"I love you, Angel."

The clash of metal rang out across the city, but no one could hear it but the combatants and their audience. Eyes watched them from the clouds, but the fighters paid no heed to the spies. Sparks flew from the point of contact between the sword and the spear. The fighter's red eyes flashed as she ducked to the left, slamming the other end of her spear into her opponent's leg. He began to buckle, but before he hit the ground, he flew into the air, hovering only for a moment before diving back down. Dystra met him halfway, slipping the top of her weapon straight past his sword and into his chest. His red blood glowed brightly as it dripped down the blade. He slashed at her, but she kept him at a distance with the spear. She stole a glance at her companion and then swung her captive over her head, grunting with the effort. She was tired, more so than usual. She shook it off and flew swiftly to the tree twenty yards away that the demon had hit after flying off of her spear. She plunged the blade into his chest once more, pinning him to the trunk. He howled for a moment, then fell silent.

Chyrit's sword lit up the night as she pushed her opponent back against a wall. Dystra retrieved her spear and headed in their direction, but before she arrived, Chyrit had run the demon through. The body slumped to the ground, and Dystra paused to assess her friend's condition. Chyrit, more than a few inches taller than Dystra, was now sporting a cut on her left shoulder but seemed none the worse for it. Her dark blue jumpsuit was cut in several places from previous battles. Dystra herself had a long cut on her right leg that had gone through her own jumpsuit, but she ignored it and headed back to the tree.

"We're running out of places to stash these," Chyrit joked.

Dystra grimaced at the ill-timed humor. She could never understand how her friend could make light of such grim circumstances. She dragged the body back to the wall and dumped it on top of the other one. Chyrit scattered dust from the small bag on her belt. Her magic made the dust sparkle like tiny stars. She spoke the name of the burial world in a language that no human had heard in a thousand millennia, and the bodies vanished in the midst of a transparent swirl of cloudy energy.

"Let's take a break and get some ice cream. I rather like that human food."

Dystra couldn't tell if Chyrit was joking or not this time.

"We don't have time for breaks. There's work to do."

"You can't kill them all in one night, Dys."

"I can try."

Dystra flew up into the night sky again, and Chyrit sighed and followed. It was going to be another long night.

Andrel stared through the gap in the curtains at the rising sun. The red glow had faded, and the orange tone of the light bathed his bedroom with an aura of stagnancy, as if everything were frozen, waiting for the dawn to be completed. Frina had left hours ago, but he hadn't slept. It wasn't that he had anything to think about. He simply could not sleep for very long. His mind was bothered by the world. It crept into his dreams and woke him with nightmares. He wouldn't call them nightmares, of course. He never woke in the middle of the night with his sheets drenched in sweat or his throat wrenched from screaming. He would wake up and sit on the edge of the bed and stare at the clock with the bright digital read-out, or he would stare out the window at the moon. He never thought about what had woken him or wondered if he should try to go back to sleep. Frina had once said that he was creepy at night because he would sit straight up and just stay there for hours, not saying or doing anything. Had she said that just last night? Or was it last week? He couldn't remember. She might have made the same comment more than once.

The clock alarm went off, buzzing noisily. Mechanically, Andrel reached for the button to turn it off. The noise cut out, and silence filled the room again. For a moment, he was tempted to continue sitting there, but he had to get to work. He didn't know why, but he knew he did. He lifted himself up off the edge of the bed and stepped slowly toward the closet on the left. He opened the door and took out the white polo shirt and a pair of khaki slacks. He laid them out on the bed and walked down the hallway to the bathroom. He reached past the shower curtain and turned on the water. As soon as the drops began to hit the floor of the shower, his mind drifted into another world. He slipped off his boxers and stepped underneath the stream of liquid, his eyes closed. He barely felt the water running off of his face and his shoulders. His mind was completely blank.

"I wonder why they don't come out during the day. It's not as if the light would hurt them."

"Don't look a gift horse in the mouth."

Dystra turned and stared at Chyrit.

"What does that mean?"

"It's a human expression. It means, 'Don't be concerned with where a gift came from. Just enjoy it.'"

Dystra turned back toward her work and scrubbed harder on the blade of her spear.

"This is no gift. If they came out in the day, we could kill more of them."

"And get ourselves killed in the process," Chyrit sighed loudly. "We're immortal, not invincible. We need rest. I'm sure they do, too. Take the daylight hours as an opportunity to get some. If you rest for a while, you'll be much more effective when it's time to fight."

Dystra paused and sighed softly.

"I know. I'm just so restless today. If only there were something I could do."

"You're restless every day, Dys. Try to get some sleep. There's nothing you can do until the sun goes down."

Chyrit laid down on a mat on the floor of the abandoned building they were staying in today. She tossed her long reddish-brown hair to the side and yawned loudly. Dystra set aside her spear and tip-toed to the window. She peered through the boards that were nailed across it, but all she saw were humans. Humans talking and laughing and walking together. She tugged lightly at her long brown ponytail and squinted her red eyes. Chyrit was right, she knew; there was nothing else she could do until the sun went down. The creatures were probably resting in their caves or their apartments or their homes back in their own dimension. If only there were a way that she could track them when they weren't using their energy…

Andrel walked slowly along the hallway, pushing the cart full of boxes and envelopes in front of him. All around him, people chattered on phones and to each other over the walls of their cubicles. He paused at Jeffries' desk and placed a manila office envelope in his mail tray. Jeffries was on the phone and playing solitaire on the computer at the same time.

"Of course, Mr. Campbell, I understand. But you don't need to worry about a thing. We're on top of the situation, I promise you."

Andrel pushed the cart onward. He passed by Klinger's office and Doren's desk and stopped at the new employee's desk. He knelt behind the cart and pulled a box off of the bottom tray that said, "Carrie Mitchell." He placed it in her tray, and she smiled and nodded at him. She was working on something on her computer. Andrel nodded back mechanically and moved on. He pushed the cart to the next cubicle and left another box there. He spent the rest of the morning dropping off all sorts of packages at different desks throughout the building. When he got back to the mail room, another shipment had come in, ready for him to load up on the cart and deliver. The other mail room worker had already sorted everything.

"It's ready to go. But lunch is in five minutes, so I say we wait."

"Sure thing. Thanks, Bill."

Andrel grabbed the paper bag that he always carried his lunch in and headed downstairs. He went out the big glass front doors and walked into the garden area in front of the building. Next to the hot dog vendor, he sat on the park bench and solemnly ate his lunch.

"You are such an overachiever. Why do you always have to be the best at everything?"

"What are you talking about, Jeanie? I'm not an overachiever. I just like to do my best at whatever I'm doing."

Frina put down the book she was studying and smiled at her friend. The librarian walked by them and scowled. The two girls giggled, and Jeanie sat down next to Frina.

"So how's your little boy toy these days? I haven't seen him in a while, but I'm assuming all is well since you've been in such a good mood."

"Yeah, everything's great," Frina whispered, glancing at the librarian's desk at the other end of the room. "I'm over at his place pretty much every night. You can call me there if you want. Unless it's after dinner. We're usually busy then."

"Really?" Jeanie's eye widened in mock surprise. "I didn't realize things were going **that** well."

The girls giggled again, and the librarian shushed them from across the room. Jeanie opened a book and set it on its side on the table to block their heads from the librarian's view.

"Give me details!" she whispered.

"Don't be so nosy," Frina laughed. "Get your own 'boy toy,' as you call them. This one's mine."

"Ooh, touchy," Jeanie leaned back and pouted. "I'm your best friend, and you can't tell me even one little thing?"

"Angel's sort of serious," Frina said thoughtfully. "I don't think he'd appreciate me telling you the details of our love life. In fact, I'm not sure he'd appreciate me telling you anything about him. He's rather private."

"Yeah, what's with that? I mean, he's not like you at all. Don't get me wrong; he's absolutely delicious. But what else do you see in him? You don't have anything in common, and he's so…well, brooding. I can't think of any other word to describe him."

"Yeah, I know," Frina sighed. "But what can I say? You can't choose who you love. Right?"

Andrel had finished delivering that afternoon's packages. He went back to the mail room and stowed the cart. Bill was already gone for the day; he had a habit of leaving early on Fridays. Andrel didn't care. He locked the mail room door and went downstairs to the lobby. Most of the offices were dark. The receptionist was just cleaning up her desk. She smiled at him as he walked by, and he nodded back. He went out through the big glass doors and walked down the sidewalk, past the garden area, and toward the parking lot. It was nearly empty.

He walked past the few remaining cars and past the office building on the other side. He took the alley in the back in order to avoid the long walk around the parking complex next door. For a moment, he wondered why he bothered. He wasn't particularly tired. But it was his habit to take the alley. It was dark, but he wasn't worried. At the end of the alley, he turned and joined the pedestrians on the sidewalk and headed for his apartment.

"The sun is setting."

Chyrit opened her eyes sleepily and stared at the face in front of hers.

"What time is it?" she yawned.

"Time? Time is of no consequence. The sun is setting! We can go out again."

Dystra grabbed her spear and headed for the door.

"Did you get any sleep today?"

Dystra ignored the question and left. Chyrit sighed and stretched. It was going to be another long night. She hooked her sword onto her belt and floated out of the room. Dystra was only a few yards away, waiting.

"Tonight, many demons will die."

"So...just like last night, huh?" Chyrit raised one eyebrow and grinned slightly.

"There's got to be a faster way to do this," Dystra sighed and rose up into the air, above the treetops.

"To do what?" Chyrit followed her. "Kill them? I think we're doing a pretty good job of that. You can't take out the entire species."

Dystra glanced at her and smiled slyly.

"Watch me."

She flew off toward the park, and Chyrit hovered there for a moment, thinking. She knew Dystra meant well, but she just couldn't seem to understand that the balance of the worlds could not be overthrown by two warriors such as themselves. At least, not if they planned on keeping the worlds intact and innocent creatures like the humans alive. They knew that from experience. Surely, Dystra hadn't forgotten.

There was a knock at the door, and Andrel opened it and turned back to his dinner preparations. He knew it was Frina. Who else would it be? She hopped through the doorway and grinned at him.

"Jeanie was asking about you today. I should have told her how distracted you've been acting. Not that that's anything different from the usual."

She peered around his shoulder at the pot he was stirring and continued chattering, "I meant to get here earlier, but Dr. Krisler wanted to talk to me after class. I want to go to a movie. It's a bit late tonight, but maybe we could go tomorrow night. I hear the new Carter Simons movie is out. Jeanie says it should be really good since it was directed by Jolie Fletcher, but you can't really tell until you see it for yourself. You wanna go tomorrow? We could grab a bite to eat at Martha's. I love the french fries there. Are you listening?"

"Why do you do that?"

"Do what?" Frina stared at him, confused. .

"Talk. You talk all the time, even when you're not saying anything important, even when no one is listening. Why?"

Frina sniffled and turned away from him.

"Why would you say something like that? If I'm boring you, just tell me to leave. I didn't mean to get in the way of your...your...brooding!"

She dashed toward the door, snatching up her coat on the way. She had just touched the doorknob, and Andrel appeared at her side, one hand on the door. He looked at her with a genuine concern in his eyes. He seemed to be paying attention to her for the first time in a long time.

"I'm sorry, I didn't mean it like that. I've just been doing a lot of thinking about things lately, and it's made me a bit...well, like you said, brooding. Come, sit down, and I'll listen to whatever you'd like to say."

He smiled, and she smiled back. That was all she needed to hear. She dropped her coat and sat at the card table, while he returned to the stove to finish making dinner.

"Actually," she began, "what I'd really like is to hear you talk. I have the feeling that there's more going on in your head than you're telling me about here. Is something wrong? I mean, you're usually kind of spaced out, but these days, it's like you're just going through the motions."

Andrel considered what she said. It was true. He was just "going through the motions." That was a good way to describe it. He just couldn't figure out why. How could he tell her that he wasn't sure he loved her the way she wanted him to? How could he tell her that sometimes he felt like his entire life was some sort of lie? Just hearing the pain in her voice earlier when he'd said the wrong thing and she nearly left was enough to make his chest ache. When she hurt, he hurt. But not figuratively, like in poetry. He felt the pain literally. When she was sad, he felt a stab in his chest, like a knife penetrating his skin. Was that love? Was his mind just manifesting some sort of physical reaction to her emotional distress? He wasn't sure, but it didn't feel right. So he couldn't tell her the whole truth.

"I've been thinking about making some changes," he spoke slowly, trying to tell her the truth without revealing too much. "Things don't feel right. It's not that I'm unhappy. I just don't feel like this life is the right one for me. Maybe a new apartment or a new job would help things."

"That's…that's good," Frina nodded uncertainly. "I mean, you should be happy. If you don't like the mail room, look for something else. And I can help you scout out a new place. But in the meantime, you're not thinking of changing girlfriends, are you?"

"Of course not," he smiled at the thought. He knew he couldn't do that if he wanted to.

"Good! Then you can make all the changes to your life that you want."

The rain began to fall again, hitting the window in a rhythmic pattern. Andrel paused and found himself lost in thought again. Suddenly, he knew what he wanted to say.

"How did we meet?"

He turned toward Frina abruptly and startled her. He stared into her eyes, and she seemed frozen by his gaze. She stammered and laughed nervously.

"Wh-what are you talking about, silly? Heh, heh, we met last year, remember?"

"Yes, I remember **when** we met. I wanted to know **how** we met. Do you remember? It seems as if we've always been this way."

"Yeah, we just fit together," Frina sighed. "Isn't it great?'

"But how did we meet? What were the circumstances?"

"It…was…at school. Wasn't it?" she looked up at him as if to coax the answer out of his own brain.

"I don't go to your school. I never have. Forgive me, but I can't recall exactly how we met."

"Oh, it doesn't really matter, does it? The important thing is that we found each other and we're together now. Right? Now quit being so weird and bring me some dinner. I'm starved."

She grinned at him, and he let the issue drop. She couldn't remember, either. So what did it matter? She was right; the important thing was the way things were now. Still, he couldn't help wondering how they got that way.

"Did you feel that?"

Chyrit stopped in mid-air and listened. She didn't hear or feel anything unusual. She looked at Dystra and waited.

"I guess it was nothing," Dystra sighed quietly. "I was sure that….Oh, nevermind. Let's go."

She flew up higher, and Chyrit followed her, glancing back at the alley they had just passed through. She hadn't noticed anything strange herself, but she knew that Dystra's instincts were not to be scoffed at. She made a mental note of where the alley was and vowed to pay it another visit when they weren't hot on the trail of such a special quarry.

The night hadn't begun as anything special. At first, it had seemed like they were going to be spending eight hours chasing down low-level low-lifes, just like every other night. But for some reason, Dystra had noticed that they were being watched. She had often had that feeling before, but tonight, she saw the eyes in the clouds. She had flown straight up, faster than Chyrit had ever seen her go, and caught one of the spies. He managed to escape, but Dystra followed him, with Chyrit close on her heels. They sped through the city, down alleys, through empty buildings, above the clouds. Dystra was even more persistent than usual tonight, as difficult as that was to comprehend. They finally lost him around the intersection of 4th and Washington, near the corporate section of the city. They continued floating around, looking for clues, and that was when Dystra had felt something odd in one of the alleys. They kept going, though; she was determined to find out who had been spying on them. They searched for another hour but found nothing. As they prepared to make another sweep, they heard a scream from a few blocks over. Dystra sniffed the air and nodded, her red eyes flashing. They flew toward the noise, leaving behind their search for now.

In a dark doorway, a homeless man huddled, clutching his tattered coat and mumbling to himself. He didn't hear the whispers just above his head. He didn't notice when the streetlamp two doors down flickered and went out. He didn't hear the voices arguing in the air around him.

"You've grown careless. They would have stripped you of every physical molecule and sent you to the burial grounds."

"You think I don't know that? I'm well aware of what those two are capable of! I've been the one watching them ever since we found them again."

"How did you let them see you, then?"

"I didn't. She's grown more alert. She's looking for us."

"Impossible! She doesn't know we're here! She can't!"

"She does. I'm certain of it now. We need to back off, perhaps choose another place."

"It's too late for that. We'll just have to work faster. We can't move now; everything's in place."

"I'll spread the word, but they're working as fast as they can."

"I'll send for reinforcements."

The wind blew down the street and ruffled the battered hat on the homeless man's head. He pulled his coat tighter around his shoulders.

"You can't mean….No….Are you certain that's…necessary?"

"As you said, they know we're here. I won't allow them to stop us this time. This is our last chance. Don't make me start thinking of you as a liability."

"Of course not. I'll work with them. You don't have to worry about me."

Andrel sat on the edge of his bed. Frina was sleeping on the other side, her back turned toward him and the window. The sun was creeping over the horizon. He could go back to bed, but he knew he wouldn't sleep. He didn't have to go to work today, but he always did anyway. The routine never broke, not on Friday and not on Saturday. A few more minutes, and his alarm would go off. It wasn't necessary to leave it on. He was always awake before it had a chance to do its job, anyway. But it was habit. He waited, staring out the window. The light had more a reddish hue today. The sun varied its routine with different colors sometimes.

The alarm went off, and he hit the button on top of the clock. Frina stirred, yawning. He went to the closet and took out his clothes, laying them on the end of the bed. He went down the hallway to the bathroom and turned on the shower. He stepped under the water and listened to the sound of nothing.

"Is there anything here now?"

"It's faint, but I'm certain there's something."

Chyrit watched Dystra as she walked the length of the alley. By day, it appeared to be a normal alley. She could see nothing unusual. But Dystra put a hand on the brick wall of an apartment building and nodded.

"Something...familiar."

Suddenly, she seemed nervous.

"We should go. I don't think it's anything we need to worry about."

She walked quickly to the end of the alley and flew up to the top of the building. Chyrit followed her up into the light. The sun was blinding after a night of fighting demons. They flew to the park and took refuge under an old wooden bridge at the far end, where fewer humans were likely to walk over them.

"What's wrong?" Chyrit whispered. "Something's wrong. Tell me."

"It's nothing," Dystra shook her head and took a deep breath. "It felt familiar. I just had a sudden feeling that we shouldn't be there. I'm not sure, but for a moment, I thought....Oh, nevermind. It's all right. Let's rest here today."

Chyrit kept a close eye on Dystra until she fell asleep. If she was rattled by something, it was with good reason. Something was in or near that alley. Something important.

Frina sat in front of the television, eating cereal out of the box, wrapped in a robe from Andrel's bathroom. She hated Saturdays. She didn't have school to go to, and Andrel worked on Saturdays. She had nothing to do but sit in front of the television. She never had any homework to keep her busy; she got it done at the library every day. Saturdays always caused her to regret being what Jeanie called an "overachiever." Sundays were just as bad. Two straight days of nothing. She needed a distraction. She stared at the telephone on the wall. Jeanie was in Vermont for the weekend on a family trip. She had no other close friends, and there was no one to go home to. Andrel's apartment was pretty much her home now.

"Soap scum? Make it gone! With Tammy's Soap Scum Remover! You'll never need anything else to clean your showers, your sinks, your…"

Frina turned off the television and wandered into the kitchen. She wasn't really fond of TV. It often made her uncomfortable. Sometimes, it made her sad. She didn't know why. She took a deep breath and determined to find something else to do. The dishes needed washing. And after that? Maybe she'd clean the shower.

Andrel finished making his usual rounds and tidied up the mail room a bit. It was quiet in there without Bill chattering away. The whole building was quiet on Saturdays. Andrel was one of the few people there who worked on the weekend. It didn't bother him. At least, it gave him something to do. Tomorrow, he wouldn't have anything to do. Suddenly, he thought of Frina, sitting in his apartment with nothing to do. She hated the weekends, and he knew it. Maybe he could get her a part-time weekend job in the mail room. Or maybe someplace else in the building. There was no reason to put her in the mail room. He decided to ask Mr. Kip about it after lunch. He grabbed his brown paper bag and went downstairs, passing the front desk and going through the big glass doors. He went into the garden area out front and sat on the park bench next to the hot dog vendor.

Chyrit stood quietly in the alley, waiting and listening. There was nothing there, as far as she could tell. But she could be wrong. She wanted to come back while Dystra was sleeping. She almost hoped to find evidence that whatever Dystra had sensed was something harmless and silly, like a litter of newborn kittens or something. But the alley was empty, and the longer she stood there, next to the apartment building wall, the more she felt that there might be something there, after all. It was faint, but she could feel it. She put one hand on the bricks and felt the energy course into her palm. There was no window on this side of the building this close to the ground. Chyrit walked slowly around the building, keeping one hand on the wall, following the trail of energy. It fluctuated from brick to brick, but it was still there. She followed it around the corner and down the sidewalk. There was a door set back from the main walkway about twenty feet from where the building jutted out. Hesitantly, Chyrit stepped toward it. She felt the energy growing stronger. She was surprised they hadn't noticed it before, but then they didn't usually use doors. She reached the plain brown door and touched the doorknob. A flash of light went through her head, blinding her and sending her reeling backwards. She shouted and nearly fell onto the walkway, saving herself a bruising by floating up into the air. Gasping for breath, she backed away. Her head was spinning. She couldn't even think clearly. She had never felt such powerful magic. At least, not recently. Not since... No, that couldn't be it. It wouldn't make sense.

Chyrit took a deep breath and determined to have a closer look at whatever was behind that door. Something in that particular apartment was oozing with power. But it was power that was trying to hide. She started for the door again and steeled her nerves for another hit from the spell, but before she got there, a light flickered on in the alley on the other side of the building. Someone had turned on a light in the apartment, and it was shining through a window. Thinking a window might be safer for her to approach, Chyrit turned away from the door and entered the alley on her left. The window was wide open, but the room beyond seemed to be quiet. She peered inside and saw a young woman with dark blonde hair wiping off a card table. There were two chairs, a stereo, and a television set in the room, and beyond that, a kitchen area with a stove and a refrigerator. Chyrit stared at the young woman and began to think that what Dystra had said about something here being familiar to her was true. That woman seemed very familiar. She didn't turn toward the window, though, so Chyrit couldn't see her face. Instead, she went past the island countertop into the kitchen area and starting preparing lunch. Chyrit hesitated touching the windowsill because she didn't want a repeat of what had happened at the door. But she really wanted to get a closer look at that woman. She moved over to the wall and phased her body out of the corporeal realm so that she could pass through the bricks. She floated toward the wall, but just as she began to phase through it, another flash of light tore through her. It filled her entire being and flung her back into the wall of the building behind her. She screamed even louder this time and slumped to the ground, shaking. She couldn't move, except for the involuntary twitches that shuddered through her body. She didn't see the feet of the people who had entered the alley after hearing her scream, and she didn't hear them speak to her, asking her what was wrong. She didn't see the young woman look out through the window or hear her talking on the telephone as she called for help. She didn't see the faces of the paramedics who lifted her onto a gurney, and she didn't hear the wail of the ambulance siren as it transported her to the hospital. She didn't even feel the needle that was inserted into her arm to pump medicine into her body. She didn't know that the magical bubble that normally shielded her from the eyes and ears of the humans had vanished.

Dystra woke abruptly. Something was amiss. She had felt a ripple in the world. Something had happened. She turned to speak to Chyrit, but Chyrit was gone. Dystra felt certain that whatever had happened, it involved Chyrit somehow. She grabbed her spear and flew out from under the bridge. The afternoon sun was just beginning to leave its zenith; the demons couldn't be involved, unless they had suddenly decided to start walking about in the daylight. Dystra paused to feel around for a sign of Chyrit's trail. She caught the scent quickly and followed its faint traces back into the city and straight to the alley.

"No," she whispered, immediately fearing the worst. She had suspected that something was there that they shouldn't mess with; now she was certain. She tried to feel for the after-image of whatever had occurred there, but it wasn't coming to her. She touched down and stood in the alley, pondering. There had to be a way to find out where Chyrit went and what happened to her. She closed her eyes and looked with her inner eyes for an imprint of Chyrit's presence. There, on the brick wall, was a handprint. It seemed to echo across the wall, toward the sidewalk. Dystra followed the trail on foot, her eyes closed. The trail ended at the front of the building, but Dystra didn't need it anymore. She sensed the powerful magic that was emanating from the doorway, twenty feet from where she stood. Knowing that Chyrit would have investigated, she guessed what would have happened next. She knew that this magic would have been too much for her friend to handle. She knew, because it was the same level of magic as her own. In fact, it seemed almost identical to her own magic. But there was no time to worry about that now. She had to find Chyrit. She flew up a few feet and quickly circled the building. The strongest scent was in the alley on the other side, next to the window of one of the apartments. There, Dystra could almost taste pain and confusion hanging in the air. Chyrit was hurt, badly. There was a faint trail of her scent leading back out of the alley and down the street. Was she wandering in confusion, looking for help?

Dystra could barely control her panic and fear for her friend. She flew quickly down the street, inches from the pavement, passing unheeded through vehicles and their passengers. The trail was disappearing, and she had no time for theatrical flying. She had to stay low to the ground just to see it. She followed it for several blocks before it vanished entirely. She stood in the intersection, looking around desperately. It was gone. She had no idea where to go. She could try a summoning spell, but if Chyrit were really hurt, it could harm her even more. She would have to try a finding spell, but those could take hours to complete. She could call for help, but everyone in their world was too busy to hear her call anymore. They didn't care about the former Peace Warriors who stayed on Earth to hunt demons. Dystra felt alone and helpless, and she had never liked that feeling. She flew straight up and peered over the landscape, hoping to catch a glimpse of energy, some sort of sign that Chyrit was out there. But there was no movement in the city. Everything was quiet.

Nearly in tears, Dystra hurried back to the alley. There were no homeless people who might have seen the incident in question, and there was no sign of a struggle. She glanced through the apartment window, but no one seemed to be home. Dystra kneeled on the ground, her hands in front of her, and tried to stay calm. She knew that she would be of no use to her friend if she lost control of herself. She tried to think of other alternatives, something else she could do. But there were no clues, no eyewitnesses. Or so it seemed. Dystra looked up into the cloudless sky. They weren't there in the day, but they could be hiding elsewhere. She closed her eyes and searched for a different kind of energy. She flew up over the building and looked all around. At first, she didn't see anything, but then she noticed a faint glow running in lines all over the city. She never would have seen it if she hadn't been looking so hard. It ran in a neat checkerboard pattern over every city block. She couldn't tell where it was coming from or where it was going, until she saw the subtly brighter glow of energy on the other side of town. It was coming from an abandoned power station that had been slated for demolition months ago. Dystra and Chyrit had often fought demons in that area, but she had never noticed the faint hub of energy that resided within the building. The chances of finding anything helpful there were slim, but it would take less time to do a sweep of the building than it would to start the finding spell.

Dystra entered the building through the southern wall. It was largely empty. Nothing seemed to have been disturbed. But the energy traces were flowing everywhere. Dystra went as quickly as she could without missing any corners. There wasn't a sign of a single demon. The last place to check was the basement. The energy around her glowed brighter as she descended the stairs, hovering just above them. She thought she heard a voice whispering in the distant darkness. It wasn't human. She mentally dimmed her energy and started walking on the ground, as softly as possible. There were several hallways branching away from the stairs, and she took the one that glowed the brightest. After passing several doorways, she approached one that had a dim light coming out of it. The voice was still whispering, and it was just as hard to hear up close as it had been at the bottom of the stairway. Dystra took a deep breath and ventured inside. The room was large and empty, except for dead power lines running all over the floor. Opposite the door sat a demon with his back to Dystra. He was whispering something into one of the power lines, infusing it with energy. Dystra guessed he was chanting some kind of spell. The language he was using was definitely not of this world. She crept up behind him and jabbed her spear into his back. He jumped straight up onto his feet, dropping the power line and turning to face her. He wasn't the demon they had chased last night, but he would have to do.

"Tell me where they are, and I'll consider not sending you to the burial world," Dystra hissed softly.

"I...I...I," the demon stammered.

"Tell me!" she shouted.

Dust fell from the beams over their heads at the sound of her voice, and her energy levels rose threateningly. The demon stared at her as if she were his greatest fear. Maybe she was, but she had no time for mind games.

"If I wanted you dead, you would be. What I want right now is information. Give it to me, and I'll let you continue whatever infernal incantation you were performing just now."

"You...you want information?" the demon's mouth dropped open. "Your kind always kill first and don't ask questions. Why are you doing this?"

"It's no concern of yours, worm. Now tell me where they are!"

"Who?"

"The ones who've been watching us! I assume that demons who spy on Peace Warriors and demons who remain active in the daylight hours must know each other. Now, tell me where they are, or I'll send you to the burial world in pieces!"

She poked at his chest with her spear, coaxing a few drops of glowing red blood from his body. He backed up to the wall and seemed to compose himself somewhat.

"I don't know," he answered. "And if I did, I couldn't tell you. They would kill me."

"Fine. I'll kill you, instead."

She dashed toward him and slammed her spear into the wall, so close to his head that she nicked his left earlobe. He screamed at the top of his lungs and didn't stop for nearly a minute. Finally, she grabbed him by the collar of his dirty t-shirt and held the tip of her spear in front of his eyes and spoke.

"Do you doubt me? I could simply cut off a few body parts first. Oh, I know you can regrow them, but it'll hurt like hell, and then I'll cut off the new parts. And I'll keep doing that, until you tell me what I want to know, or until your friends come looking for you, whichever comes first."

"They're usually with him in the day. You can't find them. Your only chance would be if one of them was making the rounds. But they do that in human form. You'll never track them!"

Dystra considered carefully. She had known this would be a long-shot. Should she chance it and waste more time on it? Or should she just start the finding spell? Being this close to a demon without killing him was making her angry and even more confused. She took a deep breath and tried to ignore his awful stench.

"How about you help me then, worm?"

He began shaking even harder, his head jerking from side to side. He managed to spit out, "No...N-no! I-I can't! You can't expect help from one of us!"

"I don't think you understand. You don't have a choice! Now, take me anywhere you think one of your friends might be. And if I think for even a nanosecond that you're leading me into a trap or that you're not trying your hardest to find your friends, I'll rip your spirit right out of your body and send it into the void."

Andrel had been in Mr. Kip's office when he'd gotten the call from Frina. She'd sounded so crazed that for a moment, he thought she'd been hurt. But it was only some vagrant who'd been skulking outside his window. The woman had apparently had some sort of seizure. Frina was at the hospital, talking to the police and waiting for word on exactly what was wrong with the woman. Andrel advised her to go back to his place, but she was determined to wait. He couldn't understand why. It wasn't as if the woman was a friend. If anything, she might have been some sort of peeping-tom character. He thought it best to take the rest of the day off and go to the hospital himself. He needed to get control of the situation. The confusion in Frina's voice had been enough to send his heart into a panic. Mr. Kip was kind enough to give him the rest of the day off and promise to consider Frina as a new employee. Andrel knew his work record was spotless and there was no reason for Mr. Kip to do otherwise, but he was glad to get out of there. Something about the whole situation made him uncomfortable. He left the building and stood on the corner to call a cab. Before he could get any words out of his mouth, though, a car stopped in front of him, and Bill leaned out the window and said, "Get in, partner. I'll give you a lift. I was just passing by and saw you."

Andrel hesitated, wondering why Bill was nearby on a Saturday, but he got into the vehicle, feeling that time was of the essence. He explained where he was going, and Bill seemed happy enough to take him there.

"You're lucky I was here. Those taxicabs cost a fortune, you know. And it would have taken forever to get there in one of them. The traffic is nuts this time of day on the weekend. But I know a shortcut."

Bill winked and sped off down a side street. Andrel considered asking him what he was doing here, but decided against it. It was none of his business.

Frina stood in the waiting room. She was too nervous to sit. She was too nervous to think about anything else. When that woman had screamed, the sound had gone through Frina's head like a harpoon. Her skull still ached. The strangest thing, though, was that the woman looked familiar to Frina, as if they had known each other. Thinking about it made her head hurt even more, but she couldn't concentrate on anything else. She couldn't explain it, but something was happening. She felt as if her world were falling apart at the seams.

She saw Andrel coming down the hallway and ran to meet him. She threw her arms around his waist and squeezed, her eyes closed tightly. He held her for more than a minute before leading her back to the waiting room and sitting down on a couch with her. The room was otherwise empty, so he didn't bother whispering.

"What happened? Why are you still here?"

She took a deep breath and tried to think of a way to explain it. She couldn't even explain it to herself.

"The doctor said she had a seizure of some sort. I heard her scream outside the window, and…and I called the ambulance. People came to help, but she couldn't even talk. I…I don't know what happened. But I had to stay."

"Why?"

"I don't know," Frina started sobbing and buried her face in his shoulder.

Andrel put his arms around her and sighed. Something was going on; he had to find out what. But he couldn't leave her here by herself. She was in no condition to be alone. She was in pain and confused; he could feel it. Her headache was contagious. He sat there with her, thinking about anything but the pounding in his head. The day had started out normal. Something had gone wrong. Here he was in the hospital, waiting to hear something about a woman he didn't know. He had never taken a day off from work before. It was probably just an unusual day, but he couldn't help feeling that the strangeness was only getting started.

They waited together for two hours before the doctor finally came into the room to give them an update. He looked as confused as they were.

"I don't have much more to tell you, ma'am. We can't tell what's wrong with the young woman. We ran a CAT scan and an MRI; the preliminary results don't show anything wrong. Hopefully, we'll know more once the specialist has had a look at them. She's asleep now; we had to give her more than twice the normal dosage to put her out, but the blood tests haven't revealed any signs of drug use or alcohol. She didn't have any I.D. on her or anything else that might tell us who she is. Are you sure you've never seen her before?"

Frina nodded silently, and Andrel spoke up, "Could I see her? That was my apartment she was lurking around. Maybe I've seen her before."

"Come with me."

The doctor led them down the hallway and through a set of doors. He paused outside of one of the patient rooms and held the door open. Andrel entered the room, but Frina let go of his arm and whispered, "I'll stay here. I've already seen her."

Andrel nodded and walked across the room and through the curtains that shielded the bed from the door and window. A young woman with long reddish-brown hair lay on the bed, propped up on several pillows, breathing softly. Her thin lips moved slightly, as if she were whispering in her sleep. Andrel's head began spinning. There was something familiar about her, but it felt like his mind didn't want to know what it was and was fighting not to remember. He closed his eyes and listened to her breathing and his own. For that moment, the whole world seemed to consist of that room. He could almost see the energy moving around her body and converging with the energy around him. It felt like he was swimming in it. Suddenly, he couldn't breathe anymore. He started to gasp and fell backwards. He opened his eyes and found himself leaning against the doctor, who had caught him when he started to fall.

"Are you alright, son? Is something wrong?"

Andrel stood up and avoided looking at the woman again. He walked quickly out the door and said, "I don't think I've seen her recently, but I feel like I might have seen her somewhere before."

"Me, too!" Frina spoke up. "That's why I stayed! I just didn't know how to explain it. It was weird."

"Well, if you think of where you've seen her, let us know. The police are running her fingerprints right now, but if she doesn't have a record, the chances are slim of finding her identity."

Andrel nodded and thanked the doctor for his help. He led Frina back down the hallway and toward the elevator. It was time to go home. He needed some rest, and by the look of her, so did she.

Dystra followed the demon closely to make sure he didn't make a break for it. He was leading her down every back alley in the city, it seemed. She tried to find a pattern to his chaotic twists and turns, but there didn't seem to be one. Suddenly, he stopped short, and Dystra nearly ran into him. He was staring intently at a bar. The door was propped open with a cement block, and rowdy voices floated through it.

"Is he here?"

The demon nodded nervously and looked back at her.

"Please. If he knows I brought you here..."

"My lips are sealed," Dystra smiled. She wasn't interested in the personal dealings of these demons; she had more important things to worry about. "Point him out to me."

The demon hesitated, then crept up to the doorway. He peered inside and quickly ducked back out again.

"He's at the bar with a young woman. He's wearing a red hat and drinking a beer."

Dystra looked inside the building. There was only one man at the bar with a red hat, and he was human. She grabbed the demon by the collar and slammed him into the wall behind the door.

"You lied to me!" she shouted through gritted teeth, fighting back tears of frustration. "That man is human!"

"No! No!" the demon pleaded. "It's him, I swear! This is how they travel in the day!"

Dystra hesitated. If he were right, it would explain the lack of demonic energy in the daytime. She squinted at him and said, "Why? And how? The techniques of human possession were lost to the ages."

"We found them. It wasn't easy, but Lord K...er, our lord was determined to find an easier way to travel in the daylight hours. He was concerned about being spotted."

For a moment, Dystra wondered why this lord would be easier to spot in the daytime, but time was running out on her. She dropped the demon and entered the bar. She kept her energy levels at a minimum and walked right up to him.

"Do you mind if I have a word with you?"

The man turned to look at her, and the look of utter shock on his face almost made her laugh out loud. The woman next to him started to protest, but Dystra gave her a glance that sent fear into the marrow of her bones, and she walked away. Dystra grabbed the man's elbow and led him out the front door. The other demon was gone already.

"What's the meaning of this? Who are you?"

Dystra glared at the man. He didn't seem to recognize who or what she was. She allowed her energy levels to rise again, but he still stared at her in confusion. Perhaps, possessing a human had altered his powers of perception.

"I am the one who has hunted you for over a year. I am the one who slaughters your kind in the dark shadows of the night. I am a Peace Warrior. Who are you?"

"How...how did you find me?"

"I have my ways. What's important right now is that you cooperate with me. You've been watching my friend and I for some time, haven't you? Are you the one we chased last night?"

She tried to see past the human eyes to find out if he recognized her now, but the barrier was too strong. Humans were annoyingly thick of spirit and difficult to penetrate. He simply stuttered nervously and shook his head.

"I don't know what you're talking about. Leave me alone."

He turned to go back into the bar, and she swung him around by the collar and threw him onto the ground. She picked him up again and dragged him into the alley next to the building, throwing him into the side of a dumpster.

"Don't toy with me! I have no time for games! I know you're a demon using human possession to escape my detection. Tell me what I want to know, and I may spare your miserable spirit."

"All right! All right. What do you want?"

"My friend, my fellow Peace Warrior. Tell me where she is."

For a moment, he stared at her silently. Then, he began laughing. He tried to control himself and managed to spit out, "You've lost her?"

Dystra's anger became uncontrollable at that moment. She yelled a war cry and flew straight toward the man with her spear. He stepped aside just in time to avoid impalement. Her spear penetrated the side of the dumpster, and she stood there, breathing heavily. He started laughing again.

"You can't hurt me. This man is innocent of our games. Your kind don't kill innocents."

"I'll make an exception," Dystra eyed him with a hunter's gaze. She tugged her spear loose and turned to face him. He backed up against the wall, no longer laughing. "Tell me where she is."

He seemed to consider whether it was worth taking the chance, then decided he didn't have much choice.

"There isn't much I can tell you. I lost her at the hospital. Too many dying humans. Makes your energy hard to track."

Dystra flew up into the sky without another word. If Chyrit was at the hospital, that meant that her shield had gone down, and the humans could see her. The situation was worse than she had thought. She flew straight for the hospital, leaving the demon behind, chuckling to himself.

Andrel lay on the bed next to Frina, but he didn't sleep. He could tell by her breathing that she wasn't sleeping, either. They were both exhausted, but the day had left them both with too much to think about. They stared at the ceiling, lost in thought. Andrel was certain now that he had seen that woman somewhere. It was a feeling deep in his spirit, like knowledge from the beginning of time. He wanted to get up and go back to the hospital and see her again. But he couldn't leave Frina.

The phone rang, startling them both. He jumped out of bed quicker than he had ever done before and grabbed the receiver.

"Yes?"

"Andrel, this is Dr. Borrowitz. I thought you might like to know that the young woman has woken up. She's not talking much yet, but seeing you might jog her memory a bit. Can you and Frina come down here again?"

"We're on our way."

Frina sat up and looked at him quizzically.

"She's awake. They want us to talk to her."

Without a word, Frina slipped on her shoes and headed for the door. Andrel followed her, and they took a taxi to the hospital. When they got there, there was a commotion outside the room the woman had been in. Two police officers and several doctors and nurses were talking among themselves. Andrel spotted Dr. Borrowitz and waved to him. He made his way through the crowd to talk to them.

"I'm sorry you came all this way for nothing, kids. She's gone."

"You released her?!"

"No, of course not. Some woman came in and just took her right out from under our noses. One minute, they were in this room, and the next, they were gone. She claimed to be a friend of the patient's, so the nurse let her into the room. We have no idea how they got out without being seen. It all happened just ten minutes ago."

Andrel and Frina looked at each other. Neither knew what to say. Andrel could feel the tension in the air. He didn't want to make things any worse, so he thanked the doctor and guided Frina back to the elevator. Once they reached the street again, he called a cab and said, "I'd like to stay and look around a bit."

"But..."

"Please, Frina. I've got a bad feeling about this whole business. I don't want you in harm's way."

"I don't feel safe in your apartment by myself anymore. If you're staying, I'm staying."

Andrel sighed. The truth was that he just didn't want her around to distract him while he was trying to figure out what was going on. But she was determined. So they both went back into the hospital. Andrel spoke to the nurse at the front desk and asked her if she had seen the woman that everyone was talking about.

"I never saw her. The nurse up on that floor told me what she looked like, and I swear I never saw her. I don't know how she got past me."

Andrel thanked the woman and went back up to the fourth floor, Frina trailing behind him. They talked to the nurse at the main desk for that ward.

"I never would have even noticed her if she hadn't nearly run into a gurney that two interns were moving to I.C.U. Gave that poor dying man quite a fright. It was like she suddenly just appeared out of nowhere. I asked her what she was doing here, and she told me she was a friend of a young woman who had been brought in here earlier today. I showed her to that woman's room and went back to my post, but I had my eye on the hall the whole time. There's no way she could have gotten past me a second time."

"What did she look like?" Andrel asked.

"A little bit shorter than me, with long brown hair in a ponytail. The odd thing was her eyes. They looked sort of red. I suppose it must have been my imagination, but I was so sure. She was dressed strangely, too. Looked like she was heading for some kind of gymnastics tournament."

Twenty minutes before Andrel and Frina had arrived at the hospital, Dystra had made her way to the fourth floor. She had managed to escape detection so far, thanks to her shield. It wasn't easy. The demon had been right about the hospital being filled with dying humans. Their energies were incredibly chaotic and could short out her shield if she strayed too close to them. She could sense Chyrit's life force somewhere close by, though. She stopped in front of the main desk and checked over the sign-in sheet, peering over the nurse's shoulder. There was an entry for a woman with no name and an unknown ailment: Room 402. Excited about the discovery, Dystra hopped over the desk and ran right into a gurney that two interns were racing down the hall with. They had come around a corner just as she landed on the floor. The man on the gurney was clearly dying; his energy slammed into her like a physical force, and her shield vanished. The interns didn't even look at her, but the nurse at the desk did.

"Who are you? What are you doing here?"

"Um, my friend was brought in this morning. I need to see her. She's the one without any identification."

"Oh, well, I guess it's all right. Maybe you can fill out some paperwork for us after you've seen her."

The nurse escorted her to the room that Chyrit was in and left them. Chyrit looked at Dystra groggily and tried to sit up.

"Take it easy, Chy. I'll get you out of here."

She reinstated her own shield and extended it to cover Chyrit. She carefully lifted her friend out of the hospital bed and floated through the exterior wall of the building. She flew back to the bridge in the park and settled Chyrit in the shade.

"I…" Chyrit tried to speak.

"Shh, lie still," Dystra said. "You need your rest."

"But…"

"I'll check your memories if you like, but don't expend any more energy."

Chyrit sighed and closed her eyes. She was asleep in moments. Dystra put one hand to her friend's forehead and closed her eyes, checking for recent memories. She zipped through the morning and paused at the point where Chyrit was checking the alley next to the apartment building. When she touched the doorknob, Dystra felt the flash and knew what was happening. But she continued watching until Chyrit tried to phase through the wall. The flash confused even Dystra for a moment, and she broke contact with Chyrit.

"It's him."

Andrel and Frina walked back to the apartment. There was no rush; they had nothing else to do. People were hurrying all around them to get somewhere, but they paid no attention to them. Clouds began to gather, bringing the day to an early close. The wind picked up a little. On they walked, not even speaking to each other. Each knew that something was going on, and neither wanted to talk about it at that moment. Frina was close to tears, and Andrel could feel it. But he didn't know what to say. He couldn't tell her it was all a dream; he couldn't tell her that everything would be all right. He knew the former was wrong, and the latter was unknown. Before they were halfway home, the rain started coming down. People around them started putting up umbrellas and running from one shelter to another. They kept walking at the same slow pace. Andrel found himself drifting into blankness. The sound of rain always did that to him. There was no sound around him but the rain falling on the sidewalk. Then, he couldn't even hear the rain. His own footsteps were all that he heard.

Suddenly, he heard other footsteps. He paid no attention to them at first, but they continued, next to him. After a few minutes, he started wondering who was intruding on his solitude. Then he knew. It was Frina's feet that he heard. He took a breath and realized that his moments of blankness had never before been intruded upon by anyone or anything like that. He could still feel his mind wandering in that place where it was safe from the world, but he could hear her footsteps as well as his own. He shook himself awake and stopped walking. Frina stopped next to him and looked at him curiously. He gazed around at the city and saw the pedestrians dashing under the awnings of business buildings and hailing taxis. He looked at the window next to them and saw the name "Pira's Electronics" painted on it. Inside the building, a television set glowed brightly, and someone was seated in an armchair in front of it, not moving. Andrel looked into Frina's eyes and tried to say something, but he didn't know where to begin. She sighed and spoke for him.

"We're not normal. We don't belong. We may not even belong with each other. I know. I can feel it, too. Something has happened, and something is happening now. I know what I feel, but I know that what I feel is wrong, somehow. I don't want to investigate; I don't want to take away what we have here. But I think we have to, don't we?"

Andrel nodded slowly, impressed by her awareness of the issue. It was as if she'd known all along what he was feeling.

"Whatever this thing is that makes us feel like this, it's the reason that we are the way we are, isn't it? It's the reason that you're so distant and brooding. It's the reason that I hate silence and being alone. My obsession with making everything as normal as possible, your daily routine…Everything we do is a reaction to something that we can't even remember. Why? Why aren't we like everyone else? Why can't we be normal?"

Frina burst into tears, and Andrel held her, his eyes closed. The rain dripped off of the awning above them, and the television in the building flickered brightly. People walked by them, talking and laughing. Cars passed by, splashing water onto the curb from the gutter. It felt like night, and Andrel wondered if it had ever really felt like day.

"That was quite entertaining."

"I didn't think so."

"Well, since it was your spirit on the line, I wouldn't expect you to." The deep voice resonated with cruel laughter and added, "Don't let it happen again."

"I didn't have any control over the situation. Your little worker bee was the one who led her straight to me. On purpose!"

"What choice did he have? He is essential to the plan. You are not. He did the right thing. You should have fought her. If you keep racking up mistakes like this, I'll start considering your replacement."

"Hey, folks! What are you doing? Waiting for it to stop?"

Bill's voice startled them, and they looked in the direction it came from. He was leaning across the front seat of his car to shout at them through the window. He laughed and said, "Come on! Get in! I'll give you a ride back to your place."

"But you're going the opposite way," Frina protested.

"It's not far. Get in!"

He opened the door, and Andrel shrugged and rushed Frina to the car. She climbed into the back seat, and he took the front passenger seat and looked back at her. She looked uncomfortable. She had never liked Bill. She always said that something about him gave her the shivers. She said he wasn't normal. But Bill was the most normal person that Andrel knew. Of course, he trusted Frina's instincts, especially considering what had happened that day. So he knew he had to find out what was really going on with Bill.

"What brings you to this part of town on the weekend, Bill?"

"Oh, just happened to be in the neighborhood."

"Again?"

"Yeah, lucky for you, huh?"

Bill laughed easily, and Andrel considered whether he should just ask him outright. Frina spoke from behind them.

"Do you know anything about what happened today?"

Bill glanced back at her and answered, "Did something happen? What's going on?"

Frina frowned and looked at Andrel for help. It was hard for her to pursue such a line of questioning. It went against everything she wanted to believe about the normal world.

"It's just very coincidental to us that you should show up twice now on a Saturday in an area of town you only visit during the work week, just in time to give me a ride somewhere," Andrel said.

Bill stared at him, waiting for the green light.

"I was just helping out a buddy. If you wanted to walk, you could have said so."

"I'm serious, Bill. Something's going on. We're just starting to figure it out. But if I find out that you knew about it all along and didn't say anything, you'll wish you'd never taken the job in the mail room with me."

"Hey, man, I don't know what the hell you're talking about, but your attitude is really starting to piss me off. You got a problem with me, come out and say it!"

Andrel was silent for a moment. Bill sounded serious. Perhaps, they were mistaken. He was ready to apologize when Frina spoke again softly, her voice barely above a whisper.

"Listen, Angel. Can you hear it?"

He didn't know what she meant at first and looked back at her. She had her eyes closed. He closed his eyes and listened. He tried to focus like he did when he lost himself in blank thoughts. He heard the rain hitting the roof of the car. He heard his own breathing. He heard Frina's breathing. Then, he heard Bill's breathing, slow and steady, as if he weren't upset at all. Suddenly, he knew for sure that Bill knew more than he was letting on. He looked at him and spoke slowly and quietly.

"I can hear your breathing. When I concentrate, I can't hear anything at all but my own footsteps. Today, I also heard Frina's footsteps. And just now, I heard your breathing. I'm not sure what this means, but I feel that it means something important. Tell me."

Bill gripped the steering wheel and continued driving. He stared through the windshield as if he were looking at something a hundred miles away.

"I could have gotten in a lot of trouble. But I was sure that someone needed to keep a close eye on you. I knew that someday you'd be needed again. I knew I had to be there when that day came, to be the one to wake you up. I just didn't know it would be so soon."

He pulled over and let his arms fall to his sides. He chuckled a little and went on.

"This can't be right. This shouldn't be happening. Not now. Not yet."

"What are you talking about, Bill? What's happening?" Andrel said through gritted teeth.

Bill looked up at him and said earnestly, "She thought she was doing the right thing. You can't blame her for this. No one else agreed with her, but we all knew that something had to be done. She acted alone, but she had your best interests at heart. She had all of our best interests at heart. Don't be angry with her."

"Who? And what did this person do?"

"All in good time, my friend. You need to rest. And get indoors. The sun is setting. I promise it will all make sense. Just give me some time."

Andrel looked back at Frina. She hesitated and then nodded. They got out of the car, walked to the front door of the apartment, and waved at Bill's car. He drove off, leaving them alone for the night.

Dystra sat, lost in thought, by Chyrit's side. The sun was setting, but she couldn't leave for her usual hunt. Chyrit was sleeping still, feverishly. Dystra tried to reach her mind, but she was still struggling with the physical effects of being hit with a direct force of energy powerful enough to kill a Peace Warrior. She was quite lucky to still be in this world. Dystra knew this because the force field that surrounded that apartment was of her own making. She had tried to convince herself when they first came across it that it was only something created by another Peace Warrior, one with abilities and powers equal to her own. But after what happened to Chyrit, she couldn't deny it any longer. There was no mistaking the energy levels. The feel of the whole spell had her name written on it, almost tangibly in her mind. This was her fault. She should have known he was here. She should have sensed it months ago. How could she make such a mistake after everything they'd been through, after all the work she'd put into making sure that they would all be safe? And what would she do now?

Chyrit began to stir, and Dystra laid one hand on her shoulder and whispered, "Shh, be still. You're safe."

Chyrit opened her eyes and said clearly, "It's him, isn't it? They're here."

Dystra nodded and lowered her gaze. She felt ashamed. It was all her fault. Everything was in jeopardy now, including the lives of the people she cared about. But Chyrit would have nothing to do with moping. She lifted herself on one elbow and reached for Dystra's face with her other hand. She lifted Dystra's chin with one finger and said, "Let's fix it."

"How?"

"You know how. It's time."

"It can't be!" Dystra shook her head wildly. "I hid them so well. Even I didn't know where they were. We can't do this! Not now! They have to stay hidden!"

"You can't protect them forever. He can hold his own, and he must. I know he's the one you're worried about the most. You did this for him. But it's time for him to wake up now."

"You're in no condition to do anything yet."

"I will be. Tomorrow."

Chyrit relaxed, laying back down on the grass, and closed her eyes. Her fever seemed to have broken, and she was resting peacefully now. Dystra floated out from under the bridge in a seated position and looked up at the first few stars of the night, peering through the vanishing clouds. There were no eyes watching them right now. For the first time, she started thinking about what the demons were up to. Something was definitely in the works on their side of things, and she didn't want to be caught unawares by whatever it was.

Andrel sat up in bed and stared into the darkness of the bedroom. Frina was sleeping next to him. He was still tired, but something had woken him. A dream, perhaps. He listened for the rain, but all he heard was the wind. He wondered if everything that had happened that day had been real. None of it made sense, but he remembered it all clearly. He wanted to talk about it some more; he wanted to ask Bill more questions. But it was late, and he was probably the only person in the whole city who was awake. He listened to the wind for a while, until he couldn't hear it anymore. Then, all he could hear was his own breathing and Frina's. He reached into his mind and his memory, searching for a sign of clarity, something to help him make sense of the day's events. He hoped to unlock whatever had taken his memories from him, the ones from years before, the ones that Bill seemed to know about, the ones that he could feel in the back of his mind like forgotten boxes in the back of a closet. His head began to throb, but he pressed on. He could feel himself getting closer to some kind of breakthrough. He could almost see it.

A flash of light tore through his mind, and he fell back onto the pillows, panting. He'd almost had it, but he lost his concentration at the last minute. It was still night. He closed his eyes and fell into a deep sleep.

"This had better be good. I'm still trying to make up for that Peace Warrior's interruption."

"I think it is good. I was thinking about what had happened to her friend, the one who was hurt by an energy shield. What if the energy was protecting something? It would have to be something powerful, something useful."

"Like?"

"Like him. We haven't been able to find him. And all reports indicate that neither have they. It might be possible that he's been here, under our noses, the whole time."

"That would be good news for us. Especially with one Peace Warrior out of commission for the time being. Find him! I want him dead before sunrise."

"This is bad. This is really bad."

"Calm down, Kam. We can handle it."

"You're kidding me, right? This is Andrel we're talking about. If we don't already have hordes of demons on their way right now to kill us all, he'll take us out himself when he realizes that we've been party to keeping him in the dark all this time."

Bill sat down on a chair in the dining room and ran a hand through his sandy-colored hair. He sighed, "Maybe it's not as bad as all that."

"What did I just say? This is Andrel we're talking about."

Kam sat next to Bill and put his head in his hands. His black hair fell over his red eyes, and he started mumbling, "What will we do?" over and over again.

"He won't kill us. Andrel wouldn't do that. He'll realize that we had nothing to do with that spell. And he'll realize that Dystra was only trying to protect him and the Prince. After we lost the Princess, we..."

Bill stopped himself. They never spoke of the Princess. It was too painful a memory to dredge up. He turned his mind to lighter things.

"Anyway, it'll be good to get back in the game. Let me tell you, passing as a human day after boring day is immensely frustrating. And I'll be glad to see Chyrit again. Hopefully, she'll heal up quick."

He winked, and Kam laughed and said, "Things won't be exactly the same."

"Close enough for me. Maybe this time, I'll have a shot."

"At getting your skull punctured, maybe."

The two of them laughed and then sat in silence.

"What's next?" Kam asked, interrupting the mood that seemed to be settling in.

"I quit my job, I guess," Bill chuckled. "No sense continuing the charade now. Say good-bye to Bill and welcome back to Dor."

The shape seemed shapeless at first. It slid across the ground, pausing at the doorstep. It could go no further. But it had a plan. It rose up and formed into a humanoid shape. It opened its mouth and shouted, "Andrel! Andrel, it's time! I have to tell you something important!"

"Bill?" a muffled voice responded.

The shape waited, holding its form. The door opened, and Andrel stepped out into the night. The shape attacked, pulling him away from the safety of his home. It smothered him with darkness, pressing him onto the ground. He fought, but his human strength was no match for the otherworldly strength of the shape. It was certain of its victory. He had nearly stopped breathing.

Suddenly, a bright light pierced the night, not from the sky or a window, but from beneath the black shape. It came from him. It glowed brighter and brighter, pushing away the shadows. The shape focused all of its energy on containing its quarry, desperate not to lose the battle. But the light was too strong. The shape was required to retreat quickly into the night to avoid complete obliteration. Andrel lay on the ground, breathing heavily. He quickly lost consciousness and didn't notice the light that was slowly receding back into his body.

Dystra woke suddenly and said breathlessly, "Andrel!" She knew that something had happened just then. She looked to the horizon. The sun was not even a hazy glow yet. It was still night. But she could wait no longer. She flew up and over the city. She passed all the usual places where she hunted the demons and went straight to his apartment. There, she found him on the ground outside, passed out. She checked his energy to make sure he was okay and carried him inside. She laid him gently on the bed next to Frina and glanced around.

"So this is how you've been living," she whispered. "You haven't made many connections to the world. I guess you couldn't. I guess it was too much to expect of a great warrior like you. What about the Prince? No, not much there, either."

She sighed and said, "Perhaps, Chyrit was right. You need us as much as we need you. I'll be back."

She left the apartment, checking the integrity of the spell before she left, and went back to the bridge. Chyrit was still resting peacefully. Dystra lay down next to her and closed her eyes, although she didn't really sleep until the sun touched the horizon.

Andrel woke late in the morning. He had never slept in before, and it left him feeling dazed. He checked his alarm clock; it seemed to be working, but it hadn't gone off. At least, he didn't remember turning it off. He went to the closet and stood there, staring at his clothes. It was Sunday. He usually wore something casual on Sunday. But he didn't know what this Sunday would involve. Things were different today. His routine was broken. He had always thought he would like his routine to be broken. For some reason, this wasn't as relaxing as he had hoped. He reached for a t-shirt and a pair of jeans and threw them on the bed. He stalked to the bathroom and turned on the shower. He stepped inside, hoping to numb the confusion and the headache. He expected to be caught up in the usual blankness that enveloped him in the shower. Instead, all he could do was think about yesterday.

When he stepped out of the shower, Frina was standing in the bathroom doorway. She looked lost and frightened. Andrel stepped toward her and offered his arms for a hug. She looked away and whispered, "It's not all right. Nothing's all right. We're not normal."

"What's normal?" Andrel chuckled, trying to calm her. He couldn't bear it if she started crying again. "Maybe we're a different kind of normal. Who knows what's really right in this world anyway?"

She seemed to consider what he was saying and turned away, mumbling, "My head hurts. I keep seeing things, pictures…"

Andrel made up his mind then that he would find out what was going on and see what he could do about fixing it. He dressed hurriedly and made sure Frina would be all right for a while so that he could go out and find Bill.

As soon as he stepped outside, he felt that something was different. It was a bright, sunny day. Birds were twittering, dogs were barking. Everything was perfect. But there were no people. No one was passing him on the sidewalk. No one was out mowing their lawn or weeding their garden. No one was driving their car down the street. The vehicles were all parked at the side of the road. There weren't even any taxis to flag down. Andrel ran through the alley to the other side of the apartment building and knocked on his neighbor's door. Mr. Anderson was always up early, usually watching television. There was no answer, though. Andrel banged on the door and called out, "Mr. Anderson! It's me, Andrel! Mr. Anderson!"

After a minute of banging on the door, Andrel went to the window and peered inside. Mr. Anderson was sitting in his comfy armchair, holding a bowl of cereal, watching the television. Andrel banged on the window and shouted again, but Mr. Anderson didn't move. He was breathing; Andrel could see his chest rise and fall. But he didn't look at the window or say anything at all. He looked pale and tired, as if he'd been up all night, doing something strenuous.

Andrel thought about going back to his apartment and telling Frina what was going on, but he hated to concern her with it when he didn't even know what was really going on. He walked around the block, taking the long way back to his apartment. He hoped to see someone, but everyone was indoors. When he looked through windows, he saw the same scene over and over again: people seated in front of their television sets, looking pale and tired, not moving or speaking. When he got back to his own door, he leaned against it and stayed there for a long time, wondering what he should do.

"We have to find them. This is a disaster!"

Kam flew around buildings, zipping down streets, with Dor close behind him.

"I know," Dor said breathlessly. "Let's split up. You look for Dystra and Chyrit; I'll round up Andrel and the Prince."

They flew off in separate directions, and Dor went straight to Andrel's apartment. He found him there, leaning against the front door. He hid around the corner and abolished his shield before stepping out into the open. Andrel stared at him with a combination of desperation and anger.

"Do you know anything about this?" he said slowly.

Dor sighed and answered, "Yes. I had hoped to get to you before you saw anything. I've been trying to reintroduce you to everything slowly. Don't want you to get cosmic whiplash or anything, huh?" He chuckled a bit, but Andrel frowned at him. He looked down and continued, "I guess we don't have a choice now, do we? You're gonna have to get back on your feet fast. We don't have the luxury of time anymore. The easiest and fastest way would be to get Dystra to break the memory spell. So let's go meet up with her."

At the sound of the name, Andrel felt a stab of pain in his skull. He knew it from somewhere, and it hurt when he tried to remember. He shook his head and asked, "What about Frina? I can't leave her here."

"Of course not," Dor said. "She has to come with us. Dys will have to break the spells on her, too."

"I'll get her," Andrel mumbled.

He turned and went inside. Frina was in the kitchen, cleaning up the breakfast dishes. She looked at him and knew right away that they had to leave. She followed him outside and said, "Hello, Bill. Where's your car?"

"We're not taking the car," he responded. "It's too slow. And call me Dor. It's my real name."

"It suits you better," she nodded.

"Hang on," he said, stepping between them and grabbing them each by the waist. "This may be a little weird for you at first."

They floated up into the air, and Frina squealed, grabbing onto Dor. Andrel stared at the ground below and then up into the sky. He looked at Dor as they began to move forward. Dor was focused on flying through the city. He took the shortest route possible, passing through buildings and trees. Frina closed her eyes when they passed through the first building and again when they passed through the first tree. When they headed for another building, she closed her eyes tightly and didn't open them again until they reached the park. Kam was floating above the bridge at the far end, waiting for them to spot him.

"They were here, but they've left," he said without a glance at Andrel or Frina.

"We have to find the...," Dor started, but he was interrupted by the sound of cracking concrete.

A cement statue about thirty feet tall and twenty feet away was falling over. It was a giraffe, and it was leaning in their direction. Kam flew in one direction, and Dor took Andrel and Frina in the other. He set them down under some trees a few yards away, told them to wait there, and flew toward the statue, which hit the ground with a thundering noise and crushed the wooden bridge. Two people were standing behind the base of the former statue, a man and a woman. They were smirking.

"So you found them," shouted the man. "Impressive."

"And we found you," shouted the woman. "Our boss will find that even more impressive."

"Who is your boss, and why should he care?" Dor shouted back. "The war has been over for some time. What we do now should be no concern of yours."

"The war is never over," said the woman. "You know that, I'm sure."

"I know you two, don't I?" Kam shouted as he came over the mound of concrete that now lay on the ground. "Yes, you were two of our top informants in the enemy army! Dreck and Sorn!"

The woman chuckled and said, "We're mercenaries for hire now. We can't help it if our new boss is interested in our old boss."

"What does your new boss want with these two?" Dor asked, waving a hand toward Andrel and Frina.

"That's for us to know, right, Dreck?" the woman said.

"And for you to find out," the man bowed slightly toward Dor and Kam. "That's right, Sorn. But it looks like they want to find out very badly."

Both of them whipped out swords and flew toward Dor and Kam. The battle was chaotic. Andrel tried to keep track of everyone, but they flew around so quickly that it was hard to tell who was hitting whom the hardest. He tried to turn Frina away from the fight, but she insisted on watching. It seemed like it would go on forever, and Andrel wasn't sure who would win.

"Are you sure you're up to this?"

"There's no time to worry about that. We have to find them."

Dystra knew that Chyrit was right. They had to find Andrel and Frina. The demons were making their move, and it was going to be big, she could feel it. And Andrel's trail was difficult to track. His scent was fading fast, as if he were moving too quickly for them to follow. At first, she worried that he might have been captured, but she knew that the demons wouldn't simply take him. They would kill him on sight. She didn't know what had happened to him, but they had to find him. They couldn't stop to worry about themselves.

"There!" Chyrit pulled up abruptly, and Dystra peered in the direction she was pointing. Several energy fields were clashing, exploding against each other. They flew as quickly as they could to the battlefield.

Two of their comrades were fighting two demons in the park, near the bridge, which was now buried under the rubble of a collapsed statue. Andrel and Frina were taking shelter under some nearby trees.

"You have to tell him," Chyrit said. "There's no more time. He'll need to know now."

Dystra nodded and bit her lower lip. She knew Chyrit was right, as much as she wished it weren't true.

"I can't just tell him, though," she said. "I'll have to undo the spells. I'll erase the memory spell first."

Dystra flew down to Andrel and Frina, while Chyrit went to join the fray. Andrel and Frina both stared at her in confusion. They both put a hand to their head, as if looking at her was painful.

"I do hope you won't be too angry with me," Dystra spoke slowly.

"Who...who are you?" Andrel stammered. "For that matter, who am I? Will you tell me what's going on around here and who I was a year ago?"

"So you've figured out that much already?" Dystra smiled a little. "Well, you'll know the rest soon enough. It's time."

She raised one hand, and a bright light passed through their minds. The park faded away, the sounds of the battle vanished, and they found themselves alone in their memories.

Chyrit didn't even glance back at Dystra as they separated. She knew her friend would handle the situation, as little as she wanted to. She looked at the fighters ahead of her. She recognized them immediately. She also saw that Kam and Dor were nearly drained of energy. They were holding their ground, but it wouldn't last much longer. They'd used all their strength fighting, but the demons were still going strong. Something was wrong. She looked around them and saw the lines of energy flowing into them. She knew something had to be done.

Chyrit landed right in the center of the battle, held out both arms, and shouted, "Stop!" Kam and Dor paused, panting heavily. Dreck and Sorn stood ready to pounce at a moment's notice.

"Are you afraid your friends will die?" Dreck hissed. "You're right, but there's nothing you can do about it."

"I want to know what you're doing here and what you want," Chyrit said. "Does it have anything to do with the power lines you have running to the power station?" She hoped she could buy enough time for her to figure out what to do about their apparently unlimited energy supply. She had to cut them off from it somehow.

"Why, Chyrit, I'm insulted," said Sorn in mock innocence. "You know that we are the top spies of both your world and ours. Do you really think we would fall for any stupid tricks or just tell you everything we know? It would be downright unprofessional, don't you think?"

"I don't care," Chyrit said through her teeth. "You're traitors. You've always been traitors, and you always will be. So why don't you just tell me what I want to know, and you can be on your way?"

"She's stalling for some reason," Dreck whispered to Sorn.

Sorn nodded and whispered back, "And I've had enough of it."

Chyrit knew then that she had hit on something. The power lines running into the abandoned power station had to be an integral part of their plan somehow. Suddenly, she knew what it was. The pieces fell into place in her mind, and she knew what she had to do.

Dreck and Sorn lunged at her in the same instant, but she flew up out of their way and rushed past them to the power lines that ran between wooden poles around the edge of the park. Dor caught Dreck and struggled to hold him back. Kam took on Sorn. Chyrit reached the power lines, raised her sword above her head, and slashed downward, cutting the cords cleanly. The two sides whipped about for a moment, spitting sparks everywhere. Finally, they lay limp against their poles, and Chyrit turned in triumph. Dreck and Sorn were boiling over with anger. She flew back to them, and they attacked her together, completely synchronized. They swung their swords in perfect rhythm with each other, but she dodged each one. She knew their moves too well. She cut Dreck across the throat with her sword and grabbed Sorn by her long black hair, swinging her around and throwing her into the ground without letting go. Dreck dropped, unable to fly, and lay on the grass, clutching at his throat and gasping for air.

Kam and Dor stood guard over the dying demon, while Chyrit dealt with Sorn. Sorn would not be so easily subdued. She twisted Chyrit's arm and escaped her grasp. She threw her weight into a blow with her sword that knocked Chyrit back a few feet. She screamed furiously and cast an energy bolt into Chyrit's stomach. Reeling, Chyrit focused her energy into a beam, aimed it at Sorn's forehead and shot her at nearly point-blank range. The demon fell, unconscious.

Chyrit floated down to the ground and turned to Dreck. He was fading quickly, but she wasn't finished with him.

"I think I know what's going on around here," she spoke softly but harshly, leaning down so that he could hear her. "But there's more that I don't know about yet. Tell me everything, or I'll rip your mind out of your body so fast that you'll fly right past the burial world."

She laid one hand on his forehead and closed her eyes. She had a good idea what she was looking for. Just when she thought she had found it, right before she could get a good look at it, something threw her out of his mind with such force that she fell back onto the ground, her chest aching from the blow.

"He's the top spy in all the universe," commented Dor. "I don't think anyone could crack that mind of his."

"Then I'll crack his skull!" Chyrit shouted.

She knelt next to Dreck, raised her right arm behind her head, and brought it down with all the strength she had left onto his head. The force she used would have been enough to turn a human skull into powder. As it was, Dreck's head was flattened into the ground.

"You squished him!" Dor said in shock.

"I still have Sorn," Chyrit grimaced and sat back. She was exhausted now, too. She had used too much energy in one hit. Sorn would have to wait.

Dor sat beside her and said, "So...how've you been? I've missed you."

"Still the same old Dor, huh?" Chyrit chuckled.

"Would you have me any other way?" Dor grinned.

"What makes you think I'd have you at all?"

Kam laughed out loud, and Dor glared at him until he walked away. He stood beside Sorn to guard her and looked up at Dystra and the others. Andrel and Frina were standing in front of her, staring blankly into the air. The three of them were perfectly still.

"It's almost time," Kam whispered to himself.

"We don't have time for this! They're becoming a bigger nuisance than we can afford right now."

"I know. They seem to have discovered our plan, as well."

"They can't possibly know everything! Still, they may suspect. Take care of it."

"I don't suppose we could move the schedule up and do it tonight?"

"Perhaps. I only need a few more things. You take care of our little problem; do whatever it takes. I'll handle the rest myself."

"Yes, my lord."

"They're coming."

"I feel it, too. Dozens of them."

Chyrit and Dor rose to their feet and looked around them. The sun was beginning to set, but the sky was even darker than it should be at this hour. She flew to Dystra's side.

"I know," Dystra said before Chyrit could speak. "But I'm not finished. The spell hasn't completely worn off yet. We need more time."

"We don't have any more," Dor said, joining them under the trees. "They're here."

They watched as the shadows dropped to the ground from nowhere, filling the park with their darkness and energy. The demons materialized and looked back at them from more than a few dozen dark faces, their red eyes glowing with malevolence. It was an army.

"There must be nearly a hundred," Chyrit whispered.

"More than we can handle in our present condition," replied Dystra.

"We have no choice," Dor said, motioning to Kam.

Kam left Sorn and started toward them, but he was intercepted by a demon that flew down from somewhere in the sky and blocked his path. Everyone stood perfectly still. The demons seemed to be waiting for something.

Then, all at once, they attacked. The Warriors were abruptly separated, unable to hold back the sudden onslaught. Chyrit, Dor, and Kam were too weakened by their previous battle to fight off the number of demons that they could usually handle easily on their own, and the number of enemies they were facing now greatly exceeded that of the typical battle. Even Dystra, who was still in top form, was overwhelmed. In attempting to protect Andrel and Frina, she found herself at a disadvantage, unable to protect even herself. She was quickly jumped by several demons and dragged away. She saw Andrel and Frina being surrounded by hungry-looking creatures and screamed at the top of her lungs, fighting her captors. But she'd lost her spear, and there were simply too many of them.

Suddenly, a bright light appeared in the midst of the dark demons. It grew brighter and larger, spreading across the park until it was lit up like daytime. The demons cowered in fear, and Dystra squinted, trying to see the source of the illumination. A man flew up into the air and dove down again like a hawk, zipping past several demons, who immediately dropped onto the ground, dead.

Dystra knew the mysterious man was a Peace Warrior. No other warrior could move like that or fly so quickly. She watched in awe as he dashed among their enemies, killing them with barely a touch. The way he moved reminded her of something she hadn't seen in such a long time, and she knew then who he was.

He flew around the park quicker than anyone could follow, until each and every demon was dead. The park looked like a real battlefield now, covered in the bodies of the dead. Chyrit, Dor, and Kam, stared at the Warrior as he floated down to the ground. Dystra glanced around and started to run toward him. The look on his face made her stop short, though. It was like pure sadness and overwhelming anger, at the same time. He flew straight at Kam, inches above the ground, and thrust a sword through his heart.

Dystra froze. She couldn't move. She couldn't breathe. She couldn't even think. Chyrit grabbed hold of Kam, trying to prop him up, but he was already gone. The Warrior withdrew his sword. Dor shouted, "No!" and ran to his friend. Frina burst into tears behind Dystra. Kam's body slipped from Chyrit's grasp and she stared at it and at the bright red blood on her hands. She looked up at the Warrior and mouthed, "Why?" But the sound didn't escape her lips.

"What has happened to him?" Dystra thought to herself finally. "Did I do something wrong? What's wrong with him?!"

Barely fifteen minutes earlier, Andrel and Frina had both found themselves living once again in a part of their lives that they had left far behind them and forgotten about, although through no efforts of their own. The last year of their lives melted away in their minds as they once more experienced everything that had happened in their former existences.

They saw their families and friends. They grew up. They watched the years roll by. They spoke in a long forgotten language that felt as familiar to them as their own thoughts. They learned and grew. They remembered things that they never thought they would forget. They re-learned all there was to know about the world of the Peace Warriors, their world. They remembered what they had known about the world of the demons. And they remembered what they had thought about the world of the humans. It was like experiencing a third life, after going through it all at once, and then living as humans during their second lives. From the day of their births, they saw it all and remembered everything.

And then came the great war.

"This peace has always threatened to fall apart. We shouldn't be surprised that the demons have attacked our homeworld, Kara."

"Of course not, Landil. But we should be shocked and dismayed by how poorly we've responded. We weren't prepared."

"And why should we have been? The people were comfortable with the peace they had experienced for the last 500 years."

"If you don't mind…"

Kara and Landil both turned to look at the new speaker. They were dressed in their fighting suits, their swords at their sides. Kara's light brown hair was swept up in a tight ponytail, and Landil's long, sharp nose was blackened slightly by the grease he had been using to shine his spear.

Andrel stepped into the conference room and glanced briefly at the other people sitting around the table. They were all Peace Warriors, conferring amongst themselves about what should be done now that a state of war had been declared. He was a young fighter as compared to the rest of them, but he had quickly earned respect all over the realm by handling the initial demon attack with skill and cunning. No one had been sent to the burial world that day, and it was he who had made sure of that. They were all waiting to hear what he had to say.

162

"If you don't mind, I have a few words for you that may help clear things up a bit. Yes, the people are used to the peace of the last 500 years. So we were ill-prepared for this attack. But they will prepare. We must be ready to lead them. The Prince and Princess are still too young to lead the people into a war. We, as Peace Warriors, are needed now more than ever. The seers are predicting the largest fight since the worlds were separated. We must stand together. We will triumph! The demons will not touch our world again!"

The room erupted in applause, as every member of the council stood and cheered him on. Even Kara and Landil, the group's most well-known malcontents, smiled and nodded. It took a few minutes for everyone to settle down. Then, Andrel sat at the table with them, and they discussed their strategy for hours into the night.

As Andrel left the council chambers, he glanced across the walkway at the Warrior training grounds. Chyrit and Dystra were practicing furiously. They were a match for each other, and their skills improved every day. He walked over to join them.

"Hey, Andrel!" shouted Dor from the other side of the training grounds. He ran to meet him, and Kam was following close behind. A few others exited a nearby building and came over to greet him. Soon, a little group had gathered at the edge of the grounds, talking excitedly and clapping Andrel on the back.

"Congratulations, Andrel, on catching the eye of the council," said a young woman enviously as she looked him over.

"Thank you, Grint," Andrel nodded politely.

"You deserve it. You have talent beyond any of us," Dystra's eyes were shining as she looked at him.

Andrel blushed slightly. Dystra's affections for him were greatly appreciated, but he hadn't yet had the opportunity to tell her that he returned them. Chyrit chuckled behind her and said, "Yeah, good going, big guy. You'll make us all look like snails if you keep this up."

She laughed good-naturedly, and everyone joined in. She enjoyed giving him a hard time, but she never meant anything mean by it. Dor made a joke about Chyrit being jealous and offered to take the place in her life that she meant for Andrel. Chyrit told him he wouldn't fit in Andrel's place, and Dor and Kam began arguing about which one of them might be able to change her mind. Andrel pulled Dystra aside, and they began whispering to each other, out of earshot of the others.

"Break it up!" said a voice.

Everyone looked up, startled. A young man walked into the moonlight and laughed, "I didn't mean you folks. I was talking to the two lovebirds over there."

Dystra's face turned a dark shade of red, and Andrel cleared his throat and approached the newcomer.

"Good welcome to you too, Kiri," he smiled. "What brings you here tonight?"

"To see my friends, of course," Kiri winked at him. "And give a few of them a hard time."

"Hey, that's my job," Chyrit protested, grinning.

"There's enough for the both of us," Kiri threw one arm around her. She shrugged it off and turned back to Dor and Kam, who were calling each other names and asking the others around them to judge which of them was the better Warrior.

"What is it really, friend?" Andrel asked in a lowered tone of voice, leading Kiri back through the entrance to the training grounds and onto the stone walkway. Dystra followed them, and Kiri glanced back at her.

"Anything you feel I need to know, you can feel free to say in front of Dystra," Andrel told him. "I would trust her with the lives of everyone in our world."

"I'm sorry, friend," Kiri sighed. "I should know that you would not associate with anyone of an unsavory character. I just can't help being a bit suspicious of everyone. Especially after what I learned tonight from two of our informants."

"Which ones?"

"The best of the best. They came to us, and they've been well-paid for everything they've given us since. And their latest news is…disturbing, to say the least."

"Tell me," Andrel said in his most serious tone of voice.

Kiri glanced around them and stopped in the middle of the walkway. He leaned close to Andrel, and Dystra followed suit. His voice dropped to less than a whisper.

"Some of our people, not many, just a few, but some of them have…changed sides."

"What do you mean?" Dystra asked.

"Traitors. They've begun working for the demons. Not even for pay. And they haven't left our world. They remain here, to see what damage they can do to us from the inside."

The three of them were silent for a moment, then Andrel asked the question that was on Dystra's mind, as well.

"Can you trust this information? Can you trust the source, considering what they are?"

"They've never given us false information. Why would they? We pay them more than they could make in a hundred years in their own world. Besides, they have an interest in how this war turns out. If we lose, they lose their income, and they lose their protection. Any number of the demon lords would be interested in separating their heads from their bodies as payback for the information they've had stolen from them."

"If we are to assume it is true, there must be a way to find these people," Andrel said thoughtfully. "They must have had contact with the demon world at some point."

"Yes, but we don't know when or where or how. It could have been at the point of entry for last week's demon attack. It could have been 500 years ago, when the peace treaty was brokered. They could have been waiting for a very long time. This rebellion against the treaty could have been in the planning stages for centuries. Our informants are working on learning more. I just want you to be extra careful. You are a bigger threat to them than most of our Warriors combined, and our biggest asset."

"We must all be careful," Andrel nodded at Dystra. "Should we tell the others?"

"We don't know who else we can trust."

"Surely, you don't think any of the Peace Warriors could be a part of this!"

"It's possible. We can't take the chance. Tell only those whom you trust explicitly. No one outside of your circle of friends can suspect what we may know. These are dangerous times. There are rumors that....Well, I will tell you more when I'm certain. I must go now. We all have work to do. Good luck, friends, and be safe."

He walked off into the shadows of the night. Andrel and Dystra stood in the middle of the walkway, deep in thought. Finally, Dystra spoke.

"I will tell Chyrit. I trust her as much as you trust me. And she can help us keep an eye out for any sign of treachery."

"I agree," Andrel sighed and turned to walk back to the training grounds. "But we should tell no one else. I am thinking now that perhaps we should wait. We can't be certain that these informants are trustworthy. They are demons themselves, after all. And it might put our friends in danger to be in possession of this information, even if it is true."

"All right, but Dor and Kam and Raya could be of use to us once we've verified the information. I'm sure we can trust them, as well."

"I wonder if the Prince and Princess have been told."

"I doubt it."

"Well," Andrel paused at the edge of the training grounds. "What was I saying before all of this interrupted us?"

"Something about my feelings for you? Or was it your feelings for me?" Dystra laughed and winked at him.

Andrel smiled and said, "When this is all over, I'll finish that conversation with you. And we'll live happily ever after, right?"

Dystra nodded, put her arms around his waist, and snuggled close to him. He held her for a minute before leaving. She watched him go down the walkway and turn a corner, and then she went back to the training grounds. Chyrit was waiting for her.

"What was that all about?"

"I'll tell you later," Dystra whispered.

They resumed their practice, finishing the night's work.

The next few nights found Andrel in conference with the high council again and again. They valued his opinion on everything from the formation of troops to enemy intelligence. Tensions were building all over the city. The demons attempted another attack one night, and two citizens were killed in the ensuing battle. One other was missing, and Dystra wondered if he might have been an enemy informant. She had seen no signs of suspicious behavior from anyone, but the demons were becoming bolder and stronger, and she couldn't afford to doubt that they might also be getting smarter and more devious. Why anyone in her world would want to join the demons was unfathomable to her, but these were dark times, indeed.

Dystra and Chyrit trained harder than ever, preparing for the inevitable moment when their skills would be needed. The Peace Warriors were kept busy, patrolling the walkways and recruiting new Warriors. There was still no official word from council on what their plans were. The Warriors were ready to strike; they were all tired of waiting for the demons to attack.

"I've heard rumors that the council is waiting for approval from the Prince and Princess," said Chyrit one afternoon, as she and Dystra walked along their designated patrol route.

"For what? The council has been put in charge of the war because the royal twins are too young to handle it themselves. What would they need approval for?"

"They're nearly 100, you know. Why does everyone say they're too young?"

"They've never been in a battle. What could they know of war?"

"You've only been in two real battles."

"I've been training my whole life," Dystra pouted. She sighed and continued, "But I suppose you're right. Everyone just considers them young. They do look very young. But still…why would the council be waiting for their approval on anything now?"

"The rumor is that something so big is happening that they won't go ahead with any major plans without running it by the Prince and Princess first. They know that the demons are planning something too big for us to deal with."

"What could be too big for the Peace Warriors to deal with?"

"I mean, it's too big for us to get into without royal approval."

"You mean, something diplomatic? I hate politics. I just want to kick their asses and send them to the burial world."

Chyrit laughed and said, "Me too, but there are other considerations. Especially, if…" she glanced around and lowered her voice, "…if there are spies among us."

Dystra thought about this and nodded slowly. "You're right. I just want this war to be over as quickly as possible. I'm not thinking clearly."

"Well, you'd better get back on track. We may be needed when the big plan is set off."

"You will be needed," said a third voice from behind them. They spun around and saw Andrel coming to join them. "I have news for the two of you. And a mission."

Dystra and Chyrit both smiled and nodded. They were more than ready.

"You know what to do?"

Dystra and Chyrit both nodded. They were nervous and excited. Their biggest mission lay before them, and it was to be conducted in enemy territory.

"You know that this may be…a suicide mission?" Andrel stared into Dystra's eyes sorrowfully. He wouldn't ask her to stay. After all, she was the best Warrior for the job. But he almost wished that she would turn down the mission.

"I know," she gave him a small smile. "It has to be done, and I have to do it. We have to."

"As long as you're sure that Sir Powl was poisoned," Chyrit spoke up.

"There's no mistaking the symptoms," Andrel sighed. "Somehow, someone slipped him a very powerful poison spell. He's dying. The healers have been working on him since last night, but they're losing the battle. Already, the force field around our world is weakening. Without his magic, its power could be cut in half. It's obvious that this was done by a spy, and a spy in a very powerful position. They would have to have been able to get close enough to the council without attracting too much attention."

"It had to be someone in the Peace Warriors," Dystra looked away. "Someone high enough in level to walk into the council chambers without anyone getting suspicious."

"That still leaves several dozen suspects," Chyrit said thoughtfully. "I could name every one of them, and I wouldn't expect betrayal from any of them."

"That's why we must act quickly," Andrel continued. "We can't afford to wait for another attack on a council member. Or maybe even…the royal palace. It's time to take the fight to them. I have official approval for this mission only from the council. They were hoping to wait for word from the Prince and Princess, but there's no time for any more deliberations."

"Let's go," Dystra prepared her magic dust, and Chyrit did the same.

"Be careful," Andrel said.

Dystra nodded, and she and Chyrit tossed the dust over their own heads and spoke the incantation together. They disappeared, and Andrel sat down in the dark, empty training building to wait for word from them.

Dystra found herself in a dark hallway. It was empty of life, but she could feel the dark energy flowing through the walls. She was in the right place. No one in the Peace Warriors had ever tried a direct raid on the enemy stronghold. It was well-known that the demons would detect an energy signature that didn't match their own immediately. But times were desperate. Chyrit would serve as the distraction, appearing in a different location, near the enemy barracks. Hopefully, by the time that the demons realized that there was another intruder nearby, Dystra would have completed her mission. It was simple: Find the leader and bring him back if possible, kill him if not.

She tip-toed down the hallway, checking empty rooms, until she came to a wide staircase. The stairs were as red as blood, and the upper level looked as black as tar. She heard voices outside a nearby window. Someone was shouting orders, and she suspected that Chyrit was still making her presence known. But there was an army here, and even Chyrit couldn't keep the show going forever. Dystra ran up the stairs, trying to keep her energy levels low.

At the top of the stairs were two doors. One felt empty, the other felt dark. She knew there were enemy soldiers behind the door, but she had to open it and go through. The demon lord was most likely on the other side as well. She raised her energy levels and her hand and sent a blast of light into the door. It splintered into a hundred pieces, and two guards on the other side were thrown into the room. She flew in and skewered one guard on her spear. The other attacked her with an electric whip. It latched onto her wrist, sending a shock of magic electricity into her arm. She nearly dropped her weapon, but she was determined to finish her mission. She took her spear with her other hand and threw it at the demon. It hit him in the forehead, embedding itself in his skull. He dropped, and the whip went slack.

No sooner had Dystra retrieved her spear, however, than two more guards entered the room from a door on the opposite side. Bolts of lightning flew from their fingers, but she dodged each one. She flew around the walls and knocked one guard into a table full of dark bottles and books. A few of the bottles broke open and ignited the table. The guard was hit by an explosive flame and disintegrated. Meanwhile, Dystra was struggling with the other guard. He shoved her into a bookcase, but she managed to push him back and hit him with a quick bolt of energy that knocked him into the fire. He too vanished in an explosion of fire and ash.

Dystra turned to peer through the doorway that the guards had come through. The room beyond was dark, but she could sense a great power lying in wait there. She stepped cautiously into the room. The door flew shut behind her, held by a dark power. As her eyes adjusted to the darkness, she saw a demon standing just twenty feet away, sneering at her. He was looking directly at her, but he did not appear ready to fight. And his energy levels were not nearly as high as that which she had sensed before. She glanced at the wall behind him and gasped, horrified. A large demon was encased in a transparent structure inside the wall. He seemed to be sleeping, but his energy was incredibly powerful. He seemed almost to be of an entirely different breed of demon.

"He is your destiny," the demon standing between them whispered. "He is the destiny of your people, and of mine. He will destroy you and make us the greatest power in the universes."

He chuckled madly and held up a small book and began to read out of it. The words were from an ancient language that Dystra didn't recognize, but she could guess their intent. Energy was flowing from the demon to the creature encased in the wall. He was trying to wake it.

"So that's your big plan," Dystra said, flying toward the demon.

She was suddenly repelled by a force field. The demon laughed, spoke a few more words from the book, and fell to the floor. The force field vanished. The demon was dead. He had poured the last of his energy into the spell he was casting. It didn't seem to have done any good. The demonic creature in the wall didn't stir. Dystra considered her options. This crazy demon couldn't have been the leader she was looking for. She doubted it was the creature in the wall, either. But she couldn't leave the room without knowing what had been going on.

There was a noise of doors being thrown open downstairs, and an influx of dark energy filled the house. Chyrit had lost the demon army's attention. Either she had been forced to retreat, or....Dystra didn't want to think about the second possibility. Anyway, she was out of time.

Against her better judgement, she left the demon in the wall and headed into the next room through another doorway in the back. Another demon stood next to a throne. He was wearing a long purple robe and looked at her with an expression of disgust.

"You're the demon king, I suppose," Dystra said, holding her spear at the ready.

The demon sneered and said in a low voice, "You will call me master when we have conquered your world. I am Dracma, lord of this stronghold, and of the rebellion against your weak and pathetic people."

"You are a demon, and you will die before you lay a finger on my world!" Dystra shouted.

She flew toward him, and he met her halfway. Their weapons clashed, and she felt his power filling the room. His energy surged through his sword, pushing her spear back. She began to lose her footing. She could sense more demons entering the room behind her. She threw a blast of energy into his chest, and he reeled backwards. She swept his sword aside with her spear, tossing a handful of dust over his head with her other hand. She began to speak the incantation, but he rushed at her, knocking her over. He pinned her to the floor and blasted her directly in the face with a bolt of energy. She found herself losing consciousness. He hit her again with another bolt. She reached out with her mind, using the last of her energy to contact Andrel.

"Can you see it, Andrel? Can you see what I've learned?"

"I can see it, Dystra. Come home now."

"I...can't..."

She passed out, knowing that her mission had been successful.

Andrel stood before what remained of the council. With Lord Powl dead, their spirits were low. But they still had a city to defend, and he had to report what Dystra had learned. The Prince and Princess had come to hear about it, too. They sat at the other end of the table, their personal guards behind them. Andrel nodded at Raya, who stood behind the Princess. She had only recently received the promotion, when the Princess' first personal guard had died defending the palace against the attack that took place right after Dystra and Chyrit had left for the demon world. Four guards and six civilians had died today, and the demons had nearly made it to the royal twins.

"You all know what the plan was. Chyrit transported to the enemy barracks to act as a decoy, while Dystra went inside the stronghold itself to seek out the leader and perhaps learn their plans," Andrel began. "Chyrit held the army's attention, killing more than a few of their soldiers, for nearly ten minutes. She was forced to retreat when the demons surrounded her. She sustained major wounds and is currently recovering with the healers."

"Wouldn't a larger force have been a better distraction?" asked the Princess.

"Yes, but we would have guaranteed ourselves several losses, and the main point of the mission was to gather information from the leader," Andrel nodded. "Dystra made it all the way into the center of the stronghold. She killed several guards and witnessed the death of a demon sorcerer. He appeared to be casting a spell that required his own energies to complete. He was trying to resurrect a creature that

I'm sure you're all familiar with. Only Peace Warriors at the council level and members of the royal family know the stories of this entity."

The council began to look around at each other nervously.

The Prince spoke softly but clearly, "Aekris."

The room was filled with a heavy silence, until Andrel spoke again.

"Yes, Aekris. He has been nothing but legend for thousands of years. But the demons are attempting to resurrect him now. If they had succeeded today, we would not be standing here now. His power is legendary. We all have reason to fear it. Luckily, the demon who gave his life in the attempt does not appear to have succeeded. For whatever reason, we have a little more time to work with. Not much, of course, for the force field protecting our world has been greatly weakened by the loss of Lord Powl."

"As have we all," said Landil quietly.

Everyone bowed their heads for a moment, and Andrel went on, "Dystra ran out of time to investigate the matter, but she went on to track down the leader of the demon armies. His name is Dracma. They fought, but he was too strong for her. She didn't realize it, but her energy levels had been weakened by her encounter with the demon sorcerer. The spell he was casting leeched energy from her body, as well. At the last moment, before losing consciousness, she contacted me to show me what she had seen."

"We've lost Dystra?" said Kara in shock. "That...that can't be."

"No, don't worry, I retrieved her myself," Andrel answered her. "She is recovering with the healers, as well."

"Wasn't that risky?" asked Kor, one of the other council members. "You're our best Peace Warrior. We can't have you conducting unauthorized rescue missions without backup."

"I had to. Dystra is as important to us as I am. I didn't go to the demon world; I only conducted a remote casting. The dust was already on her from when she threw it at Dracma. I tried to take him as well, but he was ready for that and managed to escape."

"But they will no doubt know who and where you are now," said Kara.

"That doesn't matter so much anymore. I've no doubt that the next step to this war will be full and open combat. I strongly suggest we evacuate all civilians not trained for fighting immediately."

"How do you know they'll still attack the city?" asked the Prince.

"Because they want you and your sister, Prince. I'm not sure why, but I have a suspicion that it has something to do with their resurrection plans for Aekris."

"The council could rule in our absence," said the Princess. "Wouldn't they want to get to the council, too?"

"Yes, but not for the same reason. As long as the council exists, the force field exists. They want the council dead to open our world to invasion. You and your brother they want for something else, perhaps even alive."

"That would explain why their attacks haven't killed as many people as they could have," said Kara. "They don't want the Prince and Princess to get killed in the crossfire."

"Should they be evacuated?" asked Raya.

"No, the demons will find them anywhere. Their energy signatures are unique."

"Someday they will be the most powerful of us all," nodded Landil.

"Not for a very long time," Andrel said. "Still, you'd think that would be reason enough for the demons to want them dead. Whatever they're planning for them must be very big."

"Might they still succeed in raising their champion?" asked the Princess.

"Yes, they may. We know too little about the ritual to say when or how, but it's a possibility we must prepare for. We need to strike, quickly. We have no time for further debate or discussion. Evacuate the city, and gather all forces here at the council building. The Prince and Princess will stay here in the conference room, guarded by as many of our best Warriors as we can spare. I will stand at the main doors myself. I believe the demons will attack within the next day. We must move quickly."

The city was ghost-like with the walkways and buildings all empty. Andrel took one last look around and turned to take up his post at the main doors of the council building. It had taken nearly all day to get everyone out of the city who didn't need to be there. The Prince and Princess were secure in the conference room, along with the council. Dystra and Chyrit had recovered enough to stand guard just outside the room. In fact, they had insisted on it. Andrel could feel the tension all around him. He could sense the demons coming.

The rips in the force field appeared all at once. They were barely large enough for two demons to step through at the same time, but there were enough of them to admit several dozen into the city within the first few seconds of the invasion. The battle began immediately, and Andrel found himself throwing demons from the steps of the building, only to have two more rush upon him. He could hear the clash of weapons behind him. There was a crack of thunder, and he saw Lord Dracma himself step through into their world. Andrel threw aside the demons he had been battling and approached their leader. Dracma laughed and met him with his sword drawn.

Meanwhile, inside the conference room, the Prince and the Princess were greatly distressed. Raya tried to calm them, but the Princess shouted, "I can feel it! They're reaching out for me! They're trying to take my energy!"

Raya could see nothing in the room that would be a danger to the Princess, but she didn't doubt the girl's senses.

"We have to move them!" she yelled.

Dystra and Chyrit ran into the room, and Dystra said, "It's madness out there. We wouldn't be able to get them two feet without being attacked."

"We will fight with you then," said the Princess.

She drew her sword and marched to the doorway. The Prince followed her closely, clutching his own sword nervously. Dystra and Raya ran in front of them and peered into the hallway. They went through the building in this manner, Dystra and Raya guarding the front of the party, and Chyrit and Sol, the Prince's personal guard, guarding the rear. The council stayed behind with their own guards. They didn't know where they were going; they followed the Princess' suggestions.

In one of the back hallways of the building, they were ambushed by eight demons. The Princess found herself fighting one on her own, and so did the Prince. She finished off her opponent fairly quickly and turned to help her brother. By the time all of the demons had been vanquished, the Prince was clutching an injury on his shoulder. The group rushed into a room and closed the door.

"Do you feel safer here, Princess?" Raya asked, adding with a wink, "I'll go out and beat down a few more demons if you want to move again."

"No," the Princess shook her head. "It's not safe here. But we can rest for a moment."

"Where will we go, Princess?" asked Dystra.

"Away from him," she answered.

Andrel swung his sword for the final blow and severed Dracma's head from his body. A demon who must have been his second in command tried to hit Andrel and shouted, "You will not defeat us! I will lead my people to victory!"

Andrel was ready to fight him, but he sensed that he was needed elsewhere. He flew around the building to the back. A few Warriors were battling a small group of demons. He flew past them, through the back door, and into a small room, where he found the Prince and Princess lying on the floor. Dystra, Chyrit, Raya, and Sol were surrounding them, trying frantically to wake them up.

Dystra looked up at Andrel and said, "The Princess said that someone was trying to take her energy. We ran here, looking for a safe place, and they passed out!"

"Nowhere is safe from me," said a thundering voice from behind Andrel.

Everyone turned and stared in shock and fear at the demon that floated in through the doorway. He wore a smirk on his face and a long black robe over his body. He paused in front of Andrel, and Andrel said, "Aekris. You have been awakened."

Kiri burst into the conference room and shouted, "They're here! You need to move! Now!"

"Where would you have us go?" Landil asked.

"Yes, we will stand and fight," said Kara. "We are Peace Warriors."

"They have breached the inner circle of the building," said Kiri, looking around. "Where are the Prince and Princess?"

"The Princess didn't feel safe here," answered Landil. "She and the others left to find shelter elsewhere."

Without a word, Kiri flew back through the door, leaving the council and their guards to defend themselves. He felt around for the royal twins' trail and followed it to the back of the building, pushing aside demons and skirting battles along the way. He spotted Dor and Kam fighting a couple of demons outside as he passed a rear window and entered a small room.

A demon of unusual size and strength stood in the room with its back to him. He could sense the others, including Andrel, on the other side, but he couldn't see them. He didn't stop to consider who the demon might be. He raised his sword against it. But before he could bring it down onto the creature's head, it turned and looked at him. The look in its eyes was fierce and cold. It froze him in an instant, and he knew what the creature was. He barely managed a whisper, "Aekris."

Andrel held his sword in front of him with both hands and said, "You will not harm the Prince and the Princess."

Aekris laughed and said, "I already have. That's not why I'm here."

"You will not defeat us," said Dystra, standing up. She raised her spear, and behind her, Chyrit stood and held out her sword.

"You will not exist when I am through with your world," said Aekris with an evil grin. "But I am not in this room to kill you."

"Then why **are** you here?" asked Raya. She stood and drew her magic bow, fitting it with an armor-piercing arrow, and added, "To get your carcass fried into a pile of ash?"

"Of course not," Aekris laughed. "To take your power."

He raised one hand, and an invisible force began to pull on them. They all began to feel weaker, and Dystra found herself sinking to the floor. Andrel pulled away, trying to stave off the power that was leeching the energy right out of their bodies. He gasped for air and stumbled forward, reaching for Aekris' arm. He summoned all his strength and threw what force he could muster into an energy bolt. He directed it into the hand from which the magnetic force was emanating.

When the blast hit him, Aekris cried out in rage and withdrew the force he was using to suck in their energies. He turned his attention to Andrel and drew a massive sword that was thicker than his arm and nearly as long as his body. Andrel found himself recovering quickly and flew at Aekris, slashing with his sword.

Dystra stood and turned to Chyrit, saying, "We've got to get the Prince and Princess out of here!"

"They're blocking the door, and there's no other way out!" said Sol, still kneeling next to the royal twins.

"Then we'll make a way out," Dystra said through gritted teeth. She turned to a wall that stood between them and the outside and held out both hands. She gathered her energy and directed it into a blast that ripped through the wall like it was paper. A gaping hole stood before them, and the area outside appeared clear. Dystra fell to her knees, choking. Chyrit helped her up and led the way through the hole in the wall, leaving Andrel to deal with Aekris.

At that moment, Kiri found himself unfrozen. He had seen everything, although he had been unable to move. He swung his sword at Aekris, but the demon blocked it with one arm, while fighting off Andrel with his sword. He laughed and spoke a word of the demon language. A blast of dark energy flew from his mouth and surrounded the two Warriors. Neither was able to see or hear what was happening around them. Aekris picked them both up and threw them out the door. They crashed through the back wall, flying straight into Dor and Kam, who had just finished defeating a couple of lesser demons. They helped their fellow fighters to their feet and stood ready to attack Aekris.

"Is this who I think it is?" Dor asked in awe.

"I'm afraid so," Andrel answered, panting. "We must keep him in check, give the Prince and Princess time to escape."

The four of them flew at Aekris, surrounding him. He grinned and spoke a few more words in his own language.

Dystra and Chyrit managed to lead the others away from the building. As they left the sounds of battle behind, they slowed their pace, panting for breath and trying to regain the energy levels they had before Aekris' attack. The Prince and Princess seemed especially weakened.

"If only we were older," lamented the Princess, "we would be strong enough to fight this demon."

"Save your breath," said Chyrit. "We've got to get as far away as possible."

"They'll find us," said the Prince. "They'll find us wherever we go!" His voice was shaking, and the Princess put one arm around his shoulders to comfort him.

The sky darkened, and they were suddenly surrounded by shadows. Demons formed all around them as far as they could see.

"They've come after us," whispered the Prince.

"They won't get you," said Dystra, raising her spear.

Andrel stood over Dor's unconscious form, blocking him from Aekris' view. Kam hovered in the air above their heads, ready to strike, and Kiri stood on the ground behind Aekris, nursing a severe cut in his abdomen. They were losing the battle, that much was clear. Aekris had not even broken a sweat, and they were badly injured in one way or another. Andrel had tried every attack he knew, except for one. It was extremely dangerous, but he had no other choice.

"Keep him busy!" he shouted, dashing to the side. He closed his eyes and concentrated, directing his energy into Aekris' mind. He pushed his way in, fighting with every ounce of his strength. He didn't hear Kiri cry out in pain when Aekris broke his sword arm and threw him into a wall, knocking him out. He didn't see Aekris turn toward him and raise his sword. He found himself unable to breathe as he fought to get close to the innermost part of Aekris' mind. Just when he felt he couldn't fight any longer, he spoke the ancient words and shot a powerful beam of light and energy from his mind into Aekris'. The demon howled, and Andrel fell to the ground, exhausted. He had survived the ordeal but couldn't move his body. He was completely drained.

Aekris fell to his knees and said slowly, "You...how could you know...the ancient art of mind light?! No one knows that! I...killed the last of your kind who knew it...millennia ago. How?!"

Andrel chuckled to himself. The demon still had the strength to speak, and that was not good. It would seem that his efforts had been futile. However, he had managed to weaken him.

Kam flew down to the ground and stood next to Aekris.

"He's greatly weakened, and so are you," Kam said. "Should I finish him off for you?"

Andrel tried to speak, but he couldn't make the words come out of his mouth.

"Please do," Aekris said in a low growl.

For a moment, Andrel was confused. He watched Kam step toward him and raise his sword. Then, he knew. He found the strength to speak. His voice was less than a whisper.

"Traitor. It was you."

Kam didn't say a word. He brought down his sword, intending to cut Andrel's head off. But Andrel managed to roll away at the last moment. He began crawling, and Kam laughed. He sounded like a demon. He followed on foot, in no hurry to catch him.

Andrel heard something in his mind. The sound of a battle came to him. He heard Dystra fighting for her life and the Prince screaming. He found he had the strength to stand and fly. He left Kam behind, and Kam ran back to his demon master to help him to his feet.

Andrel found the others less than a block from the council building. They were surrounded by a demon army. Although they had slain many demons, many more were attacking them on all sides. Sol lay dead at the Prince's feet, and the Princess and Raya were fighting around him, trying to protect him. His sword was nowhere to be seen, but blood was pouring from his head. Dystra and Chyrit were fighting next to them. Chyrit was holding her own, but Dystra seemed horribly drained, as if she could barely stand. The demons flew over and around, slashing and attacking. They wouldn't last much longer. Andrel was weak, but he had to do something. Seeing Dystra fighting for her life made him feel stronger. He put his hands together, palms facing the battle, and shot a wide beam of energy at everyone below him. It wasn't enough to kill many demons, but it was light enough not to hurt his friends. It weakened the demons, and they fell more quickly and easily. Unfortunately, it had weakened Andrel as well. He floated gently to the ground, landing next to Dystra, and raised his sword to fight.

The demon horde was still somewhat overwhelming, but they did manage to clear out a small circle around their group. The demons hesitated, knowing that Andrel had been the one who hit them from above. They didn't know how badly weakened he was. Dystra hugged him, and Raya said, "Where've you been? We could have used you ten minutes ago."

Before he could answer, a hush feel over the demon army, and they backed away, making a path that stretched from the Warriors' circle to the edge of the army. There, walking toward them, was Aekris. He looked very angry.

"Where's your little henchboy?" Andrel shouted angrily. "I wanted to give that traitor a piece of my mind!"

"I wouldn't expect you to have any mind left," said Aekris menacingly. He reached the edge of their little circle, and Raya stood in front of him.

"You won't touch them!" she said.

Aekris waved his hand, and Raya flew through the air, hitting the ground in front of a few demon soldiers, who grabbed her and held her back.

The Princess stood in front of her brother and backed away. Dystra and Chyrit ran in front of them and stood ready to fight. They knew they were fighting a losing battle, but they had to give it their best. Aekris waved his hand again, and they too went flying through the air. The demons tried to hold them down, but Dystra broke free and ran back to stand with the Princess.

"Fool!" yelled Aekris in a voice that shook the ground. "Do you want to die so soon? I'm not interested in you! It's the twins I want. And then that one." He pointed at Andrel and added, "He has more power than your kind deserve."

"You mean, I have more power than you can handle," Andrel coughed out.

"Perhaps," Aekris grinned, "if you were at your full strength. In any case, you must die. I will content myself with the energy I stole from you before."

There was a wave of gathering energy that swept over the demon army, and Aekris raised one hand in preparation. His palm was pointed directly at Dystra. Andrel flew quickly to stand between them, just as the energy bolt flashed from Aekris' palm. It struck Andrel instead, and he fell to the ground.

"No! Andrel!" Dystra shouted at the top of her lungs. She knelt beside him and put her hands over his head. He was losing consciousness fast. She pushed some of her own energy into his body, trying to keep him alive and awake.

"All the easier for me," chuckled Aekris. He pointed his hands at Dystra and Andrel.

Chyrit was struggling against the demons, but one of them hit her with a powerful blast of energy in the back of her head, and she passed out. In the commotion, Raya managed to slip away from her captors. Quicker than the eye, she nocked an arrow in her bow and let it fly straight into Aekris' ear. He howled with pain and ripped it out again.

"We will handle these lesser creatures," said a voice from behind Aekris. It was the demon who had served as Dracma's second in command.

Aekris nodded his assent, and the new demon leader turned to his troops. Before he could say a word, however, an army of Peace Warriors swooped down upon them. As the battle raged around them, Andrel and his friends found themselves once more alone with Aekris. Bright red blood trickled from his left ear, and he was panting heavily. But his energy level was still higher than theirs on a normal day, when they weren't mortally wounded.

"Help me," whispered Andrel to Dystra. She leaned down to listen to him, and he added, "We must defeat him."

Dystra nodded and helped him stand up. They put their hands together and leaned on each other, joining their energies together to power them up for one final blow. Aekris threw his arms to the side, sending out a huge wave of energy that knocked the Princess and the Prince onto the ground and sent Raya flying again. But Dystra and

Andrel stood together, facing him. They chanted a few words of power and raised their arms together. A powerful bolt of light flew from their hands and went right through Aekris' body. For an instant, he hovered slightly above the ground, a look of shock on his face. Then he fell. His energy level dropped to nothing, and a wail of fear and grief went up from some of the demons around them.

The new demon leader stepped forward, as Dystra and Andrel fell to the ground. Their energy levels were down to nothing, as well. They had even less left than they had thought they had when Aekris had attacked them a second time. Raya was scrambling to her feet, and she flew to their side, ready to protect them. The Prince and Princess lay behind them, staying low to avoid attracting attention. Chyrit was still unconscious a few feet away.

"Y-you…you…defeated…Aekris!" the demon lord howled. "H-how?! How could you?! He is…invincible!"

"Guess not," Raya quipped, nocking another arrow on her bow.

"We are not finished," he seethed. "There will be another window of opportunity. Time is on our side. Aekris will be reborn!"

"Not if I can help it," she said, letting her arrow fly. It hit him in the eye, and he reeled backward. But he didn't stop, or even fall to the ground.

"He will need energy," he mumbled. "He will need something to sustain him."

He looked up with a crazed look in his remaining eye and dashed quickly around Raya and the others, trying to get to the Prince and Princess. Raya followed him and slashed at him with her sword. He called for help, and two demons rushed at her, pushing her away from their leader. He raised his arms into the air and shouted, "I, Grim, will lead the demons to victory. It may not be today, but we will prevail, and I will raise our master once again to rule over the universes!"

There was a crash of thunder, and Grim tossed a handful of dark powder at the royal twins. The Princess rose to her feet and raised her sword against him, but it was already too late. The portal was beginning to open. It looked like a black hole, and it whipped the air around them into a frenzy. The Prince began to slide into it, snatching at the dirt, screaming for help. The Princess fought against the wind and grabbed his arm, pulling him back from the portal. But she found that she couldn't save both herself and her brother. In desperation, she summoned her strength and threw the Prince away from her. The effort pushed her farther back toward the portal, and she could no longer fight it. It pulled her in, and she vanished into the blackness.

"Princess!" Raya screamed, running toward the portal.

She dove straight into it and vanished. The portal closed, and Grim sank to his knees.

"Perhaps, one will be enough," he mumbled.

The Prince looked around frantically for any help that could be had.

"I cannot open the portal again, but I can ensure that you do not make my job any harder than it has to be," Grim said in a sinister tone of voice. He rose to his feet and flew over to the Prince. He pulled a dagger from his belt and grabbed the Prince's arm.

"No!" came a shout. Landil and Kara came running from the council building, their weapons drawn. The Prince took advantage of the sudden distraction, grabbed Grim's dagger, and turned it on him. Grim reeled backwards, the arrow in his eye and the dagger in his stomach. He spoke a few words of incantation and vanished.

Landil gasped, and the Prince turned to see that the body of Aekris had disappeared, as well. Chyrit began to wake up, and Kara knelt next to Dystra and Andrel.

"They need a healer, quickly," she said.

Landil turned to go back to the council building and saw a new wave of demon soldiers approaching them down the walkway.

"There's no time," he said. "We must get the Prince to safety."

"There's nowhere to go," Kara stood and pointed down the other side of the walkway. "They have us surrounded."

The two Warriors stood with the Prince between them, and Chyrit floated over to them to stand at their side. She was dizzy, but there was no time to recover.

"Wait," a voice said in Chyrit's mind. It was Dystra, trying to speak to her. She closed her eyes and listened.

"There are too many. We must go somewhere else. Andrel has used the last of his strength, but if I have a chance to recover, we may stand a better chance. We must save the Prince, too. We will have to concede the battle in order to fight the war another day. Help me."

Chyrit sat next to Dystra and laid her hands over her friend's forehead. She gave all that remained of her energy and slumped to the ground next to her. Dystra pulled herself up into a sitting position and began chanting words that no one had heard in their world since Aekris' day. She tossed a handful of dust over Andrel's body.

"What will you do?" she heard Chyrit ask in her mind.

"Protect him," she answered in kind, "for the rest of eternity if necessary."

"Send the Prince with him. He will protect the Prince."

"I will transform him to hide him among the humans. He may not know how to protect anyone but himself."

"Try."

"There may be a way. Humans protect those they love. I will cast a spell."

"It will take many spells."

"I must try. The demons will find them anywhere. I must try to be clever."

Kara left the Prince's side and looked at Dystra.

"I know what you're doing," she said. "I'll help. Landil, help us."

She gave her hand to Dystra to hold, and Landil joined them to offer his energy as well, laying his hand on Kara's shoulder. Dystra drew on their power and fed it into the spells she was casting. Kara held out her hand to the Prince, and he came to join them. Dystra threw more dust over the Prince and continued her chanting. Andrel and the Prince began to glow. The light became too bright for anyone to look at. Everyone closed their eyes, and when they opened them, Andrel and the Prince were gone.

Andrel awoke from his dream, his memories restored. He found himself surrounded once more by an army of demons, as if he had picked up right where he left off. His energy levels began to rise, and he floated up into the sky. He had failed, and his people had suffered. He was angry. But strangely, he was at peace as well, for the first time in a year. He knew who he was; he remembered where he belonged; he no longer felt a wrongness in the world around him. His mind no longer drifted and questioned. He was focused and calm. He was himself again, a Peace Warrior, fighting for his people, for his friends. It was as though a veil had been lifted from his eyes, and the dreams that had kept him in the dark were gone. In the sunlight of the truth, he could see everything clearly once more. His love for Dystra, his anger with the demons, his fear for his homeworld, it was all a part of him once more, and he felt whole again. He felt himself transforming, inside and out, his powers returning. It was time to finish what he had begun a lifetime ago.

Andrel targeted every demon in the vicinity, flying among them, practically on auto-pilot. When he was finished, he looked around and saw Kam standing among the others. The memory of Kam's betrayal now fresh in his mind, he flew straight at him and shoved his sword through his body. He heard the others cry out in confusion and fear, but he was certain he had done the right thing. He looked to Dystra and saw the worry in her eyes.

"I will explain," he assured her. "You must trust me. Please."

She nodded slowly, uncertainly. Frina walked out from behind her and said, "Andrel has a reason, I'm sure."

"The transformation spell!" Dystra said, suddenly remembering. "How...how did you break through it, Andrel?"

"I felt I was needed," he smiled at her, and she knew that he was himself.

She turned to Frina, tossed some magic dust over her, and spoke the words to undo the spell. There was a bright glow that blotted Frina from their sight for a moment, and when it faded, the Prince was standing before them.

"It feels strange to be back in my own body," he commented, looking himself over. He was wearing the same clothes, but his hair was short again. He looked up at Andrel and grimaced. "I remember everything."

"Don't be embarrassed," Andrel smiled, bowing slightly to his Prince. "We were different people, in a way. Especially you. You were completely different. And I understand why Dystra did what she did to us. It worked; we were both hidden and protected. Think of it no more. You are our Prince."

"You did your best to take care of the Prince," Dystra nodded to Andrel. "There was no way it could have lasted forever. I know that now. I tried to send you on with the best and strongest of my spells. I couldn't track you past the point where you entered the human world; otherwise, I would have followed and bolstered your protections."

"You did your best, as well," Andrel said. "I'm healed now, better than you could have imagined. I'm ready."

"Wait!" shouted Dor. "What about Kam?! He was no demon, and you killed him!"

He flew at Andrel in a rage, but Andrel sidestepped him and grabbed him by the wrists.

"He was as good as demon, my friend. I'm sorry, I truly am. He betrayed us all. Let me tell you."

They all sat down beneath the trees, and Andrel told them of Kam's betrayal of their people and how he served the demon Aekris. Dor was particularly distraught, as they had been best friends for more than a century.

"How long do you suppose…?" he began, choking on the words.

"I don't know," Andrel sighed sadly. "We may never know. But now, you all must tell me what has transpired since the Prince and I were sent here to the human world. Was the demon army defeated?"

Dystra looked down, unable to say the words. She didn't have the heart to tell him what had happened to their world, how it had changed.

"Well, you could say that you won," said a voice from the field of dead demons. "But considering the consequences, many would say that you lost."

Sorn stood awkwardly, leaning on her sword. She took a few steps toward them, saying, "I won't fight with the great Andrel here. So don't worry about me starting anything. But I don't think I could go back to my Lord Grim now, either. You defeated an entire army. If I went back alive, he would suspect me of subterfuge. I'll stay with you if you don't mind. Perhaps, I can even be of assistance. I know more about their plans than anyone."

Andrel considered and then nodded, saying, "Come and sit. Tell me what happened after I was sent here. If you tell the truth, I will let you live."

Dystra shifted uncomfortably. She determined to listen to the story and make sure that Sorn told it correctly. Sorn sat down a few paces from the rest of them, facing Andrel, and began to speak.

"Once you and the Prince were gone, Landil and Kara tried to protect Dystra and Chyrit here, who were completely drained of power. They gave their lives to keep your little friends safe, and the only reason it made any difference at all is that Dor and Kiri regained consciousness and managed to drag themselves to the battle to help. The Peace Warriors were eventually successful in fighting back the demon army, but there were few of your soldiers remaining who were in any condition to continue defending the council building. Many were dead. The city was in a state of shock and mourning. Without the royal twins, the council fell into disuse, a depressed bunch of old fighters, useless for anything. The battle had been technically won, but your people were defeated in spirit. They had lost you, their greatest warrior, and the new leader of the demons had escaped. They had lost the Prince and Princess, and the demons had promised the return of the great Aekris.

"The people continued in this manner for some time. Civilians returned to the city to rebuild it, but it was never the same. Finally, a small group of Warriors, led by Kiri, voted to reinstate the council, without the royal family to guide them, and strengthen the force field around their world. They elected new council members, as many of the old ones had died in the battle, and a new sort of government arose. Dystra and Chyrit tried to convince the new council that vigilance should be their trademark, but the council felt that chasing down the shadows of the demons was a waste of time. They had no interest in trying to track down the Prince or their best warrior, either. They knew that the human world was a mass of chaos and that Dystra's spells would hide the two of you very well. And they were afraid. Afraid of going out and finding demons, afraid they would lose this time.

"So Dystra and Chyrit left on their own. They weren't hoping to find you so much as just to make sure the demons didn't. Dystra knew they'd be looking. She was determined to prevent a demon invasion of the human world. When she arrived on the human world, she found that they had already begun. The demons attacked humans by night, feeding off of their energy, what pitiful energies they had. She and Chyrit began their nightly patrols of the human city that seemed to be the main focus of the demons' attacks – this city. They had no other choice, really. Demons were not supposed to be in the human world, let alone killing humans before their allotted time. The balance of the universes was shifting, and even the humans were beginning to notice it. They began to develop a sense that something was wrong. The veil that separated their minds from ours in the great cosmos began to tear. Dystra and Chyrit worked to return everything to its proper order. They killed demons and saved humans and maintained the veil to the best of their abilities. They succeeded for the most part, but it was obvious that even one demon could alter the balance and throw the human world into turmoil.

"Meanwhile, Dor and Kam decided amongst themselves to follow them and help if they could. Dor felt that someday you would be needed, and it might be up to him to reawaken you. He was concerned that Dystra would be too worried about protecting you to do what had to be done. He stumbled upon you, Andrel, by accident and recognized you by your face, which had remained unchanged. After that, he took on a human guise to keep an eye on you, with Kam waiting for a signal. Of course, what he was really waiting for was the return of the time of ascension, the final opportunity for the ritual to be completed and Aekris to be raised from his slumber permanently. If the ritual is completed, he will become invincible and immortal. Kam hoped to find you and kill you in your human form before that happened in order to make sure you wouldn't interfere with their plans again.

"Still, the rest of your fellow Peace Warriors remain in your world, some out of cowardice and some in an attempt to fix what is wrong with the others. If the demons were to attack now, especially with Aekris at the front of the invasion force, your people wouldn't stand a chance. They are as good as dead, unless something changes."

For a moment, everyone sat in silence, mourning the downfall of their great people. Then, the Prince spoke.

"What about my sister? What happened to her? Can we save her?"

Sorn laughed and said, "Sorry, kid, but your sister's gone for good."

"Dead?" the Prince asked, tears welling up in his eyes.

"Not dead, exactly," Sorn said thoughtfully. "At least, not completely. You see, Grim sent her into the world of Aekris, the inner world that his mind inhabits when he is not inhabiting his physical body. There, he feeds on her power, sustaining himself until it is time for him to arise again. She is unreachable."

"Raya followed her," Dystra said quietly. "What happened to her? Grim didn't want her."

"She's there," Sorn nodded. "Perhaps with the Princess. Perhaps somewhere else in that world. Aekris may be feeding off of her, as well. It's hard to say."

"If it's another world, we should be able to get into it," said Chyrit.

Sorn laughed again and told her, "Certainly. But you'd never be able to get out again, let alone rescue your precious Princess."

"Can the ritual be completed without both my sister and I?" the Prince asked.

Everyone stared at him in silence. They all knew what he was really asking.

"Of course," Sorn waved a hand at him in dismissal. "Don't be ridiculous. All it takes is one of royal blood. Twin power would have just increased his strength."

"We don't want that," the Prince said softly.

"Don't even think about it," Dystra told him sternly. "You're needed here. I have an idea that may yet save the Princess. Andrel has been inside Aekris' mind; he has some experience with it. With my spells and power and a little help from everyone else, I think we can throw the Princess a lifeline and get her out of there."

Sorn laughed scornfully, but Dystra ignored her. She looked around at everyone, and they all nodded in turn, even the Prince.

"Let's go somewhere else," said Chyrit. "We can't stay here too much longer. We need to rest up, and Grim is bound to send more demons after us."

They all stood up and started walking toward the street. Andrel suddenly remembered what had been happening in the city and turned to face Sorn.

"What are your people doing to the humans here? Where is everyone?"

"Don't you know? We're draining them of their energy in a more efficient manner – through the electrical lines. It feeds us, and it feeds Aekris, bolstering his power until it is time for him to awaken."

"Ugh," said the Prince. "I can't believe our people once came from common ancestors. Feeding off of innocent lower creatures such as the humans! You should be beaten within an inch of your life."

"Careful, kid," Sorn grinned. "You're starting to sound like a Warrior. That might attract some…unwanted attention."

She winked and put one hand on her hip, where her sword used to hang. Andrel gave her a dark look, and they all walked on.

They ended up going to Dor's apartment. They rested for an hour, but they knew they couldn't wait any longer if they were going to attempt the rescue operation before the demons did anything else. Sorn assured them that the demons couldn't do anything for another two days, but Dystra still didn't trust her word. In fact, she insisted on tying Sorn securely to a kitchen chair before they began their casting.

Andrel, the Prince, Dystra, Chyrit, and Dor sat in a circle, joined hands, and chanted the words that Dystra had recited while they were resting. A black dot appeared in the air in the center of their circle. It began to grow. They felt themselves being pulled toward it. But they had anchored themselves to the human world with a special binding spell, so the pull they felt was not on their bodies; it was on their minds and spirits. They created a mental chain, joining their spiritual hands together so that one of them could venture into the portal and be pulled back at a moment's notice by the others. Chyrit remained close to the human world; tied strongly to her body, she would serve as a sturdy anchor for the spirit chain. She held the Prince, who held Dor, who held Andrel, who held Dystra.

Dystra found herself floating in a void. Blackness surrounded her, and she called out, "Princess! Raya!"

There was a flash, and suddenly, she was standing on a walkway. Around the stone walkway, grass was blowing in a slight breeze. There was nothing else as far as she could see. A fog rolled in, and air around her gained a pinkish sort of hue. She started walking and called out again, "Princess! Raya!"

There was another flash, and she seemed to be standing on a floating platform of rock and dirt. Other platforms hovered around her, and in the distance, she could see something, or someone, lying on one of them. She jumped lightly from one platform to another, some as small as her foot, others as large as a building. When she reached the platform she had glimpsed from afar, she found two people on it. The Princess was lying down, apparently unconscious. Raya knelt next to her, shaking her gently.

"Wake up, Princess! Please, wake up!"

She was in tears. Dystra knelt next to her and put one hand on her shoulder.

"She won't wake up," Raya sniffed.

"Give her strength," Dystra whispered. She couldn't do it herself; her body was too far away, and her strength was focused on holding on to Andrel so that she didn't float off into oblivion.

Raya nodded and laid one hand on the Princess' forehead. She closed her eyes and concentrated. Dystra waited. The Princess didn't stir. Something was holding her down. She felt outwards and noticed the dark energy that surrounded the Princess. She had to break its hold on her.

Dystra mumbled a few words and sent out just a bit of energy. She hoped it would be enough.

The Princess began to stir. She took a deep breath and turned her head. Her eyes opened slowly, and Raya gasped.

"Princess! Use your strength! You have the power!"

The Princess focused her energies to fight off the dark power that held her back. She took Raya's hand, and Raya followed Dystra away from the platform.

The air began to vibrate. Everything got darker. The platforms began to crumble. A voice rose up in an ear-shattering roar. Dystra tugged on Raya's mind and led her back to her entry point.

Chyrit felt them returning and pulled on the spirit chain, bringing everyone back to their bodies, one by one. Once Dystra was through the portal, Raya tumbled after her, pulling the Princess with her. The portal closed.

"Sister!" the Prince shouted, grabbing the Princess in a tight hug.

She laughed and said, "I felt you helping me, brother. I felt everyone helping me. I couldn't have summoned my strength without you. But I still feel so weak."

"Aekris has taken a lot of your energy," said Chyrit.

"How long were we there?" asked Raya. "Sometimes, it felt like a few moments, and sometimes, it felt like an eternity."

"One year, in human time," answered Dystra.

"I searched for the Princess for a long time," Raya continued. "When I found her, she was asleep, and I couldn't wake her. I sat by her side for an even longer time. Thank you all. Thank you for not giving up on us."

"There's no time for any tearful reunions now," said Andrel gravely. "We have work to do. We must prepare for the battle ahead. We must prevent Aekris from rising again."

The city was dark and empty. A voice spoke from somewhere in the shadows above, and another voice answered it.

"We've lost the Princess. We cannot complete the ritual without her."

"What will we do?"

"We will find her. Send every available scout. The ritual must be completed tonight. The Warrior has been awakened. Time has run out."

"We should call for help," said Dor. "They would come, I'm sure of it."

"And so would the demons, most likely," said Chyrit.

"We may have to chance it," Dystra told her. "We don't know how many more demons Grim can summon. He could bring the whole demon world down upon us."

"Will they come? Are you sure?" the Prince asked.

"Kiri will come," Andrel spoke softly. "And a few others, at least."

They sat around the table in Dor's apartment, planning their strike against the demon forces.

"It's important to cut off their supply of energy," Chyrit insisted.

"I agree," Andrel nodded. "We must destroy that power plant. They'll have it heavily guarded now. We'll have to be careful."

"I could get in easily," said Sorn from the other side of the room.

"Why would you help us?" asked Dystra distrustfully. "You don't usually involve yourself this closely in things. Isn't that why you're an intelligence agent?"

"It's obvious you people are going to win," Sorn sneered. "I want to be on the winning side. I'm always on the winning side."

"I'm not so sure that we'll win," said the Princess in a whisper.

Raya, who sat next to her, lay a hand on the Princess' shoulder, brushing aside her long brown hair, and said, "We will. It won't be like last time. We'll be ready for them."

"Sorn will infiltrate the power plant and destroy their main power lines," Andrel began. "That will be the signal for us to invade. I will take the front of the building. Dystra will take the rear. We will take out as many demons as possible. We will be the distraction, and Chyrit will make her way into the building to destroy the rest of the power lines, find Sorn, and get back out."

"What will we do?" the Princess asked.

"Stay here and continue to recover. You'll need your strength later."

"Sounds like a plan," Sorn grinned.

Everyone got into position around the dark power plant. Sorn walked right through the front doors, and Andrel waited for the signal. It didn't take long. In a few minutes, the building was lit up with flashes of light, and the sound of electricity zipping through the air filled his ears. He rushed the doors and was greeted by a pair of demon guards.

Meanwhile, Dystra was doing the same on the other side of the building, and Chyrit was flying through the walls at breakneck speed, pausing long enough every few seconds to slash at power lines. She made it to the basement room, where Sorn was waiting, and the two of them started back toward the rear door on foot.

"Traitor worm!" roared a voice from the roof of the building.

A powerful force grabbed Sorn and pulled her through the ceiling, screaming all the way. Chyrit followed quickly and found Sorn in the grip of Grim himself.

"Not only do you fail to defeat the Warriors, but you ally yourself with them? Disgraceful! You will die!"

Chyrit raced to the rescue, but she was a moment too late. Grim pumped a scattering of electrical power into Sorn's body, and she went limp. He laughed, held a hand to her face, and shot her again with a powerful bolt of energy, blowing her head clean off of her body. He flung her body down and turned to face the horrified Chyrit. He wore a black patch over the eye that Raya had destroyed with her arrow a year ago, and his heavy armor seemed tailor-made to withstand metal weapons.

"Now I'll deal with you!"

"Not this time!" shouted Dystra. She landed on the roof, having flown up from the ground below. She nodded at Chyrit, and together they charged at him.

When Andrel noticed the fighting above him, he left the lesser demons on the ground and flew up to join them. He found Dystra and Chyrit battling Lord Grim, who seemed to have grown in both power and stature since the last time they had met.

"You can't stop it!" Grim shouted with a maniacal laugh. "It has already begun!"

He swung his sword at Chyrit, and she stopped it with her own. Dystra attacked him from the other side, running her spear into his neck. He howled and twisted around, attempting to cast a spell on her with a handful of magic powder. But Chyrit held him firmly, and Andrel rushed up to help.

"You won't stop me!" Grim growled. He gave one last howl into the night sky and fell at their feet. Traces of his energy could be seen leaving his now lifeless body and flying off somewhere.

Dystra gasped in horror and said, "We must follow his trail! He's sent the last of his energy to help complete the ritual!"

The three of them flew straight as arrows, following the fading wisps of Grim's last bits of energy. They led them to Dor's apartment.

"No!" Dystra shouted, speeding through the walls.

There, she found half a dozen demons holding Dor and Raya hostage. The Prince and Princess were chained together in a corner, guarded by a familiar face.

"Kara!" Andrel breathed when he entered the room and saw what was going on. Chyrit was right behind him and hovered in shock, unable to speak.

"I don't believe it," Dystra shook her head. "You died!"

"The demon lord resurrected me," Kara said in a low voice. "He brought me back so that I could serve him. He showed me the error of defending such weak and pathetic creatures as these." She waved her hand at the Prince and Princess.

"You will die just the same as your new friends," Andrel said, grinding his teeth.

"She must be under some sort of spell," Dystra whispered.

"It doesn't matter. She's dead. She's no better than a zombie."

Kara began chanting something in the demon language. The chains between the Prince and Princess began to glow. The Prince wailed in pain, and the Princess bit her lip until it began to bleed. Andrel, Dystra, and Chyrit rushed toward Kara, but the other demons moved to stand between them. Andrel and Chyrit managed to separate the demons into two groups, and Dystra flew past Kara, stopped in front of the twins, and cut their chains in half with her spear. For a moment, she felt the dark energy crawling up her spear from the chains. The twins ran away to join the others, and Kara laughed.

"We have enough of their energy to awaken Aekris! He can absorb the rest on his own!"

Dystra took a breath and charged Kara with her spear, running her through. Kara fell to the floor without even a whimper, and Dystra wiped away a tear. She looked up and saw that the other demons were dead, as well. Raya and Dor had been freed. They all looked at each other and waited, expecting the worst. Of course, they weren't to be disappointed.

His arrival was announced with the thundering sound of lightning tearing through the sky. The building shook, as an earthquake rocked the ground. The Warriors rushed outside and watched a crack in the ground grow into a massive hole. There was a flash that tore through their skulls, and he appeared in front of them. His power was even greater than before. He held out his arms, spoke a single word, and a nearby tree burst into flames.

"Take them home," Andrel whispered to Dystra. "Take them all home. I must fight him myself."

"You can't!" Dystra shook her head. "You'll be killed!"

"I'll take him with me, I promise."

"No! I won't leave you! I won't lose you again!"

"You must take them home! Otherwise, he'll take the twins' power! Now, go!"

Dystra shook her head, but she backed away, gathered the others into a small group, sprinkled her dust over everyone, and quickly whispered the incantation. Chyrit, Raya, Dor, the Prince, and the Princess all vanished, sent back into their own world. Dystra turned and looked at Andrel, her jaw set. She had made up her mind; she would stay with him.

"How touching," the demon spoke. "You will die together."

He walked slowly toward them, each one of his steps like another earthquake rocketing through the ground below them. Dystra took Andrel's hand, and they stood together, ready for battle.

Aekris threw a blast of energy at them, and they erected a force field around themselves. The energy blast blew past them, hitting the building behind them, which exploded in a rush of flames. Angrily, Aekris spoke in the demon tongue again and cast a spell. Dystra waved her hand and warded it off. Aekris reached them and raised his massive sword to strike. Andrel held up his own sword, and Dystra her spear. They separated, moving in synch until they were on opposite sides of the demon. They struck at the same time, but he fended them both off with his arms, which were well-protected by magic metal armor. Dystra cast a spell of her own, but he seemed impervious to it. He rose up into the air and spun around, throwing fireballs from his fingertips. Dystra and Andrel dodged, but the fireballs weren't made of ordinary flame. They followed the Warriors, seeking them out. Dystra was hit by one and found herself face-down on the ground, barely able to breathe. Andrel rushed to her side to protect her, and Aekris took the opportunity to stab him in the back. Andrel screamed and fell next to Dystra. Aekris floated slowly toward them.

Dystra couldn't let it end like this. Painfully, she lifted one finger, and a little spark of light flew from its tip to Andrel's head. The light spread down his body and grew until it covered him from head to toe. He pulled himself to his feet and faced Aekris.

"Enough!" he shouted, holding out one arm.

A ball of light grew in the palm of his hand, as bright as the sun. Aekris squinted into the light but kept walking. Andrel was counting on the demon's determination. He held back until Aekris was less than a foot away. As the demon raised his sword and aimed it at Andrel's head, Andrel shouted the most ancient word of power and let the energy fly from his body. The ball of light engulfed the demon, and bolts of energy flew around him, trapping him and holding him still. He howled, and his voice shook the earth. But Andrel didn't blink. He poured every drop of energy into the attack, including the strength that Dystra had given him. Aekris' body was filled with light, and it disintegrated into nothing but a bright flash and a few scraps of metal.

Andrel sank to his knees, ready to collapse. But he was concerned about Dystra. He crawled to her side and listened. She wasn't breathing.

"No, Dystra, please," he begged in a voice below a whisper, tears welling up in his eyes.

The world began to go black, and Andrel lay his head down on Dystra's shoulder and slept.

"Wake up, you two, the world hasn't ended yet," a voice floated into Andrel's mind from what sounded like an incredible distance. Yet, when he opened his eyes, he found himself staring into Raya's shining face. She smiled at him, and he managed to whisper, "Dystra..."

"She's fine," said Chyrit's voice from somewhere behind his head. "She would have died, but somehow, you shared the final spark of energy that you had with her while you were passed out. And somehow, it kept you both alive. I'll never know how, but here you are, alive and…well, breathing."

Andrel sat up and turned around. Dystra was sitting behind him, smiling. They embraced, and Dor knelt next to them and said, "The Prince sends his deepest gratitude, and he and the Princess want you to know that they'll be restoring our homeworld to its former glory. The Princess has plans to lead the new Peace Warriors herself, and the Prince is currently working on rearranging our former council."

"Thank you so much, Andrel," said the Princess, coming to stand behind Raya.

"What are you all doing back here?" Andrel asked. "How long was I sleeping?"

"One year, in human time," Dor said, then smiled, "I'm kidding. It's only been two days. The humans have abandoned the city for now, calling it a 'disaster area.' We couldn't leave you here, so Chyrit brought us all back after we ran into an old friend."

Another face joined them, smiling brightly.

"Kiri!" Andrel shouted.

"I came to help. Intelligence tells us that the demons have virtually abandoned their own world in favor of the human one. After all, it's full of abundant, easily accessible, walking energy sources. This being their new base of operations, I figured you could use a hand."

"I will be staying, as well," said the Princess, stepping forward. "My brother stayed behind to help re-organize things, but if I'm going to lead the Peace Warriors, I figured I'll need a little more field time. And who better to train me than the greatest Peace Warrior in history?"

"I couldn't have defeated Aekris without Dystra," Andrel shook his head. "We're a team."

"Okay, then, the **two** greatest Peace Warriors in history," the Princess nodded. "Even better."

"Not a bad idea," Dystra smiled. "Where shall we start? I'm ready to kick some ass!"

Dor smiled, sidling up to Chyrit and winking at her. Chyrit grinned and walked away from him, holding out her hands to Dystra and Andrel. She helped them onto their feet, and Andrel said, "Let's get going, then. There are other cities that need protecting. Aekris is gone, but the demons are lurking in the shadows, preying on the innocent."

"We can take them," Dystra grinned and held his hand. "We can take anything."

Andrel could feel that she was right. Together, they had defeated the most powerful demon anyone had ever known. Their energies were perfectly in sync, as were their minds. Although they were staying in the human world for now, nothing felt out of place any longer. A balance had been restored somehow, both for the universe and deep inside of himself. He had his friends back, his family, his comrades. He was finally at home here, and though the war was not yet over, he was at peace with it all.

ADVENTURES IN THE GALACTIC POLICE FORCE:

Trail to Omega Sector

J sighed and stared at the wall of his ship. He dropped the pen in his hand on top of the paper that lay on the table before him. Two words at the top of the page stared blankly when he looked down at them: "The Taal." He couldn't even finish the sentence. He was supposed to write a report on the people of the local star systems, including his own experiences with them, for his annual evaluation for the Galactic Police Force. He hated writing reports. Where should he start? What should he include? He'd be back at Delta base in two days by Earth time, but he was in no hurry. After all, what good was it being a Solocop if he couldn't take his time about it?

A familiar voice said, "J, we're receiving a message from Eta Sector."

"It's probably Trish," J grinned. "Let's see her." He stood up and walked out of the kitchen and into the cockpit. Sitting down in the pilot's chair, he added, "Thanks, G. Put her up."

The image of his sister in her own cockpit appeared on the window directly in front of him. They both smiled at each other. "Hey, Trish," J said. "What's up?"

"I'm on my way in to Delta base for the eval," she told him. "I thought maybe we could rendezvous and hang out."

"Cool," J nodded. Out of the corner of his eye, he saw the distant stars passing by and sighed.

"You haven't done it yet, have you?" Trish asked rhetorically. "The reports are only required every five years. You should have started working on them earlier."

"I know," J looked off into space. "I'll do it; don't worry."

"I won't," Trish smirked. "You always get things done in time. Barely."

Trish and J had been on the Galactic Police Force for years. She was three years older than he, so she had been a Solocop for eight years, while he had been one for five. They had both started training at twenty years of age and finished in a year each, a GPF record. Before that, they had both had a slightly more colorful past.

"How far are you?" J asked.

"A week at top speed," Trish answered. "Can you wait?"

"I could find something to keep me busy," J grinned. "See you there."

The image of Trish disappeared, leaving J to stare into the blackness of space. He pressed a few buttons on the console in front of him, slowing the Solo's speed by more than half.

"How long will it take us to get to Delta base now?" he asked the computer.

"At present speed, we will arrive at Delta base in one hundred and sixteen hours, Earth time," G responded. "J, that means you will be late for your meeting with Captain Smithson."

"I know, G," J leaned back in his seat, closed his eyes, and grinned. "I know."

Trish shook her head and smiled, leaning back in her cockpit seat. J had a habit of stirring up trouble, sometimes without meaning to and always when he was out for some fun. But she couldn't criticize him for it; she was the same way sometimes. She could criticize him, though, for his practice of putting off paperwork. His first evaluation report for his official entrance to the GPF had been nearly a week late. It almost cost him his career. But Trish had stepped in and spoken to the council personally, putting her name and reputation on the line in order to remind the council that the GPF needed rogues like her and her brother to handle the more unusual situations that often arose in deep space. Besides, paperwork wasn't important; skills were. And looking out for each other, which Trish and J had been doing their whole lives, especially before they were Solocops, when they didn't have the GPF looking out for them, too.

Things weren't all that different even now. The siblings saw less of each other, but when one of them was in trouble, the other was there. But Trish was looking forward to hanging out with J for a while without needing to rescue or be rescued by him. She could also use a break from her new Taal friends. It was good to be in the field, but it was also good to forget your life for a while and just reminisce or speculate or do nothing. Or just get into a little harmless trouble while having a little harmless fun. And harmless was not a word for the Taal, the cat-like people with the vicious sense of humor.

A beep interrupted Trish's thoughts. The console was indicating an incoming message from another ship not far behind her. "Speak of the devil," Trish said to herself, recognizing the transmission code as that of Rhyyzha RonTan, the Taal she often worked closely with during conflicts between Taals and Terrans. They had also spent some time together off the job, mostly because Rhyyzha was a hard person to get rid of. Trish sighed and summoned the communications screen to her window with the press of a button.

"Trish, how's it going? Want to have some fun?" Rhyyzha said quickly. "I hear there are some pirates just a sector away. I feel like beating somebody up."

"Rhyyzha, I have an appointment at Delta base," Trish shook her head. "I can't get out of it. You go on without me."

"You'll miss all the fun!" the catty Taal grinned teasingly, showing her sharp teeth. "Besides, word on the starpaths is that trouble is brewing between a couple of rival bandits, one Taal, one Terran."

"Handle it," Trish instructed. "There are three other GPF ships within days of our position. Contact them if it's too much." Her eyes twinkled mischievously. She knew a Taal had to respond to any vague doubt of their abilities by proving themselves. She enjoyed exploiting this cultural tendency whenever she saw fit.

"I'll take care of it myself," Rhyyzha practically growled and ended the transmission.

Trish smiled and flipped a switch, as Rhyyzha's ship sped off in another direction. A song started playing in the cockpit, and Trish closed her eyes to listen to it.

"I.D.," the guard demanded. He grinned when he looked at J's GPF identification. "You're three days late," he smirked.

"Really?" J feigned surprise. "Whatever will I do?" He snatched his I.D. back and strolled out of the airlock, into Delta base.

Various life-forms from many different sectors eyed him in passing, and he eyed them back. From somewhere down the throughway, Captain Smithson appeared, glaring straight at J. J turned to stare at his own reflection in a shiny wall panel. His hair stood on end in all different directions; his boots were worn and thin; his favorite jacket looked like he had pulled it out of a garbage heap. He wondered how he had ended up on the right side of the law. For the most part.

"Barker, you're a disgrace to the Force," Smithson bellowed. Then he paused and sighed, "Unfortunately, you're also a great asset. And anyhow, your sister is coming in a couple of days, and we'd have a lot more trouble with her if we dumped you than we would by just keeping you around. I trust you at least have your very late report."

J pulled a couple of rumpled, creased pages out of his jacket and surrendered them. Then he saluted casually and sauntered off down the wide hallways. For a few days, he planned on not having a care in the universe.

J wandered out to the main area of the base, where GPF officers gathered to relax. He spotted a card game starting up at a table in a dim corner. A couple of the participants were Solocops he knew from his travels, so he approached them and said, "Mind if I join you? I promise not to win **all** your money."

"J, J, you little freak!" one of them sighed. "Sit down! Troops, this is J Barker, a Solocop I met on Taal a few years back. He's with the Base Division."

The other officers at the table nodded at him, and J grimaced. No one knew that his identity as a Base Division officer was a cover;

he was really a member of the elite Samurai Division, a secretive group at the top levels of the GPF. They had their fingers in everything; they were visible to no one; and they never failed in a mission. Their skills were varied, and they worked on their own. But J had already decided en route to the station that he was going to break that last rule. He trusted Trish alone in all the universe, and she would keep his secret. She had to; she was a Samurai, too. She had told him her plans before she entered the intense training program, and they had celebrated together when she graduated.

Being Samurais was the perfect job for the two of them; it allowed them to work independently of the GPF for the most part, and it was the most exciting and challenging job in the universe. J had just graduated two months ago. He would retain his job in the Delta Sector, close to Earth and Pluto, but he was no longer tied to that solar system.

"Emperors are wild," a voice said. "Ante up, troops." The three men and two women at the table tossed their trading chips onto it and picked up their cards. J scratched at a microship behind his ear, activating the x-ray lens he wore in his right eye. He quickly scanned his opponents' cards. He was going to make a killing. As long as the base's sensors didn't detect him using some of his gear, that is.

Trish completed the docking procedures at Delta base and transmitted notice of her arrival to Captain Smithson. She noticed a bit of static that was riding on her signal. Instinctively, she instructed the computer to find out what it was. "Probably just interference," she mumbled to herself. But she had a nagging feeling that it was something more.

Smithson's voice resonated outside the docking portal just behind the cockpit of the Aria. Trish hurried out of her seat and opened the portal to see Smithson walking toward her with J in tow. As soon as he saw her, he bellowed, "Your brother is a disgrace to his uniform!"

J grinned at this and addressed her, "Hey, Trish, how's dinner sound? It's on me!"

"Of course, it's on you!" Smithson shouted. "After that un-sportsman-like....Aah! I leave him in your custody!" He pointed at Trish. "Straighten it out!" He then spun around and stalked off, disappearing amid a sea of people outside the airlock.

"What did you do this time?" Trish sighed. "Did you even make it to your eval appointment?"

"I was late," J shrugged, leaning on the wall. "So they moved it. To your slot."

"Sneaky devil," Trish grinned. "That's cool. Shall we practice?"

"Let's," her brother agreed, leading the way onto the base. "First, we'll grab a bite. I made a killing at a game yesterday, **and** the day before."

"But today they caught you," Trish finished for him. "Too bad. You oughtta be more careful." Remembering the static on the signal she had sent from the Aria, she changed the subject and asked, "Have you had any trouble with interference in transmissions since you got here?"

"I haven't sent or received any since I got here," J told her. He glanced at her to see if she was concerned about it.

"I noticed some static when I signaled Captain Smithson's office," Trish explained without looking at him. "It was probably nothing, but still..."

"Trust your instincts," he reminded her.

She smiled at him, thinking of how often they had told each other that over the course of their lives. Together, they had honed their instincts until they could smell trouble two sectors away and tell anyone exactly what kind and how bad it was. "Well, my instincts tell me we need to be on the lookout; something's going on right under our noses."

"Come to the game tomorrow," J said. "Somebody else may have noticed something."

"They're going to let you play again?" Trish laughed.

"Well, I can be very persuasive," he grinned.

They arrived at the lift and stepped onto it. "Dining deck," Trish instructed. As the lift transported them upwards, she added in a low voice, "Be careful. Let's not tell anyone what we're asking about. Someone's being very sneaky, and I think they're hiding in plain sight."

"As always," J acknowledged.

The lift stopped, and they stepped off of it and into the dining area. Cooks and chefs from nearly twenty different sectors were working at their stations, sending puffs of steam and smoke to the ceiling thirty feet above them. The smells of dozens of different foods mingled in the air, and people from dozens of different planets talked at their tables in dozens of different languages.

"What do you feel like?" J asked, pulling some yellow trading chips out of his pocket. "Insects, fish, or worms?"

"Very funny," Trish responded, scanning the huge room visually. "There's a Terran cook over there. How about a home-cooked meal?"

"Sounds good," J agreed. He sauntered over to the other side of the room, and Trish followed slowly, carefully observing everyone they passed. Nothing seemed unusual; groups of people were fairly uniform. Carbonills, green frog-like life-forms, sat together, eating what looked like roasted insects with a dark sauce. A few orange- and brown-colored Taals, known as "cat people," sat together, dining on Taal stew with five-eyed fish floating at the top. And Sigrinites, who looked like big birds with human arms and came in different-colored feathers, sat together, slurping up long strands of tocklings, a worm-like vegetation that was a delicacy on their own planet. The latter species whooped and hollered in greeting to everyone around them, beckoning for others to come and join them. Trish looked at them and shook her head politely. Sigrinites were often considered to be too friendly, and she didn't come here to make new friends.

A couple of tall bluish Loorans passed Trish and J, stuffing shoofler into their mouths. Bits of the wiggly dessert fell to the floor, leaving a trail behind the bug-eyed, beaked creatures.

"Two plates of your best vegesteak and carny pie," J told the cook behind the Terran counter. "Money is an object, but nevermind the price."

Unamused, the man set two plates in front of him without smiling. J handed over a few chips and carried the plates to an empty table. Trish sat down beside him and looked up at a security screen that monitored the dining deck. It displayed an image of each table simultaneously. A quick flash of static interrupted the pictures for a nanosecond.

"Things are sometimes more complicated than they at first appear," she whispered cryptically.

"More?" J asked without looking at her.

She nodded, and her eyes darted about to see if anyone else had noticed the brief static. No one had stopped eating or talking. A Narlan in full armor with his gangly arms swinging entered the room from the lift and stomped directly to a Narlan chef's counter, where small rat-like creatures were frying until they were crispy.

"Where have you been?" a Taal shouted at him, standing up from his seat. "You're late! Forget dinner! We have to leave now!"

The Narlan growled something under his breath and followed the Taal back onto the lift.

"When was the last time you saw a Narlan take orders from a Taal? So much for a vacation," Trish sighed. "Ready for some action?"

"Always!" J grinned. "Right after dinner. Want some more pie?"

J peered around the corner at the Taal he'd been following for the last hour. So far, nothing had happened. The creature from the "cat planet" was the most boring suspect he'd ever tailed, pun intended. All J had learned was that has name was Shalla. Right now, Shalla was entering an airlock, presumably to return to his ship for the night. J waited for ten minutes. Finally, he left and met Trish on the main deck.

"Waste of time," he shrugged. "His name's Shalla, a Narlan named Tro works for him, and he likes playing Torp. How about you? Any luck?"

Trish shook her head and told him, "I checked in every file. He's clean as a whistle. Maybe he was just angry that his Torp partner was late."

"Unless somebody's covering for them," J added. "We'll have to find out."

Trish's shipcom beeped. She looked at the display and said, "I'll be back. The Aria's done analyzing that static. That should tell us something." She hurried off and J strolled down the throughway to Simthson's office. If anyone could hide something on Delta base, it wasn't Smithson. But his assistant was another story.

J decrypted the lock on the door and slipped inside the room. The orderly office was sparsely furnished with a few cabinets and a couple of desks and chairs. The captain's desk had a few medals hanging behind it, and his assistant's desk had stacks and stacks of paperwork covering it. J casually glanced at some of it. As he expected, there wasn't anything interesting in it. He slipped on a pair of gloves and ducked under the desk to inspect the bottom corners. He was rewarded for his efforts by finding a red trading chip magnetically attached to the desk. Using his wrist band computer, he scanned the chip into the Solo's memory and returned it to its place.

A hidden trading chip in Captain Smithson's office could mean only one thing: A transaction that the captain's assistant didn't want anyone to know about had taken place recently. But J needed more proof. He sat in the assistant's chair and pressed a few buttons on the computer console on the desk. It asked for a password. J typed in "money," and file names appeared on the screen. He chuckled and scanned the files into his ship's memory. Captains' assistants were extremely predictable.

As he was finishing up, J heard Smithson's voice outside the door. He jumped onto the desk, reached up, and pushed aside a ceiling panel. Quickly and quietly, he pulled himself into the maintenance shaft and replaced the panel. He then crawled all the way to the airlock corridor and climbed back out through another panel near the docking ports. Trish was just exiting her ship.

"The static was an incoming transmission that piggy-backed onto my signal from a remote source," she said in a low voice.

"Dreeka, the captain's assistant, is in on it," J told her. "I'm gonna check out his files."

They heard footsteps coming toward them and waited. It was Shalla, with Tro following. Without even glancing at the two Terrans, Shalla marched briskly down the hall and entered an airlock at the end, Tro matching his every step.

J and Trish nodded at each other and dashed to their ships. J opened a com signal to Trish's ship before taking off, audio only. Slowly, they both maneuvered into position and followed Shalla's quickly moving ship away from the cylindrically shaped base. J scanned the Solo's memory and checked the files he had sent there. The trading chip had a manufacturing glitch that J had seen before.

"Trish," he said. "Has anything strange been happening in your sector lately? I found a chip under Dreeka's desk that was made on Taal."

"I'll check it out," Trish answered him. "You stay on Shalla's trail. I'll meet you in Eta Sector tomorrow at 1300."

J watched Trish's ship turn to enter a jump and said, "G, end com signal. From here, we should maintain radio silence."

"I do not send radio signals without an order from you, J," G responded.

"Let's see the other files," J said, ignoring the computer's sarcasm. It was his own fault for programming it with a strong personality.

He stared at the endless number of memos and financial reports that flipped past the screen. "Stop," he said, when he saw a file marked "Omega Sector." Why would anyone have financial dealings in the Omega Sector? The Sythee weren't exactly the friendliest guys on the block. "Open file." J stared at the lists in the file. Sure enough, Dreeka was trading with the Sythee for some raw materials. There were small amounts of droth, perkell, and cantor on the list, all minor explosives found only on Sordon, the Sythee homeworld. But the majority of items on the list were various higher densities of dragonite.

"Explosives and energy matter," J said out loud. "This is big."

"J, I've detected a com signal within the Taal's ship," G interrupted. "He is speaking with his Narlan friend."

"Let's hear it," J said.

"Next time, don't take so long making the exchange!" shouted Shalla's voice. "It makes me nervous when you're late."

The Narlan mumbled something J couldn't make out, and Shalla responded, "Just don't do it again, or I'll throw you in the cell!"

The signal grew silent, and J shut it off. "I don't think we'll get much out of them that way," he sighed. "A direct confrontation might be more successful. Open a com signal to the Taal's ship....Hey, Shalla, I heard back on Delta base that you sneak around 'cuz you're a coward. Want to prove it?"

Shalla's image appeared on the window, and he yelled, "Are you looking for a fight, Terran?"

"Yup," J grinned. "And I'd also like to make a wager on that fight. If I win, I get everything in your cargo hold."

Shalla laughed at the top of his lungs and said, "Foolish Terran! I will cut you to pieces!"

The transmission ended, and his ship fired at J's ship, narrowly missing it.

"Manual control," J shouted. He took the control sticks in his hands and pressed the accelerator button on the right one. The Solo zoomed past the underside of Shalla's ship and swung around to face the back of the engine ports. J pressed the targeting button on the left control stick, as Shalla desperately tried to maneuver out of range. Shalla's ship was considerably smaller than the typical Taal starship, which meant it was also quidker and more maneuverable. J gritted his teeth, pulling the Solo in one direction after another to stay on Shalla's tail. Still, his quarry managed to remain just out of range.

"I cannot get a lock on him," G piped up, "unless he slows down or gets farther away. We're too close for me to follow his movements."

"Well, he's not going to slow down," J growled. "And I'm not going to let him get away. I'll improvise."

"The last time you improvised, we almost lost a wing," G pointed out.

"Shut up!" J ordered. He followed Shalla's movements with his eyes and, pressing another button on the right control stick, fired a rapid series of nitro-missiles at Shalla's ship. Each missile hit its target, exploding half of the Taal's vessel. He was dead in space. One wing was barely hanging on, the engine parts floating nearby in a million pieces, and a hole in the ship's starboard side would take months to fully repair.

"Autopilot," J smiled and relaxed. "And send a message to our friend. Shalla, hand over your cargo. I won it, fair and square."

"Come and get it," Shalla's voice hissed. "And die for your mistake! Do you realize whose ship you have crippled? I am Commander Shalla DronTee of the Taal Empire! I will arrest you for this!"

"You don't own all of space," J rolled his eyes. "What makes you Taal think you do? Prepare to be boarded."

J cut off the com signal and said, "G, dock us. I'm going in."

"Rhyyzha, if you can't help me, I have other contacts on Taal who will," Trish sighed, glaring at the image of her friend on the Aria's window. "I have to get going." She pulled a cap over her head and adjusted her favorite jacket. "If you're lying to me…"

"I can't talk," Rhyyzha said. "Not over a com signal."

Trish flipped a switch and pressed a few buttons and said, "The channel's secure."

"I shouldn't tell you anything," Rhyyzha mumbled. "But I still owe you for saving my life two years ago. How you knew I was there and in trouble, I'll never know."

"I have my ways," Trish smiled. "Now spit it out. What have you heard?"

"There's been an uprising lately on Taal," Rhyyzha said quickly. "Small groups of dissidents are complaining that the government doesn't enforce the border of the Taal Empire. That, in fact, the Empire doesn't exist."

"I know all this, Rhyyzha," Trish sighed. "What's so unusual about it?"

"They're getting restless," Rhyyzha spoke in a low voice. "Word is, they're going to stage a coup. It could be disastrous for Taal and our relations with other worlds."

"Especially if they try to establish a **real** Taal Empire," Trish whispered.

"It's real," Rhyyzha objected defensively. "Just not enforced."

"What's being done?" Trish asked. "What's their plan? Where do they get resources? Where are they based? Who's involved?"

"I don't know anything else," Rhyyzha insisted. "There's a rumor that they're getting outside help. But that's all."

"Thanks," Trish smiled. "You never saw me."

She shut off the transmission and piloted the Aria toward Taal. She wanted to confirm the rumors. A visit to Taal wasn't exactly a pleasure trip for her, but she'd have to chance it. There was no other way.

Trish went over a plan in her mind. She'd spent more time on Taal in her youth than on any other planet in her whole life. It was the richest, most successful planet in known space. She and J had learned its ins and outs and quirks like the backs of their hands. That's one of the reasons Trish had been assigned to Eta Sector when she joined the GPF; the officer who knew the most about Taal should be closest to it.

Trish set the Aria's controls for a jump straight to Taal. For now, barring any real problems, the plan was simply to get in, snoop around, and get out. The last thing she wanted to do was run into anyone she knew or, worse yet, anyone who knew her.

Unfortunately, avoiding any people turned out to be easier said than done. As soon as she arrived at her destination, Trish was radioed by the Taal Transport Authority.

"State your business!" demanded an angry-looking Taal man in uniform.

"Just here on vacation," Trish tried to look relaxed. "Just for a day." She grinned, knowing that in Earth time, a Taal day was only about eight hours long. That would keep the TA from wondering why she was there since Terrans don't usually pick Taal as a vacation spot.

The uniformed officer waved her on and ended the transmission. Trish sighed and set a course for a remote part of the planet. At top speed, it took her only a couple of minutes to get there and land on a flat outcropping of rocks. You had to be an expert pilot to land in the uninhabited areas. Within inches of the spot Trish chose, plants of all shapes and sizes crowded around the ship. She could barely squeeze through the hatch.

On the horizon, high enough to be seen over the treetops, a few skyscrapers in a nearby city were in sight. Trish turned and headed in the opposite direction. She trudged through the thick underbrush until she reached an ancient stone building, covered in vines and surrounded by stone statues of cats. Legend had it that the Taals evolved from felines and once ruled over a kingdom of nine planets. But something happened to eight of their planets, and they ended up on Taal, swapping stories about the once-great Taal Empire. Most have forgotten that there were eight other planets in their solar system, so they seemed to think that the rest of their empire now included the outer reaches of space.

"Krynor!" Trish called out. A face peered out at her from the doorway of the old building. It was her old friend Krynor KotKin, the official historian and busy-body of Taal. "I need some info, Krynor," she said. "Something's happening, and it's big."

The smell of ionized oxygen sliced through the recycled air of the Taal's vessel. The electrical pulse from J's e-pistol hit Shalla square in the chest. Tro, his Narlan friend, held up his arms and surrendered.

"You coward!" Shalla shouted, rising from the floor. "Attack him!"

"I thought you Taal were supposed to be quick on the draw," J grinned.

"Fight me in hand-to-hand, and I will make you eat your words," Shalla growled.

"Why?" J shrugged. "I already won. Now, open the cargo hold, or I'll blast you into liquid space!"

Shalla complied, and J stared at the stockpile of GPF weaponry stashed in the old. He looked at Shalla in disbelief and exclaimed, "You bought weapons from Dreeka?!" He couldn't believe it; the Taal had always insisted that they were completely self-sufficient. Why buy all these weapons from the GPF?

"You know Dreeka?" Shalla's eyes widened. "He assured me this would be kept completely quiet! I will haul him into the Taal prisons for this insult!"

"Hey, ice it, Shalla!" J chuckled. "Don't go plasma on me! Dreeka didn't tell me anything. As a matter of fact," he added thoughtfully, "I heard it from Smithson!"

"That overpaid moron?" Shalla laughed. "You're flaming my jets!"

"I flame you not, my friend," J shook his head, pretending to be shocked. "The good captain plans to investigate and prosecute. But, uh....I could make it all go away." He winked. "For a cut, of course."

"A small cut," Shalla narrowed his eyes.

"Yeah, I, uh, wouldn't want to deprive the cause of any real resources," J nodded. He hoped Shalla would take the bait. All those weapons would be useful for only two things: a revolution or a war. And a Taal would never accept help during a war. There had never been a revolution on Taal, but there was a first time for everything.

"**You** support the cause?" Shalla glared at J. "**You** would support the new Taal Empire?"

"Of course," J smiled convincingly. "What better way to assist the revolution than from the inside of the enemy's stronghold?" He pulled his GPF ID out of his jacket and held it up.

"Brilliant!" Shalla laughed, relaxing. "But you can't be alone!"

"Did you think Dreeka was?" J asked. "How did the old trickster get mixed up in this anyway? I mean, I know he's been involved in some shady dealings before, but this is big."

"He has his own motives," Shalla shrugged. "What about you? Why did you attack me?"

"I wanted to make sure you were genuine," J defended himself. "Besides, I had to make it look good for Smithson. He sent me out here to arrest you."

"I never thought he had the brains or the guts," Shalla shook his head.

"That's how he tricks you," J grinned. "But don't worry about him; I'll take care of it."

"Choose a few weapons," Shalla indicated the cargo hold. "Then give us a tow back to Delta base, where we can load your ship. You'll have to deliver these now."

"Done and done!" J nodded. "Just give me the coordinates!"

"You'll find them in the city," Krynor pointed at the horizon. "Those upstarts don't care about their past. They only want to recreate it in their own way. I'd report them if it mattered what happens to Taal. But we are a broken race, and we must learn that before we can move on."

"Thanks, old friend," Trish smiled. "I'll visit sooner next time."

"It's hard to believe you're working for the GPF now," Krynor shook his graying, fur-covered head. "It seems like only yesterday you were a little girl, speeding around Taal on that jetship of yours, stirring up trouble, robbing the rich to feed yourself and your brother when you had to **and** when you didn't. You had the law enforcers on constant alert." He laughed, exposing his sharp teeth. "The most amazing part was that smuggling business you had going by the time you were 13!"

"Thanks for never turning us in," Trish smiled.

"Why would I?" Krynor smiled back. "You and J were my best students. The only ones who really listened to me. Besides, I knew you had big things in your future. You'd already done big things: traveled all over known space, took down three of the biggest crime syndicates in the universe. You developed a fine-tuned sense of right and wrong at an early age. I've always respected that."

"I learned from the best," Trish hugged the old man. "I have to go, but I'll come back soon."

He waved until she disappeared into the forest. When she reached her ship, she hurried inside, lifted off, and headed for the nearby city, Taal-Raal, the planet's capital. There, she set down again on a temporary parking pad.

The city was full of busy Taals rushing around. Every one of them stared at her as she passed them on the walks. Eventually, she reached an emptier part of town, where Taals only stared at her from open windows and behind chain fences. After a few more blocks, the people disappeared altogether. Here, in this strangely desolate area, she found what she was looking for: the old DronTee Corp. office building. This was their base of operations. They weren't expecting anyone to find them; there were no guards or even a simple security system. That was Taal arrogance at its very best!

Trish peered through a broken window. The first floor was empty and covered with dust, except for a wide path from the back door to a flight of stairs. The silhouettes of two Taals talking near the backdoor, their ears twitching, were visible through another dust-covered pane of glass. Trish reached through the broken window and unlocked it. Softly, she lifted the pane high enough for her to slip inside. She took a tiny spray-bottle out of her belt and sprayed the bottoms of her boots with the clear liquid. Then, she put on a pair of black gloves and sprayed them, as well. She returned the bottle to its holster and tested one finger on the dusty windowsill. It glided over the dirt without picking up a single speck or leaving behind a clean trail. Print Repellant was one of Trish's favorite tools. She slipped inside the building and tip-toed quickly across the floor and up the stairs without leaving a single footprint behind in the dust.

On the second floor, a massive shipping operation seemed to be underway. Crates and boxes were stacked to the ceiling; some were being moved in and out through the A-port, some were being repacked. They were filled with weapons and ammunition that had obviously come from the GPF. Trish hid behind a crate to watch the activities of the more than two dozen Taals in the room. From there, she saw a ship move up to the A-port and dock. She recognized it immediately. The doors opened, and the Taals started unloading more weaponry. Trish waited for an opportunity to sneak aboard the Solo.

J nervously supervised the unloading of the weaponry from his ship's hold. He wasn't used to having this many people on the Solo. He just wanted to keep them moving so he could talk to someone in charge as quickly as possible. A suspicious-looking individual in a low hood and long robe sauntered into the hold and picked up a box. But instead of carrying it out, the figure walked backwards toward J. J rested his hand on the butt of his e-pistol, just in case, but he sensed there was no immediate danger.

"Easy there, partner," a female voice whispered. "I come in peace."

J smiled and relaxed when he recognized the voice of his sister. "What are you doing here?" he asked.

"Following a lead," Trish answered. "There's nothing more for us to do here. Give me a lift back to the Aria, and I'll tell you what I've learned."

She set the box down and led the way to the cockpit. J glanced back as the last boxes were removed and said, "G, close the doors and get us out of here."

The ship's computers complied, and they flew away from the upper part of the city.

"It's a revolution," Trish said, taking off the robe and sitting in a chair behind the pilot's seat.

"I figured," J nodded, sitting beside her.

"A faction of dissidents are unhappy with the nonexistence of the Taal Empire," Trish told him. "It's nobody's business, but we should tell Python; she'll want us to keep an eye on it, just in case."

"Do I finally get to see our glorious and elusive leader?" J grinned.

"**I've** never even seen her," Trish shook her head. "Only her most trusted and oldest assistant has seen her, and I've never even seen him."

"So we leave the Taal to their revolution and fry a bigger fish?" J asked.

"What bigger fish?" Trish looked at him. "Dreeka? What's that sneaky little Carbonill up to now?"

"Something big," J's eyes twinkled. "He's trading with the Sythee."

"Why would he do that?" Trish looked puzzled. "Better question: Why would the Sythee do that? They've always taken care of themselves. They've refused all trade agreements with the other worlds. What could Dreeka have that they would want so badly? And, more importantly, what do they have that Dreeka wants?"

"Food, and explosives and dragonite," J answered her questions. "It's all in his files. He's trading wozzra for droth, perkell, cantor, and dragonite."

"Dragonite!" Trish repeated, her eyes wide. "This is big. That's the most dangerous substance in known space!"

"We should tell Python about this, too," J said. "But let's investigate further first. I want to know what Dreeka's planning."

"Me, too," Trish nodded. "G, stop at the next temporary parking pad."

207

G acknowledged her order with a beep, and J moved to the pilot's chair.

"Let's go over this," Trish said. "Dreeka sells GPF weaponry to the Taal for their little military coup, trades the red chips in for yellow ones, orders tons of wozzra from his home planet, and gives it all to the Sythee in exchange for dragonite and some explosives. To what end? And why do the Sythee need food, anyway?"

"We should go back to Delta base and find out," J said, as the Solo landed next to the Aria.

"We have to go back, anyway," Trish reminded him, opening the hatch. "We'll have to jump back to make it in time for our evaluation appointment."

J sighed and nodded. At least, he didn't have to write another paper. The physical evaluation was easy: a little target practice, some exercises. Piece of carny pie. The Samurai division evaluations were far more rigorous. They tested and strained every skill an officer had: martial arts, fencing, weapons handling, infiltration, spry tactics, spy recognition; you name it, they test it. But thorough checks were necessary for Samurai security. The rest of the GPF didn't have to do it so often; they just liked to be an annoyance. That was J's theory, anyway.

He lifted off, and Trish followed him away from the planet. After another interrogation by the Taal Transport Authority, they jumped straight to Delta base, docked, and hurried to the base's evaluation level.

"Just in time," Captain Smithson smirked at them. "I've decided to add ship evaluations to your tests, this year."

J glared at the man. He was only trying to get J riled, and it was working. J leaned toward Trish and mumbled under his breath, "We don't have time for this!"

"We have time," Trish whispered back to him. "Dreeka supervises the ship evaluations. You can keep him busy, while I check his personal vessel."

"Line up for targeting," Smithson ordered.

J and Trish stood side-by-side, pulled out their weapons, and aimed at the targets fifty yards away. J glanced at Trish's fully modernized ion-blaster, the clunkier but more powerful descendant of his streamlined, rechargeable e-pistol. It wasn't long lasting, or as accurate as the e-pistol, but the GPF loved upgrading. Trish didn't use her blaster that often, anyway, even though she was just as adept with it as J was with his pistol; she preferred hand-to-hand combat, especially swordplay. Her Samurai blade never left her; it had been hanging on her back since she was 12.

"Fire!" Smithson yelled.

J and Trish both fired and both hit bullseyes. The targets were replaced and moved back another fifty yards. They fired again and hit their marks again. Smithson waved his hand, and new targets were set up on the other side of the level. J and Trish fired again and hit the bullseyes. This time, the new targets were set in motion. But if Smithson had hoped to trip them up, he was utterly disappointed. Once again, both siblings made flawless shots.

"All right, all right," Smithson grumbled. "Let's go to combat."

They stepped into the center of the room, and two fighter bots faced them.

"Attack!" the Captain yelled, and the bots swung at J and Trish. The brother and sister launched into their own individual styles of combat, blocking and hitting with precision until the bots were down for the count.

Smithson sighed and led the way to the airlocks, where Dreeka was waiting for them.

"I'm first," J volunteered, grinning.

"I leave you to it," the Captain nodded and returned to the lift.

J entered the Solo, nodding to Trish, and Dreeka entered one of the base's fighters. J instructed the Solo's computer, "Defensive Mode. This is an evaluation. Let's give that snake a run for his trading chips. Be ready to switch to combat mode."

Trish watched through a portal as J and Dreeka maneuvered away from the base. She then turned and hurried down the corridor to the airlock Dreeka's ship, the Drondo, was docked at. She overrode the access code and stepped inside. The cargo hold held only a large trunk. Trish opened it; it was filled with yellow trading chips. She went to the cockpit and checked the transport log. Dreeka had mapped out a trip to the Carbonill homeworld and then Sordon. Trish brought up a list of recent com signals on the computer screen. The last one had come from the Omega Sector. She pushed a couple of buttons, and the message replayed on the window. A Carbonill stared back at her and said, "The Sythee are ready for another shipment, Dreeka. They can't get enough of the stuff." He laughed mechanically. "Who would have guessed that the most feared and despised race of creatures in known space could so easily develop an addiction to one of our basic food groups?" He laughed again and paused. "All right, I'll see you in a few morkas." The message ended.

"That explains the wozzra," Trish said to herself, wrinkling her nose at the thought of the yellowish, foul-smelling goop. She had thought only Carbonills could enjoy it; it was a part of their main diet. "But why the explosives and the dragonite? They could be valuable on the black markets, but are they worth all those trading chips or all that food? Surely, they couldn't be worth all that GPF weaponry!"

Trish returned to the corridor and went to her own ship. She sent an encrypted, text-only signal to Phi sector; from there, it would be sent through a vast network of informants, assistants, and spies until it reached the eyes of Python herself, the lead supervisor, coordinator, and manager of the Samurai division of the GPF.

The Solo pulled up to the base and docked. A radio signal from Dreeka told Trish, "Your turn. Move out."

Trish laid her hands flat on the control platforms in front of her pilot's chair and pressed the button under her right thumb. The Aria moved away from the airlock, and she turned the ship by turning the control platforms. A quick press of the pad under the heel of her right palm accelerated the ship to Dreeka's position, away from the base.

The fighter fired on the Aria, nicking the tip of the left wing. Trish's computer screen read, "Damage – 1%." What was he doing? Trish turned on the com and shouted, "Those aren't blanks, Dreeka! That better have been an accident!"

She watched the fighter's laser cannon train on the Aria and heard Dreeka hiss, "Is it also an accident that you disappear from the base just before your evaluation tests? I'd expect that kind of behavior from your brother, not you. And somehow, at the precise moment I notice your conspicuous absence, my associate, Commander Shalla DronTee, is attacked on his ship while running an errand for me. Did you think I wouldn't keep a tracker on him? Tell me what you know, and I'll consider letting you live."

Trish chuckled and said, "First off, what makes you think I'd tell you anything, even if I knew what you were talking about? And secondly, I'd watch who I was threatening if I were you."

There was a pause, and Dreeka said in a low voice, "I have long suspected you to be more than a diplomatic-patrol division officer. You know too much; you're involved in too much; you disappear too much. Who have you told? Nevermind. If I destroy you, I destroy the proof. Prepare to die!"

The signal ended, and Trish pressed the button under her left ring finger, switching to defensive mode. She accelerated straight for the fighter and dodged underneath it. As Dreeka turned to face her, she looped around and over him, locking her laser cannon on his targeting system. The press of a button unleashed a powerful laser that cut through the back of the fighter as if it were cotton cloth. Trish spun the Aria around and prepared a series of four nitro-missiles.

But Dreeka knew when he had been beaten. Trish watched the fighter's escape pod shoot off toward the base. A com signal flashed onto the Aria's cockpit window, and J grinned at her. "So that's why you like that little Taal ship! It sure packs a punch! And it moves, too!"

"We haven't won yet," Trish told him. "Keep an eye on that pod. I'm going to check out the fighter; my instincts tell me Dreeka's up to something."

The signal ended, and Trish docked the Aria with the drifting fighter. She opened the hatches and slipped inside. An ion-blaster fired at her from around the corner, narrowly missing her head. She rolled to the other side of the corridor and swiftly crawled to the corner of the wall. Reaching around with one hand, she grabbed Dreeka's leg and pulled him down to the floor. His ion-blaster fired again, hitting the ceiling and causing a low electrical buzz to reverberate throughout the ship.

Trish gave Dreeka's right hand a quick hit with the side of her left palm, and he dropped the weapon involuntarily. He tried to stand up, but with a quick, cat-like gesture, Trish unsheathed her sword and held it at his chest, before he even noticed she had moved.

"This is a liteshift blade," she told him. "It will slice through that body armor like a laser cannon, and it won't be dented, nicked, or dulled. Move, and I'll use it."

Dreeka sighed and relaxed. "What do you want?" he asked. "A cut? I can arrange that."

"With whom?" Trish asked him. "Are you in charge of this operation, or do you answer to someone else?"

"Does it matter?" Dreeka responded. "If you want chips or weaponry, I'm the man to deal with. I'm picking up a new wozzra shipment today."

"You answer to someone," Trish nodded with satisfaction. "Who?"

"I've never seen him, I swear," he insisted. "No one has. But he's in Omega Sector. The rumor is that he's Sythee."

"Why would a Sythee want to enslave his own people to an addiction like that?" Trish asked, not sure she believed him.

"And a deadly one at that!" Dreeka laughed. "You'd have to ask him yourself. No one else knows."

"I'll do that," Trish smiled. She stood and sheathed her sword.

A bright light flashed through the portal behind her, and she spun around to look back at the base. The escape pod had exploded. Pieces of it were floating by them. Luckily, it had been too far away from the base and the other ships to do any damage.

Smiling, Trish turned back to Dreeka, snatched the restraint straps from his tool belt, and said, "Stand up. You're under arrest."

J watched as Trish marched Dreeka into a holding cell. Smithson stood by the door, barking orders at everyone within hearing distance. Trish closed the door and walked over to J.

"Nice moves," J nodded. "But he's only the middle-man, isn't he?"

Trish nodded and whispered, "I have a plan. Let's go to Omega Sector ourselves and find the real mastermind behind this scheme. Tell G to switch to autopilot and follow us. You fly the Drondo; you're more familiar with Carbonill ships. I'll stay with you in the Aria."

J and Trish hurried back to the airlocks before Smithson could start asking questions. J set the Solo on autopilot and entered the Drondo. He piloted the ship away from Delta base and toward Beta Sector. He radioed Trish, "Will they believe Dreeka sent us?"

"I doubt they'll ask questions," she responded. "They probably don't know what he was up to."

"Yeah, Carbonills are pretty peaceable," J agreed. "In general. I guess Dreeka was the bad apple of the bunch."

They jumped to Carbono, and J sent out a transmission on a coded frequency so that whoever Dreeka was supposed to meet would know they were there. After a few minutes, a signal came back. J listened to a voice say, "Sorry Dreeka couldn't make it; hope he's not sick. The shipment's ready. Come to gate 9. You guys must really like wozzra!"

J relayed the message to Trish and led the way to Carbono's military defense base, which often doubled as a shipping port. He docked at gate 9 and opened the cargo doors. A Carbonill hopped inside and said, "Welcome! We'll start bringing in the wozzra. Is this the trunk of chips?" He indicated a case next to the doors.

"Take it," J nodded, yawning. He watched several short, armored Carbonills waddle inside, their arms full of transparent containers of wozzra. Once the cargo hold was full, J closed the doors and headed for Omega Sector.

The three ships jumped to their destination and paused to gaze at the distant black planet, Sordon. There were no visible ships or bases in the area.

"Who do we meet with?" Trish radioed in. "I don't see anyone."

Another transmission interrupted them, and a cracked Carbonill voice said, "What took you so long? My buyer is getting jittery."

"This is Sznanzo," J said, imitating the voice of a Carbonill he had once met. Dreeka's voice was too high-pitched for his throat. "Dreeka has been detained. But we have the shipment."

The transmission ended abruptly. J knew he was under suspicion. "Find him!" he shouted to Trish. "G, stay here! Defense mode!"

The Drondo sped off to the right, as the Aria zoomed away to the left. They both followed curved paths in order to meet on the other side of Sordon. On the dark side of the planet was a massive military base. A small Carbonill vessel was fleeing from it at top speed.

Trish flew after the renegade, and J followed. They took positions on either side of him and targeted some key ship's systems. J sent a signal to the Carbonill: "Give up, or we'll blast you into liquid space!"

"You like that expression, don't you?" Trish remarked.

"It's multi-purpose!" J quipped with a grin. "Now, bring your ship to a full stop, or I'll start blasting, Carbonill!"

"You don't understand!" came a plaintive voice. "The Sythee will do anything for that wozzra! Here they come now!"

Two Sythee fighters zoomed in from behind them like swift shadows and fired on all three ships. The Carbonill's ship exploded in a brilliant flash. The Drondo lost its port side entirely. Only the Aria escaped unscathed, thanks to Trish's quick reflexes.

As the ship's systems crashed and exploded around him, J managed to reach the escape pod and leave just before the Drondo split straight through the cockpit, emptying its contents into deep space. Trish had her hands full fighting off the two Sythee. Their ships were slower but more powerful. It was all she could do to keep from getting hit; her nitro-missiles were having no effect on the Sythee ships.

Terrans rarely encountered Sythee, and J regretted that they had not been more prepared. In a final effort to stave off their relentless attacks, he sent them a message: "Cease your attack! We were pursuing the Carbonill because he was a traitor; he planned to take the wozzra and escape with it. We are here to make the trade directly with you."

The Sythee paused as if considering his message. Then, they sent back a message of their own in their own language. It was low-toned and sounded like whispering. The computer's translator automatically switched on and presented J with a mechanical, monotone translation. It said, "Return to the base. We will make the exchange."

The Sythee locked onto the Drondo's cargo hold, which was remarkably intact, with a docking formation and towed it back to their military base.

"They must be desperate," Trish commented via coded transmission, while moving the Aria in to dock with the escape pod. "Need a lift? We'll pick up the Solo on the way."

J gladly climbed aboard her ship and jettisoned the pod. "I don't think the Sythee are aware of the conspiracy they're involved in," he said thoughtfully. "I think they're just desperate for their next fix of wozzra."

"I agree," Trish nodded from the pilot's seat. "So where do we find the guy in charge? Or does he find us?"

"Let's ask around," J suggested jokingly.

As soon as they were docked at the Sythee base, J activated his pocket translator and stepped inside. The place was dark and heavily guarded. The Sythee, who looked like giant black praying mantis', carried primitive weapons, such as clubs and knives. They were transporting the wozzra onto the base. One Sythee, who seemed to be in charge, said something, and the translator repeated it in English, "Your shipment is ready. The food is intact. You may go."

J glanced through a portal and saw a barge marked "Weapons Shipment." He turned to leave, but Trish blocked the door. "We should tell them," she whispered. "Maybe they can help us, too."

J nodded grudgingly and faced the Sythee in charge. His narrow, blank red eyes were creepy. "I, uh, think you should know," J told him, "that stuff can kill your people."

The eight-foot-tall Sythee gripped his dagger with one claw, and J took a deep breath and continued, "I don't know how. But your supplier doesn't care. It's your business whether you believe me or not; we just thought you should know."

There was an uncomfortable silence. Finally, the Sythee spoke, and the translator echoed him, "We will…look into it."

J nodded and said, "Yeah. Good. In the meantime, we'd like to get to the bottom of the whole mess. There's a rumor that the guy who started all this is, uh…Sythee."

The Sythee only blinked at him, and Trish stepped forward. "Is he?" she asked bluntly.

The Sythee answered her, "None here are responsible. The food appeared in our homes. When we knew it was a trick, it was too late. If you find him, bring him here."

"We will," Trish promised and returned to the Aria.

J saw a sickly-looking Sythee drag itself into the room and reach for a container of woozra. A guard swiped at it with a club, knocking it to the floor.

"Why do you distribute the food to all but that one?" J asked.

"He is the brother of a criminal," the Sythee in charge answered. "He helped him escape our base."

J considered the possibility that a renegade Sythee could be behind the whole plan. It seemed more likely than anything else at the moment, so he asked, "Where would a runaway, criminal Sythee go?"

The Sythee only stared at him, so J returned to the Solo. Trish had already picked up the barge. She radioed him, "Let's make a sweep over the planet, just in case."

J acknowledged her, and the two ships dove closer to Sordon and flew off in opposite directions.

Trish stared down at the dark, rocky terrain below her. Sythee crawled over the ground like a swarm of bugs. She could see nothing unusual. The Solo glided within her view, and J radioed her, "There's nothing here. Any ideas?"

Trish thought for a minute and said, "You know, if anyone came here to meet us and saw that scuffle we got into, he probably either took off or hid. Where would you hide?"

"In the last place we'd look," J answered.

Trish grinned and accelerated the Aria toward the Sordon sun. J followed her closely. They circled around the dim star at as low an orbit as they could risk. On the other side, a large Looran ship was hiding in the light.

Trish sent a signal to the ship, "We're here with the shipment. We had some trouble with a traitor. But he's plasma now."

"Detach the barge," said a squawky Looran voice.

Trish complied and watched the Looran ship float toward her and hook up to the barge. Then it sped off past Sordon into empty space. Without saying a word, the siblings followed it at a distance, maintaining radio silence.

After a few hours, they reached an old, patched-up jumpgate that looked like it had been discarded decades ago. Trish theorized that the Looran must have rescued it from the recycling base in order to set it up here, in a part of space that nobody ever visited. She wondered if it would handle all three ships safely; worn-out jumpgates can explode under too much pressure and send their passengers to the other side of a black hole or trap them inside liquid space between jump-points, which is why they're always recycled.

Once the Looran had vanished into the jumpgate, Trish asked J, "Want to risk it? We have no other way to follow him, since jumpgates leave no trail."

"What's life without risk?" J answered with a question of his own. "I say, stay hot or lose your edge!"

Trish grinned and led the way through the jumpgate. In a flash, they were surrounded by the wavy purple ribbons of liquid space. It was dark and made a sloshing noise as they raced through it at the speed of light, hence its name. Trish and her brother were top-notch liquid pilots, but it still took all their concentration to keep one eye on their quarry and the other on their heading. Everything had to be on manual; you had to have a good instinct to make it through, and computers had no instincts at all.

The Looran vessel passed up off-shoot after off-shoot in the long, narrow, meandering tunnel. Finally, they reached the end and emerged on the other side of Omega Sector, just a few miles from the edge of known space.

Trish gazed out into the deep blackness of unknown space for a moment and then focused her attention on the Looran ship. It flew away from the barely functioning jumpgate they had just escaped and toward a patched-together space station floating about 200 yards away. It looked like it was ready to fly apart at the seams.

Trish held her position near the gate, and J followed suit. They watched the Looran dock with the station and slowly approached him. The station was dark and appeared to be drifting aimlessly. Anyone simply passing by might have mistaken it for an abandoned junkheap. However, no one ever came out this far in Omega Sector.

Trish listened for com signals, but everything was quiet. She decided to do something bold and dangerous: dock with the station.

First, she sent a transmission to J, "I'm going in. Stay here and watch for the Looran."

Once the Aria was docked, Trish sneaked carefully on board the station. She heard low voices and followed their sound to a small room. Peering around the corner, she saw two Loorans speaking to each other, one in a pilot's jacket.

"I will return with your instructions," the one in plain robes, a female, said and disappeared into a back room. She returned in a few minutes with a memory chip. The pilot took the chip and returned to his ship, just missing Trish as she hid in the shadows. She took her transmitter out of her belt and sent J a coded message that read, "Follow him!"

J received the message and hid his ship on the other side of the station until the Looran's ship had jumped back through the jumpgate. He followed him all the way to Alpha Sector and then on to Taal in Eta Sector. The Looran slipped through security without pausing and made his way down to Taal-Raal. J followed as closely as he could without giving himself away. The Looran set down on a temporary parking pad and left his ship with a large bag. He headed in the direction of the old DronTee Corp. building.

J flew ahead of him, landed in a field, and sneaked back to the building on foot. He watched from an alley as the Looran arrived and approached the front door. But instead of going inside, he opened his bag and pulled out a fist-sized piece of dragonite and a bottle of liquid cantor big enough to blow up the entire city. He set the dragonite inside a nearby metal container and carefully poured the cantor over it. Horrified, J knew that those two elements combined would take out an area the size of three capital cities. The Looran locked his ion-blaster and set it beside the container in order to heat it up. He glanced around and ran off toward his ship.

As soon as the Looran was out of sight, J dashed to the metal container and unlocked the ion-blaster and turned it off. So the plan involved blowing up cities! Why? J picked up the container and the gun and carried them back to the Solo. He flew to the temporary parking pad and followed the Looran away from the planet. When he was past the Taal Transport Authority, the Looran waited, watching the planet. J flew right up to him and opened the com.

"If you're waiting for Taal-Raal to blow up," he said. "You'll be waiting for a very long time. If I were you, I'd bide my time by surrendering to a local member of the GPF."

Without saying a word, the Looran flew his ship at top speed toward the jumpgate. J followed him without missing a beat and fired a few nitro-missiles. Two of them hit the back of the Looran ship, taking out the navigation system.

"Stop, or you'll lose your engine!" J shouted. He knew that the Looran couldn't hope to enter liquid space and make it out alive without a navigation system, unless he were the best pilot in the universe.

Sure enough, the Looran ship slowed to a halt, and the pilot radioed J, "You are too late! The Taal capital was only the final step; the others are ready, waiting for word. He will control all of known space and much more!"

"Who?" J asked. "And where are the other sites?"

The Looran only laughed, and J knew he was in for a long, difficult interrogation.

Trish stared at the Looran standing guard in the small room. She had been all over the dark, empty station and found nothing but more dark and more emptiness. The only other living creature in the entire structure was this Looran. But she didn't seem to be in charge; she was guarding someone else. The back room had no other entrances; it was the last place Trish needed to look.

She slipped on her gloves and pressed a button on her belt, magnetizing every piece of clothing she was wearing. Quickly and quietly, she climbed up the wall like a Carbonill gecko and into the small room. She crept across the ceiling and paused directly over the Looran's head. Reaching down, she hit the Looran on the top of her head with the butt of her ion-blaster. The guard fell limply to the floor, and Trish pressed the button on her belt again and dropped down. Unsheathing her sword, Trish tip-toed into the back room. It was nearly pitch-black. In one corner, two red eyes glowed at her.

"So the man with the plan **is** Sythee," Trish nodded, pulling her infrared goggles from a pocket and putting them on. The silent shape of the Sythee loomed before her in bright colors. "But why? What do you hope to accomplish? And why not get the materials yourself, instead of going through the elaborate plan? You may as well give it up and tell me; your plan stops here."

The Sythee spoke, and Trish switched on her translator. "It has already begun," it said. The Sythee reached for a communicator, and Trish ran swiftly toward him and dashed it to pieces with her blade.

"If they do not receive word from this location at the end of their day," the Sythee spoke, "they will go ahead without it."

Trish realized what he was talking about. "You plan to use the dragonite and explosives to blow up other parts of known space?! Why?"

The Sythee glared at her and answered, "My people could rule the universe, and they cast me out of my own world. I will rule it all myself. Bow to me."

"Yeah, right," Trish smirked. "Like I said, the plan stops here."

The Sythee drew a sword, and Trish recognized it as a liteshift blade. It glimmered in the dark, and the Sythee flashed it back and forth. Trish readied herself for a duel.

The Sythee struck first with an overhead blow, and Trish blocked it deftly and rolled to the left. She hit the back of one of his legs, slicing into it, and he roared in anger and pain, the loudest sound she had ever heard from one of his kind. He turned to swing at her but was too slow, and she ducked out of the way. She spun around and landed a sharp blow to his back. The Sythee paused, and Trish watched as he regenerated his hard exoskeleton before her eyes.

He swung his blade at her and snapped at her with one scythe-like claw. She blocked the sword and kicked the claw away. But another claw grabbed her left leg, digging into her skin. The Looran dashed into the room and screamed, "You'll pay for this intrusion!" She ran toward Trish and pulled out an ion-blaster.

Trish chopped off the Sythee's arm that held her leg, ducked, and thrust her sword forward into the Looran's abdomen. She fell to the floor, gushing green, oozy blood. The Sythee, cradling his severed, scythe-like claw with its stump, flailed his remaining three arms at Trish. She blocked them all with her sword and her feet, deflecting one blow after another into the walls, until the metal was deeply scarred and falling apart. She stabbed at his legs, knocking him face-down onto the floor. She pinned his blade down with her own and kicked at his head, hoping to knock him unconscious. But his tough exoskeleton was too hard, and she couldn't hold him down for long.

Moving quickly, Trish released the Sythee's sword and stood just out of it reach. She swung her own sword down onto his back with all her strength, slicing through his abdomen and cutting him in half. The arms and legs twitched violently, and the eyes opened and closed. After a few minutes, he lay still.

Trish checked the Sythee's communicator. It was irreparable. She checked the Looran's body but found nothing. She ran back to the Aria and radioed J. There was no response.

J ducked a shot from the Looran's ion-blaster, and it hit an insulated portal. He had taken out the ship's weapons system, but the Looran himself was still kicking. J fired his e-pistol and dashed around a corner. He couldn't hit the Looran from here, but he needed a minute to think. He leaned on the cool metal wall and suddenly remembered that Loorans built their ships out of fothracite, a highly conductive metal found only on their homeworld, Setinal. And fothracite couldn't be treated like other metals to channel electricity away from the interior of ships.

J grinned and pressed a button on each of his boots, generating a protective magnetic field around them. He set his e-pistol to maximum charge, stood, and fired directly at the floor. The electricity traveled all over the ship, but most importantly, it traveled into the Looran's body. He shook violently for a minute and screamed, and then he passed out.

A beep from J's transmitter told him that G was receiving a message. He ran back to the Solo to check it out.

"Where were you?" Trish asked quickly. "Did you catch the Looran?"

"Yeah, caught him planting a bomb," J nodded.

"There are more," Trish said. "I need a list of the coordinates, now! Can you get them?"

"Hold on!" J said and ran back through the docking doors. He hurried to the Looran's cockpit and checked the computer's files. A massive list of coordinates was in a file marked "Targets." J downloaded it into a memory chip and took it back to the Solo. He transmitted the entire list to the Aria.

"I'll send a message to all of them, instructing them to abort the mission and come here," Trish said. "You contact the nearest base and have a back-up team join us as soon as possible."

"Done and done," J nodded. "We beat the bad guy, again. Want to celebrate? It's on me!"

Hours later, Trish watched GPF ships round up every ship that came through the jumpgate. A transmission from Sordon interrupted her thoughts. It was the Sythee they had met on the military base.

"I trust your ships will leave our sector soon," he said.

"We're almost done," Trish nodded. "Did you get your criminal's body? I sent it to the base."

"We received it," he answered.

"You're welcome," Trish sighed, knowing she wouldn't get a "thank you" out of a Sythee. "You know, our people might be able to help you find a cure for your wozzra problem."

"We will take care of our people," he said. "We always do."

The transmission ended, and J's voice said, "Friendly, aren't they? Well, you tried. Want to go to Sigreen? I hear their beaches are just like Earth's used to be."

"Sounds good," Trish sighed. "I could use a vacation."

She followed J toward the jumpgate and waved to the GPF ships. A signal on a secure frequency showed up on the computer's com. She switched it on and listened to the message: "You and J saved us from a potential war and learned more about the Sythee than we have learned in the last decade. You have excelled beyond your duties once again. You are to be congratulated. Both of you will receive promotions from Python, as well as her highest praise."

The message ended, and Trish radioed J, "Hey, how'd you like to be a Samurai, third class?"

"After only two months?" he exclaimed. "Plasma hot! Now that's cause for a celebration!"

The Aria and the Solo flew into the jumpgate and disappeared from view.

DAWN

They rose. Like the dead. Like wild animals stiff from the cold of the chill night. They flickered like candles and shook like ghosts. Their thoughts were whispers on the dark air. They approached the mirror as one, their forms and thoughts blurred in these early hours. They seemed not to walk but to glide in jerky, rocking movements, leaning from side to side. Their shrouds of black and mist would have made them appear to be phantoms if there had been any observers in this place of night.

The four standing as one, they gazed at the circular mirror from behind their shrouds of death and dark. They waited.

The mirror shattered, the cracks splitting their images in two or three. The mirror fell to the cold, hard floor. They turned away, their shrouds fading like mist in the morning sun.

They stood in the darkness and peered into the night air, listening to the whispers of their thoughts, to the soft drip of deep red blood that leaked from the edges of the broken mirror and pooled on the floor.

Finally, a voice broke what would have passed for silence in other company.

"A strange message. Is something happening?"

No one answered. Three heads turned toward the figure closest to the shattered mirror. The reflection of the back of his head made each glass shard appear black. The brass frame was unbroken, but the blood had stained it as it spilled out onto the floor. The deep red puddle moved slowly toward them, stopping only at a crack in the tile.

His gloved hands raised to cover his face briefly, then his arms stretched out to either side of his body, like a large black bird. His eyes looked up at each of them in turn, past their eyes, past their skulls, past their minds. When he spoke, they shivered, not only from the words but also from the very sound of his voice.

"The Beast."

The other three looked down or sideways, their thoughts turning to memories of the past. The night air seemed to transform into ice around them.

One of them struck a match on a finger and held the flame to a cigarette that hung from lips of deep red. A curl of smoke floated slowly from between the lips, as if time were slowed. The flame died, its last dance reflected in eyes of deepest ebony. He, or she, for it was impossible for any outsider to tell, raised one thin eyebrow and put one hand upon one hip. Its hair was orange and black, like flames at night, and as short as a low campfire. It wore a suit of black with a turned-up collar.

Another of their group hung back, peering past the long, straight wave of hair as dark as night that covered half of his face. His lips curled into a distasteful frown, he lifted one hand and gently waved away the bits of mist that wafted past him. He leaned uncertainly away from his companions.

In the center of their circle, a feminine figure stood, expressionless. Her long black hair, pale complexion, deep red lips, and stately black, high-collared ball gown gave her the look of a life-size china doll. She raised a hand and tilted it, the fingers locked in position as if she were holding something invisible. Then, the fingers relaxed, and the hand floated back down to rest on the abysmal blackness of her long skirt. The first of their number nodded with his eyes closed and then spoke.

"We will prepare."

Their rituals were old. Their traditions were older. Their mysteries were too old to be fathomed any longer. They were what was quaintly referred to in some circles as "children of the night." In a nutshell, they were vampires. Not the vampires of myth and legend, of course. That would be impossible. No creature could transmute its own form into that of another. No being could survive forever bound to the soil of its ancestral home. There were those, however, who were immortal. The vampires were the most famous among them. They fancied themselves to be gods. Forgotten gods, but gods nonetheless. They ruled over none but their own kind, yet any other being that met them would instinctively know that they were to be respected. Was that respect warranted? Certainly. Earned? Usually. Necessary? Without question. But deserved? Such a question would not easily enter the mind of one of these exalted beings, but what is not easily done can still be done, as he well knew.

His name was Adalgiso. It had been something else a very long time ago, but he could no longer remember either what it had been or when it had changed. Someday, he knew he would forget that it had changed at all. That was one of their oldest traditions, to forget what had been and to embrace what had become. He was obedient to all of their traditions. They were as precious to him as the rituals that had brought him into the sacred circle of his family. He was not unhappy. He was restless. Being the youngest had little to do with it. Having been adopted had less to do with it, since the rituals had made him a bloodkin. What caused his restlessness he did not know.

He tugged at the modern tie around his neck and adjusted his collar nervously. He was uncomfortable in these clothes, the clothing of his funeral and his birth. The gray tie was the only thing in the room that was not black, aside from his pale skin. It was a remnant of his past life, and it was tradition that he carry it with him always. He stood alone in front of the shattered mirror. The conduit had served its purpose, yet he felt a bit of sadness at its loss. Even in their world of forever, some things ended. Some things shattered.

He turned his head to avoid the image of broken glass and pooled blood. The wave of hair that covered the right half of his face shielded him from that side of the room. It came down in a point at his chin. He sometimes wished he could cut it off, but that was the way it had always been. So that was the way it would always stay. His roundish face grimaced, and he shivered. It was not only the mirror; something else was bothering him. Something big was coming. He knew little of the Beast, but he knew he had little to fear. Their kind did not slay one another. Tradition forbade that. But what else could be playing upon his uncertainties and sending ghosts of thoughts through his mind? He made up his mind to discuss it with his youngest sibling. He reached out with his thoughts until he found his target and then followed them out of the room and down a dark corridor of their castle.

He found his sibling in the library, lounging on a couch in a disinterested manner. A newly lit cigarette perched on the end of an ebony holder between two fingers. The fiery orange hair seemed like a beacon in the midst of all the blackness. It was the only color this member of the family had, and it was the brightest bit of color in the castle. Adalgiso spoke softly, hoping not to disturb his sibling too deeply.

"Is there something to be feared, Ridd?"

Without glancing at him, Ridd answered in a low monotone, "What could we have to fear from one of our own?"

Adalgiso was not satisfied. Ridd had responded with a question. Was there something going unspoken between them? Adalgiso breathed in the night air and listened for a whisper of a thought, but all that came to him was one of his own. He spoke again, more firmly in hopes of drawing out whatever Ridd was holding back.

"You feel it, too. There is something. Perhaps, the Beast has nothing to do with it."

He shivered at the sound of his own voice speaking the name of their ruler, their master. Even for those who had no reason to fear It, the Beast induced a certain amount of terror. It was said that the Beast was more terrible than a thousand eternities and more powerful than a thousand vampires.

"Perhaps," Ridd whispered.

That was answer enough. Ridd did not know what was coming that could warrant such trepidation, but there was definitely something in their near future. Content with that answer, Adalgiso turned and left Ridd to the solitude of the library. He returned to the conduit chamber, where a new conduit mirror was already forming from the shards of its predecessor. He would not question his oldest siblings. If Ridd was ordinarily reluctant to even speak to Adalgiso, the others did not usually deign to acknowledge him at all. If they knew anything of the future, they would not tell him. It was tradition. He had not yet performed his eternity ritual. Until he did, he was a lesser bloodkin, no less loved and respected but destined to remain in the dark on certain matters of authority. Even now, they would be performing the rituals to accept a visit from their master. The Beast would arrive in Its own time, perhaps tomorrow, perhaps next century.

Adalgiso watched the mirror forming at his feet. To honor the conduit ritual, as was his duty, he waited until the glass was nearly complete, then knelt next to it and pricked one finger on the sharp point of a remaining edge. He held the finger over the smoothing glass and dripped four drops of his own deep red blood over it. The blood hit the glass soundlessly and was absorbed into it. In moments, the mirror was complete. It was a new mirror, the frame an endless black and the glass slightly more oblong than the previous one. His blood, the blood of his family, would ensure that the conduit would function according to their will and would alert them of messages from others of their kind. He performed the ritual handsign over the glass and then gently lifted it from the stone floor and placed it on the stone wall. He gazed at his own reflection and wondered with wispy thoughts what the future would hold for his beloved castle.

Ridd sat in the library, surrounded by dark, invisible thoughts. The air was full of them. They floated and hovered and obscured. Adalgiso was correct; something was approaching the family's destiny. What it could be was still unknowable. The oldest of their circle probably did not know himself, although he was no doubt conferring with their sister on the subject. Adalgiso would not be included in such a discussion by matter of tradition, but Ridd could join them in the ritual room if it became necessary. So far, it did not seem to be. After all, they had nothing to fear from the Beast, as much as they might feel a bit of anxiety at Its approach anyway. Whatever was causing the ripples in the reflection of their fate was not an immediate danger to them. Its mysteriousness was enough to hold Ridd's attention, but it was not enough to warrant any rash actions.

Ridd did not fear reprisal from the family or the shame of ignoring the rituals. Such a thing would never happen. But Ridd's behavior was not ruled by concern for fellow vampires, even those within the castle. In fact, it was not ruled by any emotions at all. Fear, concern, compassion – such words were not to be heard from those lips nor echoed from that heart. Yet the air in the library was not devoid of emotion. Curiosity hovered lightly, and an urge to rebel hung behind it, pushed to the side but not forgotten. Ridd had once been the youngest, not to mention one of the first of the new generation of their kind, different from the older ones in a subtle but crystalline way.

The window on the other side of the room reflected back the image of the vampire sitting lazily on the long couch, surrounded by shelves of books and a single candlestick in the center of an end table. Anyone peering inside would have thought a human was seated there, blowing smoke into the air. Mortals and vampires looked remarkably identical from a distance. But closer proximity had a way of revealing the dark eternity within a vampire's eyes. And mortals did not naturally develop hair the bright shade of Ridd's orange and black. It contrasted nicely with the deep black suit, its high collar turned up and slightly out. Still, Ridd had once wondered why vampires and mortals shared so much in appearance. Sometimes, the question still hovered in the air when the smoke was making circles. Being a member of the bloodkin did not answer all questions.

Every member of the new generation had questions to which they might never know the answers. Why were they created? The endless vampires had no need to procreate as the mortals did. What had happened to the oldest of their kind, the ones that had come before even the masters? They were never spoken of and yet were destined to be remembered in the rituals of sacrifice. What had been the true power of the oldest ones, the power that had made them the masters of the earth? Such things were not spoken of. If the oldest members of Ridd's family knew these things, they did not let the secrets escape their thoughts. These questions had made those of the new generation a bit rebellious, especially during the first few millennia following their creation. They followed the rituals and traditions without question, but they did not live in the same manner as their relatives and ancestors. Their behavior did not always conform. Their habits sometimes took them into the realm of the mortals. Traveling among mortals was unnecessary but could be quite interesting. For some, it could be amusing. Mortals found Ridd's appearance to be confusing and uncomfortable, as they were unable to decipher the vampire's gender. The lanky body showed no curves underneath its suit, and the face revealed elements both feminine and masculine. The family knew, of course, and vampires would have no trouble with the question, nor would they let it bother them if they did; but Ridd kept the secret from all others. It was amusing.

The wind outside the castle howled past the window, rattling the glass in its casement. The thoughts that floated in through the walls were uneasy and uncertain. Even the Immortal realm was anxious about the Beast's impending visit. Ridd puffed on the cigarette and breathed the smoke out into the air slowly. It curled about the flames atop the vampire's head and mingled with the thoughts and questions in the library. One thought finally rose above the others, and Ridd's voice spoke softly in the night: "It should be interesting, but we have nothing to fear. I shall watch, as I have always done."

Her doll's eyes stared back at her eldest sibling's face, seeing all and yet seeing nothing. Sakra was discomfited by this.

"Give me your thoughts, brother," she said wordlessly, speaking through gestures and thoughts.

She could not reach out to him any further without offending his rank and honor. If it were meant for her to share in his troubles, he would have to extend the invitation to her first. She waited patiently. Patience was her most skilled and most important attribute. She prided herself on her ability to wait centuries for the answer to a question. All vampires could wait, of course. But Sakra could do it in the most crystalline manner. It was always clear by her very indifference that although she had asked the question, she did not care whether she received the answer, and she did not care how long it took to hear it. Few creatures of this world knew whether her apparent apathy was true or a clever façade.

She waited silently, motionless, her hands folded neatly before her. Her long black hair was perfectly arranged to fall down her back, like a cascade of night. Her long, dark ball gown, a relic from the past, did not emit a single rustling noise as it hung on her thin body. Even the emerald ring on her finger, the only color she wore, seemed muted and subdued, as if sensing the gravity of the occasion and waiting for its turn to shine. Its turn only came during the rituals. As it was Sakra's sacred duty to be the record-keeper for the family, it was her ring's place to play a vital role in each ritual that she supervised. She was the keeper of legend and lore, of history and story, of ritual and tradition. She was the link between the family as it was and as it is. The ring was her link to the family as it would be and as it should be. But only she knew this.

There were, after all, secrets that had to be kept from even the most trustworthy souls. Which was another reason that she understood the need for patience so well. Some things could not simply be spoken or given away. Her expressionless face watched her brother solemnly, as he obscured his thoughts and checked them over one by one. His patience matched hers in scope if not in depth. Eventually, he would decide that she should be told whatever was floating in the air immediately surrounding his head. There was very little they kept from one another and very few occasions when it had been necessary to keep secrets of any kind. It had always been so.

Sakra had been born into the family for the express purpose of keeping the rituals and keeping the secrets, not from members of her own kin but from outsiders and otherworlders. None could have done this job better. And none could have worked with her elder brother better. Their very thoughts seemed always properly aligned. They worked together better than a single entity could have. Why that was, only the oldest could have told them. But it mattered not. The family and the traditions were the important things. Ridd had once asked Sakra who she had been before. "No one," she had told him. "No one at all." And it was true. She had not existed before the family, before their kin.

What better reason could there be for the perfect step that she and her elder brother kept together? As the two eldest of the family, it was tradition. It was unquestionable.

Her brother turned his dark eyes and stared straight into hers, four identical pools of darkness hovering in the night air at the same height and reflecting skin of the same pale hue and hair of the same tone and texture. He spoke with a soft voice that felt like velvet, but the weight of his words was more than expected.

"I am concerned."

His face showed no concern, but Sakra knew he spoke the truth. She could feel it.

"What will happen?" she asked.

"I do not know," he answered and turned away.

That was why he was concerned. It was for the eldest among them to know what was coming and to prepare the family. If he did not know what would happen when the Beast arrived, the ritual would be broken, and the family would not be far behind it. Sakra felt the heaviness of this knowledge and weighed it carefully with her thoughts. Together, they would be strong. Together, they would support the family. But without the rituals and traditions, would it be enough? They would continue, but who and what would they be? The Beast would bring these answers, but would It be willing to give them? As record-keeper, it was Sakra's sacred duty to observe the coming of the Beast but not interact with It directly. That anxious honor went to her eldest brother. He would have to ask the questions alone and observe the rituals alone.

It mattered not, she knew. If one perished, all would perish. If the rituals died, all would die. If the Beast refused their council, the family would cease to exist. All that could be done until such a time was to wait.

Kraas finally allowed his thoughts to commingle with those of his sister. Her concern was not obvious, but it was palpable. The family was in an uncomfortable situation. To not know what was on the horizon of their destiny was the worst possible thing that could happen. The question of their fate had been hovering on the edges of their communal consciousness for a mere second in the length of their eternal night. The message of the Beast's arrival coming to them at such a time could not be coincidence. And yet, what did they, as members of the bloodkin, have to fear from one of their own? These thoughts were discomfiting. But Kraas did not share his whole mind with Sakra. As record-keeper, she should know his thoughts on the message. But it was as yet unnecessary to share his feelings or his fears.

Kraas turned from his sister and pushed his thoughts outward, touching on the drifting concerns of his other siblings. Ridd was curious as usual but patient enough to wait. Adalgiso's restless thoughts filled the conduit room as he stared into his own eyes, attempting to fathom his place in the family and its place in the universe. He was a child still, not yet fully prepared to accept their fate, whatever it was.

The question drifted between Kraas and Sakra, spinning circles around their dark heads and clouding the other thoughts. They considered its implications. To make the family stronger, they would sacrifice anything. But would such a thing make the family stronger or weaker? It was up to the eldest to choose the time of a new bloodkin's eternity ritual. Was the youngest of their number ready to completely enter their world of darkness? If he were, the ritual would strengthen the family's bonds and give them the power to see further into their own fate. If he were not, the family's power would wane, and they would be crushed by the weight of their own destiny and the will of the Beast. His own hesitation was answer enough. Kraas knew that the young one was not yet ready for the eternity ritual.

A soundless sigh filled the room, and the two siblings bowed their heads in silent defeat. The uncertainty was overwhelming for Immortals such as themselves. Their fate had always been known; it had been decided before they came to be. Something was changing.

Kraas turned and gazed into Sakra's doll eyes. Would the two siblings be strong enough to stand for the family? This was unknown. But they would follow their traditions to the last, for therein lay their strength. And perhaps, the Beast would have some answers It would be willing to share.

He inclined his head slightly, indicating that the preparation ritual should begin. Sakra obediently lifted one hand, the emerald ring on her finger shining brightly. It would focus her thoughts. Kraas raised his own arms, palms inward, and curled his fingers into fists. He crossed his forearms over his chest, where they covered the pendant he wore around his neck. Without it, only his pale skin shone with a different hue than his black clothing and hair. His straight black locks hung carelessly around his face, long enough to cover his ears but not touch his shoulders. His long black coat hung on his thin frame as if it had been fitted perfectly to the contours of his body, ending just before his feet touched the ground. The buttons ended at his waist so that it billowed around his legs when he walked quickly, often slower than he moved, time being relative to an Immortal. The pendant was a dull silver, a relic from long ago with its own secrets, and with a long, thin shapeless shape that meant nothing and everything. It would help him focus in this time of uncertainty. His eyes closed, his fingers relaxing, he let his arms and his thoughts drift away from his body. He repeated the ancient handsigns, feeling Sakra's support as she copied him. They moved together without looking at one another. An observer from the mortal realm would have seen black magic in their motions, but it was only tradition.

Together, the oldest of the family stood and performed the ritual. They did not grow weary from the effort, although the time that passed would have tired any human. Their hands moved in a constant synchronicity, and their thoughts performed acrobatic twirls in the air around them. Finally, they reached out with their thoughts and informed their younger siblings that the ritual was complete, drawing them into the swirl of tradition. It was done.

Kraas waved his sister away, and she left the ritual room to join the others outside the door. The eldest remained in place, composing his thoughts and steeling himself for the task ahead. It would be up to him to keep the family strong and centered. As the eldest, it always fell to him to maintain their traditions. He did not resent this, as a mortal would. He relished it. It was what he had come into being for. But it would be particularly difficult until he could ascertain the source of these troubling thoughts and discover what was coming that could provoke such uncertainty and fear. He knew his place. But could he keep it? If the family fell, the dishonor would rest heavily on him above all the others. The traditions must be maintained. He could not let them fail.

Adalgiso's thoughts twisted about his skull, weaving through his hair and leaving a trail behind him from the conduit room to the hall outside the ritual room. Ridd was staring at him in an unnerving manner, and Sakra seemed displeased. She did not show it by her face or her manner. But her thoughts were directed at him in a very rough fashion. Her mind snatched at a tendril of smoky thought that had reached out to her plaintively, and her eyes widened slightly. It was an almost unnoticeable reaction, but the fact that Adalgiso had noticed it was disturbing to them both. He knew by her thoughts, which were now swirling with a speed and intensity he had never felt, that his suspicions were correct. The Beast was not the only visitor that they were to have soon.

Ridd raised one eyebrow and puffed on a cigarette in one hand. Sakra made a flowing gesture with both arms and turned to await their oldest brother. The three stood outside the door silently and patiently. Everything happened in its own time in the castle. The darkness intruded on their thoughts, intertwining with the smoke and the feelings. Adalgiso found himself repeating his concerns in a never-ending whirlpool of thought, hoping for an explanation but not expecting one. The pool of blood in the conduit room had not concerned him at first. It had always vanished on its own after past messages. This time, however, it had stayed, staining the tile and expanding to cover half the floor. Just as Kraas and Sakra were finishing the ritual to prepare for the Beast, the pool had begun to recede, into the floor and the wall behind the new mirror. Who was coming besides the terrible Beast? Adalgiso didn't know. He could feel that Ridd didn't know either. If Sakra knew, she was waiting for their eldest brother's approval to let the secret out. But Adalgiso could feel the tension and knew that the answer was worse than the first message.

When Kraas finally emerged from the ritual room, he paused and, with a stony face, examined the wall of thoughts that greeted him. His eyes narrowed, and his glance fell on Adalgiso. He was not angry with his youngest sibling, but the fear that the youngest was exuding was filling the room in a way that did not become one of the Immortals. Adalgiso calmed himself obediently and awaited an explanation. Ridd leaned against the wall and waited as well. Sakra raised her emerald ring expectantly. Another momentous occasion was upon them. When Kraas finally spoke, his voice was soft, and his siblings could feel the defeat sliding from his mind and enveloping the castle. The two words he spoke felt like a death knell.

"The Twins."

The silence would have been deafening in mortal company. As it was, the hurricane of thoughts and sensations that swirled invisibly around their bodies seemed to drown out the very darkness. Nothing else moved for an eternal moment. A single thought from the eldest of their group hovered above them and suppressed all other thoughts slowly but determinedly. They must uphold the traditions. All was not lost as long as their traditions held.

Adalgiso had questions, but he knew better than to ask them. He looked to Ridd for assistance. The indifferent look on his sibling's face told him nothing, but the curiosity swirling about the orange and black locks screamed for answers. There was no time for dealing with such concerns now, however. Sakra sent them both away with a tilt of her head and followed Kraas back into the ritual room. Further rituals were necessary to receive the additional honored guests.

Adalgiso watched Ridd slip silently back down the hall, feet barely touching the ground. He followed, contemplating the significance of the latest message. He knew little of the Twins except that they were as old and revered as the Beast Itself. It was unheard of for more than one of these exalted old ones to pay a single family a visit at the same time. Something was happening. Adalgiso followed Ridd into the library and stood uncertainly in the doorway. Ridd was content to return to the couch and the candlelight. But Adalgiso was feeling an impatience rise within. He spoke softly and pleadingly.

"Tell me of the Twins."

The words hung on the air like the smoke from Ridd's cigarette. The burning light at the end of the white stick matched the orange in Ridd's hair. Adalgiso waited as his sibling considered the request. They remained motionless, both of them, for what felt like an eternity to Adalgiso. He was still aware of how time moved in the realm of mortals. Finally, Ridd spoke, so quietly that Adalgiso almost thought he was hearing his sibling's thoughts.

"I don't know why they are coming, although I suspect that our brother and sister do. The significance of the Beast and the Twins arriving within the same millennium cannot be lost on them. But I can tell you what I have learned myself in the years prior to your acceptance into this family."

Ridd took another puff on the cigarette before continuing. The thoughts flowing between their heads seemed suspended for the moment.

"The Twins together are as powerful as the Beast. There have been whisperings of a time when they were a single being, and whisperings of a time when they were rivals. A time long before the families arose. Now the Beast bows to them, as we do to It. They are just as fearsome as It is. With the three coming here, there will be more power and more to fear within these walls than there has ever been."

Adalgiso contemplated this revelation. Was his family to fall before the most feared, most powerful of their kind? But no Immortal would harm another. He was uncertain. Ridd's words weighed on his mind, especially the word "rivals." If these old ones had been rivals in the time long before the families, did that mean they had meant each other harm? If so, it was possible that they might return to such savagery someday. And what better omen than a mutual meeting at this castle of night? Adalgiso's fear grew, and he left Ridd so as not to disturb the calm eddies of thought that floated about the library. He returned to the conduit room and gazed into the mirror, hoping for a brighter message.

They moved as if they were unaccustomed to working the muscles of their bodies. Kraas and Sakra went through the motions of the ritual, their minds and bodies focused on tradition. It was an ancient dance. If there had been a single human watching them, his eyes would have missed the subtle movements of the art. Each time he blinked, the two Immortals would have seemed to move from one side of the room to another with no effort or time involved. Their arms reached out like wings, as if in welcome of some great invisible creature. Many of the hand gestures mimicked those of the earlier ritual, but the body movements were less controlled.

When they had completed the ritual, they floated as one out of the room and down the hall. They joined Adalgiso in the conduit room and called to Ridd with their minds. When the four were assembled, Kraas spoke once more, his voice calm and even, but his mind was a turmoil of fear.

"Change may be coming to us. Not only to us, but also to every family in this realm. It may even affect the mortals."

He paused, and Sakra silently bolstered his courage with her own. Her voice was not needed, but her thoughts were holding the four of them together, reminding them all of their past and their traditions.

"We cannot know what will come to be, but we have been chosen to be a part of it. For that, we can be honored. We may become a part of a new tradition. Although such things do not occur often, our stories and histories tell us that they have happened. Each time was a difficult one for our people. We thrive on tradition and ritual. But if something must change, it will be our honor to be part of it. Prepare yourselves for the arrival of the old ones. Our family will not fall until its time."

Kraas had never added the qualifier at the end of that thought. "Until its time." Such an idea was like acid inside the skulls of his siblings. Each of them digested the suggestion slowly. One by one, they surrendered to the idea that their beloved family might come to an end. The thought had never occurred to them before. Why should it? The family was even more immortal than the Immortals. Or was it? Their swirling thoughts all turned to the time before the rise of the families. There had been a time when all Immortals had been alone. Would that time come again? These questions fogged their minds, but they turned away from one another to find a lonely spot in the castle to prepare themselves mentally for the arrival of the old ones.

Adalgiso remained in the conduit room. As it was his duty to monitor and restore the mirror, he felt most comfortable here. Ridd returned to the library, Sakra to the ritual room. Kraas found solace in the highest room in the castle, the tower room. There, amongst the dust of past centuries and the emptiness of the deepest shadows, the eldest cleared his mind of turmoil and prepared himself to stand strong beside his family before the oldest of the old ones.

They could feel It coming before It arrived. It was like a siren's call across the land, through the air, reaching them through the miasma of time and space. Enough time had passed for them to prepare for Its arrival; whether that had been days or years, none of them could say. But the Beast had finally arrived. They gathered instinctively in the largest room of the castle to welcome It. Their thoughts were clear, and they moved as one. Kraas felt no doubt about the coming encounter. Sakra did not hesitate in her duty. Ridd quelled the curiosity that had drifted about the library. Even Adalgiso entertained no more thoughts of his own fear and uncertainty. They were one family.

It stepped out of the shadows as if It had been waiting there for them for centuries. The sudden brightness of Its clothing and pale skin was stunning. To the mortal eye, It appeared to be a child, a young boy, no older than 12 years. In truth, It was a creature of darkness closer to 12 millennia in age. Its skin was paler than that of any other in the room. Its clothes were white. Its hair was a golden white. It walked,

Its legs moving with clarity, but It made no sound upon the cold, dark tiles. The air felt as if it were filled with a thousand shuddering sounds, yet silence filled the room. It seemed to move in slow motion. It gazed upon them with deep black sockets that seemed to hold no eyes at all but rather the cold blackness of infinity. It stopped before them and licked Its black lips with a deep red tongue. The traditional greeting for an old one.

The family responded in kind. Kraas extended one arm behind him and leaned forward, then clasped both arms around his own torso and spun around, his coattails flying, and flung his arms behind his body. It was an old dance; it was tradition. Sakra reached out with one hand, grasping at air, then spun, her long black skirt spinning around her, her arm twisting and her head lolling to one side so that her perfectly coifed hair was flung to the side, and finally stopped and held her arms up to frame her expressionless face. Ridd leaned forward as though to bow, then flung one arm to the side, remaining in this position for some time before suddenly standing straight and clasping both hands in submission. Adalgiso held both arms up and gazed upward into the shadows in the rafters, then stepped back and to the side with one foot, lowering one arm to point at the honored guest, palm upward.

The welcoming rituals complete, the family awaited the Beast's response. After a few eternal moments, It bared its teeth and opened its mouth. As one, the family felt a sigh escape their thoughts. The Beast had accepted their ritual welcome and would now commune with them. Pulsing waves of thoughts flowed from the dark creature's mind into theirs, overwhelming their own thoughts and numbing their feelings. One by one, they became lost in the master's flow of consciousness, Its thoughts becoming their own. It planned to visit other families as well, spreading the news of a change to their age-old, beloved traditions. A new kind of Immortal reign was coming, a reign that would eliminate the need to distance themselves from the mortals. A brief flame of a thought welled up amongst the powerful ideas, a thought that seemed to come from one of the family, although it was impossible to see which member produced it. This thought formed a question about why the Immortals should care to mingle with the mortals, why they should desire to leave their sacred dark places, the places of night and eternity. This thought was quickly quelled. The Beast had spoken, and none would question It. A brief flash of terror swept through the family's mind, exhibiting the Beast's power. There would be no further questions.

Even after the deep mental connection was severed, the five figures stood in the castle, feeling each other's presence and contemplating the future. At least, the family did so. The Beast merely stood, aloof and disconnected, staring with Its soulless black sockets. It didn't move or breathe, and It didn't even seem to think. Not a single feeling or notion crept from Its skull during those interminable hours, days, and weeks. It had no need of such trivialities. It was only awaiting the proper time for a movement or a thought or Its own departure. The family dared not leave Its side; it was tradition to attend such an honored guest during every moment of Its visit.

After some time, Adalgiso felt himself slipping just a bit. In terror, he realigned his thoughts with that of his family, but the damage had been done. He found himself wondering whether the Twins were really coming and what this new reign of Immortals would be like. The family echoed his questions, with the doubts floating freely between them, until the black gaze of the Beast reminded them of their peril. Kraas reprimanded Adalgiso, and the family returned to their synchronous thoughts of obedience and ritual.

The Beast required sustenance. They would provide it. What thoughts they had left, what desires still flitted about them, what emotions still sifted through their minds, these things were drawn out of them toward the Beast. A drop of deep red blood fell from the Beast's black lips as it absorbed all these things and more. It seemed to pull the very energy out of their bodies until they were as weak as mortals. It was their duty to feed the Beast, but It seemed to take more than It needed. Once they were drained to the last, It turned from them, and they fell like rag dolls to the floor.

In this weakened state, the family could no longer maintain such a strict connection. Their thoughts fragmented and separated. Kraas could no longer feel his sister's support; Sakra could no longer sense enough of her family to record their history; Ridd could no longer muster enough curiosity to ask the questions that had pierced their concentration earlier; and Adalgiso felt only fear, a terrific fear that left him paralyzed beyond his lack of energy. Would the Beast leave them so? Why had It taken so much? He tried to control his feelings so that the Beast would not notice them, but the creature seemed to be otherwise occupied.

The Beast was speaking wordlessly to someone else, someone in a different place and time. It stepped back into the shadows and seemed to vanish, but only to the naked eye. Its presence was still among them. It was only communing with one of Its own kind, another old one.

Quite suddenly, the room became too bright to look at, although the lighting had not changed. The shadows remained as they were, and no candles or lamps had been lit. The brightness seemed to be coming from everywhere and nowhere. The prone figures of the family closed their eyes tightly but could still sense the changes around them. The tiles on the floor slowly changed color to blood red, and the drapes on the walls closed, covering all windows and doors. Two figures, hand in hand, appeared in the room before them. The Twins.

They appeared to be two mortal girls, about the same age as the Beast. Of course, they were not. They were as old and as powerful as the other. They wore old-fashioned black dresses and black lacy veils over long black hair. One whispered in the ear of its sister, and they both smiled at the family, wide grins that were longer and sharper than they should have been on such small, round faces.

The family were lifted to their feet, slowly and in jerky movements. They looked like marionettes on strings, as indeed they may well have been. They had no energy of their own, none to perform the welcoming rituals for the Twins. This was their first break with tradition, and Kraas' siblings could feel his sorrow and hopelessness. They faded in and out of reality and were finally left standing under their own miniscule power to await judgement.

The Twins turned and walked slowly, hand-in-hand, into the shadows at the far end of the room. There, they communed with the Beast, invisible and silent. Their hunger was palpable, but the family had nothing left to give. They felt wild and unstoppable, and the family cringed within themselves.

Kraas summoned a tendril of thought and spurred his siblings to reach out with him into the mortal realm. Only there could they siphon off enough energy to perhaps renew their own reserves and feed the Twins. Otherwise, it would take centuries to return their bodies to their former state. Adalgiso felt a moment of revulsion but shoved it aside. He hadn't been mortal in some time; it must have been his weakened state that made him so conscious of his former connection to them. The others felt no doubts. As one, the four minds searched the mortal world for thoughts and energy to renew the flow of their own blood. Slowly, the emptiness abated, and the darkness crept into the spaces within their bodies once more. They feared the Twins' return at any moment, but the creatures paid them no heed. Their minds tripped from one mortal to the next, wearying one, sucking dry another, taking what they needed and moving on as quickly as possible. It was barely satisfying without the time to enjoy the connection and the mutual feasting, but one tradition had already been broken. Kraas was loath to tempt fate in the breaking of another. Their quickly harvested thoughts and energies would be poor sustenance for two old ones, but it was better than abandoning the tradition altogether. He could feel the crack within the family's sphere of strength already. They must fight it, regardless of the end.

Before they had taken their fill, the Twins returned from the shadows. The Beast had gone. Where, they could not say. But they would feed themselves from the mortal realm and then go to the tower room to collect their thoughts.

The creatures were gone as suddenly as they had appeared. The family was devastated. Two traditions broken in one visit. They could feel their mental connections to one another breaking as well. Kraas broke into the maelstrom of their thoughts with vocal words.

"We must strengthen the family and repair the damage. The youngest will prepare himself for the eternity ritual."

Adalgiso shivered at these words. He was not ready, and Kraas knew it. But the best way to solidify a family was to add another member, new blood as it were. Whether this would work when the new member was not ready for the ritual, only time would tell them. The irony was evident, since time meant nothing to them. Adalgiso reached out to his family for support, and they reassured him with their thoughts. But their own feelings were tenuous as well. Their hold on each other was loosening, and the eternity ritual would either save them or doom them. For the first time since he joined the family, Adalgiso felt unworthy.

Why? Why were things changing now? Why had the old ones ignored and dashed tradition upon the rocks of mortal time? There were no answers anywhere in the dark castle. As the seconds ticked by and the Twins remained in the tower room, Adalgiso attempted to prepare himself for the eternity ritual. Becoming a full-fledged member of the family was an honor for which he did not feel worthy. As old as he was in the eyes of men, he was but an infant among the Immortals. The strongest of familial connections had not yet been established between himself and his elder siblings. If the family fell after the ritual, the fault would lay upon his honor alone.

A wisp of a suggestion stole into his solitude and returned thoughts of rebellion to his mind. "You could refuse." It was the mind of Ridd that interrupted Adalgiso's private contemplations. His uncertainty must have slithered from the conduit room where he knelt to the library, where his older sibling sat in a different private contemplation. Adalgiso considered the thought. There would be no reprisal for such a refusal since the family, including the eldest, was well aware of Adalgiso's status. They knew he was not ready and would not blame him for refusing to participate in the eternity ritual ahead of its time. But if the family fell anyway, as seemed likely, none of it would matter but that they had adhered to the traditions to the very end.

Adalgiso asked his older sibling with smoky thoughts why this idea of refusal had been sent to him. After all, the family had few choices and little time. Ridd's answer was cryptic. "We must all follow our natures, whether learned or known." There were no further thoughts on the subject, no matter how Adalgiso pleaded for them. He was left to his own thoughts once more, but he had no wish to dwell on his sibling's strange messages. The family was more important than anything to him, and tradition was all-important to the family. If the eternity ritual could restore their bonds and their strength, he must prepare himself for it and vow to make it work.

He cleared his thoughts and set about the task of organizing his own mind. He must align his thoughts and energies perfectly with those of his family, forging new connections from afar and sharing his own strength without reservation. It took an enormous amount of concentration, especially since he had not had the time usually required to grow these connections in silence and darkness. If he had been capable of the mortal ability of perspiring, his body would have produced copious amounts of sweat in the midst of his tremendous efforts. His siblings reached out to him, drawing him on, but they could not do the work for him. He opened his mind to eternity, tried to grasp its significance and its power. Each moment he felt as though he had reached some sort of enlightened state, only to feel it slip through his grasp, unable to pierce the mysteries of time with his mind. The urgency with which he made each attempt caused him to be acutely aware of the passage of mortal time. He felt the oppressive presence of the Twins within the walls of the castle and forced himself to look elsewhere, to concentrate on the infinity within them all. Immortals had a special connection to the eternal night, and he must find it. His efforts continued for years of mortal time.

Finally, they were ready. The family gathered in the ritual room, their thoughts only of support and strength. They stood as one, physically and mentally. The draperies had turned a deep shade of red from the long visitation of the Twins. Kraas held out one arm and swept all discordant thoughts from the air. The ritual had begun. Adalgiso dutifully filled the empty places with thoughts of loyalty and oneness with the family. Sakra stood perfectly still, recording in her mind and her ring the events that were unfolding. Ridd provided support for the youngest of their number, coaxing him mentally with thoughts of harmony.

Adalgiso began the ritual handsigns, abolishing memories of his long-ago mortal existence. One by one, they flitted through the air, intertwining with other wispy thoughts and vanishing in a puff of smoke. They were replaced by thoughts of the family's future and visions of its illustrious past. Reflections of his past thoughts and feelings seemed to confirm that he was destined to be among the Immortals, and Adalgiso felt stronger as the ritual took hold. Perhaps, he was ready, after all. He savored the moments from long ago as they vanished from his memory, one by one.

"There are some times when I feel as though I saw Death once and have been watching Its approach, or rather my approach to It, ever since. Indeed, I sometimes feel that I can watch nothing else. Many around me have reached, and will reach, Death first, and I feel their loss as keenly as I feel the fear that my own approach to that dark

figure elicits. Death is not a single destination, of course. We feel the chill of Its shadow when It touches someone near to us. And we feel Its icy gaze upon us when we lose a piece of ourselves: our health, our eyes, our sense of smell or reason. Such losses remind us of Death's proximity. When Death holds my attention, I can see nothing else. It fills my vision, although I do not know whether it is near or far. Sometimes this comes about because I have considered something that belongs to Death, such as a lost or soon-to-be-lost life. And sometimes Death's image appears to me quite suddenly, with little or no warning, like an unexpected mood with a mind of its own. When this happens, I am lost to this mood, and I can see nothing but Death for days. Both of these occasions occur with greater frequency with each year that passes. It is not only my own aging that I believe affects me but also that of those around me. It hardly matters, however. I can do nothing about either one, any more than I can do anything about the perceived approach of Death's dark figure."

Thoughts spoken and unspoken from his years as a mortal passed through Adalgiso's mind and touched on the minds of his family. His feelings had always been dark. Now, they would be tempered, as well.

"I once wondered what it would be like to be dead and to be found lying on my bed, where I fell, eyes open and staring and yet lifeless. I slumped onto my pillow, ceased the rise and fall of my chest, and let my eyes sit open and unblinking. I remained so for what was likely a brief time in the dark, but it felt like too long. For I was suddenly very afraid. Afraid that I was actually dead. I knew I was not, and yet the panic welled up within me, and I gasped for air and blinked wildly and reached for a light. My lungs had not yet felt the ache for air, nor my eyes for the soothing blink of their lids. Yet I suddenly needed these things as if they were life itself. And the fear remained. I was afraid I was dead. I knew I was not. Yet I was afraid I was. And I gulped down air and closed my eyes and opened them again and looked around me at the same things I saw around my bed every day. Yet they were different. And the air was different, and the light was different. And I do not know why. For they were no different than they had been the night before or would be the night after. It took some time for me to turn off the light and lay back down. It took more time for me to sleep. I feared sleep as if it were Death itself. The panic did eventually abate. However, I am still afraid. And I still do not know why. And that makes me more afraid."

A preoccupation with mortal death had eased softly into a loyalty to eternity. Adalgiso had become that which he had once feared, once when his name and his life had been different. All that mattered now was his loyalty to the family and to their traditions.

"I feel as if I've been living in a perpetual state of déjà vu for the last few years. Even when I know that I am doing things I've never

done before, it feels familiar, as if I'm reliving my life. Or as if I'm reading a book or watching a movie. And it leaves me feeling utterly bored. With everything. Every movie ends the same; every book ends the same. There's nothing I can do that will be any different from what anyone else has done. I can't even read a book anymore and truly enjoy it, because I know how it will end. I know how they will all end. There are no ups or downs in such an existence. Everything is flat because nothing and no one ever changes. Even sex has no appeal to me any longer. I can feel the urge and the ache once in a great while, but there is no satisfaction in the act itself. It is as empty as all other pleasures. I feel as if I have seen and done everything there is to see and do. And now I watch it happening all over again for the first time. Nothing means anything. Nothing is important. No gesture is grand enough to hold meaning for me. Even the changes seem familiar and well-worn. Even the changes are the same for me. The world is flat, and I am bored, lifeless, and empty. I think; therefore, I am not."

A crack. A tear. A rip in the family's oneness appeared. There was a single thought that Adalgiso could not forget. This thought was like ash in the mouths of his family, like bright firelight engulfing their very existence, eradicating it. A part of him, a part that he had not even been aware of, still could not bear to look at eternity. His fear of change was quite suddenly replaced by a fear of sameness. Kraas mentally reminded him of the purpose of the ritual, the importance it held for the family and their way. Their guests still waited in the tower room, and the Beast could return at any moment. They had to be ready, to be strong.

Adalgiso struggled with his thoughts and feelings, trying to push them away, trying to snuff out the smoky wisps that now threatened to completely cut him off from the entire castle. He reached out to his family, hoping to use their strength to save them all. Their connections were weakening. They seemed further and further away with each mortal minute. Then, it was over.

They had failed. Adalgiso had failed. He felt the shame of it, the disappointment of his family. No, not his family any more. They would never be his family again. He had not been ready. What would become of him now? No young members of any family had ever failed the eternity ritual. They had all taken the time to fully prepare themselves. Judgement could only be passed by one of the masters.

As if from a great distance, Adalgiso felt Kraas reach up to the tower room and inform the Twins of the failure. It was not necessary to do so, but it was tradition. Kraas performed his duty solemnly and with great sorrow. Sakra noted his gesture but did not react. Her role as record-keeper would be significantly less important now. Ridd took up a position by the door, appearing completely unconcerned, but the smoky trails of sadness and worry snaked about the orange and black hair in a tempest.

At first, the Twins did not respond. The family waited. Adalgiso could only guess at how long. He felt more distanced from the world of darkness with each mortal hour. Eventually, a thought floated down to them from the top of the castle. It was powerful yet soft. The Twins did not care. It did not matter to them that a young vampire had failed his eternity ritual. The old traditions were falling. It was time to prepare for new things.

The confusion was extreme. If they required air to breathe, each of the dark figures in the ritual room would have been gasping for breath. How could they abandon the rituals? Without them, the families would not exist. Some of their number would not exist. The oldest among them would no longer exist. They feared to ask further questions of the masters, but there was little else they could do. Kraas and Sakra retreated into one another, shielding each other from the fear and confusion. Ridd contemplated a trip out into the mortal world, the one place where he did not fear being alone. Adalgiso decided on his own that since the end of the family was nigh, it mattered not what breaches of tradition he now committed.

He spoke with his mortal voice, shouting high into the castle, calling for the masters, daring them to answer. "What will become of us?! How will we survive? What sort of future will there be for Immortals?"

A rush of anger and blood and hate filled the room and swept them all to the floor like a gale. They fell beneath its heavy oppression. Yet, it was not as powerful as it could have been. Only one Twin touched them, only one attacked. The other was not there. One went nowhere without the other. It had always been so. In the midst of the pain and fear, the family looked upward to the tower room and were singularly horrified by what they saw there.

One Twin was gone. Her thoughtless, spiritless body lay on the floor, drained of all energy, drained of all blood, drained of all thought. The other, filled with her sister's energy, reached out to their minds and crushed them with a thought. Her darkness overshadowed their own and cut them off from the world, from each other, from their bloodkin. Drifting in the nothingness, Adalgiso felt only despair and loss and loneliness. He had failed, and now his family had fallen. Why? He would never know.

An eternity passed, or a string of eternities. Whether mortal or Immortal, time is impossible to measure in a void of darkness and nothingness. It might never have ended. But it did end. Slowly, the four children of the night found themselves regaining some energy, some thought, some consciousness. They felt around themselves cautiously, touching on each other and strengthening their thoughts. They were still at home in their castle of darkness, the hazy shadows welcoming to their aching minds. But how? They reached gingerly for the master who had crushed them so suddenly and unmercifully.

The Twin was gone. The Beast stood in her place, simmering in her energy. It savored the taste of her thoughts and suffering, basking in the satisfaction of a plan well-executed. It allowed Its thoughts to flow freely throughout the darkness, thoughts of victory, thoughts of power, thoughts of bloodlust. Confusion overwhelmed the family once again. Tradition had been abandoned, family torn asunder, and master set upon master. Was there nothing left? Was loyalty to be forever replaced with betrayal? Tradition with power-lust? Were the Immortals to return to a savage era of blood and destruction?

Their connections to each other too weak to raise them from the floor, Kraas, Sakra, and Ridd pondered their fate. If a new way of life were indeed coming about, they would have no place in it. The Beast had not made a place for them. It had not even made a place for the Twins. The order of things was gone. Kraas and Sakra could already feel themselves fading away, and even Ridd was losing track of the thoughts around the orange and black hair. Too long among the bloodkin, Ridd was fading almost as quickly as the oldest of the family.

Only Adalgiso felt himself growing stronger. He felt the energies of the mortals flowing into his mind of their own accord. He reached out to his family, hoping to save them, to send them some of what he was receiving. But the connection was gone. They were gone. He looked up to the Beast, but his master sent him only thoughts of returning to the mortals from which he had come. He tried to remember his time in the days long ago, but he had forgotten too much. He tried to follow his master when It left for another castle and another family. But It left him behind, with only the thought that he was the first of a new breed of bloodkin. A lone breed that would resemble the oldest ones more than the families. The oldest ones had once preyed heavily on the humans, and now a former human would begin the cycle anew, answering only to the Beast, not out of tradition, but out of deference to power. That power would thrive on mortal energy, growing and feeding until all mortals would fear the name of the Beast and know Its strength.

Adalgiso was alone, left alone to deal with the changes and the sameness of eternity. He finally knew what his destiny would be, what the fate of the vampires would be. A part of him was gone with his family. He could forget them, as in the traditions of the past. But the traditions were lost, and there was no one else to record their history now. It was time for a new tradition. It was time for a new way. It was time to leave the past behind once more. It was time for a new name. He chose Dawn.

EYES OPEN AT DAWN

By P. Katherine Barkley

ISBN: 978-0-9848721-1-4

www.ingramcontent.com/pod-product-compliance
Lightning Source LLC
Chambersburg PA
CBHW071713140626
46557CB00011B/68